FRANKENSTEIN
The Monster Wakes

EDITED BY
Martin H. Greenberg

DAW BOOKS, INC.
DONALD A. WOLLHEIM, FOUNDER
375 Hudson Street, New York, NY 10014

**ELIZABETH R. WOLLHEIM
SHEILA E. GILBERT
PUBLISHERS**

Copyright © 1993 by Martin H. Greenberg

All Rights Reserved.

Cover art by Jim Warren.

DAW Book Collectors No. 935.

If you purchase this book without a cover you should be aware that this book may have been stolen property and reported as "unsold and destroyed" to the publisher. In such case neither the author nor the publisher has received any payment for this "stripped book."

First Printing, December 1993

1 2 3 4 5 6 7 8 9

DAW TRADEMARK REGISTERED
U.S. PAT. OFF. AND FOREIGN COUNTRIES
—MARCA REGISTRADA
HECHO EN U.S.A.

PRINTED IN THE U.S.A.

A MANMADE MAN—

Dr. Frankenstein's creation has spawned many offspring, both on screen and off. Now, master anthologist Martin H. Greenberg has enlisted the aid of our most imaginative, modern-day conjurers to bring you these all-new tales of man and monster....

"Frankenstein Seen in the Ice of Extinction"—His creator dead, the monster seeks a haven in the icy depths of the North, only to find his master's ghost waiting to teach him one final lesson....

"My Coney Island Baby"—The strange, gnomelike man was a keeper of the past, a keeper who just might reveal more than one reporter really wanted to know about Victor Frankenstein's creation....

"A Friend of Mine"—Stationed in the Arctic, where boredom was a soldier's greatest enemy, he began a personal quest, pursuing an Eskimo legend that had its root in the heart of Europe, two centuries past....

FRANKENSTEIN: THE MONSTER WAKES

More Imagination-Clutching Anthologies Brought to You by DAW:

DRACULA: PRINCE OF DARKNESS *Edited by Martin H. Greenberg.* From Dracula's traditional stalking grounds to the heart of such modern-day cities as New York and Chicago, the Prince of Darkness casts his spell over his helpless prey in a private blood drive from which there is no escape!

JOURNEYS TO THE TWILIGHT ZONE *Edited by Carol Serling.* Sixteen unforgettable new tales—some eerie, some scary, some humorous—all with the unique *Twilight Zone* twist. Included is Rod Serling's classic, chill-provoking story, "Suggestion."

CHRISTMAS GHOSTS *Edited by Mike Resnick and Martin H. Greenberg.* Everyone knows Christmas has truly arrived when *A Christmas Carol* takes center stage in both amateur and professional productions. Now, some of the most creative minds in fantasy and science fiction tell readers exactly what those Christmas ghosts are up to when they're not scaring a stingy old man into self-reformation.

THE YEAR'S BEST HORROR STORIES *Edited by Karl Edward Wagner.* The finest stories—by both established masters and bright new talents—published in the genre in the current year.

ACKNOWLEDGMENTS

Introduction © 1993 by Martin H. Greenberg.

My Coney Island Baby © 1993 by Matthew J. Costello.

A Friend of Mine © 1993 by William L. DeAndrea.

Frankenstein Seen in the Ice of Extinction © 1993 by J. N. Williamson.

The Comfort of Walls © 1993 by Barbara Paul.

Fallen Angel © 1993 by Peter Crowther.

The Man with the Barbed-Wire Fists © 1993 by Norman Partridge.

Skin Memory © 1993 by Tracy A. Knight.

The Man in Black © 1993 by Christopher Fahy.

A Good Head on His Shoulders © 1993 by Max Allan Collins.

Role Model © 1993 by Mike Baker.

Cyrano © 1993 by Gary A. Braunbeck.

I've Got Hugh Under My Skin © 1993 by Rex Miller.

Bride of Frankenstein: A Modern Love Story © 1993 by Richard T. Chizmar.

Special Effects © 1993 by Terry Beatty and Wendi Lee.

A Debt Repaid © 1993 by Larry Segriff.

A Loaf of Bread, A Jug of Wine © 1993 by Brian Hodge.

Piss Eyes © 1993 by Rick Hautala.

Fallen Angel, Malignant Devil © 1993 by Billie Sue Mosiman.

CONTENTS

INTRODUCTION — 9
by Martin H. Greenberg

MY CONEY ISLAND BABY — 11
by Matthew J. Costello

A FRIEND OF MINE — 31
by William L. DeAndrea

FRANKENSTEIN SEEN IN THE ICE OF EXTINCTION — 55
by J. N. Williamson

THE COMFORT OF WALLS — 81
by Barbara Paul

FALLEN ANGEL — 95
by Peter Crowther

THE MAN WITH THE BARBED-WIRE FISTS — 112
by Norman Partridge

SKIN MEMORY — 126
by Tracy A. Knight

THE MAN IN BLACK 145
by Christopher Fahy

A GOOD HEAD ON HIS SHOULDERS 159
by Max Allan Collins

ROLE MODEL 176
by Mike Baker

CYRANO 193
by Gary A. Braunbeck

I'VE GOT HUGH UNDER MY SKIN 212
by Rex Miller

BRIDE OF FRANKENSTEIN: 219
A MODERN LOVE STORY
by Richard T. Chizmar

SPECIAL EFFECTS 227
by Terry Beatty and Wendi Lee

A DEBT REPAID 234
by Larry Segriff

A LOAF OF BREAD, A JUG OF WINE 244
by Brian Hodge

PISS EYES 275
by Rick Hautala

FALLEN ANGEL, MALIGNANT DEVIL 297
by Billie Sue Mosiman

INTRODUCTION

Probably no other literary figure has been presented in as many different ways as Frankenstein's monster.

In Mary Shelley's novel, he was, of course, a figure of sorrow and pity. In the later incarnations, notably those of forties and fifties "monster" films, he was seldom more than a pathetic but ravening beast.

And then there was Mel Brooks' wonderful and unforgettable "Young Frankenstein."

It is a tribute to Shelley's creative powers that her figure can be dealt with in all these ways without losing his power or simple fascination for us.

And that's what this collection is all about: turning loose some very good writers on the very intriguing theme of Frankenstein's monster.

You'll probably like some approaches better than others, but I trust you'll find all of them fit additions to the legend and the lore of Victor Frankenstein's favorite creation.

—Martin H. Greenberg

MY CONEY ISLAND BABY

by
Matthew J. Costello

It wasn't the greatest idea for an article that I ever came up with....

"Coney Island: Yesterday and Today."

No. Where was the hook, the grabber to make the bleary-eyed Sunday Magazine reader linger on the page?

It didn't have one.

That was the problem. The amazing thing was that I sold the piece anyway. *The Daily News,* like other Manhattan papers, was eager for cheerful, upbeat stories about the decaying urban terrain.

And a nostalgic look at Coney Island fit the bill.

A trip down memory lane, a look at Coney Island when Brooklyn was the world. (Didn't they always have a guy in those World War II movies named "Brooklyn"—and he always died. Usually he was from Flatbush ... and before he died he slipped a picture out of his blood-soaked shirt. "Here—cough, cough—here's my *goil.* Ain't she a—gasp, gasp—a peach.")

Now, though, Brooklyn was like a theme park from hell, a war zone that could give Mad Max pause.

And Coney Island? Well, once it *had* been a wonderland, an immense strip of amusement parks with names like Luna Park and Wonderland and, the greatest of them all, Steeplechase. But forty years ago, Steeplechase, the last of the parks, was boarded shut, slated for demolition, the last glimmer of Coney's greatness.

The last time I had been to Coney I had to step around a dead dog lying on the sidewalk ... a dead dog ... kind of a symbolic thing, a mongrel with rigor mortis stretched out, waiting for whatever poor slob would get stuck with the task of shoveling the body into a canine body bag. (Assuming, that is, that no one wanted it for lunch.)

Still, the newspapers were looking for positive stories, and my Coney piece fit the bill.

Especially since I offered the editor a look at something new—The Coney Island Historical Society Museum, a new museum/research center right on the splintery boardwalk.

Of course, I'd have to go there.

To Coney, that is.

It wasn't Somalia.

But it wouldn't be a hell of a lot better.

There's a subway line that runs directly into Coney, an elevated line that looks like another wacky ride left over from the '50s. Ride the subway. See Brooklyn go flying by.

But nobody I knew used the subway anymore unless they were desperate. *Real* desperate.

So I took my car, my 1986 battered, blood red Escort that was worth more stolen than on the road.

Even this might have been dangerous, though, if I went to Coney in summertime. I once drove down Surf Avenue, taking a shortcut to Ungillo's Pasta and Clam House in Sheepshead Bay. It was a hot July, twilight time, the sky hazy with the salty air and the slight temperature drop of night.

And the joint was jumping. Here a drug deal, there a hooker of unknown sexuality. Eagle-eyed men watched me stop at a corner, talons out, ready to pounce.

Pretty spooky stuff.

But today, it was a still-chilly spring. With 40-degree weather promised, Coney would still be a desolate place. I could hit the museum. Score some photographs—post-WWII sailors frolicking in a big spinning drum, laughing before they got married and moved to Levittown.

Write a piece that pretended that Coney Island was a place one might still actually visit . . .

And even if the paper didn't run the piece, the kill-fee was a hefty $500.

Kind of shows my level of confidence . . .

Making a right on Surf Avenue, I saw the ocean glistening in the morning sun. I passed a line of what were once game stalls, *Try Yer Luck, Pitch a Quarter, Knock'Em Down*—all now turned into permanent tag sales.

They offered the contents of attics, garages—who knew? Maybe it was a central dropping-off point for assorted stolen goods.

Perhaps they should have advertised it as such.

Assorted Stolen Goods.

Or, *Recover Your Treasures.*

Just past this bazaar, was the carousel, justly famous for being open year-round. I saw that it was running. A thin, sallow-eyed man, the operator, looked at me as I drove past. I didn't see anyone riding a horse. The carousel just spun there, a lure.

The bumptious music, "Take Me Out to the—Boom, Boom—Ball Game"—filtered into my car, penetrating my closed windows.

Across the street, Nathan's was open. Always good for a hot dog "with the woiks," and clams on the half shell, as fresh as you could get in Brooklyn and runny with clam water, "cocktail sauce," and—since you've been good—a bag of oyster crackers.

Later . . . I told my suddenly awake taste buds. Work first, eat *later.*

The museum was supposed to be on the next block, but that block was a one-way pointing away from the ocean. And since the block ended at the beach there was no other way to access said block.

So how the hell were you supposed to get down there?

The answer seemed to be that you didn't, not in a car anyway.

I turned right, found a parking meter—neatly smashed, thank you—and parked my car beside a corn on the cob/fudge joint, a balanced meal if ever there was one.

I grabbed my reporter's notebook, locked the car . . . didn't want my tic-tacs stolen . . . and headed toward the beach, the boardwalk, and the Coney Island Historical Society Museum.

A nasty breeze blew off the water. I looked out at the ocean. There were—believe it or not—some hapless souls sitting on the chilly, sunlit beach, waiting for Godot. Me, I looked out at the expanse of the Atlantic and thought—

Go straight for 4000 miles and I'd hit Paris.

What a difference an ocean makes.

The museum was blue and white, so bright with its new paint amidst so much rot and decay. The small wooden building—it must have been a big food stand decades ago—huddled below a brick building that featured a faded arrow pointing "Down" to letters advertising the Coney Island Bath House.

MY CONEY ISLAND BABY

I wondered what fun and games went on in there these days ...

The museum sported a neatly lettered sign that said:

Coney Island Historical Society Museum
Dedicated to Remembering America's
Amusement Park
Hours: Tues and Thur, 10–2 p.m.
Contribution: $7.00
S. Solomon, Curator

With those kind of hours, it didn't appear that the museum was *that* interested in remembering America's Amusement Park.

And since it was Tuesday, after ten ... 10:15 to be exact, I grabbed the doorknob and gave it a twist.

Nothing happened.

"Shit," I said. My ears were turning red from the wet breeze. I had spoken to Solomon on the phone, he knew I was coming. The museum should be open anyway. So where the—?

"Excuse me," a voice said from behind, making me jump. You have to remember, I was all alone on the boardwalk, just me, some hungry gulls, and the wind. And then there was this gnomelike man at my elbow, hissing at me.

I turned and saw the person I assumed—correctly as it turned out—to be Mr. Solomon.

He sported extra-thick glasses (what we called coke-bottle lenses back when there were coke bottles), a wiry mustache and a face with a good three days' growth of beard.

Solomon wore a brown suit, a plaid shirt, and a grayish overcoat, open, as if he had just dashed here from a breakfast of gruel.

This wasn't like interviewing Madonna.

(Which I've done, me buckos, so don't scoff.)

"Mr. Solomon?" My eyes were watering from the wind, and getting inside the "Museum" quickly seemed like a good idea.

The gnome raised a large, wrinkled hand, waving away the formalities. "Call me Sid," he said fishing keys out of his pocket. "And you must be the reporter . . ."

"Jack Reynolds," I said while he played with the keys. I told him to call me Jack. He nodded.

And like a sullen Ahab, I stood and waited. Sid had a bit of difficulty singling out the right key from his massive key ring. He looked at me and I smiled . . . *that's okay, don't rush, I like standing out here . . .*

But then I heard the click of the lock, the door opened—and the smell of whatever was inside almost made me consider conducting our little talk on a sunlit—albeit frozen—bench.

There was one hell of a rank odor in the museum.

"Get many visitors?" I said, reluctantly following the curator.

He shook his head, and slid out of his coat. "No. Who's interested in history these days . . . traditions?"

Sid turned and looked at me.

"I run this little museum, keep the collection because it means a lot to *me,* Mr. Reynolds."

He must have forgotten that we were on a first-name basis . . .

"I get a few visitors, writers like yourself."

I was about to explain that I was journalist—not a writer. There's a world of difference, but Sid hurried on, playing with an antique thermostat, flicking on lights, bringing the wonders to life.

It was less a museum than a wacky attic.

There were giant ponies, clown suits, a sleigh from some kind of ride—all jumbled together. Sid went behind a small glass counter, and I saw a hand-lettered sign that asked for the $7.00 contribution. He saw me digging in my pocket, and waved it away.

"No, don't worry about that. You're working. Would you like some tea?"

I watched Sid plug in an electric kettle after giving it a quick slosh to see if it still contained water. I also spotted a few stained mugs that looked ominous.

"No, thanks—say, you've got some ... incredible stuff here."

Sid came out from behind the counter. "Incredible is not the word for it, Mr. Reynolds."

He walked over to one of the wild-eyed horses, the metal exposed in places where paint had flaked away. "Do you know what this is ... ?"

I was in the Louvre, getting a tour of the Impressionists. The atmosphere was that ... reverential.

"No, I don't. I mean, it looks like a horse, but it's not a carousel horse, is it—?"

Sid laughed at the foolishness of the ignorant. "No, this is one of the Steeplechase horses. The last one—that I know of. Do you know about Steeplechase?"

"Only that the amusement park closed about forty years ago." I kept looking around at the flotsam and jetsam of Coney *perdu*. "This is great, I can—"

Sid kept looking at the horse. "It might have been this horse, Mr. Reynolds, that was used the night that kid died."

"What? A kid died in Steeplechase?"

Sid nodded, his face thoughtful. "After the park was closed down, all set for demolition. What a beautiful place ... and these kids sneaked in. They rode the Steeplechase ride on its metal track that ran around the outside of the building. You know, Steeplechase had this giant building, all glass and wood, filled with slides, and barrels, and clowns. Oh, the fun you could have there ..."

I lost him again.

"And the kid?"

"Oh—he didn't know that the track was partly down. He went flying into space, riding the horse. Smashed into a storage shed, and his head was chopped off. Very sad. And it might have been this horse."

Interesting stuff, but not for the *Sunday News Magazine*. A little too downbeat ...

The horse eyes looked perpetually freaked.

I walked to one wall. For a museum there wasn't much light, but the walls were filled with photographs in cheap frames. One photo captured Coney Island filled with thousands of people dressed in Victorian finery ... parasols and top hats.

Sid was at my elbow.

"Coney Island was the place to visit ..."

I nodded, making notes, moving onto another photo, Luna Park at night ... such a beautiful place, magical—gone forever.

"Luna Park *was* a wonderland," he said.

Each photograph was more amazing than the last ... amazing, because how could so much beauty and fun turn into a decadent sinkhole like Coney Island circa 1994?

I was about to ask that question when Sid's phone rang. I was left unattended while Sid said, "Coney Island Historical Society Museum, may I help you?"

He needed voice mail.

I got up to inspect more photos now: Coney in the war years, the beach filled—from boardwalk to shore—with kids and families. In the back, the colorful rows of stands: cotton candy, corn, fudge, clams ...

Then—out of place—a portrait of a woman, young,

pretty—hand-tinted in pastel flesh tones, red lips, light brown hair.

"That's my wife ... years ago, of course." Sid was back. "My Myrna ... My Coney Island Baby. She's one of the reasons that I started the museum."

How nice. Yawn.

I remembered that I wanted to hit Nathan's on the way out of the badlands.

I saw a last photo in the corner, hard to get to because a small car from a "Whip" ride blocked it. I stepped into the chair and onto the cracked leatherette seat—how many kids' bottoms had sat there?—and leaned over to see—

"Hey—hey be careful. Don't step on the ride. You sit down!"

It was as if I were a kid again, at Playland ... doing something I shouldn't be doing, and the ride operator was yelling at me.

Maybe that's what Sid Solomon had done. Maybe he ran the bumper cars, the Ferris wheel.

Now, you sit down sonny ...

"Sorry," I said, backing off. I had only gotten a tantalizing glimpse of the photo. But it looked like a carnival midway. I had seen the words "Fat Lady"—but no more.

Sid came over and looked down at the seat, shaking his head at my gaucherie.

"I think that you cracked it some more."

"I'm sorry. I only wanted to see that picture."

Solomon looked up, and his face was no longer a happy face. Was my interview about to end? I still wanted to borrow some photos from the old guy, try to give my article a little *juice*.

"What is it?" I asked when nothing was forthcoming.

Sid turned away. "Just more of Coney ... in the old days ..."

I didn't budge. A good reporter knows when a secret is being hidden.

"But I saw—I don't know—a midway. They had midways at Coney? I thought—"

Sid stopped and looked at me. He stood there, and I think that he knew then that I didn't share his respect for the wonders of Days Gone By.

He licked his lips, thoughtful, wetting the edges of his unruly mustache.

"You wanna see it?" he said.

"Sure. It might be interesting for—"

And Sid was able to slide past the Whip chair, and snatch the photo off the wall. He blew on it, sending a spray of dust into the air—one thing the environment here didn't need.

He handed it to me.

"Take a look," he said. A small grin played on his lips, more gnomelike than ever. "Take a real *good* look ..."

And that—was when things took a very strange turn.

I looked at the photograph. There was a stall for The House of Wonders, and—in bold letters—I saw a menu that included The Fat Lady, Lizard Boy, the Webbed Man, and others too small to read. From the look of the style of dress, I guessed that the photo was taken circa 1928 ... 1929. Just before the Roaring Twenties stopped roaring.

And next to the House of Wonders was a smaller stall, offering just one attraction.

(And believe me when I tell you that—standing there in the moldy, dark room—I got chills.)

Two words ... almost ridiculous in their import ...

"See Frankenstein!"

"What?" I said, turning to Sid—with what I'm sure

was a goofy grin on my face. But little Sid looked very serious.

"It should have said, 'See Frankenstein's Creation.'" Sid cleared his throat. "Victor Frankenstein was a scientist, an educated man. We don't know where he's buried today, but . . ."

I laughed, but the dry sound drew a glare from Sid. "Wait a minute. You're telling me that somebody was able to convince people that Frankenstein, a story made up, was *real*, that there was a monster? And people paid money to see it?"

Sid took the picture from me.

"It *was* real," he said quietly.

Oh, I thought, wondering if the bus for Wingdale had pulled up yet.

"I thought it was a novel." Duh . . .

"It is a novel," Sid said. "But that woman—Mary Shelley—she based it on a real event. It was all true. She was only a girl. She thought it was funny."

Sid put the photograph back on the wall.

And I was thinking: now *this* may be a story. "When Frankenstein Appeared at Coney Island."

Except it was too ridiculous, even for New York.

"Well, that's an amazing story, Sid. Who'd a *thunk* that Coney Island had been home to such a . . . historic personage."

He scrambled back to me.

"*You* don't believe me."

I smiled. "No, I believe that maybe you think that the sideshow had someone, something—and maybe *you* think it was Frankenstein—I mean his monster."

"His *creation*."

"Okay, his creation. But it was probably only a dummy, fitted up with stitches and—hey, wait! Didn't the monster, the creation die in the Arctic? That's what happened in the book."

Sid walked back to the counter. He looked preoccupied. Had senility taken its toll on the old curator?

His answer surprised me.

"That was true. Frankenstein's creation ended up in the Arctic, trapped on a berg. And he probably died there."

"*Probably* died?"

Sid nodded. "But he was *found*. Found frozen, and brought back. The Captain knew who it was, and he brought the body back—encased in ice. He sold it to the highest bidder, a promoter."

"And it was kept on ice?"

Sid nodded. "For years . . . but when the Depression hit, somehow it wasn't taken care of, and the body was allowed to dry. It became desiccated, shriveled."

Sid shook his head. "Who knows—maybe they could have revived the creature again."

"If they had the manual," I said. "That, and about 2000 volts from a high Bavarian electric storm."

Sid startled me by banging on the glass chest.

"Still joking, eh? All just a story, a myth, huh?"

And Sid brushed past me, moving toward the back of the museum, into dark recesses that hid more chunks of rides long gone, more photos, posters, to a back room . . . and a door.

I heard the key ring jingle, then a click—and Sid disappeared. He quickly returned, but not before relocking the room he had exited.

What goodies did he have in there, I wondered.

Sid gently lowered a tattered, leather-bound book down on the table.

"There, Mr. Wise Guy Reporter. There's your evidence."

I touched the book—the leather was so ancient and sere it left a fine dust on my fingers.

"Certainly old enough," I said.

MY CONEY ISLAND BABY

I turned the book around. I opened the cover.

I wasn't sure—with the fancy Gothic lettering, the "s" that looked like a large "f"—but it looked as if it were written in Deutsch.

"My German's a bit rusty," I said.

Sid pointed at the words. " 'Notes and Commentary, Dr. Victor Frankenstein 1786–1787' . . . it's all in there. Everything Frankenstein did."

I had to admit that this looked genuine. It was old enough, that was for sure. And I began to wonder if maybe my cynicism wasn't misplaced. Perhaps there was more here than met my jaded eyes.

"Th–this is great. Are there more things like this, back there?" I nodded in the direction of Sid's secret room. And his alarmed, wild-eyed reaction told me that, *yes* . . . there might indeed be some more wonders in his back room.

"No . . . I—I really can't talk anymore."

Sid pulled the book away, our interview time apparently ended. "I have to take Myrna—my wife—for her walk. She likes the afternoon sun. There are things I have to do."

I wondered what Sid would do if some other customers were to come.

But more than that, I wondered what he had hidden in his inner sanctum. Long-gone amusement parks were nice . . . but very weird stuff was even *nicer*.

I began to get an idea of what I might do.

"Well, thank you, Mr. Solomon. Thanks for showing me everything."

Sid nodded, clutching his book tightly. He obviously regretted his indiscretion.

"Can I call you—if I need more information?"

Another nod, and Sid led me out of the maze to the front door, ushering me out to the chilly boardwalk.

* * *

I was eating a Nathan's chili dog and sipping from a plastic cup of beer when the plan jelled. It was after the second homeless person hit on me and I turned away, that I knew what I would do.

Said plan had its unethical side, but I was desperate.

Not "Coppers, you'll never take me alive!" desperate, but as I said, I was a journalist. This was the Nineties. You have to make your dollars where you can.

So after finishing my adorned dog and brew, I walked back to what seemed an even chillier boardwalk, and staked out the Coney Island Museum.

I checked my watch. At 2:00 p.m. Sid should leave the building, lock it up and return to some other fun-filled aspect of his life.

I waited. Two came, then 2:15, and I wondered if he hadn't closed early for the day.

But at about 2:30, the gaily painted blue and white door popped open and Sid, with his overcoat buttoned tightly this time, came out ... pushing a chair.

With someone in it.

Myrna, I guessed. Letting his wife catch some afternoon rays. It did look like a woman, curled up in the chair, a blanket on her lap.

The chair wasn't a wheelchair, but some kind of wicker vehicle—again, a genuine Coney heirloom from the days when people promenaded on the boardwalk.

I crouched down by the Aquarium, hidden by a protrusion from a *Spin to Win* booth ("Win a Carton of Luckies!"). I worried that Sid would wheel his old lady this way, necessitating a rather comical departure.

Instead, Sid headed north.

I waited until he was blocks away, and then I popped out of my hiding spot and cavalierly walked to the museum.

MY CONEY ISLAND BABY

I wondered if the museum might have a security system of some kind. That would be very bad news.

But Mr. Sid was such a traditionalist that I doubted it.

When I got to the door, I checked that Sid was nowhere in sight and then I removed a small metal pin that I kept for such emergencies. Years of penny-ante investigative reporting had left me with a moderate skill in jimmying locks. The door proved no problem.

I quickly entered the museum and shut the door behind me.

And there was that foul smell again—ripe, rancid.

Like a whole warren of rats had curled up somewhere in here and died.

I forced myself to breathe through my nose.

Now, for part two of the plan.

The back room.

From the way Solomon crept back there, unlocking the door, creeping in, and then creeping out, I guessed that there were some *primo* goodies back there ... things even stranger than old Frankenstein's notes.

I moved through the darkness, banging my shin on the Steeplechase horse.

"Damn," I said. My voice sounded weird in the dark room. Then—more carefully—I continued to the back room.

Solomon had a standard issue Yale lock on the door.

"Piece of cake," I said.

Had it open in 35 seconds, my personal best time *ever.*

I looked over my shoulder, just to make sure that the coast—as they say—was clear.

Then—back to the door. I slipped the lock off its ring, pocketed it, and then—taking a foul breath—entered the inner sanctum of the Coney Island Historical Society Museum.

* * *

The room was black. I hadn't seen Sid turn on a light—he must have simply used the ambient light to find Frankenstein's notes.

But there was one thing that I knew . . . I had found the source of the stench that filled the joint.

This was—to be sure—the olfactory mother lode.

My eyes crossed from an aroma that could be described as completely nauseating. My chili dog rumbled in my gut, and I considered a dash outside to gulp some fresh, salty air.

But no—the curator might be on his way back.

I had to find a light, see what was interesting, maybe grab a sample, then dash away all . . .

I took a step into the black room.

My left thigh banged into a table of some kind.

"Ow," I said, the pain irritating in its sharpness.

My hands fondled the wall, first left, then right, searching for a light switch.

I whispered . . . "Got to be a fuckin' light switch here . . . somewhere . . ."

I leaned into the table again, more gingerly this time.

Maybe there was a table lamp here of some kind. I reached out, into the darkness, about to grope the tabletop.

I hit something soft, a bit spongy . . . cloth, like a sack of something. I felt it, running my hand up, feeling something like . . . like flesh—

"Oh, shit," I yelled. "Shit."

I leapt away, bouncing with each expletive. And I banged into another table—where my butt told me that there was nothing on it.

I considered leaving.

But my hand touched a table lamp and I turned it on . . .

MY CONEY ISLAND BABY

And I saw the body. He was a big fellow, well over six feet tall, maybe seven feet. His skin was dry, almost like a mummy's, and cracked—except where I could see the telltale signs of stitching.

For a moment, I wondered whether Sid Solomon had a sideline ... killing people, storing them in the back of the museum. But this thing was *old* ...

"I know what this is," I said.

It was good to hear a voice, even if it was my own.

The body, the stitched-together corpse, had been dead a long time. If its innards were as dry as the skin, just moving it would cause it to fall apart, the brittle bones cracking, the internal organs so much dried shoe leather.

"The monster ..." I said.

"No."

The voice made me jump a good six inches into the air.

Solomon was in the doorway.

"I told you, Mr. Reynolds. Not a monster, but a *creation*. Frankenstein's attempt to make the dead live again."

Solomon shook his head sadly.

"It was in a crate, in a warehouse. An old Midway display. I'm sure they thought it was made out of rubber and cloth, pigskin, just a trick ..."

"And it's not?"

Solomon shook his head. "No, he's quite real." Sid walked to the table and took the dead creature's hand in his own. The "creation's" hand was enormous, a large, worker's hand, rough, and grayish. I couldn't imagine touching that skin again.

"Just as the book is real," Solomon said.

"I believe you now."

What a story, I thought. Frankenstein's Monster ... Found. It could be a Geraldo special. They could do an autopsy on television. I'd have to negotiate exclusive rights, film, TV, print. The whole deal. And Solomon would make out like a bandit, too. He could open a gigantic museum, go look for more bits of Coney Island memorabilia.

I shook my head back and forth. "This is great, Sid. This is going to make us." I turned to him. The creature seemed less terrifying, now that it was going to be my ticket to a beach house in Malibu.

Sid licked his lips.

He spoke slowly.

"I'm glad you believe ... everything now. It makes it so much easier ... you'll understand."

Understand? What was the curator talking about?

Sid backed out of the room. Good, I had to get to a phone, call my agent. Tell him that his faith in me had not been misplaced. His client was "The Man Who Found Frankenstein's Monster."

What a story!

I heard the squeak of wheels.

The chair, Sid's wife ... he was wheeling her into the room. I saw the dark brown wheelchair, the small rubber wheels, Myrna's blanket-covered legs, then—

Myrna.

Eyes open. Mouth shut. Pleasant-looking woman.

Dead as a doornail.

I think I yelped.

There was a line of stitches that ran across Myrna's forehead.

Events were outdistancing my ability to understand them.

Sid blocked the entrance with the chair.

"When Myrna was dying ... I felt as if I was losing my world. There was so much we shared together."

Right, I thought. So you're keeping her as a memento. Very nice, now let me get to a phone and—

"Then—before the end, I found the book, the crate, mixed in with hundreds of other things ... just so much garbage. I told Myrna what I wanted to do ..."

Sid looked up ... to something above my head. I turned around, and there was a shelf, a giant bell jar—and floating inside—a brain.

A piece of masking tape was pasted across the jar, the word ... "Myrna."

"It had to be removed. I knew that. Removed, preserved, while I found everything I needed, good healthy organs, no cancer. Frankenstein's notes told me what had to be done ..." Sid grinned. "And I wouldn't need an electrical storm. Con Ed could take care of everything ..."

O–kay, I thought. Time to get the check.

"Unfortunately, there is only one way to get healthy organs ... heart, liver, lungs. One way—"

"Which is—?"

Sid looked up at me. "I've locked the front door. And there's no one to hear if you decide to make any noise."

I got the picture. Frankenstein's book, Myrna's brain and *my* body, *my* organs—and a mighty big electrical bill.

"I think I'd better go—" I said.

To which Sid responded by bringing out a syringe, glistening in the yellow light, its tip wet. Before I could react, he jabbed me in the arm.

"You have," he said, "about sixty seconds left of consciousness ... the muscle relaxant, of course, works immediately."

Of course ... I discovered that when I tried to push by the chair, and I slipped to the floor like a gumby man.

"Oh, God—" I groaned. Then, to show I wasn't a complete dolt, I said, "You arranged this—"

Sid looked guilty. "Curiosity..." he said, leaving the aphorism unfinished.

Or did I just not hear it?

Because after that, my mind went blank.

Which, considering what was in store for my body, was probably a good thing...

A FRIEND OF MINE
by
William L. DeAndrea

One

Every day they were locked into the room below the ice. They sat in their swivel chairs and looked at the screens. The men had been psychologically matched for compatability; the chairs were ergonomically designed for comfort, the screens a soothing orange-on-gray to ease eyestrain. The people who'd designed this system didn't want something as avoidable as human discomfort to lead to any ill-considered actions.

There was no way to engineer out the boredom.

"Don't you ever wish somebody would *launch* a goddamn missile once?" Corporal Mike Alvarez asked.

Sergeant Hank Peeters scratched his nose. "Who?" he asked. "Us? That's up to the boys in the mountain in Colorado. All we do is watch the screens."

"You got that right. All we do is watch the screens. No, I didn't mean us, I meant them. It would make it seem worthwhile sitting around here, at least."

"What do you mean, 'them'? There is no 'them' any more. The Cold War is over, and our side won. We're sort of like a leftover."

"A frozen leftover," Alvarez said. "Doesn't it ever bother you that we spend our whole lives on, in, and around *ice?*"

"The compound is warm enough."

"I'm not talking about the compound, man, I'm talking about the fact that we're sitting on a glacier a quarter of a mile above the nearest earth. It's like floating in space."

"Depends on how you look at it," Peeters told him. "Ice is a mineral, you know. And ground is made up of minerals, right?"

"You like it up here, don't you?"

Peeters was silent for a few moments. "Yeah. Yeah, I do."

"I heard you signed up for another hitch up here."

"It's not allowed. They're afraid we'll go stir crazy."

"Hah! But you tried it, didn't you? You went to the old man and asked to stay, didn't you?"

"What if I did?"

"Don't you miss civilization? Goddamn, man, the *Greenlanders* don't even come around here."

"There's a tribe not too far away."

"I'm not talking about a tribe, I'm talking about *you*."

"No, then. If you absolutely have to know. I don't miss civilization. Civilization has become a big ugly mess of crime and dirty politics and people whining about how hurt and victimized they are, and how society ought to be restructured to help *them*. There's not a kind of person out there who's not doing that."

"Except your kind, right?"

"I don't know. I don't even know if I have a kind. But I suspect that if I go back there, I'll be pissing and moaning just like the rest of them. And there's nothing worse than being the kind of person who makes you sick."

Alvarez looked at him for a few seconds, then said, "I was just kidding, you know."

"What about?"

"When I suggested I wished somebody would actually fire a missile. I didn't mean it."

"I know you didn't."

A FRIEND OF MINE

"I just wanted to make sure. Because, my friend, you are getting strange enough to do it yourself."

Peeters smiled. "Never happen," he said. "I just said I was sick of it. Didn't say I wanted to destroy it."

"Maybe so. But I think our hitch up here has lasted long enough. Maybe if you re-up they'll put you on some desert island someplace. Then you can be lonely *and* warm."

When the shift was over, Peeters had attended to his paperwork, then checked out a halftrack for a little drive to clear his head. That wasn't strictly according to regulations, but the CO understood the grind here, and he knew that a little open space—even a little frozen-solid open space on top of a glacier—can be better than fifty bottles of tranquilizers.

It certainly was for Peeters. As usual, he invited Alvarez along, and some of the other guys, but, also as usual, they were busy playing ping-pong or watching videos, or, in Alvarez's case, looking at the sunny scenes on the postcards his mother sent him from Miami.

Peeters was just as glad. There was something he had to do, and he couldn't share it with anybody, yet.

It was May, so daylight wasn't a problem. He gassed up the crawler and warmed up the engine until the heater would almost melt lead. He grabbed a couple of extra twenty-liter jerry cans, just in case, checked the compass on the dash, and headed off. North. There was something he had to check on. Something he had seen the last time he was out this way.

He'd been about fifteen klicks north of the base when the blizzard came up. In Greenland, a blizzard isn't something the weather boys can warn you about. Peeters had learned, to his surprise, that it is possible for blizzard conditions to prevail without a snowstorm being in progress. A blizzard, it turns out, requires only low temperatures, strong winds, and snow, but the snow doesn't have to be falling from the sky at the time. God was frugal here in the Arctic Circle. He could make the same snow do for any number of blizzards.

Anyway, the wind had kicked up, and Peeters' soothing vista of bright blue sky and weird, wind-sculptured ice was gone in seconds, replaced by a nightmare of white streaks as the snow rose and blotted out the weak sunlight.

Peeters shrugged. He reached for his clipboard (when you go anywhere in that country, you make sure you keep track of how you got there, because there's no highway back), and was just about to turn the crawler around, when something thumped heavily against the glass cab of the arctic vehicle. Then another thump came, then another. Somebody was throwing rocks at him.

A freak shift in the wind gave him an instant of visibility, and he saw ten or twelve figures in anoraks running across the snow at him.

It was Eskimos, for God's sake. Attacking him now with gloved fists and clubs, yelling at him. Angry. Hostile.

Peeters had tried to pull away, but he was afraid to gun it, for fear of running over one of them or something worse.

The glass was case hardened and thick, and the locks were good (these things were designed to be polar bear-proof), but Peeters was getting nervous anyway. Every so often, a club would rattle the glass. The angry faces outside showed no sign of letting him go.

And there was something else. This was not just a

A FRIEND OF MINE

hunting party. There were women and children, along with men climbing the crawler, trying to get inside.

Then a sound came. Peeters told himself it was the wind. He'd been telling himself ever since it was the wind, howling through some whistle it had carved for itself in snow and ice. There were arctic wolves, and Peeters supposed they howled, but no wolf had ever howled this loud or this low.

Whatever it was, the Eskimos heard it, too, and turned as one to face it. Then, as quickly as they'd attacked, they climbed down off the crawler and disappeared into the wind.

Peeters looked over his shoulder all the way back to camp.

He duly reported the incident. The CO scratched his crew cut and said, "Well, Sergeant, I'm damned if I know what to make out of it. The Eskimos aren't hostile."

"Yes, sir."

"Far from it. They're the friendliest people on Earth. The non-fraternization rules are to protect them from us, not us from them. Hell, the first white men who came up this way kept getting the use of the Eskimo wives. It's like a custom. At least it was."

"Yes, sir."

Though the interview wasn't over, Peeters already knew two things. He wasn't in trouble, and this report wasn't going to go any further than this office. He was pleased at the first, not so happy with the second. What had happened out there had been *weird*. An anthropologist or somebody else who knew about these things should check this out.

Peeters said as much.

"Sergeant," the CO said, "I know you've got the best interests of the service at heart. But keep in mind the song and dance that we have to go through with the

Danes and now the U.N. to keep this place open, won't you? That we're not having an adverse effect on the 'indigenous peoples'? That we're not screwing up the ecology?"

"Yes, sir."

"Those are good rules, Peeters. I believe in them. Though how the hell anyone could screw up this godforsaken ecology is beyond me.

"In any case, some pencil pusher who goes home to a wife every night might take a report of what happened to you out there today and twist it so that you've done some irreparable damage to their noble primitive psyches or some such crap, and then we'll all be in the soup. You'll get a black mark in your record, and I'll have to put an end to crawler excursions, morale will drop, men will become lackadaisical at their tasks. Some nut in Moscow will get nostalgic for Communism. He'll fire off a missile. We'll miss it. Washington will be destroyed. One thing will lead to another, and all the missiles will be fired. The human race will be destroyed, maybe all life on Earth."

"Yes, sir."

The CO looked at him.

"Peeters," he said.

"Yes, sir?"

"Have you been listening to a goddamn thing I've said?"

"Yes, sir. The human race will be destroyed, sir."

"I was kidding, Sergeant, okay? You were supposed to laugh."

"Sorry, sir."

"I was trying to lighten things up a little around here. Don't go back to the men saying the old man thinks the human race is about to be destroyed, will you do me that favor? Because I don't really think that."

A FRIEND OF MINE

"Certainly, sir. I didn't really think you did."

"Sergeant Peeters, you're a good man, and your record speaks for itself, but you've got to loosen up a little. If we can't laugh in a posting like this, we go nuts."

"Yes, sir."

"What happened today was probably some sort of welcoming ritual or something, or initiation, you know? I'll pass along your report if you want me to, but I think the best thing is just to let it drop. All right?"

"I won't push it through channels, sir."

"Excellent, Peeters, excellent. Now go to the rec room and watch a dirty movie or something."

"Yes, sir."

Peeters went to the rec room, but he didn't watch a dirty movie. Instead, he sat down at a computer terminal—not to play Tetris, but to plug into one of the truly amazing array of data bases this little machine at this isolated outpost could reach.

He started simply; he dialed up an encyclopedia program and looked up ESKIMO. That gave him a cross reference: see INUIT AND RELATED PEOPLES.

Peeters cussed himself. He should have known that much. He read the article, but it didn't tell him much he didn't know. A lot about hunting for seals and whales and the like, some stuff about ice fishing. A lot about Alaska and Canada, just a passing reference to the peoples of Greenland and Russia.

But at the end, there was a bibliography. He followed that up, then chased down *their* bibliographies. It took him every free moment for several days, but finally, he found a reference to a paper entitled "Description of Some Aspects of Unexplained Religion-Caused Behaviors Among Inuit and Related Peoples," by D.K. Olsen. He tried its data base call up number, and from the bowels of some computer somewhere, the information scrolled up on the screen.

In Danish.

The CO would have approved. Peeters sat there and laughed for about twenty minutes. Well, he thought, it was a good try. He scrolled through it anyway, hoping that somehow combining his native English, his grandparents' Dutch, and the German he'd learned in college, he could make something of it, but no dice.

Well, it had been a good try.

Wait a minute, he told himself. There was a note at the end that seemed to say the article was also available in German, English, Russian, and Japanese.

He tried for the English version, but it wasn't there. Okay, he thought, last chance, and punched the numbers that would bring him the German version. Even if he could read Russian or Japanese, he doubted this terminal could show the characters on the screen.

And then, *ach du lieber,* there it was.

Peeters rubbed his eyes—he was going to go blind, peering at a CRT for hours at a time like this—then plunged in. It was tough slogging. His German was rusty, and each sentence he decoded had to be decoded again from academic jargon. That part was harder than reading the German.

Peeters didn't want to have to do this again, so he took notes.

Beginning in the 1930s, when polar exploration settled down to becoming less of a race to some arbitrary geographical spot and more like science, there had been reports of rare but real anomalies in the behavior of various tribes of what were for many years called Eskimos, but more recently have come to be known by their preferred name of Inuit peoples.

Since the Inuit represent a number of more or less

A FRIEND OF MINE

discrete populations, numerous variations in language and culture were to be expected, but *in general,* their religious beliefs tended to be a form of animism, ascribing spiritual traits to the wind, the snow, and the various animals they deal with in their lives, as well as a belief in the survival of the soul after death.

Except.

Except some tribes admitted to having known a personified god "long ago." He was a giant called Veektuk, and he rescued abandoned hunters from ice floes. He provided meat when hunting was bad. He loved children. And he disappeared after the white man came.

The amazing thing about Veektuk is that those rare tribes who knew him weren't imprecise about *when* they knew him. It was frequently pinpointed as during the lifetime of a member of the tribe, more often as during the lifetime of a parent or a grandparent. There was a mosaic of Veektuk reports totaling a hundred fifty years or so, from the 1840s to within a few decades of the date of the report.

The other remarkable thing was that the tribes who knew Veektuk were scattered haphazardly around the pole. This wasn't a story that diffused in the normal manner of folklore. It was a story that arose again and again, at widely scattered locations throughout the Arctic.

And that was about it. This was one of those academic papers that was basically a call for help. Before Peeters let the thing go, he checked the date of the report. Nineteen seventy-nine. He wondered what, if anything, had happened in Veektuk scholarship in the ensuing fourteen years. If anything.

He knew that if he played his cards right, though, he'd be able to add to it. Not that he cared.

What he cared about confirming was his sight and

his sanity. He hadn't told the CO his whole story, and a good thing, too, considering the reception he'd gotten. He hadn't told about what he'd seen through a split-second break in the blizzard when the people had been storming the crawler, a glimpse too quick to leave much more than an impression. The possibly-imaginary sight of an impossibly huge man, howling in the snow.

As the crawler chugged along, Peeters made a fetish of watching the compass, of matching exactly the route he had taken the last time. He wished he had more to concentrate on, because the rest of his brain was racing madly.

What if he ran into the Inuit again? What if it got back to the CO? Hell, his hitch here would be done even sooner than it was doomed to be.

But how could he *not* go? He had a chance to track down a god, a small "g" god, to be sure, but how many people even achieved that? And a benevolent one, besides. Peeters didn't even want to think of the need he had discovered in himself to find somewhere, anywhere, a benevolent god.

Gracious. Going out to call on a god. I should have worn dress blues.

And, of course, as a contrapuntal bass line to the whole composition was the stubborn and undeniable knowledge that he was a fool. That he was chasing a lie, or an optical illusion around which some tiny minority of the tiny slice of mankind known as the Inuit had created a myth. If he found so much as a crude ice sculpture in the form of a man, he'd be lucky. As it was, he probably wouldn't find—

He found dogs.

Four of them, staked down by leather leads and bone

rings into the ice, at almost the exact point he'd come to before.

He'd nearly run them over as he approached, in fact, because they were sleeping, buried in snow to keep warm. Their keen sense had warned them of the approaching crawler, and they'd sprung to their feet, barking and snarling at him.

Peeters knew enough about the people who lived here to know that they killed only what they hunted. But life was cruel, and polar economy was harsh. A dog too old to pull a sled was staked out like this and left to starve.

One dog at a time.

This was different. These dogs weren't old or sick. They were young animals, prime specimens, strong and square and active even now.

Peeters needed air, even in this frigid weather. He pulled the snorkel of his parka tight around his face, and opened the door of the crawler. Before he climbed out, he clipped a rope to his belt, in case a sudden blizzard sprang up on him again. He jumped down from the tread, and his boots crunched snow.

Peeters had loved his stay in the Arctic. His days spent staring at a radar screen served to remind him of the absurdity of so-called civilization and why he hated it. The rest of it was order and simplicity.

Until now. This made no sense at all. What was this supposed to be, a sacrifice?

But that was nonsense. Those same harsh economies that dictated the death of an aged dog precluded the needless death of four superior dogs like this. The people here just couldn't afford it.

Peeters stood there, feeling useless. The thought of the waste of the dogs' lives oppressed him, but there was nothing he could do. The animals were bred for strength, not for gentleness. If he approached, they would certainly tear him to pieces. If he somehow did manage to set them free, they'd still starve. Or they'd run into a bear and go down fighting. A better fate, but still not an enviable one.

Air Force issue cold-weather gear was good—Peeters didn't feel cold, just numb with helplessness and bewilderment.

He forced himself to think. What did he have?

Well, he had a gun in the crawler. He could shoot the dogs. That way, at least, they wouldn't suffer. But the dogs would be just as dead.

Then he thought of what else he had in the crawler. He had emergency rations—MREs, the great-grandchild of the K-ration. According to the Pentagon, MRE stood for Meal Ready to Eat, but in the service it was widely understood to mean Meals Rejected by Ethiopians. They were horrible, but they might seem pretty good to a starving husky. Even with a hefty dose of morphine from the emergency medical kit in each one.

Sure. He could dope the dogs, tie their legs and muzzles in case the dose wore off en route, throw them in the crawler, and hightail it back to base. He'd catch hell for it, but it would be worth it.

Of course, it also meant giving up the Great Veektuk Hunt, but that had been foolish on the face of it. Besides, if he got through the hiding that awaited him from the CO, there was always next time.

It would be nice to dope the dogs, if only to shut them up. Their howling and yapping had attained amazing volume. He turned back to the crawler.

That's when he saw the bear.

It wasn't the biggest polar bear in the world—it was about as high as the bottom of Peeters' rib cage at the shoulder—but it would do. And it meant business, eyeing Peeters and the dogs alternately, getting ready to start that almost comical shamble that turned into a lightning fast, deadly lunge at the end.

Peeters started telling himself exactly how big a fool he was, but he realized there was no profit in it and made himself stop.

He wasn't getting back to the crawler—his path would brush the bear's nose. The thing to do was to back around the dogs, get the dogs between the bear and him. *So much for saving the dogs, you hypocrite.* He excused himself partially by telling himself that if the dogs tied up the bear, he'd be able to beat it to the crawler in time to get the rifle and save all of them.

He kept telling himself that until he slipped.

Men were not designed for walking backward on ice. Peeters slipped and went down. He heard a kind of slapping noise—no more—as the bear ran for him. He smelled hot breath and felt pain, across his chest, across his face.

Then the howling came, the noise he'd heard before. What came next was like a magic trick. His vision had been filled with the open jaws of the bear, approaching his head. Then they vanished, leaving him with a vision of a clear blue sky. Snarlings and gruntings filled his ears, with the dogs yapping background vocals.

Painfully, Peeters twisted his body to see what was going on. What he saw was a nightmare vision—a fur-clad giant wrestling with the bear, holding it to him with one arm, pushing back on its head with the other.

Peeters heard the crack, then the bear flopped forward like a rug.

Peeters flopped himself, back to the snow. He had no strength. This, a part of his brain knew, was a fantasy concocted in his last split seconds to keep the horror of his death from himself.

It was quiet now. He was going. The last thing he saw was the scarred gray face leaning over him.

Two

"Don't try to move," a voice said. It wasn't hoarse so much as stiff, as if from lack of use.

Peeters sank back down. He didn't especially want to. His head felt heavy, his whole body tired, as if he'd been drugged. Or dreaming.

That's it. Definitely dreaming. The warmth I feel is the freezing-to-death feeling. The whiteness above my eyes means I don't have enough blood left in my eyelids to make things look red in the sunlight. He resented it that his last dream should be of a strangely accented voice telling him not to try to move, but at least he wasn't in any pain.

Then he did move. And the pain was staggering.

"I warned you," the voice said. It wasn't quite "I vond you" but it was close. "If you must move something, move your left arm. That has not been injured."

Peeters had heard something like this voice before. Sure. It was like a slowed down version of Arnold Schwarzenegger, with echo effects. Whoever this was had an Austrian accent.

"Sprechen zie Deutsch?" Peeters asked.

"Ja, gut," the voice said. "Whichever you prefer. You have been crying out mostly in English; I assumed that was your language."

"It was," Peeters said, then he heard himself, and said, "Am I dead?"

There was a strange noise, something between a bark and a wheeze. It went on for a long time, and Peeters had trouble recognizing it as laughter. "Do you ask me that? Do you think I am God, then? It would take one wiser than I to stake out the line between life and death. What is your name?"

Peeters told him. "How about you."

A FRIEND OF MINE

Shadows on the sky told Peeters he'd been mistaken. His eyes had been open all the time. He was in an ice cave, or an igloo—an igloo, more likely because smoke from the fire whose reflection he could now also see dancing on the ceiling didn't fill the place—lying on a bed of soft furs. His boots were off. He tried to turn his head to look for them, but the pain was too much.

"I warned you," the voice said again. "Just your left arm for now."

Peeters listened this time. He raised his left arm, which didn't hurt, except for the fact that it weighed a ton. He brought it to his face, and found, to his surprise, that he had a good start on a beard, some two weeks' worth.

"I've got to get back to base."

"You are too ill to go anywhere. Besides, I must talk to you. I must decide."

"Decide what?"

"What I am to do with you."

Peeters was suddenly cold. "What you're going to do with me?"

"That is what I said."

"If you wanted me dead, you could have left me with the bear."

"I know. I should have. Compassion, of necessity, is alien to me. I have left others to die as you were going to die."

"For now, at least, I'm glad you changed your mind."

"Do you know why?"

"I don't know anything."

"I watched you, you and your ... engine. I watched for a long time. You had come too close to me before—that was you, was it not, some weeks ago?"

"I suppose."

"And now curiosity was driving you back. I could have killed you, but it would do no good. I would have to leave here, cross the pole yet again. I have done it too many times. I am weary of it."

"But you saved me, anyway." Peeters tried to sit up in his excitement. Pain forced him back down. "Ow. You saved me. From a polar bear. No weapons."

"I have a large knife. Do not concern yourself with that."

"I'd like to know how you did it."

"I am very strong, and I have had much practice."

The way he said it dissuaded Peeters from pressing the point. "Okay," he said, "*why* did you save me?"

"I do not know. I think it might be because you were taking a large risk to give the dogs their chance. In reality, the people of this place staked them out there as a gift for me—I need good dogs—but you had no way of knowing that. I could see you suffering over their plight, ready to take a risk for them, when you owed them nothing.

"It has not been my experience before now that a European would have such a gesture in him."

"I'm an American."

"I know of your wars, but you remain Englishmen."

Peeters decided these things didn't make sense because he was too weak.

"And so I decided," the voice said, "to give you the chance you were giving to the dogs. I brought you here and kept you warm, and bound your wounds as well as I could—I sewed you up with seal gut and a fish bone."

"Listen, you've got to get me back to my people," Peeters said. "I thank you for what you've done, but I need antibiotics quickly."

"What do you need?"

A FRIEND OF MINE

"My wounds are going to fill with pus; I'm going to develop a high fever and die."

"No. I know of these things. The People got the proper medicine from the missionaries. You have no fever now, do you?"

Peeters felt his forehead. "No," he said. "I don't think I do."

"And, of course, I boiled my instruments. My ... teacher was ahead of his time in that regard."

Peeters decided to stop trying to make sense of it.

"Are you Veektuk?"

Again, the laughing noise. "That is what the People make of my name. If you must call me anything, call me Victor."

"Victor."

"After my father. Victor Frankenstein."

Victor Frankenstein, Peeters thought, and he found it all very encouraging. Obviously, he was *not* in some igloo on top of Greenland's ice mass; he was in some military hospital somewhere, probably back in the States. There were probably pretty nurses running in and out, giving him the shots of morphine or demerol or whatever that were giving him such interesting dreams. The bear'd fucked him up, no doubt about that, but they'd found him and plunked him back to the States, and now he could lie on his butt and dream and accumulate his pay until he was in shape to spend it.

Of course, there was another possibility. What if he was lying in that hospital bed and the pretty nurses were running in feeding nutrients to him through a tube in his nose because he was in a permanent coma. What if he was going to spend the next thirty to forty years inside his own head? My God, the *first* thing he dreamed up was Frankenstein's monster. Where did he go from there?

"I wish I knew," he said aloud.

"Wish you knew what?" his host responded.

"Never mind. How did you get to be a god?" He *was* a god, right? Sure. Veektuk. That was from before the bear, wasn't it? Unless he was imagining the whole thing.

He made himself stop. He was, as far as he could tell, physically paralyzed, at least temporarily. Too many doubts would freeze his brain, and then he would be as good as dead. Just stay calm and take things at face value.

"A god?"

"Sure. You've become obscure folklore. You turn up in stories all around the Pole, rescuing Inuit, bringing them food in hard times."

"I do what a decent man would do for his neighbor. It costs me nothing. It gains me fine furs and good dogs that they leave for me in gratitude. Fair trade, Englishman. Isn't that your creed?"

"You're kind of out of touch, if you don't mind my saying so. How long have you been doing this?"

"What is the year?"

Peeters told him.

"Then I have made my home in the Arctic—it is hard to keep track of time here, since I do not age—for something over one hundred eighty years."

"Of course," Peeters said. "The book came out in 1818."

"I am glad I rescued you. You represent a problem to *think* about. I have solved all the problems of mere survival long since."

Peeters laughed. "You think *you've* got a problem to think about."

"Yes. For one thing, why are you so unafraid? You can see, can't you?" The great, gray, scarred face loomed over Peeter's.

"I can see."

A FRIEND OF MINE

"And yet you do not draw away. Am I not ugly to you? Once, all fled from me for my ugliness."

"My mother used to say, 'Beauty is as beauty does,' and you saved my life. Besides, I—" Peeters was going to go on to say that he probably didn't look so hot himself, after being mauled by a bear, but a strange noise cut him off. The creature was sobbing.

It went on for a long time. Finally, the Austrian-flavored tones returned. "I am sorry. I have always believed that to be true. I—I once needed very badly for it to be true. But the world showed it to be a lie. Perhaps men have learned since I walked among them."

Peeters thought it over. "A little, maybe. Some people have learned to be ashamed to hate for no reason. Little enough. Too damned little."

"That is another puzzling thing. You accept all I say. Are you humoring me?"

"No. Myself, a little, maybe."

"I think I must tell you my story, so that you can understand."

"I think I know your story," Peeters said, and he went on to tell the story as best as he recalled it from his teenaged reading of the book.

"How could you know this?"

"The book I mentioned. *Frankenstein, or: The Modern Prometheus*. Mary Wollstonecraft Godwin Shelley, 1818."

"Godwin! Of course! The anarchist. My father knew and corresponded with him! News of Frankenstein's death on the whaling ship undoubtedly reached that family."

Peeters could see the creature's shadow shuffling uneasily. "It is well known, this book?" he asked almost sheepishly.

"It's a classic."

"Then people will understand."

"No. I'm sorry, they won't. They see you as a soulless, murdering monster. Most have never read the book, just corruptions by popular storytellers. They miss the point."

"I should not have killed the child, Frankenstein's brother. I have been tormented for years that I killed the child. But I was *myself* a child, and I was banished and denied. It is not right to reject those for whom you are responsible. They call me the monster? Well, perhaps they are right. And since it seems I do not age, I may not die; thus I may never know if I have a soul. If I do, it undoubtedly is corrupted by hate, for to this day I hate Victor Frankenstein for what he did to me."

The creature's voice got very soft. "But I also know this. My hatred is no deeper than the love I could have given him. He could have taught me, ugly as I am, to be a man. Instead, he drove me to be a monster."

"That's the way I always read the story," Peeters said.

"Here, drink this. You must sleep some more now."

Peeters drank and slept. There were no dreams.

Days passed. Peeters grew stronger. He could sit up, now, if he supported himself with his good arm.

He was also coming to grips with the idea that this dope dream of his (if that's what it really was) had a quality of consistency no other dream he'd ever heard of posessed. There was just the igloo and the fire and creature. And the talk. Hours and hours, about everything imaginable. Peeters' host had a hunger for knowledge, especially about science and technology. He had a low enough opinion of mankind that no history of war or brutality surprised him.

"Tell me more about the flying machines," the creature would say, "I have seen them." What impressed him most about men going to the moon was the idea of carrying air to breathe in bottles.

The time came when Peeters could sit up and feed himself. That day, there was little talking. Victor—Peeters had come to think of him as Victor—sat brooding, staring at Peeters sometimes, flexing his great, strong hands.

"Tell me," he said at one point. "With all the wonders men have achieved, are there—have there been—others like me?"

"No. I think people are afraid."

"Afraid of making monsters?"

"Perhaps. But also afraid of not being able to help treating them the way your father treated you."

"You are honest, Peeters. Perhaps too honest."

"You owe it to your friends to be honest with them."

That brought a few hours of silence. Then Victor said, "You call me your friend, Peeters. Don't you know I have been sitting here trying to decide whether to kill you?"

"See? You're honest with me, too."

"There have been more of the flying machines. Many more. The kind you told me are called helicopters. They are looking for you."

"My body, you mean. They must figure I died weeks ago."

"If they keep looking, they will find us."

"If they find my body, they'll stop looking. Is that the way you're thinking?"

"Why are you not *afraid?*"

"I don't know. I don't want to die, but from your point of view, I wouldn't blame you if you did kill me." Peeters didn't tell him that a part of his own mind was still convinced he was already dead.

Victor said, "Look at me."

Peeters struggled to a sitting position and looked

Victor in the eye. The eyes were the only part of him that looked alive.

"I have considered," Victor said, "bringing you to them."

"You have?"

"Yes."

"Don't do it."

"You want me not to? It would save your life."

"They'll catch you and cage you and cut you up to see what makes you work."

"Is that so bad? You say I am already famous, or a version of me is. Perhaps I could write my own book. And tell the truth."

"Victor. It would be awful. Don't do it. They won't fear you now, but they won't respect you either. Here, you're nearly a god. If you came back to civilization, you'd just be another guest on the *Oprah Winfrey Show*."

"The what?"

"Never mind. I'd rather have you strangle me and get it over with than submit you to that." Peeters bit his lip. "God, I don't want to go back there myself. That's why I volunteered for Arctic duty in the first place. I don't fit into the world I was born into any better than you fit into yours."

"You must go back."

"I what?"

"You must go back. Your world is your responsibility, just as I was the responsibility of my father. If it is monstrous, it is because you—and all the other men and women—have driven it into being monstrous. Am I not the living evidence of the sin of turning one's back on one's responsibilities? You must go back. You will go back and fight for a better world. If you and enough others do that, I shall not mind captivity or curiosity or whatever awaits me so much. Perhaps, someday, I won't need to be a monster or a god. I will be a man, which is all I ever wanted."

"Victor, don't do it."

"I have decided. After you have slept, I will bring you south, to your people."

Peeters had had no choice but to drink, but he fought off the sleepiness. He had to stay awake, had to think of something to do. Victor slept, he knew that. He was sleeping now, in fact.

But what difference did that make? He couldn't overpower him, couldn't restrain him, even if Peeters were in the best condition of his life.

Whatever he did would have to be simple and stealthy.

He had an idea that made him smile. It was simple, and he could manage it easily.

He crawled over to where Victor lay and made his preparations. Then he slipped into furs, some of his and some of Victor's giant-sized ones. He pushed open the snow block that plugged the entrance and stepped outside. The cold, fresh wind was intoxicating after God knew how long breathing seal-oil fumes.

The dogs that had frightened him so weeks ago were now well trained and docile. They dug out from under the snow and took their place in harness in a matter of seconds.

Peeters found the whip, cracked it, and they were off, in the direction Peeters best judged to be south. He heard a bellow from the igloo.

Over his shoulder he could see Victor trying to chase him, but stumbling and falling. No shoelaces in the People's-style boots Victor wore, perhaps, but it was still possible to tie someone's ankles together with a leather thong. It took only a second for Victor to break the leather. He scrambled to his feet and yelled, "Come back, you fool. Don't die for me!"

"Good-bye, my friend," Peeters yelled back. "And thanks."

Peeters had no stamina. He was exhausted in minutes, and close to death in an hour. He had fallen off the sled and was lying in the snow when, miraculously, they found him. Alvarez was part of the search party.

"Hank!" he said, "Hank, you sonofabitch, you're alive! Where have you been? Where'd you get them clothes? Who sewed you up? You're a mess, man, but you're alive! We'll get you fixed up, don't worry about that."

Even as Peeters muttered thanks, he felt a twinge of fear. This was the first time of thousands those questions would be asked. What could he say? What could he do to let his friend keep the role he had heroically created for himself on the fringes of the humanity that had scorned him?

Then it came to him. It would mean time and treatment in a mental hospital, but he could take a year or so of that—long enough for Veektuk to work his way around the pole to another place.

It was an answer that would stand up under any test—lie detector, truth, drugs, whatever.

"I've been with Victor," he whispered. "Victor saved me."

"Who's Victor?" Alvarez demanded.

Peeters put a childish smile on his face and said, "Victor is a friend of mine." Then he began to chant. "Victor is a friend of mine, he resembles Frankenstein..."

FRANKENSTEIN SEEN IN THE ICE OF EXTINCTION

by
J. N. Williamson

It was fitting for him to come to live among the Eskimos because, believing in dual existence, they thought all creatures were capable of becoming human beings. To the people who somehow existed north of the Arctic Circle, the face of a man was merely a visage to be raised into place.

He did not know any of that when he first found himself among them, too weary to travel farther. He knew only that if he did not rest, receive nourishment, and spare his great body from another day's exposure to the merciless cold, he would not be able to defend himself against attack. Among the many things he had learned by now was the faultless knowledge of how far he could be pushed without recognizing the need to kill.

And taking human life at this point of his existence would make a mockery and sham of his last encounter with Dr. Frankenstein.

It was after he'd paid his final respects to the man of science, the man who had created him, that he'd vanished into the frozen wastes with nothing impelling him except a combination of almost worshipful grief and a supremely subtle perception of freedom—in addition to an all but consuming purposelessness. The single human being to whom he had, in any manner, belonged was forever gone and had taken with him the only guidance or direction the Monster had known, save for that he discovered in his studies.

So it had seemed cruelly appropriate for him to journey in solitary misery over the ice and the frozen waters of a land with an ocean that both opened south into the Atlantic and was joined, by the Bering Strait, with the North Pacific ocean. A directionless, uncharted land where time was as mysterious and alien as his own awareness of it.

The fact that his travels were cruel to him simply matched his apprehension of life amid the human species as bewilderingly savage, because he had found every hour of it uncharted, enigmatically puzzling, and cold.

Constantly clad in the boots called "mukluks" and a voluminous parka that came to a hood concealing everything about his appearance but a sliver of his face, he had finally reached a location where he was allowed to dwell in peace with the shivering, stolid, similarly-costumed community of man. Of course he realized he could not and never would be *of* the community; but the shorter, darker Eskimo people at first permitted him to live among them—on the fringes of their igloo village. No one spoke to him then, of course.

For a period of time he believed to be weeks but could possibly have been months, the creature was the happiest he'd ever been. Because he had never been allowed for long to engage in social intercourse with any gathering of men and women, this new isolation was acceptable. Never at any minute a source of solace or intellectual satisfaction, but perfectly acceptable. Effecting a rude, makeshift lean-to composed of scraps of tin and wood he'd thought to bring with him before wandering off into the icy wilderness, he was able—

since his arrival coincided with that of the frozen island's spring—to while away the hours poring over his many books. These, too, he had borne with him in a knapsack slung over one broad shoulder. For sustenance he was content to dine on shrubs or insects abruptly exposed by the minimal melting snow and on dead things he stole, on occasion, from beasts. He was not an epicure. Without a purpose for existence or extinction, he wholly lacked the capacity for discrimination or preference but for what the Doctor, and books, had taught.

Still, in a corner of his mind it was clear he would not be able to prolong his existence under such Spartan circumstances when the brief summer died and interminable winter began. He might well have confronted the fact except that any attempt at reflection or planning he made beyond that stimulated by his reading immediately returned to the forefront of his thoughts a panorama of memories involving his origins and his originator, the dear, damned, dead Frankenstein. When such memories intruded, he always found himself becoming conscious of the glacial coldness of his present life with such agonizing intensity that it set his teeth to chattering violently and aroused the despised feeling of fear. *The cold,* he'd mused after recovering from one onslaught of the unsought recollections, *is as merciless in excess as fire, and man.* And, gripped by that thought: *There is surely a point of conjunction between the extremes of heat and cold. Is the product of that meeting man, or death? Life—or cessation? Or . . . an other?*

Thereby devising for himself a new direction of thought, and instead of planning a means of survival for the rebirth of winter, he'd recorded his countless questions in a thickening commonplace book. Once, he had considered it his journal, or diary. Now he knew it was just a vain record of his impressions of and his wonderments about life, and liked it more.

On those mornings after he had found enough to eat and then slept dreamlessly, innocently, he gave himself enjoyment by playing. ("Morning" was always the time when he awoke, ate what he had left; it lasted until he was once more hungry, or sleepy.)

He played with living things.

He supposed it was as if he were granting himself a childhood, of sorts—returning to a past he had not, in fact, lived. Yet in a fashion he was unable to grasp, it also appeared to him to be a revisitation to a happy period of time he'd shared somehow with many boys. No matter in any case, because his morning pastime entertained him.

He liked to position his big, awkward body in the parka and mukluks on a patch of sturdy ice several safe yards from his lean-to abode, spread his long legs, and wait to hear the honk of geese approaching from the distance. Sometimes, in the Arctic, the birds flew astoundingly low, whether in preparation to land or the certainty that they could easily escape from the half-frozen two-legged beings below them. He was quite convinced that if he exhibited enough patience, he might one day reach up and capture the dangling leg of a particularly prideful goose. He had no desire to slay or to devour the bird when he succeeded, but he supposed he would.

As days formed weeks while the Monster stood perfectly motionless, waiting with a smile no living thing saw, various members of the Eskimo community became aware of what he was doing. None of them had heard of a man capable of immobilizing himself for such periods of time in temperatures that were surely freezing his unseen face, and there was no reason they could conceive for a human being to endure such torment.

One by one, the Eskimos drew the conclusion logical to their belief in dual existence that the tall and powerful stranger among them was not human.

In all likelihood, they reasoned, he had the *inua*—the spirit—of a polar bear.

With the proper deduction made, most of the neighboring Eskimos lost interest in the motionless figure on the ice—until the morning came when he made his catch.

The Monster had been on the verge of abandoning his game mere minutes beforehand. Already that day he'd flapped his arms futilely at several gulls arcing overhead, then, hearing quacking sounds, had soared into the air in a valiant attempt at capturing the feet of ducks flying by. Indeed, he had felt his fingertips graze the downy belly of a duckling scarcely able to achieve the altitude requisite to safe flight. He'd decided to wait only another hour or so—"hour" representing the quantity of time required for the pain in his upturned face to surpass the anticipated pleasure of actually catching a goose or another flying creature—

When a young falcon that had dived in vain for the duckling nipped the creature's fingers, and he closed them swiftly enough to capture it in his hand!

For an instant he was sure he had crushed it. Instead, when he loosened his hold with caution, finger by finger, he spied the youthful falcon's bright, black eyes staring defiantly up at him. It was not only alive, it was trying to flee from his grasp and attack him! He admired that. Then a closer evaluation of the bird's well-being informed him that his instinctive grip had, indeed, damaged one wing. The falcon was striving to will its wing to flap just as (the Monster saw) the other one still did, but very little was happening.

He laughed at its plight and decided to keep it instead of eat it.

Those who witnessed the snaring of the falcon and heard the stranger's terrible laugh when raw wind brought the sound to where they silently watched from outside their igloos wondered if even his identification as a great white bear was adequate, and what the fellow might be instead. Before the following day, most of the Inuit people for a mile around claimed to have witnessed the remarkable catch or to have heard the inhuman laugh. Some began to carve cedar masks with the likeness of a being with a face that was half human, half polar bear, painted to depict skin gone snow-white from exposure to the cold of summer.

And the man whose face they had not seen at all devoted much of his effort toward healing as well as taming the young falcon. He was relieved to discover it would eat most of what he, himself, would eat; and as more time passed, the bird ceased fighting the tether to which he had snared it and began to exhibit its willingness to let him approach it. Gradually, its wing appeared to be healing and it was able to raise itself off the earth a foot or two, always short of the tether becoming taut and yanking it back down. This delighted its sole observer, who appreciated its cleverness and began to plan for the morning when he would let it fly as far as the cord permitted. If he continued to be patient, he might succeed in training the falcon to hunt with him!

In spite of the easily discernible way that temperatures were beginning to drop, the Monster could almost have imagined he was content.

But he could not believe that because, quite apart from the presence of the bird, he sensed that he was not entirely alone.

Stripping the brown feathers from a ptarmigan he

IN THE ICE OF EXTINCTION

had stolen from a weasel primarily by shouting boisterously at the little animal, masticating its breast and tossing small bites to the falcon, he did his best to put his unwelcome thoughts out of his head. He had thought he was done with the past—done with the only close relationship he'd known. Done with the man who was both friend and master. That man, without doubt or question, was dead. And yet ...

When the two of them had both walked among the living, it had always been a matter of the doctor's dreams taking shape through him. Frankenstein had said as much. And now, with each day shortening and darkness once more demanding its right to rule, there were incessant dreams; nightmares. A shadow voice he could not quite hear when he awoke—yet he recognized the inflections, he'd *known* the note of gentle reproof—had greeted him, he believed, possibly warned him. There was also the sensation by moonlight when he crouched with the tethered, patient falcon beneath the insufficient lean-to, shuddering with a coldness that permeated brain and body, that Frankenstein was once more struggling to *live,* through *him*—

And might at any second materialize before his eyes.

The Monster was badly haunted.

So he began to study in earnest, hurling himself feverishly into a life of the intellect in the belief that it would hold at bay the time when he might have to go before an altered and elevated, even more imposingly knowledgeable edition of the scientist and doctor who had bestowed life upon him. Indeed, if he wasn't finding just enough food to sustain him and the bird, or exercising it—giving it more and more rope—he was immersed in passionate learning. He read that the short summer had probably melted enough of the icebergs to endanger shipping in the region, that the sea was replete with whales, salmon, seals, shrimp, and cod. He found that the Vikings were those who became the first recorded Arctic explorers, and that Eric the Red had established a settlement in Greenland about 982 A.D.

The creature also expended his fervent effort to learn the language spoken by the people among whom he lived. It was called "Eskimo-Aleut" and spoken in suffixes, using only three vowels; the *i, u,* and *a* as in "pit," "put," and "pa." Afterward he began to read of the Eskimos' belief in dual existence—

And was again sharply reminded of he who haunted his remorseless sleep.

Nevertheless, for a considerable period of time he never heard the doctor speak to him when he was awake. He told himself this was probably a courtesy, meant to give him time to get accustomed to a very troublesome likelihood: that the doctor and he remained inseparable, even by the special and peculiar properties of that which was called "death."

Now, how that could be, he did not possess an inkling. Certainly he himself had seen nothing which he killed regain life or anything approximating it. Of course (he rationalized), that might be because he consumed most of what he slaughtered. It was obvious that doing so eliminated the receptacles to which the perished might otherwise have returned. And there was also the possibility that the outward appearance of death was not, in fact, death itself, and that people did not wait a long enough period of time for the "spirit" to reoccupy their bodies. For all anyone except a great scientist such as Frankenstein might know, that could take centuries—longer!

The objection to displaying such patience appeared to be that those beings declared deceased had a tendency toward rotting, then emitting an odor that the living thought unpleasant. This reasoning angered the Monster, made him wish to strike his fist upon something or someone. How would impatient people feel if *they* died and, when they were allowed to resume a "life" they had known only a few days before, they discovered their bodies had been burned, hopelessly sunk into the earth, or chewed to pieces? What would *their* reactions be when they learned the reason for their plight was that, through no fault of their own, they had begun to stink?

Here in the North where he dwelled now, it was possible for a thing that seemed perfectly dead—due to its motionlessness and lack of response to kicks and shouts—to look far better than the dead things he'd seen at home. Before long (he knew), he himself would stop moving— frozen by increasingly colder temperatures—and he believed he'd endeavor to resist with all his might any kicks, commands, or bites coming his way. Customarily, most of the living left unrelated dead things alone, unless they wished to devour them. He knew he himself already looked close to dead, facially—on his way to or from death—but he'd never mastered the art of absolute motionlessness. Being frozen in place would almost certainly be a help.

On the day that the falcon flew without its tether, then returned to perch painfully on his wrist in response to his piercing whistle, the dead Dr. Frankenstein once again spoke to him.

For an instant he did not know who was speaking. But he recognized his own language and stood deathly still while blood drawn by the falcon's clutch dripped soundlessly from his wrist to the absorptive snow. *Look,* the shadow voice said with urgency.

Turning his head slowly, he saw—a startlingly short distance away—a lone, gray wolf stealthily stalking a child squatting in the snow just outside its igloo. Because his studies had taught him that such animals rarely attacked or wished to eat human flesh, he continued simply to stare at the unfolding tableau. Then, he understood! This wolf was badly limping and its ribs showed clearly beneath its rough covering of fur. It was starving, and desperate—probably half-mad with hunger.

Now, though, it would assuage the cramps in its belly. The child was a boy no older than three and was oblivious to the approach of the lame but silent beast. The onlooker turned his head back, stroked the falcon's sleek head.

But—*Look!* cried the voice in his own head, and he knew he must obey the command.

The wolf, as if suddenly sensing the presence of the big, totemlike being to its right and intuiting the possibility of interference, chose that moment to seize the small boy in its jaws and begin dragging him away. But its aging fangs (noticed the reacting onlooker) only sank into the parka at the scruff of the child's neck, and squeals of fright annoyingly shattered the day's silence.

You must save the boy! insisted the Monster's internal voice. *You must!*

Swinging both arms to the sides, dislodging the falcon, he took two immense strides and placed himself in the gaunt wolf's path, snarling at it.

Then, presumably reacting to his efforts to make the sinewy bird a partner in hunting, the young falcon flew directly in the wolf's face—alighting with razor-sharp claws digging for the eyes. The child's squeals became shrieks of absolute terror.

Distantly aware that elder Eskimos were emerging from their homes, shouting, the creature reached the bleeding and confused wolf in two further steps. Raising his locked hands above his head, he brought them down atop the animal's skull. Simultaneously, the fal-

IN THE ICE OF EXTINCTION

con lofted itself into the air and the wolf let the boy fall harmlessly to the frozen ground.

Ignoring it completely as he realized belatedly that the beast's flesh would nourish him just as satisfactorily as the little Eskimo would have served the animal, he set about stamping the wolf with his enormous mukluks. Very possibly it was dead after his first great blow, but he strove to be thorough and he was enthusiastic about this activity. He went on pounding the wolf with alternating feet until its skull was decimated, reduced to shards of small bone, and the little boy's family was tugging him away from the animal.

With ease and grace, he threw them off his arms and turned to the closest man, clawing his hands in the manner that the falcon had used its feet—

And was startled to perceive that the father of the child wished to embrace him. Too amazed to offer resistance, he tolerated the hug around his waist and also the grateful pats on his broad back, mustering a smile to show he understood.

Unfortunately, more of his face than generally showed had been exposed by his expenditure of effort and the Eskimo family's expressions of gratitude. Above the head of the man who was embracing him he saw clearly that the mother of the rescued child was peering at him with her own features contorted in a grimace of shock.

That did not, however, prevent any of them from welcoming him into their igloo.

Nor, after they had persisted in persuading him to remove his parka, did the clear sight of his face move them to expel him.

They simply sat—unharmed boy, an older daughter, the parents and an extremely aged woman—staring at him.

He knew what they were seeing. Whether he forced

his lips into a smile or just allowed them to droop at the corners as his mouth seemed to want to do, his face was a horror to others and his head resembled a skull. Upon the latter grew a remnant of hair—at least, hair was *there;* he did not remember having more or less of it—sprouting improbably from portions of his pate, above one ear but not the other, with several strands above the jawline that could once have been sideburns. Healed but puffy scars gave his cheeks a bloated appearance in one sort of light, hollowed them hideously in another. A few angling teeth protruded from his mouth, in repose or not, while the others that remained were pointed and as jaggedly arrayed as a barracuda's. And, whether the light of the sun or in a room was bright or faint, all the flesh of the face and head which was exposed to sight was abnormally pale and pasty. He thought his best feature was his eyes, but even they—risen near the surface now that the region of his countenance between the bridge of his nose and his creased white forehead was sunken—appeared both dull and ripe for being plucked out by some passing beast.

Upon impulse he spoke several words to the members of the family in a crude approximation of the Eskimo-Aleut tongue he had so ardently studied, and their stunned stares turned to pleased surprise. However, for a long moment, no one in the igloo replied but for the small boy he'd saved crawling a few feet to sit beside him and play with his large, dangling fingers.

Then, without warning, the leathery crone seated apart from the others leaned forward at the waist and raised a trembling arm. Looking directly at the Monster, pointing, her red-rimmed eyes opened wide, she whispered two harshly-rasping syllables.

And the father of the small child nodded his head in

IN THE ICE OF EXTINCTION

recognition as he, too, pointed at their visitor. Both the man and his mother wore expressions of awe. " 'Ns Gawd," the former said distinctly, "*you* 'Ns Gawd?" And he added the words meaning, in English, "You're back?"

After a brief consideration, the creature tapped his chest with his fingertips and smiled. " 'Ns Gawd," he agreed with a delight that grew as the minutes passed.

Now he had friends and a *name!*

He did not have the slightest notion whom the Eskimos had imagined him to be until he returned to his lean-to later in the day and had slipped a makeshift hood over the falcon's small but ferocious head. The bird had already torn away shreds of the wolf's dead hide while his master was inside the igloo, and " 'Ns Gawd" thought he had eaten more than enough for the time being.

Then, inside a dog-eared volume of the encyclopedia he'd brought with him, before it was too dark to read, he found a reference to a Latin scholar who had succeeded in rendering the dialect of Eskimo-Aleut as a written language. Apparently the Inuits had heartily endorsed his work.

The man had been named Hans Egede.

Now the intelligent Monster reasoned through the mystery, preferring problem-solving to the other thoughts likely to be evoked as night came on—night, and a darkness that soon would be virtually absolute for many months. His neighbors, utilizing the vowel sounds available in such words as *put, pit,* and especially *pa*, had remembered the scholar through the generations as " 'Ns Gawd."

And they believed the being who had killed the crippled wolf and saved their child from becoming a meal was that *same* Hans Egede—

Though "Ns Gawd" had, in fact, adapted their language from Latin in the year 1721! *Because,* he understood the rest of the mystery as he finished eating and attempted to avoid staring at the murky shadows making life-size shapes just outside the freezing lean-to, *they have seen dead and rotting men before, but not one who slays marauding wolves.*

The appearance of death is not death itself, the familiar voice in his head declared. *You deduced that yourself.*

"I merely wondered about it," said "Hans" aloud.

Perhaps there are times when wondering assumes the appearance of fact, if it is accompanied by belief, the shadow-voice of Frankenstein mused.

The creature pulled the hood of the parka tightly around his head and strove to conceal his face from the dreadful cold. "How could that be?"

You wondered if you were listening to my voice, and, when I ordered you to save the boy, the doctor answered, *you did. Your belief made it a fact. My belief in you, and my wonder, have brought you friends—a new name!*

The Monster was about to scoff, if he found the courage to defy the doctor, when he saw the Eskimo who had called him 'Ns Gawd poking his head and shoulders into the lean-to. The fellow was smiling. "Come," he said simply in the new language "Hans" had learned.

And he slept with the family in their igloo that night and for many nights—none of them with true mornings, except for the way he eventually awakened—to come.

And when they built another igloo, together—all the members of the family and other people from the community working beside 'Ns Gawd—they presented their old igloo to him.

He felt he might cry, but he did not know how. Then

IN THE ICE OF EXTINCTION

the father and mother, the old woman, the daughter, and the small boy who waved a gloved hand at him, were carrying their meager possessions to their new home and he was left to take his falcon into the igloo that would save their lives from the deep-frozen winter of night that was upon them.

Neither the Eskimo friends who continued to live nearby nor the books "Hans" continued to read when he wasn't searching with the falcon for something to eat explained to him that his neighbors believed their debt had been paid to him in full.

Exceedingly hungry, more intolerably bored with each fact he learned and for which he had no practical use than he'd ever been before, the Monster began to consider killing the falcon. He told himself the act would be done for food, for his own survival, but knew he primarily would just like to kill it. It wasn't that he hated it; he simply found himself dwelling on how interesting it had been to stamp the skull of the wolf into nothingness. Besides, it might have been the fortunate one. It had done what everything inside it said to do, even succeeded in spite of its ruined leg—till something altogether manlike had interfered, behaving with the obtrusive and imperious character of the species! Man, forever looking after his own, even at the cost of lesser beasts who lacked his deceit, upright construction, or audacity!

Or, the words started taking shape like someone speaking in his brain, *his power.*

The Monster closed his eyes, determined not to answer, not to make this a dialogue. It was warmer in the igloo, he could not, in fact, freeze to death there; but the single room's lack of variety combined with his own inactivity and solitude made it feel increasingly claustrophobic, and as colorless as extinction. So it was not really the inevitable that was happening now;

it was not the visitation he'd dreaded for an unguessable period of time that had left him—

He lifted the sparse, spidery lashes of one eye to look across the barren igloo, and found the full-length image of Dr. Frankenstein showing grayly on the wall.

The man, or what remained of him—the life-giver, the scientist and physician who had simultaneously been friend, mentor, and godlike figure—was like a long stain in the ice. It wasn't that his features, hair, limbs, and clothing could not be discerned, it was a *flatness* of the ghost, an absence of substance or depth. Close to the creature called 'Ns Gawd, the falcon tugged at his tether, flapped his way as near to the exit of the igloo as he could get, and strained at his restraint.

You yourself seek autonomy, and that is only another word for power, the doctor intoned. *But all the autonomy Man possesses is dominion over the lesser creatures, who do not have the ingenuity to deceive themselves as we do.* It was abruptly colder in the ice-enclosed room and becoming colder. *It is only in our misuse of autonomy that we err, and only when we forget our other, special gift that our errors become grave.*

The Monster struggled to his feet. Stiff from disuse and the absence of proper nourishment, his legs allowed him to advance only lurchingly toward the originator. After a few steps, he felt enfeebled in many ways, paused with his chin lowered. "What is the other special gift, Doctor?"

Frankenstein sighed, or appeared to do so. The perceived sound rustled like many leaves in his creation's big head. *Fool that I am, I dared hope you might have discovered it yourself.* He hesitated, then spoke more loudly, commandingly. *Soon, very soon,* he said—*you shall.*

IN THE ICE OF EXTINCTION

"Hans" wished to ask the doctor what it was like where he existed now but was afraid to pose the question. In the old days, when his master hadn't replied obliquely, the answers had often sounded horrendous. Now the doctor might reply that he was in torment; if so, the creature had no hope whatever. So he dropped his head lower, his gaze as well—

Until he heard the falcon alighting softly again on the hard-packed igloo floor, at which point he opened his eyes and raised his trembling head.

He saw nothing left on the wall; not a trace of the ghost.

But soon, it had sworn, very soon he was to discover the nature of Man's gift which, when it was forgotten, made all his errors grave. He supposed that it was the quality called "love," but surely Frankenstein had not supposed he could learn it alone, without his master's teachings and guidance. And if it wasn't love or some human attribute akin to it, how could he hope to discover it in this land of ice, this frozen universe with its featureless horizons and all but featureless life? Yet he *had* to find out in time what it was and not let the doctor down again—for he was bound to return, now that he'd found him and a doorway from the other world, and Frankenstein *had* to be placated, alive or dead—he had to *approve* of what his creature did if he was ever to belong, and to be warm and content, even for a moment of his life!

For at least three days he waited and reflected, studied and thought, never once indulging himself in contemplation of the joy he might experience from murdering his pet. In fact, he fed most of the steadily-dwindling supply of food in the igloo to the falcon, now and again freezing into immobility in the vain hope that he might hear the whispered sound of Frankenstein's heartfelt approval in his head. He understood now it was part of his task not to be deceived about the freedom he'd imagined he possessed, for to do so would only reinforce the doctor's undoubted conviction that he was just one of the lesser creatures. "Autonomy," the dictionary said, was "self-rule," and Man was entitled to that only over those who *were* lesser; "Dominion," however, was "the power to rule," and despite Frankenstein's remarks, he had never particularly wished for that. Consequently, he decided, it was still his task to prove to Dr. Frankenstein once and for all that his status was not with the lesser creatures but with Man, who looked after his own. . . .

A morning came when he was awakened by the clamor of human voices raised in a variety of what people called "emotions." There was a common undercurrent he recognized instantly as unhappiness, or sadness, though there were threads of other feelings running through the mixture of male and female voices. Again it was "morning" because he'd been brought to consciousness; but beyond the igloo now, each new day looked very much like night except for the austere moon and reflections from the ceaseless snow and ice. Because he wasn't yet aware of being hungry, he continued to lie where he was for many more moments, waiting until the people outside had fallen quiet.

Then, believing there might be none of them in the immediate vicinity, he shuffled to the low-lying exit from the igloo, fell to his hands and knees, and peered out at the strange blackness.

When his vision had adjusted, the Monster saw, at a short distance from him—where the sea itself began as a narrow strip of glacially cold water that widened until it would appear to become the world—the bent and aged woman who was the first to declare that he was the brilliant scholar, Hans Egede.

IN THE ICE OF EXTINCTION

He was astonished to see her seated on an ice floe that was already being blown by the crisp and cutting winds out to sea! From where he knelt, she looked alive and as calm of demeanor as if she sat upon the deck of a mighty ship!

" 'Ns Gawd" drew himself back inside the igloo with a shudder. During the travels that had brought him to this arctic world, he had not cared what became of him. Frankenstein had perished and he was alone. Yet he had never for an instant lost sight of how abominably cold he was, nor, when he had been obliged to trap fish and to dip his hand briefly into the waters of agony, how terrifying it was to think of ending his existence by accidentally falling into the murderous sea. Fire had been frightening to him and he had learned to respect its power, but in its destruction there might be a cleansing of sort. Freezing numbed, clutched, and stole your life, but *boasted* of it—ice held you up for inspection, as an exhibit or display, and did not even permit itself the pleasure of devouring you. The Monster could relate to fire; freezing was manlike, and he had come to fear and respect it above everything but the ghost of Frankenstein.

"I dared hope you'd discovered the other gift yourself," the doctor's words returned to the creature in memory; and once more in recollection only. "Soon, you *shall*."

He rushed from the igloo with a mournful shout and charged toward the old woman on the floe with a brain that churned with as many ambivalent thoughts as the voices of the people awakening him had contained assorted emotions. The footprints he left in the snow, then on the slight bank above the frigid waters, were as long as and deeper than those left by beasts who sought only prey. With no further consideration for his deeds, he waded out in pursuit of the drifting cake of ice, scarcely noticing that he was able to stand. His focus upon rescuing the crone was so intense that his scientifically revivified skin almost failed to inform his brain that he had never felt so horribly cold.

But when he saw the expression on the Eskimo woman's face that told him she was not only still alive but seemingly irate, the inky sea waters suddenly rose to his waist and the only way he would not have been aware of his exquisite agony was if he had been dead.

Terrified now but fiercely persistent, 'Ns Gawd dog-paddled after the crone, fully unaware that he was emitting a shrill whistling noise between his cold-compressed lips. Drawing within a short distance of her, beginning to lose his feeling in his feet and legs, he heard the old one shout at him and saw her wave her arms as if motioning him back! Man and Woman, he thought, were ultimately beyond comprehension.

Then he caught her as she shouted angrily and began to throw herself into the sea.

Locking a gentle arm round her waist, ignoring the harmless blows she gave him with her fists, he managed to swim with the ancient till it was possible to stretch out his legs and, pinning her to his back with one arm in order to spare her further exposure, walk the remainder of the way. His own legs and entire lower body felt as if they were becoming the roots or trunks of the trees he knew, then, he badly missed, and his strides toward the bank were taken wholly on the strength of the instruction and guidance of his originator, living and dead. He had no idea whether the aged woman was still alive when, unaided, he clambered to safety.

The rest of the family whose child he had saved, then shared and given their home to him, was ranged in a semicircle that the Monster found almost threatening. Father, mother, nearly-grown daughter and the boy himself—larger, now; "Hans" was surprised he had not noticed how the two children were growing—scowled at him through the darkness of Arctic day.

Gently, almost tenderly, he slid the grandmother off his back and lowered her to the snowy earth as if to explain to his neighbors what he had been doing. On his knees, desperately needing to get into his igloo and warm himself, he listened to the crone's heart as he had seen the great Frankenstein do. "It is beating," he told them in his crude imitation of their language. He squinted up at them through the gloom, searching for a smile that would infect them with the joy he believed they should experience. "She lives!"

For an answer, the children's father approached 'Ns Gawd and the blue-lipped elder and, from behind his back, produced a club. The creature knew they sometimes used it to kill seals and other animals for food and braced himself.

The man brought the club back and struck his mother in the head with it.

His wife took it from him, emitted a single sobbing sound, and duplicated the man's deed. Then she held the weapon out to their daughter.

The Monster hugged himself and stared, too late to act, too frostbitten and surprised to move in any case. He watched the girl accept the club, glance fleetingly at each of her parents, then smash her grandmother's head with a blow more devastating than that bestowed by her parents. 'Ns Gawd looked at what was left and saw that the old woman's skull had split in two; it bore resemblance to an apple that had been cut open down the middle. The snow was a pretty pink round her ruined head and shoulders as the girl passed the weapon to the family's youngest member.

Frankenstein's creature cried *"No!"* at the boy and tottered partway to his feet.

And the child—whom he had not thought strong enough to participate in his family's rites—brandished the club at *him*, at the scientific construct that had saved him from the wolf.

Between boy and Monster, the father stepped, reviling the latter with words for which he knew no translation. The sole parts of his indignant message that were successfully conveyed were "Go to your igloo" and "Leave us always, for you have brought dishonor."

Straightening to his full height, atrociously cold, he thought perhaps to seize the club from the child and wield it against them all. *It is in the misuse of our autonomy that we err,* he thought, or heard, no longer caring about the distinction. In spite of that, he reached round the Eskimo man and touched the sticky club with his fingertips.

"You're not 'Ns Gawd," the small boy said in his language, slashing at the towering creature with the brutal weapon. "You're not!"

He turned without a word and wended his difficult passage to the only home he had at a ragged, haphazard lurch.

Once there, he tore the hood from the falcon's head and watched without surprise as it flew out of the igloo. It was not a mistake that he hadn't covered the opening that served as a doorway, but he did so now, happy to be in a place without the endless complexities of life.

Removing the icy and stiffening parka and allowing it to fall, he wrapped himself in rags and blankets left by the abode's prior occupants, lay down as far from the freezing winds tearing at the door covering as possible, and ordered himself not to shake to death. He did not mind if he died, but the spasms coming over him since emerging from the sea waters shook him with a force that appeared supernatural in their intensity.

You must save the boy! came the voice of old, in

IN THE ICE OF EXTINCTION

memory. "So he may club me?" mumbled the Monster. *The appearance of death is not death itself.* "Then the old woman can walk about without her head?" he said aloud. *My belief and wonder have brought you friends, and a name!* "It was taken from me," he replied; "you have brought me to this—being threatened by a boy I could throttle with one hand!"

Trembling, he slept. Having slept dreamlessly, he awoke.

The doctor sat by the doorway of the igloo, not more substantial than before, lifting the creature's parka to show it was dry. His smile was benign, even affectionate. There could have been tears in his eyes. Although he still lacked all color, the gray hue of his countenance and garb was brighter then the unbroken mornings of night. *You haven't as yet discovered it,* he said softly. The doctor still held the warm parka, but it wasn't possible to be certain he was thrusting it toward the Monster. *The other, special gift which we must not forget when we have misused our autonomy.*

He worked himself into a seated position, allowing himself the slightest display of ire. "I saved the woman!"

That was not it, Frankenstein said brightly. *An act of love is preceded and motivated by a* feeling *of love.*

He got to his feet, too heartsick and alone in his world to revere his maker that moment. "How can you know I did not love the crone, the family?"

The doctor also stood, the picture of nonchalance and control. *Because you are mine,* he said briskly, the parka draped over one all but dimensionless arm. *There is but one you can ever love—*

Bellowing, the Monster ran at him with his long arms outstretched.

—And it is not you, the ghost finished his remark as his creation collided with the wall of the igloo, bringing a shower of icy fragments down upon himself.

He caught the parka before it landed on the floor, donned it, and rushed out of the igloo.

Then, moving as blindly and without a planned destination as he had done after Frankenstein died, he turned north, heading in the direction where all the hunters of the community went—except during winter. No one went where, desperate enough to attack even an armed man in order to survive, the big game gathered, shivering like starving convicts in a compound sealed against every possible escape. To the extent that he was thinking at all, he went there precisely because nothing remotely manlike would dare to be present.

He knew the doctor was right as he always was. Unloved except in some perverse fashion by he who had given him the semblance of life, the Monster did not love himself, and could not love the Eskimos. Frankenstein had said he had not learned the gift that living things possessed which they must use when their autonomy was misguided. He supposed that applied to his attempt to save the aged woman's life, but the sole understanding he could draw from his failure was that the Eskimos weren't lesser creatures either and he'd kept them from fulfilling their own ill-used sense of autonomy. *Perhaps,* he mused as he trudged many miles into the wilderness, *all this is linked to what the doctor told me once concerning the mistake he made in creating life, and me. That the true Creator gives human beings the freedom to do what they will, and only asks them to abide by His laws. Perhaps a human being who cannot love anyone except, on occasion, himself interferes simply when—*

He stopped walking, and ponderously probing for the truth, at precisely the second when he was a single moment too late.

Before him rose the most enormous being the Monster had ever seen. Previously blending in to the world of ice and snow where it belonged, the polar bear was a sixteen-hundred-pound shaft of white light that appeared to reach to the gray skies. As it stood facing him, its forelegs were twice the circumference of his arms, and they wafted out to him in a deliberate manner that was nearly a wave but seemed to deny him passage. The beast growled deeply in the throat yet did not show its fangs, as if knowing there was no good reason for it to enhance its unarguable might.

He'd believed nothing remotely manlike would be encountered where he had dared to go, but the polar bear stood erect with as much apparent, natural ease as he, and the rumbling sound emitted by it was as unwelcoming as the remarks of Man. *And it's not* you *you can love,* Frankenstein had said when, at last, he'd wanted to grapple with the doctor, even force him to reveal his maddening secrets. A "special gift," indeed! Perhaps what he needed was to chance encountering the doctor on the other side of death; there, if he was fortunate, the definitions of autonomy might not yet have been made!

He roared at the white bear and charged headlong at it, locking his powerful arms as far as they would go around the beast's middle. At one and the same time he combined squeezing with a shoving effort meant to bend the animal back, either to break its spine or to knock it to the earth where his greater nimbleness and quickness might give him the advantage.

The polar bear raked the claws of one paw from the nape of his neck to his buttocks, leaving his flesh open in gaping wounds.

Livid, raging, he pummeled the beast's snout with all the power he had in one arm and, when it roared in ferocity and hurt, he began to pound its sugary face and head with both large fists.

It dropped its forefeet to the ground! Swiftly, he slipped to one side of the bear, locked his hands under its muzzle, and started pulling back. He also succeeded in working one of his feet behind the closest rear leg to prevent it from standing or running. He knew he might soon snap its neck if he could hold it in place, and if he did not lose consciousness because of the searing pain in his back. It was as it had been with the wolf— the sense of a contest or duel, the excitement, the growing certainty he had that he was the superior combatant, *not* the lesser creature in any way!

And he saw the polar bear cub, tumbling over itself in anxiety and bewilderment. One round little ball of fur, watching everything that was happening high above him. Had the Monster taken another step before its mother warned him, he would have kicked or stepped upon it.

Glancing heavenward, he saw his falcon wheel in the frigid air, ready to return and become a second spectator from his lofty realm.

The Monster released his hold and sat down beside the fluffy white creature, extending his hand to stroke it. Maybe it had not been the doctor's voice telling him to save the Eskimo child. But perhaps, he reflected, Frankenstein or he had been correct in knowing there was a special gift to which one might resort when the exercise of freedom was either unhappily enacted or denied to one. "I love you," he expressed his discovered new hope to the quizzical white cub, and its mother's freeswinging paw tore his ugly head from his shoulders.

After the female polar bear had inspected her cub for possible harm, the miniature version of her came upon the detached and smiling skull several yards away. He played with it as long as he could, but the falcon flew away almost immediately and lived until some Eskimos recognized it as the former pet of the Monster. Then they killed it.

THE COMFORT OF WALLS
by
Barbara Paul

At one time I amused myself by memorizing truisms. Walls have ears. Happy are they whose walls already rise. Death is only an old door set in a garden wall. I believed every word.

And why should I not? Abandoned by my Creator at the moment of my birth, I had none to instruct me—nay, none to provide even those barest physical necessities to keep the spark of life glowing within me. I now understand that He hoped I would perish . . . or at least vanish into the wilderness where I would cause Him no embarrassment. He created, He looked, He turned His back in disgust. I have not seem Him since.

But I discovered within myself a certain unwillingness to die in order to accommodate His wishes. Gratitude has its limits, especially when modified by subsequent events. I loved Him for bringing me into being; I hated Him for repudiating me. A father who deserts a child in need is less human than even I. "Foul demon," He called me, as if He Himself had reached into the bowels of hell and plucked me forth. I come from neither hell nor heaven; I exist only because of the lure of science, because of the hypnotic enticement of laboratory experimentation, so tempting to a young mind away from home for the first time. I exist because of the frenzied, self-absorbed enterprise of a very clever schoolboy showing off.

Left alone in a world I did not know, I proceeded forth in search of human contact. Oh, the mixture of eagerness and anxiety I felt then! But all too quickly I was made to see exactly what I am. They cursed me, these strangers, and hurled stones at my head. And then they ran away. I wandered from village to village, looking for that one place where I would not inspire fear and hatred.

Alas, that place does not exist. A wall stands between humanity and me, a wall I cannot breach. They will forever dwell on one side; I, the other.

That was your scorpion gift to me, Frankenstein. Life, but no way to live it.

I learned to keep to the forests and the foothills, sparsely populated environments with a plenitude of hiding places. I concealed myself during the daylight hours, venturing out only when cottagers and townspeople were safe within their walls at night. Daylight invited mishaps. I once saved a child from drowning and was rewarded with a bullet in my side. I took a different child's life and was not punished for it. Clearly, the ramifications of one's acts had nothing to do with moral justness; it was a world of chance I lived in.

But what intrigued me was the ease with which I performed both deeds. I found pleasure in neither act, but nevertheless was nonplussed to learn that taking a life was no more arduous than saving one. How fragile their bodies are! The boy struggled as I squeezed the vitality out of him, but his exertions had no more consequence than that of a feather striking at a mountain. But he was one of their young; I would not know the measure of my own strength until it had been tested against that of a full-grown man. I had yet to determine what feats I was capable of performing.

THE COMFORT OF WALLS

Therefore I became a creature of the dark, a peerer through windows, a lurker on the fringes of other people's lives. I longed for confrontation and simultaneously dreaded it; what if I were to encounter a strength superior to my own? At one village the men banded together to hunt me down, and I discovered I could feel fear. And so I vacillated between wanting to kill them all and wanting—yes, I admit it—to be one of them. Perhaps the two desires are not so incongruous as they appear.

I would undoubtedly have continued in this manner for some time if it had not been for a chance encounter with a traveler one inclement summer night. Whenever the wind howled and the rain plummeted down, it had become my habit to shelter in caves, of which a multitude were convenient to hand. That night I sat near the mouth of my chosen cave, watching the wild beauty of the jagged lightning fragmenting the night sky and listening to the powerful crash and roar of the thunder as it echoed through the mountain passes.

Then a flash of lightning revealed a figure struggling against the wind as he climbed the slight escarpment toward my cave. I edged back, away from the opening. My guest slipped and slid his way inside, where he uttered a sound of relief and proceeded to shake himself like a dog; I was close enough to feel drops of water on my face. Then, with a sigh, he settled himself to wait out the storm.

A few minutes passed in this fashion, neither of us able to see the other and he thinking he was alone in the cave. Then I must have made some sound because he cried out in alarm, "Who's there?"

So my presence was known. "A traveler, like yourself," I answered hastily, "sheltering from the storm."

My answer did not calm him. "Why did you not make yourself known when first I came?"

"I did not know what manner of man you were," I replied. "Nor do I know now. Have you come to rob me?" Humans, I had learned, looked kindly on those who were quick to defer to them.

"Why, no, man," he answered in a less agitated voice. "I am no thief of the road. But you are right to practice caution. A night like this invites mishap. How came you here?"

"You have named it," I said. "Mishap. I was making my way to Beinsdorf"—a nearby village—"when I lost my way. The road forked and I chose the wrong branch."

"Ah. I live in Beinsdorf and was on the way there myself when my horse threw me and bolted."

"Then you have lost your horse?" I put much sympathy into my voice.

"I fear so. He is an untried colt and was frightened by the thunder."

I made some appropriate response, and we fell into an informal discourse that made the time pass more pleasantly. I was no longer so ingenuous as to think I had found a friend; the daylight would quickly put an end to his provisional acceptance of me. But not only did I value his company, I also enjoyed the game. By feigning an interest in the mundane particulars of his life, I could prevent his asking me about mine.

Before long he was holding forth on the subject of his house, a structure that had been years in the building, as he was desirous of making every detail exactly right. He spoke lovingly of the large dining hall, the children's playroom, the nursery. I asked him how many children he had.

He was silent so long that I assumed he had not heard me. But then a sob came out of the darkness. "I have no children," he said with a choked voice. "I have

THE COMFORT OF WALLS

no wife. No family at all. I thought building the house would . . ."

I waited, but he did not finish the sentence. "I am sorry for your pain," I said. "You want a family, yes?"

"All my life I have wanted a family," he replied. "I am no longer a young man. My last hope was the house, my beautiful house. But even that was not enough to entice a member of the fair sex into matrimony. If this cave were not so dark, you would know why instantly. You see, my friend, I am the ugliest man in Beinsdorf. No woman will have me."

This struck me as wonderfully entertaining. My fellow fugitive from the storm was a milder version of myself, a living creature exiled because of his repulsive appearance. "Then prepare to abdicate your throne," I said to him. "Because once I have made my way to your village, you will be only the second ugliest man in Beinsdorf."

"What's this?" he cried. "A man uglier than I? It cannot be! I must tell you, my friend, that I have traveled widely, and nowhere have I encountered a physiognomy more unsightly than my own."

"Would you care to place a wager on the question?" I asked him. "You and I will stand side by side in front of a mirror. If you agree I am the more hideous of the two, I win the wager. I leave the judgment up to you."

He laughed in the darkness. "What shall we wager?"

"If you win, I will replace the colt you lost tonight." It would be easy enough to steal one.

"And you? What do you want if I agree you are the uglier?"

I considered. What did I want? "You will allow me to stay in one room of your beautiful house for a time." In case he was suspicious, I added, "Until I can find permanent lodgings of my own."

"That is no wager, my friend," he said kindly. "You

85

are welcome to stay in any event. But if that is what you wish, so be it. You must dine with me tomorrow evening. We will settle this matter then." He gave me instructions as to how to find his house.

Eventually the fatigues of the day overcame him and he fell asleep. I waited until the first glimmer of dawn began to glow over the eastern mountain tops and slipped away. Another cave somewhere, another hiding place ... until it was time to keep my dinner engagement and select a winner in our bizarre competition.

That evening I arrived before our appointed hour as I desired the chance to explore the lay of the land, so to speak. My host had spoken truly; his was indeed a beautiful house, far and away the grandest I had seen in Beinsdorf. It was situated in a charming dell, framed by a gentle woodland that ran down to a serene pond of water. He had built himself good walls. The nearest neighbor was half a mile down the road, giving the place a semi-isolation that should appeal greatly to the newly wed. The surroundings were perfect for embarking upon a lifelong matrimonial journey; how wretched for my host that no new bride had ever crossed his threshold.

Even more curious about him now, I approached a lighted window and peered inside. He was remunerating the woman who had prepared the meal for him; not once did she look him in the face as he counted out the bills into her hand. For he was ugly—oh, yes! He was ugly. Twisted body, narrow-set eyes beneath shaggy brows, a perpetual sneer upon his face caused by a scar along one cheek ending at the corner of his mouth ... there was nothing of grace or appeal about him. But worst of all, my host was a hunchback. He was an evil-looking creature, yet the words he had spoken the night before were gentle and sad. I wondered if he would make the effort to understand that I was one such as he, only far, far worse.

I stepped behind a cluster of yew trees when the woman left the house, and there I waited until I was confident she would not be returning for some forgotten article. Only then, as the daylight slipped away, did I approach the door. I knocked, three times.

He screamed when he saw me—a piercing, woman's scream. I forced the door open all the way and stepped inside as he shrank away from me. I pushed the door to behind me and stood there wordlessly, towering over the deformed little man.

Finally he found his voice. "What . . . what are you?"

"I am your dinner guest," I said, "come to settle the question of which of us is uglier, you or I."

I waited for it to dawn on him that he had spent the night alone with me in the cave. When it did, he fainted.

Leaving him where he fell, I went to the sideboard and lifted the lid from a steaming dish. What intoxicating aromas! I had survived by eating berries and what food I could steal, but never had I tasted anything on the order of what my host had been prepared to serve me. I filled a china plate and then, for the first time in my life, I sat down to a proper dinner at a proper table.

The meal was delicious, better than anything I could have imagined. I was filling my plate for a second time when my host moaned and stirred. He sat up and pressed the palms of his hands against his temples. He slowly looked around . . . and learned to his horror that his nightmare had not disappeared. He scrambled to his feet and bolted toward the door.

But I was there before him. "You are neglecting your duties as host," I told him. With one hand I grabbed his hump and lifted him off the floor; he screamed again, whether from pain or from fear I could not judge. I put him down in an empty chair at the table and brought him a plate of food. "Eat," I said.

He sat staring at me as I ate, not touching his own food. His mouth worked several times as if he were trying to speak, but no words came out. His crooked frame trembled and tears ran down his cheeks.

"A mild summer we're having, isn't it?" I remarked conversationally.

He had to try twice before he could answer. "Much milder than last year." His voice was high and constricted.

"This is excellent wine," I said, holding up the decanter. "Local?"

"N–no. From Italy."

"Really? Remarkably smooth." As if I knew about wines!

I have to respect him for one thing; he did try. He sat there doing his best to make inane conversation until I had eaten my fill. But at last the tension grew too much for him and he blurted out, "What do you want?"

"Why, you know what I want," I replied, wiping my mouth with one of his linen napkins. "I want to resolve the question of who is uglier. You remember our wager. If you are the uglier, I am to provide you with a new colt. If I am, then you are to provide me with lodgings for a brief period. And you are to rule on the winner."

His voice came out a squeak. "Then I rule that you owe me a colt, for I am the uglier! You cannot stay here!"

My heart grew heavy; he had failed the test. "I thought I had found an honorable man," I said sadly as I rose from the table. "But I see that I was mistaken."

"W–what are you going to do?"

THE COMFORT OF WALLS

"I like your walls," I said.

It took only one squeeze of my right hand to snap his neck. Alas, this was still no test of my strength; the ugly little man had put up less resistance than the child I'd killed. I carried my host's lifeless body outside where I weighted it down with stones before throwing it into the pond. Idly I wondered what his name had been.

Then I went back inside the house and discovered for myself the wonders of sleeping between linen sheets on a real bed.

For a fortnight I stayed inside my house, reading books from my library, admiring my paintings on the walls. No neighbors came to call, no tradesmen knocked at the door. It was lonely, but loneliness was my natural state; there was naught I could do to change that. But then the food supply started to run low, and it was time to go foraging.

I waited until the early hours of the morning when the whole village was sure to be asleep and then left with a light heart, because now I had a warm and comfortable refuge to return to when I was done. There is no way to break down a door quietly, so I disturbed the sleep of a few of those worthy villagers as I helped myself to provisions from their larders. But I moved quickly; none caught sight of me.

One cottage had yielded up a meat pie baked for the following day, its heavy crust still releasing scents that were so tempting I decided not to wait. I found a small shed stacked with wood behind one dwelling; I rearranged the logs to make myself a place to sit. The night was unusually warm, the meat pie was exceptionally good, I was strangely content.

But I must have fallen asleep there, leaning my head back against one of the logs, because suddenly I realized daylight had arrived and I was still far from the safety of my home. I gathered up the remainder of my newly-acquired provisions and started making my way back to the house by the pond. My progress was anything but straightforward; I would dart around a building and wait until someone passed. Then I'd run a few steps to conceal myself behind a cart until someone else was out of sight.

The hour was early, but the entire village was up and bustling! I had never before seen so many people abroad at once in Beinsdorf; something was afoot. I began to grow anxious; if I were seen, they might start looking for me. They might even look in the house by the pond. Oddly, most of the shops seemed to be closed. I broke into the barrelmaker's and positioned myself by a window that gave me a good view of the main road that ran through Beinsdorf.

After about an hour I began to hear music. At the far end of the road a group of people appeared, and then more people, and then even more. Young girls were carrying garlands of flowers while even younger ones scattered petals in the road. Everyone in the village seemed to be there—laughing and talking, as the musicians played and children scampered around to their hearts' content. And in the center of it all was a beautiful young woman, with long golden hair, a shy smile, and a blush on her cheek.

It was a wedding procession.

I crouched down beneath the window as they passed, the sounds of their gaiety and celebration washing over me like a wave. An event that drew the entire populace together! How wonderful that sense of community must be! I had never seen such a thing before, nor would I be permitted to see it now. But suddenly I wanted to see it, I *needed* to see it. A wedding was something I'd only heard of, never witnessed.

THE COMFORT OF WALLS

Before long the sounds of the music began to grow fainter. Leaving my provisions hidden in a corner, I left the barrelmaker's shop and started following the procession, keeping well behind so that none would see me. The celebrants led me to a pretty, well-kept church and its attendant graveyard. By the time I reached the little church, the music had stopped; silence now reigned within its walls.

The church windows were fitted with stained glass in rather simple designs; with a little searching I discovered one section of plain glass through which I could see. A man was speaking; I paid no heed to his words as I gazed upon the others listening to him. The couple seeking connubial bliss knelt before the speaker; they looked like angels, the groom as young and comely as the bride. Their faces were flushed and happy . . . and somehow serene.

Many of the congregation had that same expression on their faces. Others were weeping softly—tears of happiness, I assumed. Even the children were entranced by the scene they were beholding and sat quietly in their places. I thought of the ugly little man I had killed and wondered if he would have been welcome to participate in these nuptial festivities, he who had built a lovely home for a bride who never arrived. How he would have envied the handsome young groom!

Then something the speaker said caught my attention. "We are all God's children," he pronounced solemnly.

What is this? We are *all* God's children? All of us, even I? A child of God? I?

Suddenly I was filled with a rage like nothing I had ever known before. I hated them, I hated them all! I hated the pretty bride and her pretty groom, I hated the smug congregation with those looks of boastful satisfaction on their faces. I hated their hypocrisy, which let them call themselves children of God while naming me demon and monster. I hated the very walls they built around themselves to give themselves comfort. I strode around to the front of the church, pushed open the doors, and stepped inside.

"Children of God!" I cried. "Shall we put it to the test?"

The screams of terror that greeted my appearance were gratifying in the extreme. *This is what I am; see me, and know me.* I marched down the center aisle between the hastily emptying pews. Mothers were pulling their children to them while others scrambled to get out of the way. A little demonstration seemed in order. I took hold of one of the wooden benches; it was bolted to the floor, but a slight wrench was enough to pull it free. I heaved the bench through the nearest window, and the screaming broke out anew as everyone tried to escape the flying glass.

Two men approached me; one was carrying a stout walking stick while the other held a shard of stained glass in his hand. I cracked their skulls together with a resounding crunch that shocked the screamers into silence. Then I lifted up the two corpses, one in each hand, and held them high over my head for all to see. Now I knew my strength! Now I knew what I could do! And I had been *hiding* from these puppets?

I could smell their panic as they pushed and elbowed their way toward the open door; I let them go. When the church was at last empty, I dropped the two dead men and looked around. A rectangle, two long walls and two short ones holding up a roof, that was all. Still, a house of worship—the most comforting set of walls man had yet devised. I walked over to the long wall with the broken window.

My first push convinced me the resistance was not

THE COMFORT OF WALLS

insurmountable. I pushed harder, and a crack appeared in the wall, starting high in one corner and running diagonally down to the floor. Then I put my full strength into it, and the wall groaned and made an angry grinding sound ... and then collapsed.

I had to move quickly to get out of the way. With one long wall gone, the two shorter end walls could not support the weight of the roof, and both walls came tumbling down in a roar and a cloud of dust and debris with the roof caving in on top of them. All that was left standing was the other long wall. I walked around to the other side and gave it a good push.

Standing there in the church graveyard and looking down on the pile of rubble that had once given the illusion of refuge, I felt as if shackles had suddenly dropped away from me. So much for your comforting walls, humans! I turned my back on the wreckage and walked boldly away. I had nothing to fear. I was my own wall.

But I was not my own comfort. The thought came from nowhere, and it troubled me. My triumph at the church was not diminished by it, but the thought did serve to make me acknowledge that that triumph was not quite complete. I had witnessed that day a ceremony that would never be performed for me, but that did not lessen my need for it. For all my newfound ability to dominate the puny humans left me even more an exile than ever. So I decided then and there that I would refuse to deny myself any longer the companionship of another living creature.

I had a house that was built expressly for a new bride, and a new bride it would have. Not a pretty, frail creature like the young woman who had knelt in the church. Nay, I needed instead a bride who was strong and fearless, who could look upon me without horror because she herself was every bit as hideous as I.

Barbara Paul

A bride who needed me as much as I needed her. Yet no such bride had ever been born, nor ever would be.

But one could be made. A bride could be manufactured out of old bits and parts and then galvanized into life, the same as I. A bride who would not be abandoned at birth, as I was. One who would be welcomed, and cherished, and never left alone. A bride who was my kindred spirit in every way.

There was only one human on earth who could work this miracle, one human who must be hunted down and persuaded. It would not be easy, but it must be done. I had a journey to make, a quest to pursue.

I am coming, Frankenstein.

FALLEN ANGEL
by
Peter Crowther

At first Yellen thought the man was watching *him*.

He pulled back against the hedge, folding his body into the sharp branches, and waited. The man staggered a little and bent down. Yellen stared, trying to make out his movements through the gloom. The man had rested something on the ground and was now straightening up, muttering. The sounds of indistinct words floated across the street. Yellen glanced quickly to left and right to see if there was anybody else around. The street was deserted.

Yellen had been casing a small one-up-one-down that stood out among the other houses by virtue of a gleaming silver satellite dish, standing proud on the patchy stucco like a ripe boil. He had heard the sound of footsteps and had dodged gracefully across the sidewalk into the hedge. He looked back at the man and wrinkled his nose. The hedge smelled of pee.

Across the street the man rose to his full height and took two faltering steps forward ... then another one back and slightly to one side. He wore a long topcoat which, as he swayed side to side, feet held so firmly in place that they could have been nailed to the sidewalk, flapped open to reveal a dark jacket and light-colored pants. His shirt collar was unbuttoned low, necktie sprawled to one side in an explosion of crumpled material. The top half of his body continued to ripple as though an electric current were passing through it. Yellen recognized the current as being 80-proof. He slid his right hand into his jerkin and eased the .38 out of his waistband while the man shuffled around so that he faced the wall, his back to Yellen, and made a big deal out of unzipping his fly.

A faint hybrid sound of pooling water and bursts of mumbling echoed through the night. It sounded like someone trying to tune into a distant radio station.

After what must have been a full minute and a half, the man shook himself, bent forward, fumbled up his zipper, and then turned around. He looked straight across at Yellen, but his eyes clearly didn't see anything except the night and the loneliness and the New Jersey air. The man threw his arms into the air and shouted to the sky.

"Thus st—strangely," he stuttered hoarsely, "are our souls constructed . . ." He paused, shook involuntarily, and then continued, "And by such . . . by such slight ligaments are we bound to posterity or ruin!" He staggered back a step or two and, as if attached to a single string which had suddenly been severed, his arms and head fell forward to sides and chest. He kept this way for several seconds, swaying, and then lurched down sideways to retrieve whatever he had set on the sidewalk. Yellen retreated further into the hedge and concentrated on the object as it came into view. It was a bag.

It looked like a doctor's bag but bigger. One of those old black valises that carried prescription pads and Valium and pain-killers. *And what else?* Yellen wondered. *Maybe a few uppers?* He held the gun down by his side so he could bring it up at full arm's length and fire if he were forced into it. He almost wished he would be. But, no, the man hoisted the bag up under his arm and leaned an unsteady head so that it met the object . . . and kissed it tenderly. Then he turned around to face the way ahead.

Yellen squinted. The bag looked heavy. Important. Precious.

The man started to shuffle his one-two-one way along the sidewalk and Yellen moved forward from the hedge, sliding the gun into his jacket pocket. He watched the man for a few seconds and then turned back to look at the house. It was still dark. He knew what was in there. VCR, television set, bunch of compact disks, receiver. The usual. It was the sign he had grown accustomed to looking for. It usually meant objects which he could easily turn into cash. He looked back at the man's weaving figure, heard a distant belch, and his eyes locked onto the black bag. But maybe there were better pickings to be had.

The man reached the end of the block and turned into the next street, shuffling back before proceeding, like a bad vaudeville act or Snagglepuss the old cartoon lion. Then, with a throaty *burrrup* and a stream of Shakespearean-type mumbling, he was gone.

Yellen rechecked that he was still alone and unobserved and then took a final look at the house. His mind was already made up even before he acknowledged the decision. He folded himself into the air and the shadows and ran crouched and silent-footed across the street.

He got to the end of the block and peered around the corner. About fifty or sixty yards up the sidewalk the man was doing more of his soft shoe shuffle, trying to make a ninety-degree turn over the shards of a large fence. He negotiated the barrier with difficulty and staggered off the sidewalk. Yellen followed.

He followed the man across some stumpy grassland, festooned with ditches and rocks so concealed by the night that even he, stone cold sober, experienced some difficulty in maintaining his balance. The man, however, now seemed to have found his feet and glided effortlessly across every obstacle with seeming surety.

Eventually the steady hum of humanity, that almost indiscernible and often reassuring presence of civilization, faded behind them as they picked their way across the barren land. Here a tree sprouted from the earth, there an occasional bush; up a small slope, down a sharp ravine . . . until, at last, the sound of the man's shoes clattered again onto man-made material. Yellen stopped and watched, breathing heavier now.

The man was on a street. It ran straight to the right and into the far distance where it joined the main drag down into Westfield. To the left it ran a few yards before curving away and down what appeared to be a hill. Yellen couldn't be sure. The light was very bad, fed only by three streetlamps, unevenly spaced, and a gibbous moon that played hide and seek with the passing clouds.

The man stamped his feet, almost losing his balance in the process, and then crossed the road he was on and walked toward a large house that seemed to fill the whole horizon. A thick patch of cloud slipped across the moon and then slid off toward distant Miami, the sudden increased glare of light catching the full splendor of the property and etching it against the dark sky to the north. The house stood alone on the road. Yellen looked at it and marveled.

The tapering roof of an octagonal tower adjoining one side of the main roof—a choke-topped chimney rose from the other—gave the house the appearance of a clenched fist, its index and little fingers stretching up in a combination of exclamation and caution. It was, Yellen recognized from his college days, a Queen Anne style mish-mash of tower, bay windows and porte cocheres. There were many examples of the period around Westfield, but this, surely, would qualify as being one of the finest. Possibly *the* finest.

Moonbeams glinted like fairy dust down a tapering roof which alternated between rows of fish-scale shingles and rectangular slates. More shingles adorned the gable, and the porch—within which the man now fumbled in coat pockets, the bag still held firmly beneath his arm—featured a frieze of spindles and inverted taper columns, up which a veiny confusion of ivy tendrils had crept. The windows were a patchwork of Elizabethan straplines, with small multicolored panes surrounding a larger clear-glass center.

And there, attached to the highest tip, a jumble of thick cables stretching and bowing down from it to the darkened depths of the grounds, was the biggest receiver dish that Yellen had ever seen.

As he crept stealthily across the road and into the drive of the house, Yellen kept his gaze fixed on the object, watching its perspective change and its size increase until, as he crouched behind a thick bush, the thing seemed to dominate the sky. It was at least three—maybe four—times larger than the usual dishes householders fixed to their properties. Black or dark gray in colour, it boasted a stamenlike centerpiece of glass pipettes which themselves formed a fairy-ring periphery to a thick and bulbous apparently metallic protrusion that angled into space. As he watched, Yellen thought he saw the spike glowing. A sound from the porch made him crouch lower and fumble in his jacket pocket for the gun.

Through the bush, Yellen could see that the man had now turned from the door, which now stood partly open, to face the drive and the road beyond. He held the bag tightly to his chest with both hands, stepped out onto the path and looked up at the receiver dish. "As I stood at the door," he said, loudly and in now more succinct tones, "all of a sudden I beheld a stream of fire issue from an old and beautiful oak, which stood about twenty yards from our house."

As if on cue, the spike now proceeded to glow and throb and a distant symphony of metallic *tings* sounded through the gloom. "And as soon as the dazzling light had vanished, the oak had disappeared," he continued, "and nothing remained but a blasted stump." The man staggered a little and then, resting the bag on his outstretched left arm, he unfastened the clasp and pulled the sides apart. Looking inside, his voice lower now but still distinct, he said, "I never beheld anything so utterly destroyed."

And then he reached into the bag and pulled out, his hand clasped around one leg, what appeared to be a floppy doll. The object flailed at the movement, its free leg and both of its arms and its head swinging freely.

The man dropped the bag to the ground and held the doll aloft. Turning his head so that it faced the dish—or, perhaps, Yellen thought, some greater entity far beyond the confines of the house—he intoned, "Yet from whom has not that rude hand rent away some dear connection, and why should I describe a sorrow which all have felt, and must feel?"

He turned around and lowered the doll, taking it into both hands and pulling it to himself. "Nay, ne'er mind *describe* . . . why must I *countenance* it? Why *should* I countenance it?" And then he turned back to face the house and went inside, pushing the door closed with his body.

Yellen waited, heart beating fit to burst, and watched the porch. The door banged against its casing and then, slowly, drifted open once more. He removed the gun from his pocket, felt the reassurance of body-warmed metal, and then replaced it again. With a quick look around him he stood up and ran to the porch, up the few steps on tiptoe, and through the doorway into the darkness beyond.

Once inside, Yellen flattened himself against the wall behind the door and listened. He could hear echoing footsteps fading somewhere in front of him but, his eyes not yet conditioned to the impenetrable blackness, he couldn't make anything out. *Why doesn't he turn on a fucking light?* Yellen thought. Suddenly the sound of the footsteps changed. The man was on some stairs. But was he going up or down? Yellen put his head flat to the wall and closed his eyes, straining to hear. It was up.

He removed his shoes and placed them carefully by the door. Then, his vision improved, he moved forward deeper into the house.

The doorway opened onto a pentagonal hallway from which a series of doors, all but one closed, stood in the center of each wall with the main door behind him. The open door led onto what seemed to be a corridor. It was there that the footsteps could be heard. He checked his gun again, walked across the floor to the corridor, and slipped stealthily through.

At the end of the corridor was a cross passage. Once there, Yellen glanced carefully around the corners. To the left, the corridor led to what seemed to be a rear entrance to the house. The righthand wall of this smaller corridor featured a series of picture windows which showed a long, rambling garden, completely untended and overgrown. At the rear of the garden, adjoining a wide, rough pathway, was a car. Its wheels had been removed and the axle ends rested on small piles of stone. The car appeared to have no glass in its windows. The glass door at the end of the corridor opened onto a small room, also completely glassed, and Yellen could make out various handles and pieces of equipment.

In the other direction, to the right at the end of the main corridor, a shorter passage led to another open area, though this one was considerably smaller than the main hall. Yellen saw a banister end leading upward to the right and out of sight. Now, at least, he knew where the stairs were. He started to move toward them.

As he walked, straining to hear the footsteps and continued mumbles from somewhere overhead, Yellen was suddenly aware of the state of the house. It had been allowed to go completely to ruin.

From all of the walls large strips of wallpaper hung free, reaching to the floor and myriad piles of broken plaster and fast food wrappers and containers. From all around he seemed to hear soft scurryings, scratchings and rustles, and the almost soundless movement of gently billowing material. As he reached the foot of the stairs he checked the gun again and moved around the banister to face the risers leading upward.

The flight of stairs had, approximately, 25 risers and Yellen could clearly see the next floor. The stairs opened onto another cross corridor before continuing around to the right, up again. He started up, suddenly sharply aware of a pungent smell.

The smell was not exactly unpleasant, but it was strong. It hinted of body odor, a thickening draught of parmesan cheese sitting atop a bowl of steaming hot vegetable chowder. By the time he had reached the top of the stairs, it just smelled like shit.

The cross corridor led, to the left, to a long passage which featured three doors, two on the left, one on the right. The right one was glass paneled and led onto a small balcony overlooking the rear garden. At the far end of the passage was a wall and, on the left, a dark patch which suggested the corridor made a sharp turn to further rooms.

To the right, the corridor ended, by the foot of the

next flight of stairs, at a door. The door was open and a light was shining from inside. Somewhere, something was humming. It was an equipment-type hum, the sound of confident strength, of well-tended machinery.

Something small ran over Yellen's feet and it was all he could do to keep from crying out. He kicked out and skipped toward the door. As he passed the next flight of stairs, the smell he had noticed earlier hit him like a hot sheet thrown over his face. He stopped and looked up the stairs.

The flight led to another level, another blank wall and, presumably, another cross corridor. Looking up, he could hear sounds ... groans and moans, shufflings and—he turned his head to one side to concentrate—an occasional clank, like bottles, or glasses being chinked together in a gesture of good health. But the smell coming down from up there spoke of anything but good health.

Yellen glanced over at the open door, listened, and then stepped onto the first stair.

His heart was now beating like an electronic drum, faster than should be humanly possible.

He took the second stair.

And then the third.

Each step led him deeper into that smell of depravity and filth. It was as though he were descending into a blocked sewerage system and not simply climbing a staircase.

When he had reached the top, he looked back. There was nothing much to see, just the faint glow coming from the small room to the right of the foot of the stairs. He turned around and swallowed hard to keep from throwing up.

This time, the corridor ending at the left and front, a passage led to the right and along to a large pair of doors across which a heavy plank had been fixed into two large, rusting metal hooks. The moans and groans were coming from behind the doors.

Yellen considered going back downstairs and out into the night. The temptation was strong. Hell, if he were so bothered about finding out what was behind the doors, he could even come back another day, tomorrow maybe. With help. In the light.

Because the night, and particularly this house, spoke of monsters. *Monsters!* Why should he think of monsters, for crissakes. He hadn't even used the word since he was a kid and couldn't get to sleep because of the big man who could fold his body into sections and sleep in the large bottom drawer of his chest. The drawer where his mom put Yellen's underwear and socks. The drawer which Yellen would never go into unless the penalty was sufficiently dire. After all, what were a few skidmarks in your smalls or the occasional lump of toe-cheese rattling around your socks when the alternative was to have a spindly arm and toothy grin telescope out of the colored interior of a chest drawer to grab you and kiss you, and pull you into the feigned softness of what was, in reality, a material hell.

Something shuffled up to the other side of the doors and bumped into them, letting out a tired groan. The doors had rattled briefly, softly, and were still again. Whatever it had been could now be heard shuffling away again.

Yellen took a deep sigh, strode to the doors, and lifted the plank free. He placed it against the wall and reached for the handle. As he did so, the left hand door opened slowly.

Yellen wasn't even aware of throwing up.

His gorge moved quickly and without deliberation, traveling from his stomach, up his throat, and into his mouth from where it splashed in one silent burst and then dribbled in two or three additional pulses.

Yellen shook his head at the thing that faced him in the gloom. It was—or once had been—a girl, maybe 14 or 15 years old. She stood before him as if in supplication or submission, completely naked, scrawny breasts covered in sores and scratches, a thick pubic thatch hanging from her crotch like a Scotsman's sporran.

The girl's skin was yellow, like matted breakfast cereal, boasting a series of sores, tears, lumps, and criss-crossed stitches that wept thin funnels of matter into crusted configurations on her cheeks and jowls. One of her eyes was closed in a puffy ball of rainbow hues. The other, a watery orb that started, seemingly without recognition nor emotion, out of a thin and skeletal white socket, blinked once and fell still. The skin on her cheeks and down onto her neck was stretched so tight that Yellen could see the musculature flex and vibrate as she turned her head, first one way and then the other. It was with profound regret and shame that he saw he had been sick onto the top of her head, where his vomit ran and mixed with long tendrils of thinning hair.

The girl opened her mouth wide, separating lips so black they looked like heavy pencil slashes gouged beneath a turned-up nose, and let out a soft, querulous hum. Then she turned from him and shuffled back into the room. As she moved away from him, slopping her trailing feet through rivers of brown and yellow and green ooze, Yellen saw the caked mess of shit on her backside.

Now, in spite of the smell, Yellen moved into the room.

There were maybe fifteen or twenty of the unfortunates in there, some standing, some sitting, and some lying down amidst the debris and the filth. Some were younger, some maybe older than the girl who had admitted him, but all were children. A handful in the far corner, beneath a series of barred and whitewashed windows, were only babies or toddlers. One of them watched Yellen, his black-rimmed mouth a shitty stain, as he paused in the act of eating a long runny stool that dripped onto his legs. It would, he thought, be crediting the child with too much to say that there was a spark of intelligence in those watery eyes. His actions were purely reactive.

A sound behind him made Yellen spin around.

The man stood in the doorway, swaying slightly, a beatific smile etched on his face. In the current circumstances, the smell of bourbon was tantamount to being the finest Chanel perfume.

The man held onto the door with his left hand and waved the other expansively to the scene inside the room. "With how many things are we upon the brink of becoming acquainted," he said in a slow, deliberate voice, "if cowardice and carelessness did not restrain our enquiries?" One of the children moaned and the man lifted a finger to his mouth and shook his head paternally.

Turning his attention back to Yellen, he said, "To Monsieur Frankenstein, this was a rhetorical question, my friend. I, however, put it to you fully." And with that he stepped back and ushered Yellen out of the room. Yellen walked as if in a dream, back onto the landing, and the man closed the doors and lifted the heavy plank back into its place.

"What are they?" Yellen asked as he followed the man down the stairs.

"They are the chosen ones," he replied, the words drifting over his shoulder like motes of dust. "I know what you are thinking, my friend."

"I'm not your friend," Yellen snapped.

The man reached the foot of the flight and nodded. "Quite so. But I do know what you are thinking. 'Its astounding horror would be looked upon as madness by the vulgar.' " He spoke the words reverently and Yellen saw that they were slightly out of the flow of the man's first sentence.

"Are those . . ." Yellen waved his hand. "The things you keep saying, are they quotations?"

The man nodded again, bending slightly from the waist as though before a dignitary. Standing straight again, albeit falteringly, he said, "Shelley."

"The poet?"

"Mary Shelley. The author *and* poet. *Frankenstein*. Are you acquainted with the work?"

"I've seen the movies," Yellen said.

The man sniggered. Then he gestured to the room at the foot of the stairs. "Come," he said. "All will become clear."

As he walked toward the room, the man removed a hip flask from his jacket pocket and, throwing his head back dramatically, took a deep swallow. Then he returned the flask to his pocket.

The room was huge and bare.

In its center was a padded black table, above which hung a chandelier-type object bedecked in wires and tubes. The wires ran from the head of the object and across the ceiling to a high point on the wall below which a window looked out onto the path by which they had come to the house. Yellen, patting his pocket for the reassurance of his gun, recognized the scene and surmised that the wires were attached to the receiver dish.

On the table itself lay the doll which the man had carried in his valise. Only it wasn't a doll.

The child was perhaps five years old, his skin pale

and withered, a single heavily stitched scar traveling the full width of his stomach. Yellen stared at the child, not daring to believe what he was seeing. "You're mad," he said. The words sounded so ineffective, so cliched and so entirely inadequate.

The man walked in front of Yellen to the shelving that covered the walls surround the room. Yellen now saw that the shelves bore what might well be hundreds of large bottles and jars and tanks, each with something floating in thick-looking solutions. " 'I hope the character I have always borne will incline my judges to a favorable interpretation, where any circumstance appears doubtful or suspicious.' " He reached down a bell jar, containing what Yellen thought could be livers or kidneys or something similar, and unscrewed the top. "That was what Justine Moritz, the closest of close friends to Elizabeth Lavenza, Frankenstein's virtual sister, said as she stood accused of the murder of Elizabeth's son, William." He took a rubber glove from the shelf and pulled it on with a loud squeaking sound. Smiling at Yellen, the man said, "Nobody ever understands." He lifted one of the things from the jar, replaced the lid—one-handed and with difficulty—and returned it to the shelving.

"What are those?"

"Things no longer required by their previous owners," the man replied. "You could say they're not wanted on voyage." He chuckled and stepped across to the table where he dropped the piece of tissue or whatever it was into a round surgical tray which lay beside the child's body.

"Where do you get them?"

The man turned around and leaned against the table, removing the hip flask with his ungloved hand. " 'A churchyard was to me merely the receptacle of bodies deprived of life, which, from being the seat of beauty and strength, had become food for the worm.' "

"Oh, my Go—"

The man threw the flask across the floor. "Oh ... spare me your platitudes and your pathetic pleas for help." He moved toward Yellen, waving a finger at the ceiling. "There's nobody there, can't you people understand that? The lights are on, but there's nobody home. God?" He laughed, making the word sound like an invective. "He doesn't exist—or, if he does, then he's singularly lacking in compassion.

"*I* am the light ... *I* am the way. It's because of *me* that those children still survive."

Yellen shook his head.

The man turned back to the table and began rubbing a cloth across the corpse. "The girl that you saw is my daughter." He stopped and leaned on the table, head bowed. " 'I saw the yellow eye of the creature open; it breathed hard, and a convulsive motion agitated its limbs.' " He returned to the washing. "She was my first," he added. "Fourteen years old, raped and stabbed to death, her vagina clipped almost up to her abdomen with cutting shears. I try not to think of what order her injuries were sustained ... try not to think that the killing insertion to her heart came last."

He dropped the cloth back into the bowl and pulled a cord overhead. The chandelier began to lower slowly. Turning to face Yellen, he said, "And yet you talk of God." The words came in a haze of spittle and disgust.

"You *are*—"

"Mad? So you said. 'All men hate the wretched; how, then, must I be hated, who am miserable beyond all living things.' " He suddenly concentrated his gaze on Yellen and frowned. "Incidentally, why are you here?"

Yellen shrugged. "To steal."

The man copied the shrug. "Makes no matter." The

chandelier beeped and came to a shuddering halt. "Ah," the man said, "we're almost ready." He waved for Yellen to join him. "Here, you can help."

"You gotta be joking!"

"I never joke, Mister Thief. Hold not another in contempt lest you are yourself free from blemish. I, my dishonest guest, live to give. You, on the other hand, are a taker."

Yellen removed his gun. "Well, I'm going to do some giving right now."

The man watched the gun impassively. "And what do you propose to do with that?"

"I'm ... I'm going to go back to that hellish room and put those things out of their misery. Will bullets—"

The man dropped to his knees on the floor and clasped his hands together. " 'She died calmly—' "

"Shut up."

" '... and her countenance expressed—' "

"I said ..."

" '... affection even in death.' "

"... SHUT UP!"

" 'His yellow skin scarcely covered the work of muscle—' "

Yellen ran across the room and swung the gun against the man's face, sending him sprawling against the table. The table skidded away and then held against two restraining straps fixed to the floor, jerking its passenger off to land with a dull thud.

"Jesus Chri—"

"There's no him, either," the man said, holding a shaking hand to the gash below his left eye. "There's just you and me, thief. Do what you must."

Yellen lifted the gun and fired. And he kept firing.

The first shot went through the man's hand and cheek, splaying brain onto the floor milliseconds be-

FALLEN ANGEL

fore the back of his head touched it. The second and third went into his chest. The fourth, his stomach. The fifth strategically placed—Yellen had walked while firing and was now standing directly above the man—in the center of his forehead. There wasn't a sixth, only a click ... followed by many more clicks until Yellen's finger eased from the trigger.

When he went back to the room at the top of the house for the final time, he carried the cold body of a small boy. He had already dragged the man's body up the stairs and propped it against the door beside two cans of petrol that he had found in a small hut in the garden.

On the top of the can sat two books: one containing matches and one containing words.

Entering the room again he smiled frequently. Nobody inside responded. Nobody tried to leave.

He placed the boy's body with the other toddlers and dragged the man into the center of the room.

Then he walked around spilling petrol everywhere, singing, "Hush little baby, don't say a word, daddy's going to buy you a mocking bird." It was a song his mother had sung to him many years ago.

As the flames took hold, he flicked through the pages of the other book, trying to find something appropriate.

He found it and paraphrased: "Farewell my beloved friends: may Heaven in its bounty bless and preserve you; may this be the last misfortune that you will ever suffer."

Then he left the conflagration and rejoined the night.

"When I placed my head upon my pillow, sleep crept over me; I felt it as it came, and blest the giver of oblivion."
 —Mary Wollstonecraft Shelley (1797–1851)

THE MAN WITH THE BARBED-WIRE FISTS

by
Norman Partridge

She said we should bring that stuff down to her shack by the creek 'cause we had to give her that stuff if she was gonna do what Jimmy Tibbs wanted her to do. And we didn't know then that she was a witch so we brought that stuff down there. Us kids did. That was before the aqua duck when there was still a creek there. And Jimmy made me tote the big spool of barbed wire 'cause I was stronger than he was and 'cause I was a nigger and he said that niggers was like Ygor in the picture and did what they was told. He was littler than me, but back then I figured he was right 'bout that Ygor stuff so I didn't bellyache.

That particular year it was a dusty summer. Hot and dry and miserable dusty. The creek bed was all buzzin with gnats and the rocks that was used to bein underwater was hot like little fryin pans and my socks was all itchy with brambles. And on top of that I was sick of the whole thing 'cause Jimmy had done had me runnin back and forth along that dry creekbed with notes for the witch all week long. Anyhow, now everythin was settled and us kids was all finally gonna go and get turned into growed ups. Jimmy was way ahead of me 'cause all he was carryin was his daddy's RCA radio and the plug cord was draggin 'tween his

THE MAN WITH THE BARBED-WIRE FISTS

legs like Satan's tail. Mary Hannah wasn't too far behind Jimmy. The poke with lipsticks and powders she stoled from her daddy's five-and-dime was scissored tween her arm and her chest and her cheeks was all shiny with lipstick in thick stripes like she was an Injun chief. And she was real eager to come with us fellas 'cause she said that since her daddy took sick he had to live upstairs all the time and her mama sometimes did that stuff with the truck drivers who brung goods to the store so she wanted to know how to do that stuff too 'cause now the truck drivers was startin to look at her sometimes too. And after Mary Hannah come Rusty and all he had was the keys to his daddy's Ford, but Rusty was lazy so he was slow and I knowed he was frettin on account of all the trouble he could get into 'bout them keys if his Daddy found out that he stoled them. And b'sides, he was sneezin on account of the dust from the itchy brambles us kids was kickin up.

And Jimmy laughed, singin, "Sickly child, sickly child . . ."

I was last. The spool of wire was heavy and I was wearin gloves and two coats to keep from gettin scratched and I didn't like to think what Pap was gonna do when he found out the barbed wire wasn't in the barn no more like it was supposed to be. But Jimmy said to me, "Little Pete, your daddy is just a stupid nigger so he ain't even gonna know it's gone, and even if he does know it he's gonna know better than to holler that someone stoled it, 'cause God knows where that kinda yellin gets a nigger round here, Little Pete."

Little Pete. That's what they call me 'cause I'm hunched up like Ygor. But I wish they would call me like they did the little boy in the picture. Peter. That's what Mama used to call me before she went off to the sportin life. And I wished I was like Peter in the picture too, all brave like nobody's business and off huntin rhinocerasses and alligators and havin adventurers 'bout the giant who stoled my story book and that soldierman with the rubber arm who rescued me.

But this wasn't no adventure like that. Like I said, it was hot. Not cold and rainy and gloomy like in the picture. The witch's shack was a teeny bit of a place out behind the big house and it was all leanin sideways and ready to fall over like the big house was too and like the houses in the picture. Jimmy said that she wrote him in a note that we had to meet her in that shack cause the big house was too grand for the likes of us little folks and little folks got to meet her in a little place. So we climbed up from the creek bed over the hot fryin pan rocks that was real smooth even though, like I said, there wasn't no water in the creek. This was before the aqua duck, 'cause since we got that there is always water there and you can't walk down that way no more and there ain't even no stones in the bottom of it accordin to what people say and now there ain't no grand house or even little house there no more, either, 'cause I guess them houses finally leaned over too far and just fell down and somebody hauled them away. But back then there was still a creek and two houses and when us kids come up through all that manzanita and then through the rusty barbed-wire fence what was all tangled-busted and needin fixin bad we was practically on the little porch which belonged to the shack. It was pretty rickety with a hole in the roof and I thought 'bout the picture and the hole in the labboratoree roof where Ygor pushed a boulder through and almost hit Jimmy.

But it wasn't Jimmy he almost hit, it was the doctor in the two-tone coat. Jimmy said the man was Frankenstein's son, like the picture's called. I said that Peter was Frankenstein's son, but Jimmy just said I was stu-

THE MAN WITH THE BARBED-WIRE FISTS

pid 'cause Peter was the grandson. But then when I asked him how come the picture wasn't called *Grandson of Frankenstein* he couldn't even give me a right answer. It's the same way as when he tried to tell me that Ygor was the same fella as Dracula and that the Frankenstein Monster was really the Mummy.

Anyway, "You bring it all?" was what the witch asked and Jimmy allowed how we had. "Boy, you better not be lyin," was the next thing she said.

"I ain't lyin," was what Jimmy said.

Jimmy lied all the time, though. He always said we should go to the picture together, but then he wouldn't sit with me when we did go even though we went plenty of times 'cause it was the only picture they showed for weeks and weeks. He told me he was my friend plenty of times and then throwed rocks at me when he seen me walkin by myself while he was with Rusty and the other fellas. I knowed he did it 'cause I was a nigger and I was always gonna be small like Ygor, anyhow. Even though back then I used to pray it wouldn't be so, specially when Jimmy and Rusty called me a nigger dwarf circus clown.

And for sure Jimmy lied bout that stuff with Mary Hannah too, even though he said that he really didn't hate her 'cause of what happened though after it happened he said she was just like the witch.

"I had to say it," was what he said 'bout that back when I was still talkin to him. "I had to make up that story 'bout us kids runnin into that barbed-wire fence that was covered up with weeds and manzanita. You don't want folks to know what really happened out there, now do you, Little Pete? You don't want that man comin after us, or talkin to your pap, do ya?"

"No."

"Well, that's thinkin straight. 'Cause you and me know we got to keep that a secret 'tween us, just like

Ygor and the Doctor kept their secret bout the Monster in the picture."

I didn't say nothin to that even though I wanted to say that Ygor and the Doctor didn't keep their secret too good. But I didn't say it 'cause I knowed that Jimmy didn't understand 'bout that witch and her barbed-wire man and it wouldn't do no good to argue 'bout them if he didn't even understand bout Ygor and the Doctor.

Anyhow, us kids was in the shack with the witch and Rusty was still coughin and snifflin 'cause of the itchy dusty brambles and the witch asked, "He ain't got TB, does he?" and Jimmy just laughed and said 'bout the brambles. So she forgot 'bout that and then she started lookin over our stuff, checkin the tubes in Jimmy's daddy's radio and twistin up Mary Hannah's stoled lipsticks to make sure them lipsticks wasn't empty. Next she got hold of Rusty's belt and pulled him up close right tween her legs with her red dress all wrinklin up round him. "These keys go to a car now, don't they, little man?"

Rusty nodded quick and she just laughed and laughed with her rosy lips a big circle and then a big man stepped out of the shadows and he was laughin too. He looked like a nigger, but he looked just like the Monster too—I mean to tell you he looked like Frankenstein, but Jimmy always said that ain't right 'cause the Doctor is the one who's Frankenstein and the Monster ain't got a name at'all 'cause he's dead and nobody gives a name to things that is dead—and the Monster Man was grinnin at the way the witch had a hold of Rusty's belt and the way he was squirmin. And then he stepped up to us kids and said over his shoulder, "Hey, now, Viletta, this un ain't even no boy" while he ran a big thumb over Mary Hannah's war paint.

THE MAN WITH THE BARBED-WIRE FISTS

Jimmy piped up, "She's as good as a fella. She does everything that us fellas do."

The Monster Man just laughed some more when he heard that. Real hearty, he laughed. He pulled Mary Hannah toward him by her overalls and then commenced to smearin her war paint into two rosy circles.

"No," I said, and I grabbed hold of his arm just like Ygor did in the picture and it was a hard arm like a fence post. "She's my friend and you ain't gonna make her a circus clown."

He looked at me sort of puzzled and then he made questionin eyes at the witch and shrugged his big shoulders. She said, "Leave the little gal be. When I was young I used to like to run with the fellas too." She winked. "And you see how good I turned out."

He allowed how she had turned out pretty good. She said that as everythin seemed right we might as well get down to brass tacks and me and him should run along and might as well take the radio up to the big house and enjoy it for a spell. And then later we could come back cause she didn't spect Jimmy or Rusty to last very long and then it would be my turn since I didn't bring nothin that was so grand as a radio or keys to a car, but I already done that thing that Jimmy and Rusty wanted to do anyway even though they didn't know 'bout it so I didn't mind even though I still didn't feel growed up like a man. But still I couldn't figure out why the witch said that 'bout comin back since she knowed I already done it 'cause I done it with her.

Anyway, the Monster Man said okay and bent down and the witch kissed him with them rosy lips of hers and even her tongue. Later on Jimmy said that was the worst part of it. Seeing that a white woman was in love with a nigger. I said that maybe the Monster Man wasn't really a nigger 'cause his skin just happen to be black like the Monster's skin just happen to be green (you can tell that from the poster at the picture show). Maybe he was part nigger and part Monster, I said. Like Ygor was part Dracula and the Monster was part the Mummy. But Jimmy just wrinkled his nose at that and said, "Jumpin Jesus Christ, Little Pete, that fella wasn't nothin but a big dumb buck nigger. Next you'll be tellin me that you seen a coupla bolts stickin out of that dumb coon's neck."

But he didn't have no bolts. And since I knowed that from then on I knowed that Jimmy Tibbs was a pretty stupid fella. I told him so right then, and I told him there wasn't nothin bad bout bein a nigger cause I knowed after what happened at that witch's place that Jimmy was deep-down scared of niggers. And that was the last time I wasted my time talkin to Jimmy Tibbs who thought he was a big man right then but sure enough found out he wasn't as the years went by.

So back we went into the heat. Me and the Monster Man. He was takin long strides and it was hard for me to keep up 'cause I could hardly see over the radio and I almost tripped in a coupla postholes that was by the front steps. He said "Just watch it now" and I did while I hopped round them holes and them holes was wet at the bottom and the ground down there was black-red like an old sore that ain't healed over after a long time and them holes was crawlin with worms and all of a sudden I didn't want to look at them holes no more 'cause they stunk and they made me think of what that boilin pit must have smelled like in the picture cause it was full of sulphur. So we got up to the porch of the big house and there was a big patch of shade up there so I set down my burden in the middle of it. We both happened to wipe our brow at the same time and that made the Monster Man chuckle. "Hey,

THE MAN WITH THE BARBED-WIRE FISTS

shortcake," he said, "how 'bout some lemonade fore we go back?"

I allowed how I'd like that. So he got us some and I seen that his was a touch darker than mine and I was gonna trouble him 'bout it but before I could he asked, "What's wrong with you, anyhow?"

"I can't say as I know," I said soundin kinda puzzled and quiet like Pap always does when folks ask him bout me. "I was just born this way."

"Uh-huh," he says. "I heard 'bout stuff like that. Your ma took a bad scare while she was carryin you, I 'spect."

I didn't say nothin cause I didn't know 'bout that. Maybe it had somethin to do with the lightnin was what I thought that summer, 'cause I recollect in the picture where Ygor said the Monster's mother was the lightnin. And I wanted to know if the big man was the Monster and knowed 'bout that, so I asked him straight out. "Naw," he said. "I seen that picture too. That man ain't *really* big, like me. He ain't really a monster. He's wearin elevator shoes and a jacket stuff full with pillows. That Frankenstein is a scrawny little white man, just like everybody else in that picture. It ain't nothin but make-believe."

I was gonna tell him 'bout the difference tween Frankenstein the Doctor and the Frankenstein Monster, but I didn't want to get him riled. So I just asked him what his name was and he jingled Rusty's daddy's keys in front of my face and said, "Today my name is Jesse James, shortcake, but you can call me Jess."

"Okay, Jess," I said. And then he asked me what they call me and I said "Peter" cause I like that boy in the picture. His name is Peter and he wears sailor suits and hunts all manner of stuff. And when he gets in a fix someone comes right quick and helps him out of it like the soldierman with the rubber arm helped him and his daddy helped him too.

I took to lookin at them postholes while I drank my lemonade, waitin to see if a worm dared to poke its head out in the sun and what Jess would do to a worm that dared. But that didn't happen. Nothin happened 'ceptin Jess drank some more lemonade and patted the top of the RCA. He said, "I sure am sold on radios, yes, sir."

"Me too," I said. "And this radio is awful grand. I wish my Pap had one like it. I bet *Amos and Andy* sounds awful grand on a radio like this one."

Jess wrinkled up his nose. "That's just a couple of white men on that show, Peter," he said. "You know, the only kinda white folks you should mix with is the ladies." And then Jess seen Jimmy come out of the shack all puffed up like a rooster and he patted the radio once more and chuckled in a way that made me know he thought the RCA was awful grand too. "Hey now, Peter, you come and watch how to mix with white folks."

Jess drank down his lemonade in one big gulp then stepped off the porch and dust puffed up all round his boot just like a bomb goin off in a war picture. My, he was big and his stride was long. Long as the space 'tween them postholes with the scabby dirt and worms, which was a good bit long. "Hey, boy," he hollered to Jimmy. "You come here."

Jimmy looked up sharp and when he seen who was talkin to him his ears got awful red. But he come ahead anyway. And when he got close enough Jess squatted down real low till he could look him in the eye. "You like that over in there?" he asked and Jimmy kinda looked away but he was smilin. Then Jess said, "Well, it sure didn't take you long."

Now Jimmy's whole face got red and Jess said,

THE MAN WITH THE BARBED-WIRE FISTS

"Yeah, well, don't never take a cherry very long. I figure that was 'bout four ... mebbe five minutes, countin unbuttonin and buttonin time. Now, you tell me, boy, was that worth your daddy's RCA?" But Jimmy didn't say nothin so Jess said some more. "Well, I'm sure gonna enjoy that radio."

Jimmy was lookin at the dirt, but he said in a loud voice like they do in the gangster pictures, "It ain't for you, it's for the lady."

Jess curled up a fist and smacked Jimmy's ear real good like Joe Louis does and the blood come like Jimmy been cut, and while Jimmy was swayin all woozy Jess said, "The lady is mine and I'm hers, so it goes to figure that your RCA is mine *and* hers." He took hold of Jimmy's shirt and pulled him close and I seen Jimmy cringin away from Jess' lemonade breath. "Now, you listen up, boy. And you do like I say unless you want your daddy to find out where you been playin."

Jimmy listened real good now 'cause I reckon I should have told you before that his daddy was a soldierman like the soldierman with the rubber arm in the picture 'ceptin Jimmy's daddy didn't have no rubber arm. Anyhow, I never seen anyone talk to Jimmy like Jess did, and I 'spect no one ever had 'ceptin his daddy. But Jess didn't just talk, he dragged Jimmy over by the old busted fence that we come up through when we come up from the creek bed over the hot fryin pan rocks. He give Jimmy some wire cutters and told him to cut the rusty wire off them old posts, but Jimmy tried to give them cutters over to me.

"I paid with my radio to do what I wanted to do," Jimmy said. "I ain't gonna do no nigger work for you." But Jimmy looked kinda sick when he said it somehow, and I knowed his stomach was feelin like mine always did when he throwed them rocks at me, and I was gonna say so when Jess said, "What kinda nigger work you think I'm talkin 'bout, white boy?"

"Buildin a new fence," Jimmy said. "Look here, I know you got a whole spool of wire in there on account of that's what Little Pete brought. I thought you aimed to sell it to somebody, but if you think I'm gonna—"

Rusty came out of the shack just then wipin his nose on his shirttail. I grabbed hold of Jess' hand feelin like Ygor in the picture when he grabs hold of the Monster and sends him after them fellas who hanged him and busted his neck but didn't kill him through and all of a sudden I knowed just how wrong Jimmy was 'bout Ygor. "Him too," I said, pointin at Rusty. "Him too."

In a minute Rusty was cryin 'cause Jess had told him what he imagined would happen if Rusty's daddy found out bout the missin car keys. So Rusty got real busy quick workin the posts out of the ground. It wasn't hard work 'cause them posts was already leanin and wasn't set in cement like they set posts in these days. But like I said, Rusty was a lazy sort and so it was hard for him and it didn't help when he got to sneezin again.

"Look here." Jimmy pulled Rusty away from his work and stood up to Jess 'cept he was so small standin in Jess's big shadow that he was silly lookin. "We paid you, mister. We ain't gonna build no fence."

Jess just laughed that same real hearty laugh, mainly at that "mister" stuff I 'spect 'cause it come right out of the blue.

'Bout then was when she come out of the shack. The witch did. She was holdin Mary Hannah's hand and Mary Hannah was as pretty as could be with powder and lipstick and you could see how she wasn't no little girl no more.

"Now don't you be scared," was what the witch

whispered to Mary Hannah. "There ain't one thing to be scared of."

Jess looked Mary Hannah over with a big grin then he says to Jimmy and Rusty, "Now you remember what I said 'bout your daddies." And then he took hold of Mary Hannah's hand and took her up to the big house.

I sat down in the dust, in the sun, right tween them two postholes, listenin to the radio and lookin at the worms squirmin in the black-red mud and tryin to recollect how things went when I'd brung Jimmy's notes to the witch.

All of a sudden I smelled sulphur.

Soon enough the witch got Jimmy and Rusty busy with a shovel and them old posts and that old rusty wire. Their hands got cut up somethin awful cause they didn't have no gloves, and she just shook her head at Rusty when he begged for somethin to drink. She said, "You boys wanted to make men, didn't you?"

Like the Doctor in the picture. That's what I got to thinkin. He said he wanted to make a man. But that ain't what he ended up makin. He ended up makin a monster. A giant that stoled storybooks from nice little fellas like Peter. But Peter thought that giant was nice and Ygor thought he was nice too. And Mary Hannah always said how sad he was and how he never did nothin bad that those other folks didn't make him do 'cause he was really just gentle as could be. And I watched Jimmy and Rusty and I thought Jess was pretty nice and I recollect diggin them two holes by the porch after the witch took me inside the shack. And then I took off my gloves and looked at the scabs on my palms and recollect how she told me to hold that last note to Jimmy real careful so I wouldn't get no blood on it.

Rusty finished makin his barbed-wire man first. The

witch pushed him up against it and then pushed him away and she started rubbin on the barbed-wire man with her red dress all wrinklin up round her like before. And then Jimmy finished and she did the same thing to his barbed-wire man and Rusty started cryin then. But I think it was just cause he was scared 'cause he couldn't have knowed what was gonna happen to him 'cause of that man.

And then the radio went quiet and Jess come out of the house with one arm round Mary Hannah and the other round the RCA. He walked right over to Jimmy and handed him the radio, sayin, "I was just spoofin you bout keepin it, boy. We sure wouldn't want you to get into trouble with your folks."

The witch laughed at that and then Jess give Rusty the keys to his daddy's Ford and Rusty stopped bawlin so I knowed for sure he didn't really understand.

"Skedaddle, now," the witch said and Rusty and Jimmy did just that real quick, runnin down the creek bed over the hot fryin pan rocks, runnin like they was so happy to be free and didn't have a care in the world like you can still see them boys runnin today.

Then Mary Hannah come over and took my hand, and she had little scratches on her hand. And the witch went round them postholes and slid her little hand into Jess' big one. I looked up at him and I was all mixed up 'cause I didn't know if he was the soldierman with the rubber arm who come to save me or the Monster or the giant who stoled my storybook or maybe all three, like Ygor was Dracula and the Monster was the Mummy. But I looked at his eyes and I looked at them two big holes like sores in the ground that was dug by me when I made my barbed-wire man and I knowed that I was never gonna grow up to be a man 'cause Jess had done that for me and I was grateful 'cause I bet it was somethin I never coulda done by myself anyhow.

And Mary Hannah had a hold of my hand. She said, "C'mon, Little Pete, I'll take you home." And she picked up the witch's shovel and the poke of lipstick and powder and I got the spool of barbed wire. Off we went 'tween Jimmy and Rusty's barbed-wire men and that rusted wire was startin to sigh and then we was climbin through what was left of that busted-down fence and it was singin in the hot breeze.

And the witch waved goodbye and said, "Thank you for my man, Little Pete."

And I looked one last time at Jess who looked mighty happy and big and strong as anybody could ever want to be and it was like lookin into a mirror and seein somethin that was never gonna be.

And I smiled at the witch and said "Thank you" right back.

FOR ALAN M. CLARK

SKIN MEMORY
by
Tracy A. Knight

Rivulets of blood streamed from the woman's palms and dripped onto the wooden stage.

"As you continue to feel your wounds, the wounds that represent the pain in your life," Dr. Errol Tompkin said softly, looking down at his female subject, "you can relax with the understanding that even as your wounds shall quickly heal, the healing of your life can occur just as elegantly, just as rapidly, just as completely..."

The audience—three hundred psychologists, psychiatrists, social workers, therapists, and counselors—was as reverently rapt as if witnessing the exultant appearance of an ascended master. Physically, however, Dr. Tompkin didn't as much assume the likeness of the Maitreya as he resembled a hip Burl Ives. He blazoned his three-hundred-pound girth with a royal blue silk suit. His long gray hair was gathered in a ponytail which hung halfway down his back. Silver whiskers commingled with hints of rusty auburn in his close-cropped goatee.

By now the blood flowed less copiously from the stigmata on the subject's palms. "Now just allow yourself to relax again deeply as your attention remains upon your wounds," said Tompkin, "and as your unconscious mind lets you know that the process of healing is happening and will continue till complete, you can begin to awaken, feeling relaxed and refreshed, feeling better than before."

Tompkin arose from his chair on the stage. "Ladies and gentlemen, I hope you have found tonight's presentation and demonstration helpful and instructive. From my clinical experience, I can tell you honestly that the Tompkin Technique will prove amazingly effective with a wide range of client conditions, and may be the key needed to unlock your most difficult clinical cases. I encourage you to integrate this technique into your practice and witness the astounding results."

A storm of applause filled the Cedar Ridge, Illinois, Civic Center auditorium as Tompkin took a bow. Soon his female subject arose slowly, looked briefly at her wounds, wiped one hand against the other and smiled broadly.

After leading his subject off the stage, Tompkin unbuttoned the top button of his shirt, loosened his tie, and gestured toward the microphone situated in the middle aisle. "We have time for a few questions."

A young female therapist stepped to the microphone. "Dr. Tompkin, how did you develop your unique approach to psychotherapy?"

"I'll let you in on a little secret," Tompkin said with a chuckle, "I was inspired by my dermatologist. Really! I had gone to him because I suffered a rash on my wrist, beneath the buckle of my watchband. The doctor explained that I possibly was allergic to nickel, but went on to say I might try switching the watch to my other arm. I asked him why that would help. He said the initial reaction might have been due to my sweat intermingling with the nickel and there was a chance it wouldn't happen on my other arm. But here's the clincher: He said my left arm would remember the reaction and would tend to produce it again. *'Remember'*—that was the word he used."

"The Tompkin Technique grew out of a wrist rash?" the therapist said with mock incredulity.

Tompkin nodded, flipping his ponytail. "Research has repeatedly demonstrated that hypnosis can enlarge breasts, make warts disappear, produce blisters, effect all sorts of physical changes. And with what the dermatologist told me, it suddenly was clear to me that skin itself must be able to *conceptualize*. Right? In order to remember, it must first conceptualize. So why not combine the two insights? Why not utilize hypnosis to allow patients to give visible physical expression to their emotional problems? Perhaps by providing them with that experience, I reasoned, a beneficial shift in the central psychological conflict would occur. And I'll be damned, it worked."

Heads in the audience bobbed up and down as they muttered to one another, socially acceptable genuflection to this psychologist who had, in a few short years, become the darling not only of the psychotherapy field but of the popular culture as well. His recent cover photo on *Newsweek*—heralding the release of his book *Becoming a Newborn: The Tompkin Technique for Personality Reintegration*—was proof enough of that.

"Another question?" Tompkin said in his mellifluous voice.

An older gentleman approached the microphone. "Dr. Tompkin, I'm a physician, so I'm interested in what your approach has taught us about the mind-body connection. What's been one of the most fascinating physical changes your technique has produced?"

"Well, they're *all* fascinating." He paused for a second, tapping his goatee as he searched his memory. "I do remember a case about a year ago, a supremely successful dentist who was nonetheless chronically depressed. When I induced the technique, his face distended and turned purple. His eyes swelled shut.

SKIN MEMORY

And some interesting hysterical symptoms developed, too: His jaw locked closed and he was functionally deaf. Don't be mistaken—I was worried at first. However, in just three or four days, the symptoms cleared. As it turned out—he hadn't told me this beforehand—he was horribly abused as a child, his only defense then being to hide in his closet and psychologically shut himself off totally from the household's chaos. Once the physical effects of the technique cleared, his depression was completely lifted. And since you're a physician, you might be interested in my next book, in which I theorize that if we are able to penetrate certain barriers in our physiological functioning, there may be no limit to the physical changes humans could learn to induce in themselves. Imagine it: Hypnotically-actuated face lifts! Trance-induced tummy tucks! Altered-state-produced nose jobs! I've been practicing on myself, but it's not gone well—how do you think I managed to gain a hundred pounds in the past year?"

The audience laughed appreciatively.

"How do you guard against burning out?" another audience member asked amidst the waning titters.

"Simple. By basking in the warmth of successful therapy," Tompkin said. "Believe me, if I'm ever convinced I'm not enriching my patients' lives, I'll not only burn out, I'll probably become so thoroughly toasted I won't know my *ash* from a hole in the ground!" Satisfied with the audience's approving groans, Tompkin flashed a warm smile. "Now, we have time for one more...."

Before he could finish the sentence, a gangly man in his early twenties, with wild eyes burning above an aquiline nose, sprinted up the aisle, knocking aside several attendees and leaping onto the stage. Just as his hands met Tompkin's lapels, five bodyguards sprung from their places in the front row and wrestled him to the floor.

Absolute silence shrouded the audience as they witnessed the unthinkable. Dr. Errol Tompkin, a therapist who had saved so many lives, righted so many psychological wrongs, attacked? Why, it was like a leper eye-gouging Jesus.

Muffled shouting and crying seeped out from between the bodies of the five burly bodyguards as they pinned the man to the floor.

Tompkin smoothed the front of his suit coat, cleared his throat, and said, "It's okay, nobody panic. This man apparently has something to say. Sir," he said, looking down at the squirming mass of men, "if you can behave yourself, I . . . *we* will hear you out."

The rhythm of the struggle on the floor slowed, then stopped. Tompkin nodded to the bodyguards and they arose, revealing the thin young man. He sniffled as he surveyed his torn white dress shirt. Still shaking from the melee, he got up slowly and walked to the edge of the stage. He wiped a finger beneath his large nose and said in a thin, reedy voice, "This is bullshit—all this stuff about healing people. You ruined my sister." He turned to the audience and swept his trembling finger across the sea of attendees. "You all ruined my sister."

"What's your name, son?" asked Tompkin gently.

"Fred. Fred Archer," he muttered.

"Fred, tell us what you mean."

Fred grimaced, his lower lip bowing downward as if he might begin either crying or spitting invectives. Surprisingly, he spoke in a soft, cracking voice. "My sister Anita saw a therapist six months ago. She was having a lot of problems, even tried to kill herself a couple of times. And why wouldn't she?" he said, spreading his hands, looking up with clear blue eyes to Tompkin. "Our parents beat us and starved us when we were little. The state took us when I was seven and Anita was three. We lived in a bunch of different foster homes. Both of us were abused in some of the foster homes—sometimes by foster parents, sometimes by other foster kids. The state finally let us go a year ago and we've lived together ever since. We had a hard time, but we were making it ... until she saw one of you damn therapists." His face reddened, his jaw clenched. "He did some kind of hypnosis mumbo-jumbo on her and she suddenly believed we'd been raised in a satanic cult for several years, where we had to help sacrifice people, chop up babies and eat them, do all sorts of disgusting stuff. It didn't happen! I was there! But she sees it in her mind, she thinks she remembers it, and she's convinced evil is waiting to come back into her life, no matter how much I try to talk sense into her."

Tompkin eased his portly body off the stage and walked toward Fred Archer. As he approached, the young man flinched, jerking up an arm in front of his face.

"It's okay, Fred," Tompkin said, "I just want to talk to you." Tompkin reached out and placed a hand on the young man's shoulder. "I happen to share your disgust with much of today's therapy. You're correct in your implication: A lot of therapists are creating disease—that's right, *creating* it—in order to make a fast buck or work out their own issues. Many of them have not been properly trained in the vagaries of human memory and imagination, and fool themselves into thinking that when they hypnotically regress a patient they're simply retrieving actual, unedited memories, uncontaminated by imagination. They're dead wrong. But you listened to me tonight, right?"

Fred nodded.

"Then you know my approach isn't anything like

that. I'm not hypnotically regressing patients or anything of the sort. The Tompkin Technique is simply a way to give the person's emotional problems physical expression so he or she can heal psychologically, an effect induced by the inevitable physical healing." He closed his eyes, paused a second, then nodded to himself. "I'll tell you what, Fred. In every city where I give a workshop, I volunteer my services and see one client free of charge. Usually it's a particularly troublesome case that a clinician in the audience presents. But tonight—considering the poor treatment she's received in the past—I'm going to see your sister. How's that?"

Fred didn't respond immediately. He looked down his lanky body to his cowboy boots for a few moments. "I guess so," he finally said.

The audience erupted in an enthusiastic ovation. Several attendees came to the front and circled young Fred Archer, patting him on the back and offering to hug him, offers he declined with a bewildered look on his face.

Tompkin pulled the rental Cadillac Seville into the driveway. After turning off the ignition, he reached into the pocket of his trench coat and removed a flask. He took a sip, then tipped the flask toward Fred. "Have some brandy?"

Fred shook his head. He hadn't said a word since they left the auditorium a half-hour earlier.

Tompkin let the liquor slide down his throat. He patted his round belly. "Ah, my inner child likes a nip now and then, you know? Show me the way, my boy."

As they walked to the front door of the house, Fred turned to Tompkin and said, meekly, "Anita hasn't even left the house in a couple of months. She just stays in her room."

"Don't worry, Fred. I can help her."

SKIN MEMORY

They entered the house and walked to Anita's bedroom, where a dim lamp glowed with dirty golden light.

The small young woman sat on the floor in a corner of the room, knees pulled up against her chest, body cocooned in a thick blanket. Only her liquid brown eyes and shimmering mane of black hair were visible.

"Anita?" Fred said. "Anita, this is Dr. Errol Tompkin. He says he can help you."

Her eyes widened as she pulled the blanket more tightly around her.

"It's okay, Anita," Tompkin said, almost whispering. "Your brother told me how rough a time you've been having. He said you've been very depressed and you're scared of people hurting you, so you won't leave the house. Is that true?"

She nodded.

"Let me tell you what I can do for you." Tompkin then turned to Fred. "Wait for me in the other room."

Fred backed out of the room slowly, pained concern darkening his young face.

Tompkin described his technique to Anita, all the time embedding suggestions that she become more relaxed and open. Soon she let the blanket fall to her shoulders, revealing her delicate nose and full, pale lips.

"Good, very good," said Tompkin. "Now, Anita, I'd like you to lie down on your bed and just let yourself relax."

She complied. Soon, Tompkin noticed her breathing settling into a slower, calmer rhythm. She kept her eyes focused on the ceiling, allowing herself only an occasional furtive glance at the psychologist.

"What do you feel like, Anita?" said Tompkin. "How can you describe yourself most accurately, most vividly? Use your imagination. Help me to visualize it."

She considered Tompkin's question for a full minute before responding. Her lips quivered as she answered in her mild melody of a voice, "Patchwork. Like a messed-up patchwork doll. Every place I lived made a little part of me. A lot of the parts hurt. And when I saw that therapist, he said I was something different, that my life was something completely different than I thought. Now all the parts don't fit together."

"Good, very good."

"You ever read that book *Frankenstein?*" Anita asked suddenly, arching her eyebrows as if an insight had only now dawned upon her.

Tompkin nodded. "Certainly. Mary Shelley, right?"

"Mm-hmm. I used to read that book when I was in foster care, read it so many times some of the pages fell out of it. I always felt sorry for the monster. He was a lot like me. People created this patchwork girl and then rejected me, hated me."

"I'm impressed," Tompkin said. "You know yourself well, Anita. Now, just allow yourself to relax."

Tompkin began the hypnotic induction. Anita quickly let her eyelids drop closed. After ten minutes of suggestions for deeper and deeper relaxation, Tompkin moved to the next phase.

"You can ask your unconscious to make your conception of yourself manifest, to allow it to come to the surface and be seen by you and by me . . . so it can be faced . . . allowing you to move beyond it, allowing you to heal."

He continued the suggestions another twenty minutes, subtly varying them, employing a host of different forms and emphases. Soon, Tompkin noticed the changes. They weren't dramatic at all. Anita's face flushed slightly. She whimpered in hushed tones as a thin red line appeared across the width of her forehead and began weeping blood.

"Good, Anita. That's good."

The scratch bled briefly, then began to clot. Tompkin took out his handkerchief and dabbed at Anita's forehead until it was clear of everything but the long, thin scratch.

"Continue to relax," Tompkin said softly, "and when your unconscious recognizes that your healing has begun, you can slowly awaken."

Thirty seconds passed. Anita's eyelids fluttered open. A single shining teardrop slid from her eye and down her cheek.

"How are you feeling?" Tompkin asked.

"Kind of strange but better . . . I think." She pulled up the covers to her chest.

"You can rest now, Anita. Things *will* be better." Tompkin bent down over her and said, "I'm renting a cabin down on the Mississippi River for the next two days, until I have to leave for my next workshop in Nebraska. If you need anything, here's the phone number." He scribbled the number on a business card and laid it on her stomach.

Tompkin left the bedroom and encountered Fred pacing back and forth in the front hallway. "Things went well," Tompkin said. "It's funny, but I usually find that folks like Anita—passive, with a murky sense of identity—make the best patients for my treatment and produce the most visible results. She surprised me. There were a few physical changes but nothing as dramatic as I expected. Maybe this means her difficulties weren't as profound as they seemed. At any rate, I left my phone number with her. If either of you need to consult with me before I leave, please don't hesitate to let me know."

"Thanks, Dr. Tompkin," Fred said. "And by the way,

I'm sorry if I insulted you at the presentation tonight. After what she'd gone through with the therapist, I'd decided that she'd be helped the most if I just loved her and listened to her and was here for her. I was mad at therapists ... all therapists. I shouldn't have taken it out on you."

Tompkin smiled with understanding. "You're a good brother, Fred. Sometimes, though, you need a professional. To make things happen."

The next evening, Tompkin was drinking a brandy on the cabin's front porch, just relaxing, feeling the warm summer breeze and watching the soft smear of orange and purple sky left behind as the sun drifted behind the Iowa horizon across the gently rolling river.

Already he had added Anita's case to the notes for his next book, and looked forward to sharing his treatment of her with his audience in Nebraska two days from now.

Inside, the phone rang. Tompkin got up with a grunt and entered the cabin. His state of meditative relaxation and mild inebriation was punctured when he heard the panicked voice on the other end.

"Doctor, this is Fred Archer. You ... you gotta get over here right away! Something's happening to Anita!"

"Whoa, hold on, relax, Fred. Tell me what's going on."

"I don't know ... but you get over here and help her!"

The line went dead.

Tompkin *harrumphed* as he gathered his jacket, wishing now he had driven on to Lincoln.

He arrived at Anita's house twenty minutes later. He ran to her front door, knocked, then rang the doorbell when no one answered. Suddenly from inside he heard a cry, a full-throated wailing so eerie his initial impulse was to run away. But there was much pain in the loud mewling; he was impelled to try the door. It was unlocked. He stepped into the dark house.

When he closed the door behind him, the volume of the cries subsided, leaving only the sounds of low-pitched gibberings and heavy breathing that seemed partially clogged with thick phlegm.

He tripped over something on the way to Anita's bedroom. Taking a few more steps, he waved his hands in front of him until he found a floor lamp and flicked it on.

Fred lay on the floor, unconscious and bleeding from one ear.

Tompkin bent down and shook the young man by the shoulders. Fred's head bobbed limply on his neck.

From the bedroom poured more cries, now intensifying, becoming deep, mournful howls so thundering Tompkin heard the windowpanes reverberating in their frames. He covered his ears as he stood.

He crept toward Anita's bedroom. The door was slightly ajar. He pushed it open carefully, entered, then slid his hand along the wall until he found the light switch and flipped it up.

Tompkin cried out, falling back against the wall in shock.

He could scarcely recognize the thing lying in the bed. No longer the petite rag-doll of a woman, Anita had grown. Her legs had thickened three-fold, rippling muscles now straining against taut skin. And she was taller, too, much taller; her grossly swollen feet extended well beyond the foot of the bed. Her clothes were ripped to shreds, exposing withered breasts and skin which now was pale yellow and dry, appearing almost like ancient parchment which any moment would curl and flake and flutter to the floor.

With a finger and thumb of her bloated left hand, Anita held a large sewing needle from which dangled thick black thread. As Tompkin stood rigidly in place—terrified to the point of mental and physical paralysis—Anita pushed the needle into her forehead, right next to a large, tattered gash which, as Tompkin watched in horror, tore itself open farther and farther, spilling dark blood down her swollen face. Curling her thin black lips, she cried out again.

Her sunken, milky eyes upon Tompkin, Anita—or the monster which now lay in her place—shoved the needle through the shredded skin to the other side of the leaking gash, then pulled the loop of thread taut. She took a deep breath, coughed until some yellow matter spilled from her mouth, and let loose of the needle. The needle dangled from the oozing fissure, swinging back and forth before the creature's wandering eyes as she looked up to meet the psychologist's frozen stare.

In an impossibly low-pitched, rumbling voice, the monster said, "I expected your reaction, Doctor, though I don't understand it."

Tompkin couldn't move, couldn't say a word.

The monster moaned as it struggled to turn onto its side. It let one of its massive legs drop off the side of the bed. Sluggishly, moving its arms as if they were dead weight, it pushed itself up out of the bed. Slowly it stood.

The monster that had been Anita Archer was nearly eight feet tall. It raised its gigantic hands to its face, examined them closely. It reached up and felt its disheveled jet-black hair.

"Stay away from me, Anita," Tompkin said, gasping between words, trying to edge closer to the door.

"You did your duty toward me," the monster said, shrugging as it took two shambling steps toward Tompkin. "Do not detest me." Its dark lips spread to reveal pearly white teeth. "I think I *am* better." The naked monster looked down impassively as several more wounds appeared across its chest, its stomach, its legs and feet. Each rift in its flesh tore wider and wider, until dark blood poured freely, streaming down the monster's body.

Tompkin felt he would vomit at any moment. He wanted to run but didn't dare turn his back on the vile creature, not for even a second.

It took another step toward him.

Tompkin held out his hands, a feeble shield. "Anita, listen to me. You hurt your brother. That's not what you want. Please—lie down on the bed. Perhaps I can help you."

"Maybe you're right." Looking down its blood-drenched body, its smile flattened out and a puzzled look settled onto the spoiled face. When it sat down on the bed, the frame broke with a loud crack and the creature spilled to the floor atop the mattress. "I'm clumsy," it said, shaking its large head. "I should be better. I'm tired. Make me not so tired. Make my wounds close." It fell back on the mattress, laid its swollen arm over its eyes. "Help me more. If I can be helped. If I'm good enough. I need you."

Seeing his opportunity, Tompkin fled the room. He leapt over Fred, who had regained consciousness but still lay dazed on the floor.

He moved his obese body faster than he ever had before, hurtling out of the house and into his car.

Tompkin spent the next two hours driving aimlessly around Cedar Ridge, deliberating over what he should do, if anything. Periodically, guilt's needle teeth nibbled at his guts; but each time it did, he was able to refocus himself, to push away the dull ache and return to the vital business of practical problem-solving.

It was well after midnight when he returned to the cabin. Immediately he began packing his clothes, deciding his best bet was to rest up and leave for Lincoln first thing in the morning.

He drank three snifters of brandy quickly, hoping to induce enough drowsiness to allow sleep and, perhaps, forgetfulness.

Tompkin had no more than started a fire in the fireplace and lay down on the couch, still fully clothed, when someone began beating on the front door of the cabin. He tried to ignore it.

"Tompkin, open up! I see you in there!" Fred Archer cried.

Realizing no escape existed, Tompkin arose reluctantly, walked to the door and opened it.

Fred reached through the doorway and grabbed the front of Tompkin's shirt. "What did you do with her?"

"What do you mean, Fred? I didn't do anything with . . ."

"Where is she?"

"I . . . I don't know. You both were at your house when I left. Anita was resting. She seemed better."

"You liar!" Fred shouted, shoving Tompkin to the floor. "She's gone! I called the police. I told them that a large man attacked me—I couldn't tell them it was Anita. They had already seen her running through town, but they couldn't catch her. When they tried, she killed a policeman." Fred's shoulders slumped as tears filled his eyes. "Dr. Tompkin, that was my sister."

"Believe me, Fred, I've been using the technique for over five years. I've never seen anything like this. It must have been something . . . something with Anita."

"Oh, great," Fred said, gritting his teeth as anger

SKIN MEMORY

blazed in his eyes, "blame *her*. That's just great. Maybe the reason you don't see things like this is because you blow into town for a one-day show, do your damage and then take off. You don't have to take responsibility for what you leave behind. You know what you are, Tompkin?" Fred looked down at his forearm and picked off an insect he saw crawling there. He held it up to Tompkin's face. Its legs squirmed as it struggled to escape. "You ain't no better than this thing!" He threw it to the floor and stepped on it.

Tompkin wiped his face and sighed. He couldn't force another word from his mouth.

The front door of the cabin was torn from its hinges in a screeching cacophony.

The creature who had been Anita Archer bent its head down through the doorway until its face loomed in the room's flickering firelight. Water dripped from its naked body. Its parchment skin was now almost completely covered with tattered, bleeding wounds, several of which had large needles stuck into them. Apparently the creature had tried to stitch itself up but could not keep up with its body's rending.

The monster bellowed in a voice so low Tompkin felt his bones shudder within his skin. "I swam along the river until I found you!" It carefully stepped into the cabin, rising now to full height.

Seeing his sister's condition, Fred ran to the creature's side. "Anita, I'm sorry, forgive me. Please." He wrapped his arms around the creature's abdomen, which was eye-level to him. "I was trying to help," he whimpered.

The creature shook its head slowly, then grasped Fred with its gargantuan hands and lifted him until his head bumped against the ceiling.

The creature roared, "Look at you. You are tiny and weak. You don't understand me. You don't see how much better I am!" And before Fred had a chance to apologize again, the creature fell to one knee and brought down the young man's body against the other. As his spine snapped sickeningly, Fred folded backward, nearly in half.

The creature shoved Fred's broken body to the floor and stood. "Come here!" it thundered.

"Please, Anita, please don't hurt me," Tompkin pleaded.

The creature frowned; its bushy eyebrows almost covered its eyes. "I don't understand," it said. "I wanted to find you. To thank you for healing me. I'm better now. If only I were stronger, perhaps I'd stop bleeding." With that, it turned, pushed its gigantic body through the doorway and shambled out into the cool summer night, turning back briefly to call, "I'm sorry if I disappointed you. I'll wander until I'm whole. Or perhaps I shall die and my burning miseries will be extinguished. Either way, my spirit will find peace. Farewell, Dr. Tompkin. And thank you."

Tompkin ran to the door and saw the creature's figure bathed in the light of the full moon as it lurched toward the river.

He ran to the bedroom and grabbed his suitcase. As he walked back through the living room, Tompkin looked down at the dead body of Fred Archer. It struck him that from what Fred had told him, Tompkin had never been connected to Anita and the creature she became, the thing the police saw. Naturally they would assume that Fred Archer had been killed by the incredible monster.

Then Tompkin felt a rush of paranoia sweep through him. Could he be tied to the murder scene in any way? He decided at that instant and took a burning log from the fireplace, which he held beneath several of the cab-

SKIN MEMORY

in's curtains until assured that the building would soon be nothing but a smoldering heap of ashes.

He walked outside and as he looked across the Mississippi to Iowa, he spied the monster as it swam the rippling river under the moon's silver gaze. It windmilled its giant arms, sending great sprays of water into the midnight air, glittering droplets that arced through the moonlight briefly before settling into the creature's wake.

Tompkin threw his suitcase into the car and got in. As he drove away, he saw the cabin in the rear-view mirror, bright flames licking the outside walls.

If he drove fast enough, perhaps he could make it to Lincoln by morning.

If he drove fast enough, perhaps he could outrun the memory of Anita Archer and her brother Fred. Perhaps he could still the squirming guilt in his gut and the faint, echoing voice inside which told him what he had become.

The next afternoon, an Iowa State Policeman discovered what he thought was an abandoned rental car on the shoulder of Interstate 80. After taking a look into the vehicle, he ran back to his cruiser and grabbed the handset of his two-way radio.

"Base, this is Unit Twenty-Three."

"Go ahead."

"Got something real strange out here on I-80, Al. Gonna need an ambulance ... I guess. Found a car along the road. Inside there's a body, burnt to nothing."

"Car fire?"

"No, no. The body's all burned up, but the interior of the car is barely scorched. You ever read about— what is it called—spontaneous human combustion? When people just go poof? Well, that's what it looks like. Jesus, there's not so much as a tooth left in this body; it's just a big, weird-shaped ... ash statue. And I'll tell you something else, Al, as long as you promise you won't certify me insane and have me locked up in the Ha-Ha Hotel. It doesn't even look like a human body. There aren't any arms or legs, not really. There's about six or seven ... spindly things wrapped around the steering wheel. The body's all bloated and round and the head's no bigger than my fist. Al, it looks like ... now don't you laugh ... it looks like a goddamn giant tick burned up in there."

THE MAN IN BLACK
by
Christopher Fahy

I encountered him only twice, both times on the strand.

In the summer of 1816, Shelley and I and my stepsister, Claire (who followed us everywhere) took a cottage on Lake Geneva's shore near the villa occupied by Lord Byron. Shelley and Byron became fast friends, and engaged in many an evening of heated debate on the subjects of poetry, philosophy, and politics, in which, to my great dismay, they were joined by Byron's physician, Polidori, a shallow and vain young man who considered himself their match—because of his medical training, no doubt. I, who was not quite nineteen at the time, felt equal to this buffoon, but far behind the other two, in spite of the fact that I had been raised in a highly demanding atmosphere, and I usually sat in silence along with Claire (who was madly obsessed with the roguish Byron), content to ride the eloquent twists and turns of thought of these passionate men, who seemed so much older and wiser. And Shelley at the time was but twenty-four!

The season began auspiciously, with sunny days of garden walks and rowing on the lake, but then the rain set in. One might have expected such weather to work in my lover's favor; the gloom negating the lure of the water and hills, he would turn to the core of genius inside and produce great reams of verse. But day after dreary day crept by, and nothing issued forth. "Oh, for a ray of sun!" he cried at the end of the first week of slate-dark skies. "A single ray!"

Byron was not affected thus. *Childe Harold* was going splendidly, and nothing could slow the pace of his fervent (and, some might say, twisted) brain. His cheer was unflagging, which tended to make Shelley sulk. Our evening intercourse became quite strained. To break this mood, we would read aloud from a volume of supernatural tales which Polidori (that arrogant fool) had found in the villa's library. One evening, after I'd taken my turn, Byron, tilting his handsome chin toward the ceiling and raising an index finger, said, "We will each write a ghost story."

Few could oppose a command of Lord Byron, and none of us did that night: all swore an oath to write a tale with supernatural elements—even the pompous Polidori, even the scatterbrained Claire. A gleam came into Shelley's eye. He sees this as the way to break the paralytic grip that holds his muse in check, I thought. But I was wrong.

Almost from the time we met, Shelley had urged me to write, as the juvenilia I'd shyly shown him convinced him that I had talent. I was far from convinced myself, as his own superb efforts were so far above my productions that I was prepared to capitulate and assume with contentment the role of wife and mother. But Byron's challenge inflamed Shelley's ardor to make me set pen to paper.

Each morning (oh, how gray and desolate they were, with the rain beating down on the tiles of the roof, streaming over the panes of the casements), Shelley would say, "Have you thought of a story yet?" And I, in misery, would say, "Not yet," and blush with mortification. His story was going well, he claimed; he would show me a part of it soon.

One morning, my spirits depressed by the endless

THE MAN IN BLACK

clouds and lack of inspiration, wishing with all my heart that Byron had never proposed his game, I went out alone to the shore of the lake, hoping that exercise would jog my muse, or, at the least, rouse my sluggish and fretful blood.

The air was a penetrating mist, which hid the snow-capped peaks, the farther shore, and most of the lake's expanse. My soul was claustrophobic, smothered in fog, and my stroll, instead of providing the elevation which I desired, served to oppress me further—the more so when I came upon a fish, dead, washed up on the sand.

It was beautiful, silver with tinges of green and gold, and of good size. I knew not what variety it was; I only knew it seemed a shame for it to die and lie here in the cold. I stared at it, my thoughts on how I, too, should end like this; how my dear Shelley, my dear friends should end like this—when suddenly a loud voice startled me:

"How soon the worm determines that the vital spark is gone!"

The man was small, a little taller than my height. His trousers and his coat were black, and somewhat frayed. I sensed he was close to Byron's age (which was twenty-eight) but had suffered the ravages of disease: his frame was bent, his brow was lined, his face was gaunt and pale.

"The worm," I said.

"Observe the eye. Oh, how it feasts!"

I regarded the fish again, but with more diligence, and yes, a worm—thin, white—was threaded through the creature's eye. I thought of the dream that had plagued me after the death of my infant daughter the year before. I dreamt that I had rubbed her chalky skin before the blazing hearth and her eyes had opened, gazed on me—and then I awoke once again to the terrible truth. The dream had returned to me last night when Shelley and Byron (and Polidori, who offered his "expert" views) had speculated on galvanism: if it might someday be applied to bring the dead to life.

"Oh, that the vital spark could be restored," I said, "and once again this fish could swim in all its beauty and its grace."

The small man stared at me, his eyebrows raised, his dark eyes shining bright. "Do not wish *that!*" he said. "Never, never wish *that!*"

Perplexed by this fervid response, I said, "And pray, why not?"

He proceeded to tell a fantastic tale: of a friend of his from the town of Zurich, a medical man, who had raised a corpse from the dead. He insisted this story was true, and more: insisted this creature constructed of parts from the tomb and the charnel house still roamed the world. His cheeks, so pale at his narrative's start, were brightly flushed by its end, and his eyes had the beady glitter and shift of a raven's. Mad, I concluded, and shivered from more than cold.

"The fish is dead, and must remain so, as all who die must remain in that state and return to dust," said the man in black. "Do you understand?"

I replied that I did, wanting ever so much to return to the cottage, my lover, the warmth of our hearth.

"Heinrich Berger," he said, extending his hand, and I took it; the fish could have been no colder.

"And you, my dear madame . . . are?"

Releasing his cold, dead hand I said, "Mrs. Shelley."

"Mrs. Shelley," he said with an odd, jerky twist of his head. "*Mrs*. Shelley. I see."

I sensed he knew it was a lie. My name was Mary Godwin still, as Shelley did not approve of marriage. More to the point, he already had a wife, who lived in London with their sons.

THE MAN IN BLACK

"I devoted myself to science," the small man said, "and neglected life's social side. And now, I fear, the pattern is solidified." He waved his hand impatiently. "Well, that is of no consequence, if only I—"

Then suddenly he craned his neck and said, "He's here! He's followed me! I shall never, never escape!"

I searched the fog, but saw nothing at all.

"He's here! Go, go, it isn't safe!"

With this, he turned his back to me, and raised his arms. "Begone!" he cried. "Begone, foul demon! Plague me no more! Return to the moldering grave from whence you came!" Swinging toward me again, he shouted, "Why do you stand here after I've warned you? Go! This minute! Now!" Then he strode forward into the fog, screaming horrible oaths. Soon he was swallowed up and I heard no more.

I shivered again and hugged myself and walked back up the strand. Every so often I glanced behind, but saw no man, and certainly no "demon." When I entered the cottage, Shelley looked up from his place by the hearth, smiled slightly, and asked: "Did your outing help? Have you thought of a story yet?"

His superior tone, his imperious high pale brow made me suddenly understand why his schoolmates had taken such great delight in tormenting him. I crossed to the fire and held out my hands, remembering my poor dead babe. I turned to the chair where Shelley sat, still with his haughty smile.

"I have thought of a story, yes," I said with a little smirk of my own.

Shelley quickly abandoned his story. Polidori, to our great surprise, managed a rather decent vampire tale, while Byron (competing with his brash physician?) created a vampire sketch of his own—and created a fetus in hapless Claire, whose condition dashed all desire to write—and even, at times, to live. Only I, of the five who had taken the oath that sodden, windblown night, wrote a book.

It was published more than two years later, thanks to great effort on Shelley's part. He had tried, while a student at Eton, to call up the Devil by chemical means, and the theme of my novel entranced him. He made me expand and embellish my early draft, then hounded Lackington & Hughes to bring it out.

Its first reviews were dreadful, but, despite these harsh pronouncements by the learned arbiters of taste, the public chose to enjoy it. *Frankenstein, or, The Modern Prometheus,* sold quite well—much better than any of Shelley's work, which created a certain friction between us. But Shelley was glad for the money, indeed, as Harriet, his wife, had drowned herself, and now he had charge of their two young sons as well as our own sweet William. Yes, I *was* now Mrs. Shelley.

I encountered the man in black again in 1822. By then we were living in Spezia, in the midst of savage native folk who howled at the moon at night. Often Shelley would join in their naked romps in the waves—his friends, the two Edwards (Trelawny and Williams), keeping a watchful eye on him, as (unbelievably for one who sailed so much) he could not swim.

Claire's daughter by Byron, Allegra, had died of typhus, and we had been forced to abandon Pisa, taking Claire, afraid that she might bring harm to the dissolute Lord, who lived nearby, as she managed to put the blame on him for Allegra's death. I was pregnant again, and not feeling well, when we moved. The doctor advised me to stay in my bed, but I refused; I found that a walk beside the Gulf would ease my pain and raise my spirits, and one penumbral afternoon, returning from such exercise, I suddenly heard from behind, "Mrs. Shelley." I turned.

He had aged to a shocking degree: his hair was white, his arms were sticks, his waxen skin sagged on his cheeks. He seemed to be clothed in the very same garb as the first time I'd met him, and now it was tattered and torn.

"It is you, I am not mistaken?" he said, his watery dark eyes shining.

"Mr. Berger," I said.

"*Doctor* Berger," he said. "Your memory is excellent." He took my hand. Again, his was so cold.

A pain ran through me then; I winced, and his eyebrows rose.

"A slight discomfort," I said. "I am pregnant, you see."

"Ah, yes," he nodded. "Your first?"

"My fifth," I said. "Three other children of mine have died, two since I saw you last."

"The curse!" cried Berger, clutching his vest. "I prayed that it would spare you, but, I see, to no avail! It is *him*, of course. Anyone who has even the slightest association with me can be caught in his spell. Oh! What have I done?"

"My children died of fevers," I said, "not of a curse."

This remark was completely ignored. "And how were you to know, when you transcribed the tale," said Berger, trembling now, "what horrors you would bring upon yourself?"

At this, I blushed. "The tale. You've read my book?"

"Of course."

I had altered his story, setting it in Geneva instead of Zurich, adding more characters, adding new scenes; and yet, it was *his* story. "I am truly surprised it has traveled so far," I said. "I expected it not to leave England."

"*He* learned of it," said the man in black. "It was *he* who brought me a copy, left it on my bedstand while I slept."

Poor Berger was still quite clearly mad. I contrived of a way to escape.

"He used to follow *me*," he said, his finger pointing to the sky, "but then I followed *him*. What difference? Either way we are bound to each other—till death! But now—" and here his grin grew wide, his stained teeth showed—"but now I have finally outwitted him, now I have trapped him. With luck . . ."

Then, tilting his head and staring at me with those red, wet eyes, he said, "Do not stay here. Though he is trapped, he has his ways. For the sake of the child that still survives and the child you carry, quit this place!"

I thanked mad Berger for his concern, then said I must rest, and bade him a quick farewell. As I made my way back to our villa, the dank and decrepit Casa Magni, his words reverberated in my brain, and I found myself constantly looking across my shoulder. I thought of the night before, when Shelley, out on the terrace with Williams and me, had suddenly cried, "Look! There it is!" and pointed to the sea. He insisted he saw the dead Allegra perched on a moonlit island, clapping her hands. But Williams and I saw no island, saw nothing but waves; and now, as I looked behind, the man was gone, and only a handful of moon-mad natives occupied the sands.

I reached our odious abode, and all at once my strength abandoned me. Shelley ran over and clasped my hand and pressed it to his breast. "A chill," I said, and straightaway took to my bed.

The pains commenced soon after: racking, horrible pains that would not allow sleep. Feverish, I tossed and

THE MAN IN BLACK

turned, my mind obsessed with thoughts of the man in black. On the fifth night the bleeding began.

Claire and Jane Williams did what they could, applying towels to stanch the hemorrhage, yet still I bled. We were far from a doctor; one had been summoned hours before, but had failed to appear. I lapsed into coma and, in the depths of that shadowy state, encountered my precious William and Clara again. Oh, happy reunion! I shrieked with joy as we embraced, then felt the cold. Such cold! For Shelley had somehow procured some ice; its application stopped the flow; by the time the doctor arrived, I was back from the brink.

For several days, I was terribly weak. At times I feared I should perish and go to that better place where my mother, who'd died giving life to me, dwelled. I nurtured a piece of her rationalist soul in my all too unworthy breast, and gave no credence to demons and curses and spells. And yet, another child of mine was lost—and I thought of the man in black.

I had barely begun to regain my strength, when Shelley announced that he and Williams were sailing across the Gulf to meet their friend Leigh Hunt. No, he could not desert me! I cried, and lapsed into histrionics worthy of Claire. He reasoned with me soothingly; assured me he would soon return; explained that he could not leave Hunt, who'd just arrived, alone in a foreign land. He had hired a young but experienced sailor, Charles Vivian, to help with his week-old boat. His argument calmed me; I said he should go. But when on the following dawn I saw him ready to take to the wide black sea, I was shaken by fear, and once again begged him to stay. Now, though, he would not be swayed.

The days were long, the nights were longer still; with natives dancing 'round their fires and howling like wolves as I tried to rest. The skies turned dark, the waves turned wild, my heart was sick with fright. Then a letter arrived from Hunt—confirming that Shelley had started back at the very height of the storm!

Trelawny was the first to hear the news: three bodies had been washed ashore far distant from one another. In accordance with local law, they were buried in quicklime.

It was good Trelawny who arranged for the exhumation; he who built the funeral pyres, each on a separate shore. It was he who notified Byron and Hunt—who attended the burning—and he who collected the ashes and placed them in casks of his own design. It was he who rescued my husband's heart from the eager, merciless flames.

Disconsolate and inconsolable, I hid in my room in the horrible Casa Magni with hardly a thought (with what shame I admit to this) for my only surviving child, small Percy, who, thanks to Claire, was cared for well. (For once Claire had made herself useful.)

For weeks I was sunk in a pit so dark I scarcely desired to live. Trelawny, Hunt, Lord Byron, even Jane—whose husband died along with mine—I had Claire turn away. Why I did not bring an end to it all with a draft of laudanum, as Fanny, my older sister had, remains a mystery. I felt, though, even in the blackest gloom, that I was destined for some great and noble task; and one bleak morn, while gazing at my husband's heart in the jar on my bedroom shelf, the nature of that task grew clear: through his work, he must live again. Whatever time remained to me would be spent in securing his fame.

One sleepless night, as I lay with the ceaseless pulse of the murderous waves in my ears, I was jolted straight up in my bed by a thump at my door. Claire, of course. The lateness of the hour could only mean

THE MAN IN BLACK

one thing: she was caught once again in the grip of hysteria.

"Claire, please," I said. "I have no strength—"

With a creak of its hinges, the door swung inward, then crashed to a stop. A huge black shadow filled the hall. With my heart in my throat, I turned up the wick on my lamp. The shadow, stooping to avoid the jamb, came forward, into my room.

It was eight feet tall at the very least and its shoulders were four feet wide. Its flesh was gray, its lips were black, its eyes oozed yellow slime. It raised its arms; its limbs were clothed in rags. "I have waited so long, so very long," it said in a rough wet voice.

My mind had not been strong for weeks, and now I knew: I was mad, as mad as the man in black! My brain had conspired to make my contrivance real! I gripped my shoulder, squeezed it hard; it hurt. Yes, I was awake.

I smelled him then; he reeked of death; I clutched my throat. He said: "I love you. Now you will be mine."

"Foul vision, let me be!" I cried. My heart was wild now.

"I am no vision," he replied. "I am the one you love. For only one who loves me could have told my tale so well." He showed his cracked and jagged teeth; he issued forth a hiss. "The last remaining obstacle between us is gone," he said. "My creator is gone."

"Your creator," I said.

"Doctor Berger," he said.

I gasped.

"Yes, Berger was your 'Frankenstein,' " he said. "He had no 'friend,' *he* gave me breath—but did not make me whole. And I, his flawed creation, took the breath from *him*."

"You killed him!" I said.

At this, he grinned. It was dreadful to see.

"He thought he had outwitted me," the harsh voice said. "As my creator, he had powers over me, and lured me to an island and stranded me there. But I have powers, too. I knew the boat would someday come, and I was right. The three of them were no match for my strength and I hurled them into the sea."

"My husband!" I cried.

"Your husband and both of his friends!" said the monster. "I stole their spark, then sailed for shore and caught my creator unaware, before he could weave his spell." At this, he held out his massive hands and made a twisting thrust.

"You killed . . . them all," I said. "You killed . . . my love!"

"And took his spark. And now you must love *me!*"

"Love *you!*" I cried. "You killed my world!"

"I *am* that world," said the fiend in a rasping voice. 'For I contain your husband, babes—"

"My babes!" I said.

"I contain all you love!" said the demon, grinning again. "And now you must come to me!"

I grabbed the lamp and held it out, praying with all my heart that the light would banish this apparition. No: it remained. I thrust the flame at the creature's wet, dull eyes. They widened with alarm; he sucked in breath; he shielded his face with his hand.

"You killed the greatest poet in the world!"

The fiend drew back, his arm still raised. In a voice akin to a wind on the moors, he said, "But I *contain* that poetry. I hold inside me all you love, and I love *you!* Love is the vital spark! It makes me whole! Without it we wither! Without it we die!"

My heart was filled with hatred and revenge, and yet this creature's words were so infused with pathos that,

THE MAN IN BLACK

for an instant, my fury wavered. Sensing my conflict, he advanced again.

The stench of the grave rushed forth on his breath. "You gave me a second birth," he said. "A *noble* birth, in your book! You, who never met me, understood!"

I gagged, I groaned; I pressed the lamp against his wrist. He shrieked with pain.

"Begone!" I cried.

"No, no!" he wailed. He tore his hair and gnashed his teeth. "You love me! You do! You must!"

Again I singed him; smelled his flesh; the dark room stank of death. "Begone!"

He howled, he fled, his feet like thunder on the stairs; the whole house shook.

I quickly went to Percy's room. The babe still slept, unharmed. I set the lamp beside his bed and sank to my knees, hands clasped.

The sea banged loudly on the shore, but otherwise, the house was still. My nervous disposition made me prone to vain imaginings; had all this been a dream? My heart beat on, then seemed to cease. I fell into a faint.

I awoke in the morning to screams: hysterical Claire. At once I ran to her and found her pale and gasping at the door that led to the terrace. She pointed down, and there, on the stones, was the source of her consternation.

A severed finger, purple, oozing putrifactive blood, and I too caught my breath. The finger was huge and could only belong to—I had not dreamt!

I locked the door and led poor Claire to the table. There we sat, trembling, hand in hand, as I told her my gruesome tale. A knock on the door made us frantic. To our vast relief it was good Trelawny—with grisly news.

Feet, hands, arms, legs in a state of mordant decay

and of monstrous size had appeared on the strand overnight. They seemed to belong to different persons—to a race of giants, he said. In addition, the corpse of a Zurich physician had been discovered, his neck snapped so badly it lolled on his shoulders. A terrible shipwreck was suspected, as for days now the sea had been rough, but so far no fragments of any boat had been found.

I thought of the monster; heard once again his pathetic wail. "There was no wreck," I said to my noble friend, "unless it was the wreck of a tortured soul."

Trelawny frowned, saying, "Mary, forgive me, for I do not understand."

"The vital spark is love," I said, and flung both hands against my breast. "The vital spark is love!"

A GOOD HEAD ON HIS SHOULDERS

by
Max Allan Collins

Louie Carboni was no monster.

Some people thought he was. He knew that. But they were stupid people. Ignorant people. Insensitive people. Uncultured. Unschooled.

As Carboni drew back the curtain to look out on the lake, the sky thundered and lightning threw a silvery glow on the baby-smooth surface of his round, thick-lipped face; his bright dark eyes glittered under heavy black brows and prominent forehead, thinning black hair slicked back over a massive skull. A thick five-dollar cigar smoldered between the similarly thick fingertips of a hand heavy with ruby- and diamond-encrusted gold rings. Wearing a LC-monogrammed scarlet silk smoking jacket over creamy silk pajamas, his feet in soft lambskin slippers, the short, wide, solid mob boss looked like a beast somebody had dressed up for a joke. Of course, Carboni didn't see himself that way.

Carboni saw himself as a modern Napoleon, as a wall of books on the Little General and several busts around the otherwise rustic den of the cabin indicated. He was proud of what he had accomplished by the young age of thirty. He felt he'd smoothed his own rough edges, without losing his touch where keeping discipline was concerned.

Louis Alberto Carboni had come out of a rough

Brooklyn neighborhood; his pop, who came over from Naples at the turn of the century, was a barber whose shop had been a hangout for the local Black Hand boys. Good connections like this put Louis and his boyhood pal Carlo Gazia in solid with the Five Points Gang. By the time he was sixteen Louie was one of the most prosperous pimps in Brooklyn.

He'd come to Chicago to help Danny Torello run whorehouses. He and Carlo were Danny's righthand men, and when Prohibition came in, it was Louie and Carlo who convinced Danny to expand, even if it did mean war.

War was the natural process by which civilization found out who its real leaders were. That was Carboni's creed. He had waged every kind of warfare known to man—openly attacking some enemies in certain cases, and in others weeding out the competition from within. Deviously. Like that guy Machiavelli laid it out in *The Prince*, a book whose philosophies would have been beyond the intellectual grasp of his late friend Carlo Gazia.

Carlo had been no dummy—he had a good head on his shoulders; but what good did it do him? After all, Carlo couldn't even read. Made an "X" for his signature, and not a very good one. Tall, skinny, mustached, a real ladies' man, Carlo had street smarts, but that was it.

Carboni heard a rustling outside the window and returned to draw back the curtain again, but figured it was just the fall wind, shaking the shrubs and bending the trees down by the lake. Lightning cut the sky like a jagged Z and turned the surface of the restless lake silver-gray.

"Exquisite," Carboni said, pronouncing the word slowly, correctly.

He'd set himself a goal: three new words a day. Ten years solid, he'd stuck with this program, and not even

A GOOD HEAD ON HIS SHOULDERS

when the streets were running red with blood and the bodies were piling up like kindling did Louie Carboni not find a few minutes a day to improve his vocabulary.

He walked to one of his Napoleon busts and placed a hand on the shoulder of the Little General.

"It's hard being a leader of men," Carboni said. "You have to make sacrifices for the common good. Right, pal? Fuckin' A!"

He sat in the deeply padded brown leather chair. Before him, in the cobblestone fireplace, a fire snapped, crackled, glowed orangely; he basked in its warmth. But in the flames he saw faces. Faces of men he'd killed, or had killed.

He shook them away.

"It's all right," he told himself. "Only a monster has no conscience."

He was sorry about them, or at least a few of them. Not the soldiers—a lot of them fell in any war. Pawns to be sacrificed. But some of the generals, who were getting too powerful and had to be gotten rid of, they were pals, and killing pals was never a picnic.

He'd killed Carlo in this room.

Carboni shivered a little, rose and threw a log on the dwindling fire. It perked up again.

Doing it here, just three months ago this weekend, killing this friend who'd been like a brother to him, dispatching him in this haven of trust, had been such a hard thing. Well ... pulling the trigger hadn't been hard; he'd made up his mind, when he heard Carlo was cutting side deals, that his near-brother needed killing. And he'd staged that phony flare-up with the Giannis to have somebody to blame.

But when he'd fired the .38 and the round black hole appeared in Carlo's throat, and Carlo's eyes got round and wide, Louie had seen something terrible in those eyes: betrayal.

The shocked disappointment that had registered in Carlo's eyes before he dropped face down, revealing a bigger, more gaping and bloody wound in the back of his neck, had haunted Louie Carboni. When he was alone in this room, here at the secluded cottage near Lake Geneva, he should feel safe, secure, in a womb of warmth and trust.

But now, whenever he came here, he felt Carlo's accusatory gaze was always on him.

It had been business. It had been a necessary maneuver in maintaining the proper power structure. Nothing personal. Certainly not the monstrous act of some madman.

Yet those lousy stinking editorials (from the one "dry" paper in town, that conservative piece of shit, the *Sentinel)* dared to call him that. Just last week they'd compared him to that *real* madman, the Medical School Mangler. Imagine! The nerve! Comparing the Napoleon of the North Side to some mass-murdering slob!

He was offended by the ... (he thought for a moment, his cat mind chasing the mouse of a right word) the *carnage,* the sheer brutality of this monster. And killing doctors—professors of medicine. Why do such a savage thing? Those guys were healers; they helped people, and more than that, they trained other people to help people.

This was the kind of beast the feds should be tracking down—not him. He was a business tycoon, not some homicidal mental case. This was the kind of fiend the papers should be stirring the public up about.

Well, actually, they were. The papers had been full of the Medical School Mangler. Seven deaths to date in as many weeks. Bodies torn apart savagely. Limbs

A GOOD HEAD ON HIS SHOULDERS

flung around the quiet studies of cozy bungalows near Hyde Park like a butcher shop that got upended.

One of the boys said a cop on one of the scenes told him that blood was splashed around like the work of some crazy modern artist.

How could that fucking piece of shit *Sentinel* editor put Louis Carboni in the same sentence with such a madman?

And with this thought came the image of Carlo Gazia with betrayal in his eyes and a hole in his throat.

His cigar had gone out; he lighted it with a horsehead lighter and thought to himself, *I'll just sell the goddamn place*. Maybe it was childish, maybe it was weak, to be haunted by something; to feel . . . guilty. But that, Carboni decided, was what separated him from the monsters.

He was a man who could make hard decisions and suffer the consequences with dignity.

The sky growled and cracked, and the room was momentarily bright with lightning, then rain began to batter the windows, like thousands of demanding, drumming fingers.

But after a while the very incessantness of it became oddly soothing. He'd just drifted off to sleep in the comfortable leather chair when the sky exploded again, and as his eyes popped open, the room was washed with lightning's whiteness. At this very moment, a knock came at the door, and made him jump.

"Yeah?" he boomed irritably, making his own thunder.

Vinnie popped his bullet head in the door; the narrow-eyed, needle-nosed, mustached hood was in rolled-up shirtsleeves and a loosened tie. He and the other boys were out there playing poker, Carboni knew.

"I know you said not to bother you, boss . . ."

"I require solitude, Vinnie. I told ya that."

"Yeah, boss, but . . ."

"Did I even ask you to have a girl sent out? No. Does that say anything to you, when I don't want female companionship? It does. It says, I require solitude."

"It's just that Doc Stein's outside."

Carboni sat up, confused. "What the hell's the doc doing here? We ain't . . . haven't sent him any 'patients' in weeks."

Vinnie raised his eyebrows. "I dunno, boss. But he's acting kinda strange. All sweaty. Nervous. Looks like shit."

"I don't want to see him."

"Boss . . . he says it's urgent."

Carboni didn't like anybody pushing him or contradicting him, and the heavy sigh he swallowed didn't taste good at all. But Doc Stein—minor minion though he was—knew where the bodies were buried. Hell—he'd *buried* most of the bodies! What was left of them after the doc's farmhouse crematorium got done with them, anyway.

And the doc was usually anything but pushy. Timid, even. If Doc Stein came around saying something was important, something was urgent, chances were it was. Important. Urgent.

Carboni stood, waved a pudgy hand; the jewels on his rings winked with reflected firelight. "Send him in."

Vinnie went away and a moment later was opening the door for the slender figure of Dr. Victor Stein, his wet fedora in hand, dripping, his raincoat dripping, too, onto the wood floor.

"Get his damn coat, Vinnie! Have some fuckin' manners!"

"Sure, boss," Vinnie said, and did.

A GOOD HEAD ON HIS SHOULDERS

Stein was an average-looking man in every way—about five eight, slight of build. Rather weak-chinned with ordinary features but for piercing dark nervous eyes magnified by heavy lenses in dark frames; he was the kind of person who looks like a pair of glasses coming at you—you barely noticed the man behind them. Tonight, as usual, he wore his white doctor's smock which was touched with splotches of red as if the doc had been operating and suddenly called here.

Carboni, still standing, gestured to a wooden chair against the wall. "Pull up a seat, doc. You look damp. Sit by the fire. Warm your bones."

"Thank you, Mr. Carboni," he said. "You're very kind to see me at such short notice. I hate to impose."

"Doc, you're an important part of the team. Always time for you."

For the Carboni mob, a "staff" doctor was a vital team member indeed; when the bullets started to fly, you had to have somebody who could make the necessary repairs, and wouldn't be reporting gunshot wounds to the cops.

"I'm gonna have a little snifter of brandy, doc. It's good stuff. That is . . . excellent vintage." Carboni rose and moved to the liquor cart. "Care to join me?"

"Certainly." Doc Stein was sitting now, closer to the fire than Carboni; he was holding his palms up and out, warming them. His face was orange from the flames; there were angles in Doc's face that Carboni had never noticed before.

"I have to ask you to be patient with me, Mr. Carboni."

He handed Stein a snifter of brandy. "Sure, doc. As long as I'm not *a* 'patient' of yours." And he laughed.

Doc looked at him, either not getting it or simply unamused. "You're going to find what I have to tell you . . . incredible. Fantastic. I'm afraid—unbelievable."

With an expansive gesture and a benevolent smile, Carboni settled himself back in the deep leather chair. "Doc . . . I may just be a street kid made good. But I'm not a stupid man. I've educated myself." He gestured to the wall of books. "Give me a little fuckin' credit, okay?"

"I meant no disrespect. I ask only that you grant me fifteen minutes to present my case. Then, you may toss me out on my ass, as your boys might say."

"I'd never do that to you, doc."

"Good. But again—I ask your patience. My story is a strange one. . . .

"I believe you are under the misapprehension that I am a defrocked doctor (Stein began), but in fact I am a failed medical student. I had the highest marks in my class. I was attending on full scholarship. The dean of the medical college was my mentor. It was all too perfect, like something out of storybook.

"I was a week away from graduation, ready to begin my internship, when I was . . . if I may use the phrase again . . . thrown out on my ass. Why? Because of my experimentation into areas where man is not meant to go . . . or so have said the unimaginative, petty medical minds of this so-called enlightened century.

"One would think that the peasants who launched witch hunts against my forebears were endemic to the nineteenth century. Unfortunately that is not the case. They exist, these feeble-minded modern-day peasants, amongst the highest level of supposed society, and the upper reaches of academia.

"But I race ahead of myself.

"I know, Mr. Carboni, that you have assumed I was either German or Jewish, or a German Jew. In fact I

A GOOD HEAD ON HIS SHOULDERS

am neither. My roots are in Geneva ... and I do not refer to Geneva, Wisconsin, but Switzerland. My family name was once illustrious. It was distorted—courtesy of a cheap popular novel of another age, which unfortunately has endured—into something quite literally horrible.

"My great-great grandfather, after whom I was named, was Victor Frankenstein.

"And 'Frankenstein' was not a monster ... no matter what school children who've seen that cheap, recent Hollywood monstrosity may believe. Frankenstein was a *man*—but more than just a man: a scientist, the most brilliant scientific mind of his age.

"Oh, you've heard of the novel? You've *read* it? Yes, you're right ... Mary Godwin Shelley's alternate title for that unfortunate work *was* 'The Modern Prometheus.' I had forgotten, for a moment, how well-read you are, Mr. Carboni. But I would encourage you to seek more enlightened, enlightening literature in the future than such travesties as Mrs. Shelley's Gothic mockery.

"Forgive my bitterness. I'll try to control myself. No ... no more brandy. This is fine.

"I will not bother you with any further critique of Mary Shelley's work. It would take hours to point out every lie, every distortion, each complete fabrication. Suffice to say that my great-grandfather did, indeed, manage to construct a living man out of bits and pieces of dead ones.

"It is also quite true that he and his creation became ... adversaries ... and that they were lost to mankind, to science, on some polar ice cap, long ago....

"No, no, you're right ... that wasn't in the film. It's not important, Mr. Carboni. Please let me continue.

"My father was not a scientist. He was ashamed of his heritage ... it is he who dropped the prefix from our family name, condemning our family to a lifetime of Jew-baiting. A foolish man, my father. Perhaps vision skips a generation.

"At any rate, I stumbled upon my great-grandfather's papers in a trunk in our attic, when I was but sixteen. I already had a keen interest in science, and reading these brilliant, exciting documents inspired me further. I made medicine my goal—not to be some meager M.D., but to do medical, scientific research, in the tradition of my great-grandfather.

"And even at that tender age I formed the ambition to confirm, and to continue, his data. To repeat, and perfect, his grand experiment.

"It was toward this end that I was working (cadavers weren't difficult to come by) when the powers-that-be at the medical college discovered my research. The dean—my supposed 'mentor'—instigated the proceedings that deprived me of my career before it had begun.

"I was out in the cold, told that I was lucky the 'good name' of the school had to be preserved, or I would have been turned over to the authorities, after which (so said the dean) I would be languishing in a prison or, more likely, an insane asylum.

"The only good turn my father ever did me was put me in touch with your late friend, Mr. Gazia. My father worked in the garment district and had business dealings with Mr. Gazia, and this was how I became a part of your family, Mr. Carboni, your 'team.'

"Mr. Gazia said there was need for a medical man in your organization, and I was set up with my farmhouse surgery and since, when? 1928? I have been patching up bullet holes and stitching up knife wounds and, on a number of occasions, disposing of patients who didn't pull through.

"Here, Mr. Carboni, is where you may truly lose patience with me. Here is where ... frankly ... I have possibly done you a disservice. I ask only that you withhold your judgment until my tale is told.

"It is from the refuse of your organization, the soldiers who have died in battle, that I have found the ... spare parts? The materials I needed to pursue my experiments. To be candid, these experiments have been dismal failures. These stitched-together patchwork men have remained useless piles of protoplasm on my laboratory table. One after another, they have been consigned to the crematorium.

"Until three months ago.

"My great-grandfather kept his notes in the language of his native land—*Schwyzertutsch,* Swiss-German, a dialect difficult for a speaker of true German to even understand; as a child, we'd spoken, even written, the language at home, to a certain degree. But my abilities were below that, I would say, of the average Swiss schoolchild. Later, I took a college German course, and felt I was capable.

"But in truth I was not.

"I took a crucial portion of my great-grandfather's notes on his key experiment to a native speaker of the tongue. Out of context, these scientific ramblings were of no import to this woman; but to me, they were a revelation. They amounted to the key to the secret of creating life.

"With the correct translation in hand, I set out to assemble one more patchwork man. Last winter you had that outbreak with the Gianni brothers, remember? We lost five soldiers in that skirmish. They gave their lives to your cause, Mr. Carboni, but they gave me their limbs, their organs, their life's blood.

"I created a giant. Your men were chosen for their physical prowess—remember Tony Lombardi? His torso became that of my giant. Remember Ange

Berini's massive arms? Those formidable biceps, those powerful forearms? They are now my giant's.

"You look as if you doubt me. Or my sanity. I can understand that. My story is almost over. Bear with me. . . .

"My giant was like a child. He had no memory of his former life. But he was not a baby: walking came easily, and just hearing my speech awakened something in his own speech center. We were conversing, normally, by the third week.

"He wanted to know his purpose.

"Can you imagine, Mr. Carboni? Look at that world out there—the rain lashing the windows, thunder cracking the sky, lightning making the night momentarily day. Can you imagine being face-to-face with the God who created all of that, and who created you?

"Imagine how humble my giant felt in my presence. Unlike you and I, Mr. Carboni, my giant could face his creator. He could ask him the *purpose* of his life . . . a question we can ask the sky until it falls and never get an answer.

"But I had an answer for him: *revenge*.

"I had brought him into this world to serve me. And the goal I wished him to reach was complete, total vengeance upon those who would subvert science, those who called me mad, those who felt so threatened by my genius that they had to tear the future from my hands and fling me into the trash heap of humanity.

"But I fooled them. I fooled them all.

"He killed the dean first. In front of the man's wife, who I instructed the giant not to touch, although I understand she is quite mad, now. She witnessed her husband's arms and legs being torn off as a naughty child might those of a grasshopper or beetle. The living room was sprayed with his blood, littered with his

A GOOD HEAD ON HIS SHOULDERS

flesh, was filled with his screams, and he was only the first, the dean was.

"There have been six more. Teachers. Board members. Those who wronged me. Those who denied the world ... or *tried* to deny the world ... my medical and scientific genius.

"But a few days ago, something ... unfortunate occurred.

"You see, in my great-grandfather's notes, he indicated that his creation's memory remained a blank slate. His creation knew only the *now*—had been 'born again,' but not in a Christian sense, and was a sort of eight-foot child.

"I assumed this would be the case with my giant, but after a time, he began having flashes of memory. At first, I deflected his questions, but finally he became ... irritated with me.

"Something else my giant knows that you and I never shall, Mr. Carboni, is what it feels like to pick your creator up by the throat and scare the living hell out of him.

"I requested that he put me down and pledged to answer his questions completely and honestly. I told him who he had been, and it acted as a sort of triggering mechanism ... a floodgate of memory opened, and the face of Nicky De Luca lighted up as the eyes of Willie Manzoni filled with the memories of Carlo Gazia.

"Yes ... Carlo Gazia.

"You see, Mr. Carboni, as I mentioned before, your soldiers were men picked because of their physical nature. They were wonderful brutes, and perfect specimens for my research purposes in every way but one: their deficient mentality.

"Fortunately for me, your good friend, your partner, Carlo Gazia was shot and killed just at the moment that I needed a man of superior intellect. Which, compared to my other prospects at least, Mr. Gazia certainly possessed. In addition to which, he'd been shot in the throat. So many of your deceased who passed through my hands and my farmhouse were shot in the head. Which of course makes their brains quite unusable.

"The problem we both have, now, Mr. Carboni, is the brain of Carlo Gazia. It is filled with what I schooled my giant in, in his first days, when he was taking his first steps: revenge.

"And Mr. Carboni, it is my unpleasant but necessary duty to tell you that the object of my giant's quest for his own, personal vengeance is you, sir."

Carboni was standing now. He looked down at Doc Stein, whose face in the firelight was as orange as a jack-o-lantern, and said, "This is all true?"

"Yes, sir."

"I thought you were mad for a while, but . . . Mother of Mercy, can it be true?"

"Oh, yes."

Carboni's tongue felt thick in his mouth; he went to his desk by the wall of books and got out his .45 Colt automatic. Worked the action—checked the clip.

"If it is, doc—I owe you one, warning me like this."

"Think nothing of it."

He smiled tightly. "And unlike those medical-school bums, I take you seriously. I can see the benefits—a whole army of men like your mangler and there wouldn't be a mob on the face of the earth that could stop me."

"That's probably true."

A crack of what Carboni at first thought was thunder interrupted them. But it was from the room beyond, where Vinnie and the boys were playing poker.

Someone had kicked in the door.

Immediately, there was a barrage of ghastly sounds:

A GOOD HEAD ON HIS SHOULDERS

screams, gunshots, thumps, overturning furniture, more screams, horrendous screams the likes of which Carboni had never heard, and he had heard some.

He put one hand on the doorknob, the automatic tight in his other fat fist. A hand touched his arm.

Doc Stein, his eyes childishly wide behind the thick lenses, was waggling a lecturing finger.

"I wouldn't go in there, if I were you."

Whap! Something hit the door, impacting wetly. It was a sound that repeated, as something, or somebody, was being thrown here and there, against the door, against this wall, against that one, and through it all, the men were screaming. The gunshots had stopped.

And then, finally, the screaming stopped, too.

A noise that might have been the front door slamming made Carboni look searchingly at the doc.

Doc Stein nodded. "I think he's gone."

Carboni sighed. He cracked open the door, then he barreled in, ready to shoot.

He was not a squeamish man, but all of his supper came up almost at once.

The large outer, lodge-style room, its poker table incongruously in place, was strewn with body parts, streaked with blood. One bloody arm was hanging over a stoic elk's head, sleeve caught in the antlers. An armless, legless torso that was Vinnie had its hysterical eyes open and was trying to talk but could only gurgle.

Carboni backed into the den. The .45 trembled in his fist. He shut the door. Hard.

Doc, who had not even ventured out there, said, "Not a pretty sight, I'd wager. He's strong, my giant is."

Carboni grabbed the little man by the front of his white smock. "How can I kill him?"

"I'm not sure. His organs are all technically dead,

although I suppose well-placed shots of sufficient caliber might stop the heart from pumping. Trouble is, a side effect of my great-grandfather's creation process is a toughening up of the skin ... a leathery effect, which most bullets can't even penetrate. Sorry."

Carboni slapped the doc, who went down hard.

"You didn't come here to *warn* me," the gangster said. "You came here to lead him *to* me!"

The little man shrugged. "I am sorry, Mr. Carboni. I had to. He did my bidding, seven times. I owed him this much."

"The only reason I'm not killing you," Carboni said through clenched teeth, waving the .45 at Stein, "is I might need you later. Stay put! I gotta get the hell outa here...."

Carboni went to the window, where the wind and rain were still rattling the panes. The storm was pelting the lake, as if God were firing down infinite machine guns; trees, barren of leaves, seemed about to snap. He put his hands up on the lock, to open the goddamn thing and climb out, when the awful face was suddenly before him.

Stitched-on ears. A skull-cap stitch-line where the brain, Gazia's goddamn brain, had been dropped in. Bits and pieces of various of his men were standing outside the window, staring at him, a grotesque face streaming with rain that might have been tears, and hands that used to belong to who-the-hell-knew crashed through the glass and reached in and big fingers clutched Carboni's fat neck and squeezed, and lifted.

Carboni's head came off like the cap on a bottle of shook-up Coke, and his blood geysered the same way.

His body did a brief, shuffling dance before stumbling and falling, face down, except there no longer

A GOOD HEAD ON HIS SHOULDERS

was a face attached to the torso, the neck of which was spilling red like an over-turned paint can.

The giant, who was wearing a raincoat and dungarees, crawled through the window, workshoes crunching the glass underfoot, carrying Carboni's head by the left ear, the eyes in it moving wildly, as the howl of the storm provided accompaniment. The giant's footsteps shook the room as he strode to a pedestal where a bust of Napoleon rested. With a massive forearm, he swept the bust off and it shattered into countless pieces on the wood floor. He stuck Carboni's head on the pedestal, moving it around until blood and tissue provided some purchase. Carboni's eyes and his mouth were still moving. That would stop soon.

A thoughtful hand to his cheek, Dr. Stein considered this for future research. Reflex action only, or could Carboni's brain still be functioning, until the oxygen loss put a stop to it? A worthy topic to pursue....

"Ready, doc?" the giant said. "We don't want to be here when the cops show."

"No, we wouldn't. What now?"

He patted his ex-partner's round skull with a huge hand.

"Now?" the giant said. "Now, there's gonna be a *new* head man in town."

ROLE MODEL
by
Mike Baker

Paul Shine first began to doubt the stability of his eight-month-old marriage, as well as his wife's sanity, the day that Andrea brought home the brain.

Paul didn't usually get home from work until after six, sometimes even later if the rush hour traffic was particularly bad. Today, though, he'd joined many of his coworkers in leaving early; with the bosses off at a convention in Florida, there wasn't any reason to stick around.

It was just after three when Paul swung his Jeep Cherokee into the driveway of his and Andrea's two-story, four bedroom Silverlake home (which had been a wedding gift from Andrea's father). Spotting Andrea standing by the front door, keys in hand, Paul smiled.

Leaning against one of Andrea's shapely legs was a plastic grocery bag from the local supermarket. Beside it sat a large glass jar filled with a dusky, greenish liquid. Pickles, Paul thought as he killed the Jeep's engine. She bought me pickles.

Like a child caught with their hand in the cookie jar, Andrea looked up from the door, her eyes wide with surprise.

"Hi, honey," Paul said as he climbed out of the Jeep. "Looks like I'm just in time to help with ..." Paul's words trailed off, and the smile vanished from his lips, when he noticed the contents of the jar; instead of those kosher dills which he could never seem to get enough of, it contained a brain.

"Jesus Christ!" Paul exclaimed. "What the fuck is that?"

Andrea glanced down at the brain, then up at Paul. "Homework," she said, smiling shyly.

"What!?"

"It's a study aid," she explained. "I've got a test on the central nervous system Monday."

Paul tried to look away from the brain and found that he couldn't; like iron to a magnet, it held his gaze. Though he had known she was a medical student—and a brilliant one at that—when he had married her, Paul still wasn't totally comfortable with the fact that Andrea spent a good part of her day poking and prodding dead people. A woman's place was in the home, caring for the needs of her husband, not dissecting the corpse of some shmuck who'd donated his body to science.

"I'm sorry, honey," Andrea said. Stepping away from the door, she headed across the driveway toward Paul. "I didn't expect you home so early."

"I wanted to surprise you," he said, smiling thinly. "Looks like I'm the one who got the surprise instead, doesn't it."

Reaching the Jeep, Andrea stood in front of her husband, blocking his view of the brain. "It'll never happen again, honey," she told him. Managing to look both contrite and sexy at the same time, she planted a quick kiss on Paul's cheek. "I promise."

The instant Andrea's lips touched Paul's flesh, all her sins were forgiven, wiped forever from his mind.

Drowning in his love for her, Paul helped Andrea unload the groceries from her Honda Civic. And to show just how much he really cared, he even carried the brain in for her.

Mike Baker

* * *

It had been a classic case of love at first sight when Paul met Andrea at a dinner party a little over a year ago. It didn't matter that she was six years his junior, or that he was already married, or that he had two children, or that Andrea was the younger sister of his wife Patricia's best friend; Paul had to have her, regardless of the consequences. This was the woman he'd written countless sonnets about; she was his soulmate, the one he'd been searching for all his life.

Paul filed for a divorce from Patricia the day he moved in with Andrea.

Paul liked to consider his marriage to Patricia as an unfortunate consequence of youthful ignorance. They had met in a Creative Writing class at UCLA during Paul's sophomore year. He was the teacher's pet, the brash young poet with a bright future. She was a transfer student from a Northern California community college. They hit it off instantly. Patricia had been attracted to Paul's intelligence and wit; he liked her tits.

Three months after he had first laid eyes upon her—and two months, three weeks and four days after he first laid her—Paul threw caution to the wind and proposed to Patricia. (Paul later blamed his uncharacteristically-spontaneous behavior upon the bottle of wine and two joints he'd consumed earlier in honor of the sale of a poem to a literary journal.)

Much to Paul's surprise, Patricia accepted. They were married later that year, during the summer break between classes.

Not long thereafter, Paul began to notice changes in Patricia, in the way she treated both him and his writing. Subtle at first, these personality alterations gradually became more and more pronounced. Before long the shy, bookish, perpetually-horny Patricia who'd heaped mountains of praise upon Paul's work was gone, replaced by a loud, demanding, soap opera-addicted harridan who looked upon his poetry with disdain because, "that kind of crap don't pay for shit."

Paul swiftly grew to despise his wife, to loathe her with a passion one usually reserves for certain noxious in-laws. Patricia became Paul's scapegoat; any facet of his life which displeased him was blamed on her. For example: It was Patricia's fault that Paul had forsaken his dream of achieving the lofty title of America's poet laureate and become an advertising copywriter instead; her constant whining had driven him from the ivory towers of his youth and into the mundanities of 9-to-5 suit-and-tie world. It was also Patricia's fault that the burden of fatherhood had been thrust upon Paul, who'd long held the belief that children served no useful purpose whatsoever; they were loud, obnoxious, smelly, and, most importantly, expensive to maintain. If only Patricia had stayed on her pill like she was supposed to. But no, she'd forgotten. And along had come Tiffany, bills trailing behind her like an umbilical cord. Then, less than a year later, it happened again.

A week after he found out that Patricia was pregnant again, Paul got a vasectomy.

The day Paul left Patricia, he sent her a bouquet of dead roses. Attached was a note which read: "Roses are red/Violets make me itch/I'll see you in court/You money-sucking bitch."

The divorce settlement was swift, and, in Paul's eyes, quite fair. Patricia ended up with the house, the cars, the kids, and half of Paul's money.

Paul got something far more important: his freedom.

Two weeks after what he liked to think of as the "brain incident," Paul was visited at work by Mitch Petron, a plainclothes detective from the Los Angeles

Police Department's Homicide Division. After ushering him into the privacy of a nearby office, Petron informed Paul that his ex-wife's body had been found earlier that morning floating in one of the garbage-filled waterways which the city of Venice, CA liked to refer to as its canals.

Restraining the urge to shout for joy, Paul struggled to keep a somber expression upon his face.

Sitting down across from Paul, Petron pulled out a notepad and a pen. "If it isn't too much bother, Mr. Shine, I'd like to ask you a few questions."

"Certainly."

"Where were you between the hours of nine p.m. and midnight last evening, Mr. Shine?"

Thinking that Petron's technique was about as subtle as a sledgehammer, Paul answered the detective's question, explaining in meticulous detail how, from the hours of 8:00 p.m. until nearly 3:00 a.m., he and Dan Mitchell, one of the firm's Account Executives, had had the less-than-enjoyable honor of escorting a client, a devout churchgoer from the Midwest who liked to watch topless women wrestle in whipped cream-filled pits, on an alcohol-sodden crawl through some of Los Angeles' sleaziest nightclubs.

After Paul's boss, and Mitchell as well, corroborated his story, Petron's interest in Paul as a suspect dropped considerably. Saying that he'd be in touch, and reminding Paul not to leave town, he left.

Keeping the facade of grief he'd so carefully maintained in place, Paul asked for, and got, the rest of the day off.

Before heading home, Paul decided to stop by his favorite bar for a couple of celebratory drinks first.

Paul ended up spending the rest of the day at the bar. Arriving home a mere half-hour earlier than usual,

ROLE MODEL

Paul parked his Jeep on the street instead of the driveway. Snatching up the bouquet of roses which lay on the seat beside him, he headed for his house. In his mind was a simple plan: he'd sneak inside, surprise Andrea, and break the good news to her.

Taking great pains to be as quiet as possible, Paul unlocked the front door and stepped inside. Smiling, he headed for the kitchen; from the sound of things, Andrea was hard at work preparing his evening meal.

Peering in through an open doorway, Paul spotted his wife. She was standing with her back to him by the sink on the other side of the kitchen, chopping vegetables on a cutting board with a large, gleaming knife. The blade rose and fell, neatly bisecting already small pieces of carrot with uncanny precision.

Andrea was so engrossed in the meticulous dissection of the vegetable that she failed to notice Paul's arrival.

Finishing with the carrots, Andrea set upon some celery.

"They're fools," she muttered as she worked. "They don't understand. They don't see."

Moving faster, the blade became a blur.

"Like her, I have the power to create, to bring forth life," Andrea said as she chopped. "I have examined the causes of life, and death as well."

Paul could see the tension in his wife's body. The muscles in her shoulders and neck stood out like cords, and she gripped the knife with white-knuckled intensity.

"If they only knew what she did." Sighing, Andrea examined the celery for a moment. Apparently not happy with what she saw, she resumed her chopping. "Like her, I became acquainted with the science of anatomy, but it wasn't sufficient. So I did as she did, and observed the natural decay and corruption of the human body."

Paul wanted to go to Andrea, to hold her, but he held himself back. She was wound up so tight, there was no telling what she'd do if he made any sudden movements. No, it was best if he just left her alone, let her calm down a bit.

"Remember, I am not recording the vision of a madwoman," Andrea proclaimed as she attacked a radish.

Leaving as silently as he had arrived, Paul returned to his Jeep, bought a six-pack of Heineken at a liquor store, and headed for Griffith Park. Later, after he grew tired of watching children play soccer, transients dig through garbage cans, and drug deals go down, he went home.

Paul had discovered Andrea's amphetamine stash a month after the wedding. One evening while she was off at the library studying, he had suffered an intensely painful sinus attack. Nose clogged, head throbbing, he's stumbled into the bathroom and grabbed what he'd thought was his prescription sinus medication. Dry swallowing some pills, he crawled back into bed to await the relief they would soon bring.

Relief came, but it wasn't what Paul had been expecting. A fire flared to life in Paul's heart and swiftly spread through his body, imbibing it with strength. The fire burned in Paul's brain as well, filling his mind with a powerful desire to get things done. Paul's sinuses still hurt, but he didn't care anymore; trivial bullshit like that was beneath him now.

By the time Andrea showed up four hours later, Paul had vacuumed the house, rearranged the living room furniture, and alphabetized his entire CD collection.

Grabbing his wife as soon as she shut the front door,

ROLE MODEL

Paul carried her upstairs to the bedroom where they made passionate love for the rest of the evening.

Paul never confronted Andrea with his knowledge. He understood the pressure she was under and sympathized with her. Medical school was no picnic; the amount of work Andrea's professors expected her to do on a daily basis was truly staggering, far more than Paul could have dealt with had he been in her shoes. Andrea persevered, though, and Paul was immensely proud of her for that. So what if she needed a little chemical pick-me-up every now and then; as long as she got good grades, and cooked dinner on a regular basis, he was happy.

Besides, Andrea wasn't a junkie. That kind of thing just didn't happen to people like them.

The next week was tough for Paul. Andrea had midterm exams all week long, so she was even more high-strung than usual. Then there was Monday's dinner fiasco; attempting to cook and study at the same time, Andrea had burned the pot roast, turning the once-tender meat into something which resembled a giant charcoal briquette. Keeping his anger in check, Paul had relieved Andrea of her dinner chores for the rest of the week; until midterms ended, he'd subsist solely on junk food.

The next day, when he showed up for work, Paul was told that Bob Richards, the firm's other copywriter, had suffered a fatal heart attack the night before. The search had already begun for a replacement, Paul's boss informed him; in the interim, though, Paul would be expected to carry the additional workload.

The kicker occurred on Tuesday afternoon. Paul was winding down after a meeting with one of Bob's accounts, an obnoxious gentleman who called Paul's ad copy "childish" and "stupid," when his lawyer phoned with what he assumed was good news: when Patricia died, the lawyer told Paul, custody of his children automatically returned to Paul; all he had to do was say the word and they would once again be his.

Paul shivered at the thought of once again living under the same roof with his son and daughter. "Who has them now?" he asked his lawyer.

"Your ex-wife's older sister," the lawyer replied.

"She can keep 'em," Paul said, then hung up.

By Friday, things had calmed down a bit. Paul was finally getting a handle on Bob's accounts, an offer of continued monetary support had purchased his children a new set of guardians, and Andrea was taking her final test, an all day affair.

Slipping out of the office an hour early, a stack of projects which needed to be done by Monday morning under his arm, Paul headed for home. During the stop and go freeway crawl, Paul used his car phone to make a call.

Arriving at his house just as the delivery boy was pulling up, Paul hurried inside to set up his surprise.

Paul was in the basement attempting to choose a wine to go with dinner when he heard the front door open above him.

Grabbing the closest bottle, Paul headed for the stairs. As he did, he spotted something out of the corner of his eye. Sitting on a shelf across the room, partially hidden by other items, was a familiar-looking jar.

"Paul?" a voice called from above. "Where are you?"

Leaving the jar for later, Paul ran up the stairs and into the kitchen. Andrea was standing in the dining room, staring at what lay before her. A lace tablecloth covered a table set with their finest china, silverware, and glasses. The lights were off, and a pair of lit candles illuminated the room.

ROLE MODEL

It was a classy, romantic setting all the way, with the only incongruity being the cardboard pizza box which sat in the center of the table.

Wine bottle in hand, Paul stepped into the dining room. Pulling back one of the chairs, he turned to Andrea. As much as Paul hated to admit it, she looked awful. The pills, and sleepless nights, had taken their toll on her; not even makeup could hide her unhealthy pallor and the bags under her bloodshot eyes.

"Sit," Paul told his wife. "I'll pour."

Smiling, Andrea did as she was told.

"How did the test go?" Paul asked as he uncorked the wine.

"I aced it," Andrea told him. She fidgeted, playing with her silverware with a trembling hand. "They think that they're all so smart, when in reality they know nothing."

"Sounds like a lot of people I know." Not wanting any spills on his grandmother's best tablecloth, Paul only partially filled Andrea's wine glass.

As dinner progressed, Paul noticed Andrea growing more and more relaxed, as if someone had opened a valve and bled the tension out of her. He smiled; with any luck she'd pass out soon and get the sleep she so desperately needed.

After they'd finished eating, Paul ushered Andrea into the living room, informing her that it was her duty to decide how they'd spend the rest of their evening as he did.

Returning to the kitchen, Paul stacked the dirty dishes in the sink. Despite their value, he absolutely refused to wash them; he'd bribe Consuela, their cleaning woman, to do that odious chore when she came in on Monday.

Flipping off the lights, and blowing out the candles,

Paul joined Andrea on the living room couch. "So, what did you decide?"

"Movies," she replied.

Big surprise, Paul thought. "Which ones, honey?" he asked, even though he already knew what the answer would be. When it came to movies, Andrea was like a little kid; she could watch the same film over and over again, never seeming to grow tired of it.

"*Gothic* and *Haunted Summer*," Andrea said, grinning broadly. Lifting the remote control, she punched a button and Ken Russell's *Gothic* began.

Snuggling close to Paul, Andrea laid her head on his shoulder. "I love you," she whispered.

"I love you, too," Paul replied. "With all my heart."

They watched the film in silence until Julian Sands, who played Percy Bysshe Shelley, made his first appearance. "You're just like him, you know," Andrea said.

Andrea's statement confused Paul; he didn't look anything at all like Julian Sands. "Who?"

"Percy Shelley," she replied. "The greatest poet who ever lived . . . other than you, of course."

Paul couldn't help but be flattered by Andrea's compliment, even if he didn't agree with it; when it came to early nineteenth century poets, he'd always considered his work to be more on par with Lord Byron than Shelley.

By the time the film reached the halfway mark, Andrea was asleep.

Not caring what was unfolding on the screen—he'd seen the film at least five times before—Paul's mind began to wander. He thought back to dinner, and how the wine he'd chosen had actually gone well with the meal. And to think that he'd just grabbed a bottle at random; who'd have guessed that a burgundy would go well with pepperoni.

ROLE MODEL

Suddenly, an image flashed in Paul's mind: the jar.

Like a fish on a lure, Paul was hooked. From that moment on, no matter how hard he tried, he couldn't get the jar out of his mind.

Three-quarters of the way through *Gothic,* Paul made up his mind to go downstairs.

Sliding out from beneath his wife, Paul rose to his feet. If she wakes up, he thought, I'll say I had to go to the bathroom.

Looking down at Andrea, Paul couldn't help but smile. She looked as content as a sleeping babe, relaxed and at ease with the world.

Tiptoeing out of the living room, Paul headed for the kitchen. Leaving the kitchen light off, he flipped on the basement lights and headed down the stairs, taking care to avoid the ones which creaked.

Across the basement from the stairs was a floor-to-ceiling walk-in freezer/meat locker. A remnant of the house's previous owners—a frugal minded couple who, Paul had heard, bought their beef by the truckload—the locker was pretty much ignored by Paul and Andrea; their standard-sized freezer served them just fine.

The shelves Paul sought were over by the locker.

As he crossed the room, Paul noticed a humming noise coming from the meat locker. I would have sworn we'd turned that thing off, he thought. The damn thing sucks power like you wouldn't believe.

By the time he reached the shelves, Paul had noticed something else new about the locker: there was a shiny new padlock dangling from the door.

Turning away from the locker, Paul directed his attention toward the shelves. Reaching up, he slid a can of paint to the side, revealing the large jar he'd glimpsed earlier. Floating in the jar, bobbing like an obscene ice cube in the green-tinged liquid, was the brain.

Paul's evening, which had been perfect up until that point, suddenly took a turn for the worse.

Anger flaring inside him, Paul lifted the jar from the shelf. Wondering what Andrea would say when confronted with the brain, Paul turned to head back to the stairs. Then he stopped.

Setting the brain on the floor by his feet, Paul stared at the locker. I wonder, he thought as his eyes came to rest upon the padlock.

It took nearly ten minutes of searching, but Paul finally found a set of heavy duty bolt cutters. A triumphant grin upon his face, he stalked across the basement. Snapping the lock took a greater amount of physical effort, and made more noise, than Paul thought it would, but he succeeded nonetheless.

Laying the bolt cutters on the floor beside the brain, Paul lifted the now-worthless lock from the door.

Shivering from the cold emanating from the metal handle, Paul opened the door.

The meat locker was like a giant refrigerator; when the door opened, the overhead lights came on.

Reacting to the wave of cold which rushed out to meet him, as well as the sight which greeted him, Paul gasped. Lining three of the locker's walls were neatly-stacked body parts encased in plastic bags. Affixed to each bag was a white card.

Stepping into the freezer, Paul squatted down and read the writing on a card which was attached to a bag containing a frost-rimed hand. Caucasian female, the card said. Transient, aged 44. Cause of death: exposure.

Paul recognized the handwriting on the card instantly; it was Andrea's.

Rising to his feet, Paul turned to face the far wall.

ROLE MODEL

Resting against it was a metal cart over which was draped a white sheet.

Lying atop the cart, hidden from prying eyes by the sheet, was what appeared to be a body.

The breeze from the air conditioning units which cooled the locker made the sheet flutter and rustle, billowing it occasionally so that it looked like the figure beneath was stirring.

Maybe it is stirring, a tiny voice inside Paul's mind said. Maybe it was just resting, waiting for someone stupid enough to open the door and set it free.

His breath forming a cloud in the air before him, Paul took a hesitant step toward the cart.

Moved by the breeze, or lifted by an unseen hand, the sheet shifted, then dropped back to its original position.

A piece of machinery in the locker's wall pinged, startling Paul, almost making him scream.

When his heart rate had returned to a more sensible level, Paul took a moment to evaluate his situation. Convincing himself that he had nothing to fear from the shape under the sheet, he strode purposefully across the locker, grasped the sheet, and lifted.

Then the door slammed shut.

And the lights went out.

Leaving Paul alone in the darkness. Alone with the monster.

Crying out in surprise, Paul spun about, jostling the cart as he did.

Cold, hard fingers brushed against Paul's leg.

This time Paul did scream.

Desperate to escape from the hand before it seized his leg in a death grip, Paul lunged toward where he thought the door was.

Paul struck the locker's wall instead. Stunned, he

fell onto a carefully-arranged pile of plastic-bagged torsos.

The locker door opened. Light flooded into the room.

Looking up, Paul saw Andrea standing above him. In her hand was a syringe. "You shouldn't have done this, Paul," she said as she jabbed the needle into his arm. "It wasn't your time yet."

The needle's sting shocked Paul back to reality. Crying out in pain, he yanked his arm away from Andrea, but not before she'd emptied the syringe's contents into his body.

Paul rose to unsteady feet. "Why?" he asked his wife.

"As it once was, it will be again," she cryptically replied.

The room began to spin around Paul. He was having difficulty thinking, much less standing. "What," he said. His voice sounded funny, like a 45 rpm record played at 33. "You're not making sense."

"Mary Shelley was one of the greatest women who ever lived," Andrea told him. "She's my role model, my inspiration."

Leaning against the wall for support, Paul stared into his wife's eyes. Her pupils were dilated, and the whites were even more bloodshot than before. She's popped some more pills, he thought. Had a little pick-me-up before coming downstairs to see who was disturbing her "homework."

Glancing at the cart, Paul saw that, with the exception of a pallid, heavily-stitched hand and forearm which had fallen free, most likely when he'd bumped the cart, all was as it had been before.

"*Frankenstein* wasn't a work of fiction," Andrea told Paul. "It was fact."

Paul's legs went rubbery beneath him. "Help me,"

he pleaded as he sank to his knees. "I love you, Andrea. Don't do this to me."

"But I have to, my love," Andrea said as Paul collapsed by her feet. She knew that he could still hear her; the drugs she had injected him with would render him immobile while keeping him more or less lucid. "Fate decrees it. The similarities between my life and Mary's are far too great to ignore; if I am to ever be as great as she once was, I must relive her pain."

Grabbing Paul under the arms, Andrea dragged him from the meat locker, across the basement, and up the stairs. When she reached the kitchen, Andrea stopped to rest. "Mine is a pain-filled life, my love," she told Paul. "If you only knew the suffering which Mary and I had endured, then you would surely shed a tear."

Even though Paul's body was numb, it wasn't totally without feeling; he'd felt every jostle and bump of Andrea's agonizingly-slow climb up the stairs.

Lifting Paul once again, Andrea dragged him across the kitchen and down the hallway to the guest bedroom. "Patricia didn't understand about fate," she said as she maneuvered his body through the doorway and into the bedroom. "She didn't realize that it can't be ignored. She was fated to drown in the Serpentine, to die in the same manner as Harriet, Percy's first wife."

Just outside the doorway to the guest bathroom, Andrea paused to catch her breath.

Once she had regained her composure, Andrea knelt beside Paul. Cradling his head in her arms, she kissed him. Then, wiping a tear from her eye, she dragged him over to the bathtub.

"I'll never be the same after this day ends, my love," she told Paul as she draped his legs over the tub's edge. "Believe me when I say this, though: I shall remain true to you until the day I die; I want to be Andrea Shine on my tombstone."

Sliding one arm under Paul's waist, and the other under his neck, Andrea lifted. Straining from the effort, she slid her husband's limp body up the bathtub's side, over the tub's edge, and gently lowered it inside.

Andrea adjusted Paul's body so that his legs were raised, and his back was flat against the tub's floor. When everything was just as she wanted it to be, Andrea turned on both the hot and cold water taps and lowered the lever which activated the plug in the tub's drain.

The tub slowly began to fill with warm water. Paul could feel it seeping into his clothing and lapping at his skin.

Andrea waited until the tub was nearly full before she shut off the water.

"Farewell, my love," she told her husband as a tear rolled down her cheek. Falling from her face, it struck the water, landing amidst a cluster of bubbles which had just broken the surface. "I shall return eleven days from now to give you the burial you so rightly deserve."

Refusing to succumb to grief, to yield to the seemingly endless pain which filled her life—Mary hadn't given in, and neither would she—Andrea rose to her feet and strode from the bathroom, turning out the lights as she did.

A final bubble broke the water's surface as darkness filled the room.

CYRANO
by
Gary A. Braunbeck

"I am going to seek a great Perhaps."
—Rabelais on his deathbed

... now that virtue has become to me a shadow, and that happiness and affection are turned into bitter loathing and despair, in what should I seek sympathy? asked the knife-edge of his conscience as he lay alone fighting wakefulness. Slumber, even brief and uneasy, granted him stay from the innate afflictions of his wretched heart, and for that he was thankful; though toward what or whom this gratitude was or should be directed he dared not imagine.

The sea-roar gave way to the memory of the words he had screamed at R. Walton before springing from the cabin window of the ship and landing upon the ice-raft which was borne away on icy hyperborean waves. Time thereafter was measured by the burgeoning strength of anguish which, meeting no resistance, continued to poison those vestiges of the "soul" he was still foolish enough to believe within his attain.

I was, then, a monster, a blot upon the earth, from which all men fled and whom all men disowned.

His unmerciful nightmare continued with the Siberian village of hovels where, despite the villagers' screams and the stones with which they bruised him, he assembled the materials for the funeral pile he later constructed upon a larger, thicker ice-raft, one that could endure the heat of conflagration without collapsing into the sea.

The flames crackled and hissed, consuming his filthy rags and blackening his charnel-house skin, the stench filling him with the writhing pain of a Death beyond the death he sadly called existence.

Oh, earth! How often did I imprecate curses on the cause of my being! Even Satan had his companions, fellow devils, to admire and encourage him, but I am solitary and abhorred.

His flame-charred flesh slithered from bone, drooping like the sleeves of a dark cloak, when suddenly he beheld near him a hunched and shivering figure wearing only a dressing-gown, slippers, and nightcap. He pointed at the figure and perceived with a start that he was, indeed, wearing a great black cloak whose hood concealed his hideous countenance. No cursed flesh covered his skeletal hand.

The cowering figure raised its head and cried, "Ghost of the Future! I fear you more than any specter I have seen. But as I know your purpose . . ."

He cringed.

The dressing-gowned man uttering these words was Victor Frankenstein.

The creature gave a loud gasp and lurched forward, wrenching himself from sleep, momentarily disoriented until he caught a glimpse of a life preserver marked *SS Cotapaxi* hanging on a nearby pillar.

A book tumbled from his lap and onto the ship's deck, falling open to the title page: *The Reclamation of My Honor: a journal by Ebenezer Scrooge*.

"A splendid work," said a voice behind him. "It is one of my wife's favorites."

The creature turned in the deck chair to see the ship's captain standing beside him. "I apologize, sir, but my dream was of a rather unsettling nature and I fear I have awakened less than rested, so forgive me if I seem ill-at-ease with your unexpected presence."

To his great surprise the captain—a tall, healthy-looking muscular man—did not turn away in revulsion. "I am Roderick Usher, captain of this vessel. It pleases me to tell you that, despite the rough weather encountered two days ago, we will arrive in Italy on schedule." He lowered his voice, as if taking the creature into his confidence. "I must confess this is a great relief to me. Many of our guests are ambassadors and other assorted government officials, and must be in Padua in time for the world conference."

"A world conference? Toward what purpose?"

Captain Usher smiled, displaying a mouth filled with dazzlingly bright teeth. "My good sir, have you not heard? The conference is to commemorate the signing of the Russo-Japanese Pact five days hence by Nicholas II and Emperor Meiji. Such a covenant not only ensures peace between their warring nations, but crushes the budding revolution in Russia, as well. I understand the pact has prompted several like agreements among smaller allying countries."

"Ah," said the creature. "I seem to recall an article of news which concerned a similar pact between Reza Shah Pahlavi of Persia and President John Brown of the Confederate States of Mexico."

"Indeed," said Usher. "Even now Brown's esteemed Vice-President, Miguel Hidalgo Y Costilla, journeys to Italy on this very ship. But enough talk of politics." Usher's face grew pensive. "Since you were afflicted with fever when brought aboard, I found it necessary to isolate you from the other passengers. The medical officer informs me that your crisis is now past. I wish you to know that, having been made aware of your tragic circumstances, I will do everything in my power to ensure that you arrive safely to your beloved."

"My beloved," whispered the creature, placing one of his gigantic hands against his breast and feeling the bulk of the letters within his pocket, letters he had read countless times before this day and would read countless times again before reaching his destination.

"Have you time, Captain, to indulge me with some answers?"

"If they are mine to offer."

"There are certain . . . inconsistencies in my memory of the last several months, caused by the post-surgical fever of which you spoke. The man who purchased my passage, did he offer a name?"

"Yes. And what a splendid, amiable fellow he was, of a decidedly distinguished background. Dr. Jonathan Merrick of the Treeves Institute in Dublin."

"I never knew his name," whispered the creature, "only his charity, and the goodness of his soul."

"He seemed to hold you in great esteem. When I pressed him for details, he informed me that he had been giving a series of lectures at the University of Krasnoyarsk when a commercial fishing vessel beheld a fire on a nearby ice-isle and discovered you among the wreckage. As he is considered a maverick in the field of treatment for burn victims, and was only a few days' journey away, he was sent for at once."

The creature looked at his hands, still overcome by their power and beauty. How truly miraculous were the skills of Merrick!

Why could you have not been my creator? he thought.

A flash of memory, then: Merrick's sad expression as he said, *"The damage was restricted to your torso and legs. As much as I wanted to give you the new face you so desperately wished for, it was unravaged by the flames. I had no choice but to leave it as it was. Please understand it was only through the grace of Provi-*

dence we were able to obtain enough tissue to restore those areas destroyed by fire. To have constructed a new face for you under such circumstances would have been perceived as a vain cosmetic indulgence and thus trivialized everything I as a physician believe in. I hope someday you will find it in your heart to forgive me."

From the lower deck a sultry female voice chimed into the air, announcing that breakfast was now being served.

"Such a sweet voice," said the creature. "One cannot help but wonder if—"

"The sweetness of her voice withers against the truth of her delicate beauty," said the captain. "That is my wife, Madeline. Both she and my sister Camille work the ship alongside the crew. You must dine with us this evening. I insist."

The creature rose from the deck chair and approached the safety rail, his massive body, well over eight feet in height, dwarfing the formidable figure of Captain Usher. Leaning forward to allow a burst of sea spray to bathe his face, he said, "I thank you for your proposed kindnesses, but I have never been afforded the luxury of knives, forks, spoons and plates, so my manners would be ... questionable at the very least, and undoubtedly offensive to your wife and sister."

Joining him at the rail, Usher placed his hand on the creature's immense forearm and said, "It seems to me that unrefined table manners are not what keeps you a solitary soul. I would not be so insistent, but the well-being and contentment of all my passengers is of the utmost importance to me. I suspicion that your hesitancy to imbibe of the joy which marks this voyage is a symptom of a deeper distress."

"Though your suspicion is correct—and a testament to your perceptiveness and leadership—I can only respond by again thanking you for the invitation which I cannot accept."

Usher, whose outward composure failed to mask his feelings of insult, said, "You disdain the companionship?"

"On the contrary. Nothing would please me more than to sit at a clean table with fresh linen and partake of an agreeable meal in the company of friends. For so long I have fantasized of such an occasion—the aroma of the food, the bouquet of the wine, the pleasant murmur of surrounding voices engaged in conversation, the ghostly wisps of pipe and cigar smoke filling the air afterward."

"The pleasantries of such an evening await. Why deny them to yourself?"

"Because that is only part of the fantasy I have constructed from the fragments of my hope. Shall I tell you the rest?"

Usher, whose expression compassionated the creature, gave a silent nod of his head.

"Very well. The scene goes like this: I put down my emptied brandy snifter and turn to the woman seated next to me. How to describe her beauty to you? It is not so much a physical loveliness, though she is undeniably pleasing to the eye, as a bloom that bespeaks the humble-mindedness at the core of her nature. She possesses time's gift of perfect humility, and it is that gifting which makes her so alluring. I ask her to join me for a dance and she rises gracefully, not at all repulsed by my countenance. I fill myself with the fragrance of her perfume and, as her eyes meet mine, I feel as if I am Da Vinci, staring through the face of one of his exquisite madonnas, staring past the layers of marble and dust into the burning heart of some godly truth I have always been seeking. My senses heighten with the satin touch of her hand in mine. I revel in the sparkle of her laughter as it mingles with my own to become a singing our hearts cannot contain. I pull her closer to me and she does not resist, for I know this time, this breath, this moment is filled with the heat of a thousand secret flames. Then, at the last, after the euphoria of her gentle velvet lips brushing moistly against my cheek, she places her hands on my shoulders and whispers, in a voice so delicate that crystal cannot compare, 'Now you can come home from your ghost so that I may cherish you for the rest of our days.'

"Do I disdain companionship? you ask. No, good Captain, not at all. This scene of ridiculous fancy has been my only sanctuary from the loathsome truth of my being for so long that I cannot afford to have it tainted by the brutal truth of reality. Do you not understand? Look at me, Roderick Usher, and tell me truthfully that you do not believe your Madeline and Camille would be overcome with horror at the sight of me! The grave-pallor of my face, the stink of lime and rot that surrounds me, the dull pustule-yellow of my eyes. Could any woman not born of fantasy look upon such an obscenity as me and feel tenderness?" He reached into his breast pocket and snatched out the letters, thrusting them toward the captain's face.

"Upon awakening in your infirmary I discovered these in my pocket. Written by the hand of a young woman of such refinery and exquisiteness my heart bursts at the thought of her *beaux yeux,* they tell the tale of her painful solitude which was relieved by the first of many missives delivered to her from the northern extremities of the Earth. This tender courtship through words has continued over these past three years, filling her heart with such hope and love I found myself weeping at the yearning which guided her hand as she scrawled her fragile dreams upon the page. She claims to love me with a depth and passion usually attributed to poets and gods—and I know it is me she loves, for her narrative betrays she has been made aware of the circumstances under which my grisly and wretched birth was induced."

"I don't understand," said Usher, his eyes glistening with sympathy. "If she knows of your history and claims to love you in spite of it, why are your feelings in such chaos?"

"Because *I did not write to her!* The missives she speaks of were composed by another."

The Captain blinked, then turned away for a moment, his demeanor growing deeply thoughtful. Momentarily, he turned to face the creature. "My dear, dear fellow. I think the answer to this conundrum is within your grasp. Dr. Merrick gave a letter to the ship's chaplain, with instructions it be delivered to you upon your recovery. You will find the chaplain's office on this very deck. I will take you."

The creature affectionately grasped the captain's hand, taking care not to employ too much pressure lest he injure this man who had been so kind. "Good Captain Usher, I thank you for your compassion, but if I am to be given the solution to this enigma I prefer to be alone. So many of my days have been spent thus."

"I know. And my heart breaks for it. Even my dear Madeline has wept at the thought of the misery which has for so long been your only companion."

"Farewell, then, Roderick Usher. It pleases me to call you my friend."

"And your friend I shall remain. But I will not accept a 'farewell' from you, for you will dine with myself and my family this evening. The rancor and malice you have encountered in the world does not exist in this heart, nor in those of my wife and sister. None shall cringe at the sight of you, nor scream and turn away. On that you have my most solemn word."

"Until this evening, then," said the creature.

"Which cannot arrive soon enough for my satisfaction," replied the captain who, with a respectful, affectionate salute, continued on his rounds.

Making his way toward the chaplain's office, the creature chanced to encounter a little boy who was playing at shuffleboard. It did the creature's heart well to see this child who, though alone except for his imagination, was nonetheless enjoying himself. Perhaps, to some, aloneness was not a curse, and the knowledge achieved from imagination hung around their necks like pearls instead of chains. The creature was almost envious.

Without warning, the boy suddenly stopped playing and spun around, glaring.

Never before had the creature experienced such an overwhelming dislike. Had he been pressed to describe the boy he would have been struck dumb, but there was, nonetheless, something wrong with the child's appearance, something displeasing and downright detestable. He could not say why he so disliked this seemingly innocent child, only that, for the first time in years, the urge to kill came over him. But such impulses had been his damnation once before and he would not, could not succumb to their seductions again.

"Methinks I know you, horrid beast," said the child with a sneer creeping onto his face. "Indeed, there is such a mark on you."

Seeing in this child an all too familiar evil, the creature stumbled backward into the rail.

The boy's voice was the hiss of a serpent. "I should call you father, would that Fate had bequeathed us a different lot."

The creature pressed a fist against his mouth to repress the shriek lodged in his throat, thinking that this terrible boy must be deformed somehow, for he gave a strong feeling of deformity though it was impossible to specify its origin.

Swallowing back the scream, the creature pulled his fist away and said, "If ever I were a perversion, I would appear almost Divine under your shadow."

The boy smiled. "Is that how a murderous abomination addresses one whose life has been inspired by him?"

Before the creature could respond an angry female voice shot through a far cabin window. "Edward! Edward Hyde! If you are not in front of my eyes in one half-minute, I shall thrash you within an inch of your life!"

The boy glanced in the direction of the voice, then hurled into the creature, grasping his hand and kissing it. Then he was gone.

Shaking with such force he feared his body might shatter into fragments, the creature stumbled toward the stern, his throat clogged in terror at the knowledge that the violence, so much a part of his accursed nature, was not limited to himself, that it was infecting the world like a malignancy, seeping into the psyches of mere children, turning them into the unholiest of demons. But did such a thing exist before his own birth, or was it through him that the malignancy entered the world?

"May God damn you to an eternity of torment, Victor Frankenstein! Through my anger and violence you have begat the seeds of humanity's self-destruction. All in the name of your filthy science!" He stood at the end of the ship, shaking with hatred and self-loathing, and so screamed at the horizon: "Did I solicit thee from darkness to mold me Man? Or was I, like the doomed Iscariot, simply a vessel used to carry out the will of One more powerful even than your science?

Here I stand, an ABOMINATION! SHRIEKING TRAVESTY! WHERE, THEN, IS HOPE? WHERE REASON? WHERE TENDERNESS? Or is it all a diseased illusion? If there be Any who hears these words, I say this to You: will my sufferings forever endure, or is there an end to it?"

He dropped his head, weeping, unable to staunch the flood of faces and memories that assailed him; the cries of those he had killed—Clerval, William, the dear Elizabeth—underscored the deaths of Justine Moritz and Alphonse Frankenstein who, were it not for the creature's grief-maddened actions, would breathe still. The anvil of guilt so long a part of his every breath weighed even heavier for the glorious sight of the sea before his gaze: what right did he, unholy brute, have to enjoy anything so wondrous?

He thought of the blind De Lacy and his children, and missed them intensely.

He thought of the image of his doomed mate, torn apart by Victor Frankenstein before she could be instilled with life.

He covered his face with one hand.

He remembered the loneliness of all the days leading to this one.

Imagined the loneliness of his future.

And, deep within himself, he screamed.

And he screamed.

And he screamed.

Then a tiny hand touched him, and he blinked away tears to see another little boy standing beside him, only where the child Edward had carried the sense of deformity, this poor boy's affliction was apparent to even the weakest eyes. A more dreadfully misshapen being had the creature never seen, and where the previous boy had filled his heart with disgust, this one filled it with empathy.

The creature knelt, pulling the twisted child to him. "Have you a name, sad little man?"

"Erik," whispered the boy through knots of crusty and discolored flesh. "I have been sent for you."

"And who is it that would send such a ... fine ... lad ... as ..." The creature's heart brimmed and he could speak no more, only embrace this boy whose heart, he was certain, had been broken as often and as mercilessly as his own.

"It's all right, now," whispered the boy. "No one is so wicked or ugly that they do not deserve a chance at redemption."

"Thank you, dear child," choked the creature as a shadow fell across his sight.

A woman of chiseled ethereal loveliness touched the child upon its head and whispered, "Such a serious little boy you are, Erik. How often have I told you that your face will not shatter were you to allow a smile to cross it every now and then?"

The child turned from the creature and said, "I have found him."

"So you have. Such splendid work cannot go unrewarded."

The child's face tensed in anticipation.

The woman touched Erik's cheek with great love and said, "You may go to the music room and play the piano until it is time for lunch."

"Oh, thank you!" he said, throwing his arms around her neck and kissing her cheek with hard, little-boy glee, then bestowed the same affection on the creature before taking flight toward the stairs.

The woman, smiling after him, looked at the creature and said, "I hope you know, sir, that even though Erik is only my ward, I could not love him any more were he my own son."

"That you feel such affection for him, dear lady, is

proof enough I need not pity the misfortune of his form."

"His soul is pure and full of music. His skill at playing and composing are nearly godlike. How could one not treasure him?" She extended her hand. "I am Christine Daaé, fiancée of D. Gray, chaplain of this vessel. I know well who you are, sir. Jonathan Merrick spoke glowingly of you when he gave this to my betrothed." She removed an envelope from her pocket and placed it in the creature's hand. "I hope the contents gives your tortured soul some degree of peace. If not, then please, please seek out my loving Dorian. He will do for you all that he can, even if it crumbles against the weight of the pain previously inflicted on you." She touched his hand then, flooding his system with warmth and promise and a hope of deliverance he had dared not imagine.

"The sight of your devotion to the child has already given me some measure of peace."

"I am glad for that. More than you can ever know."

And with that, she left him there, the envelope and its mysterious contents clutched in his hand.

Heart pounding, breath staggered, hands shaking, he broke the seal on the flap and slowly removed the folded pages.

He read:

My Dear Friend, Child-of-None:

How to even begin this? Shall I say that your tragedy has moved me to such a degree that I will measure the remainder of my life as blessed? Or would it be more fitting to say that nothing thusfar in my thirty-one years has compared with the effect you have had on both my heart and my—if you'll pardon my using this next word—science? Suffice to say this: you have moved me deeply, and it will be only upon the moment of my death that you shall be elsewhere than the forefront of my thoughts.

There is much to tell you and my time is short (the ship sails in less than five hours) so I will dispense with any further declarations of respect and affection, save for this last: know that, whatever may befall you come the next dawn, you are, and always shall be, welcome in my home and my heart should you ever choose to return to Ireland.

You have doubtlessly found the letters which I placed in your jacket while you were suffering from fever. The young lady whose hand composed them was and is the daughter of an esteemed Italian scientist who, though well-respected in the community of his fellow scientists, was recently and posthumously stripped of several honors when it was discovered his quest for knowledge (much like that which possessed your Dr. Frankenstein) led him to commit an act so cold-blooded in its conception, so heinous in its disregard for individual human life, and so atrocious in its consequences, that many of us in the medical community have officially stated our belief that the discoveries he made and the serums he created, though ultimately beneficial, are almost totally negated by the appalling manner in which they were achieved. I tell you this because the girl consistently failed to make mention of these facts in any of her letters—motivated, no doubt, by her fear that, should you recognize her name, your heart would grow cold. And who can place blame on her for that, knowing, as I do, that she herself was the unknowing (at first), then unwilling subject of her father's experiments, which rendered her life, as yours, a painfully lonely one?

Before continuing with a listing of further facts surrounding the girl and her letters, I think it is necessary to tell you of a very strange occurrence which took place after our arrival back in Dublin.

A private wing of the Institute Infirmary had been isolated solely for the purpose of your care. Know that you were well-attended by every member of my staff during this period. (I say this because you were unconscious during the journey from Siberia to Ireland, and remained thus for several weeks after our arrival.)

One evening, shortly after the midnight hour, I was awakened in my chambers by an orderly who informed me that you had regained consciousness and were asking for me by name. My curiosity and unease were beyond any measure at that moment, for I had never introduced myself to you and had given specific orders that, upon your revival, no one but myself was to speak to you. I dressed quickly and climbed the tower stairs to the private wing.

Imagine my shock when, upon entering, I saw you standing by your bed, examining the intravenous drip attached to you. When I inquired how you felt, you turned to me, smiled, and said, "I suspicion that he is fine, Dr. Merrick, being deep in a coma as he is."

"Is this some jest?" I asked.

"Would that it were," you replied, in a voice very unlike the one I recalled hearing when first I saw you in Siberia.

"Have you a name?"

"In life I was known as Victor Frankenstein."

"Victor Frankenstein is dead, having succumbed to fever and infection aboard the ship of

Robert Walton. His death has been documented in newspapers and medical journals world-wide."

"I know. And for what will he be remembered when all the facts surrounding the circumstances of his life and death are made known?" Your hands balled into fists, striking at your chest. "For having remade Man. The dubious morality of the act itself is not why I am now being punished, Dr. Merrick. I am being punished by my Creator for having given life to this tragic form you see before you and then, in ignorance and selfishness, turning away from it in denial and revulsion. My sins against him are multitudinous, but none so fierce and harmful as that of having disallowed him compassion. Because of that refusal he became the tortured killer who robbed my life of meaning. And why not? I gave no thought to the meaning of his life. But I digress.

"Sit down, Dr. Merrick, take the writing pad and fountain pen from your desk. I am about to pay my penance and, insomuch as it can be done now, right the ghastly wrong which I have committed."

It was through him that I learned of the girl, a childhood friend of Victor's from his early years in Italy. Then he bid me write to Professor Pietro Baglioni at the University of Genoa. I complied, writing the words which he dictated, and did soon receive Baglioni's reply. The professor, a very intelligent fellow possessing a singularly dry wit, yet often stale in his manners, was quite happy to provide the facts behind the girl and her father—who, at that time, lay on his deathbed.

Over the ensuing months Victor Frankenstein returned to you every night. Having obtained all the information about the girl from Baglioni, Victor informed me it was time we wrote to the girl herself, now that she was orphaned and completely alone in the world. Night after night did your Dr. Frankenstein dictate the most passionate, poetic letters to me, missives so overpowering in their honesty and desire I often found myself on the verge of tears, having been reminded of my own youth and first love.

We—or, rather, I—sent these letters as quickly as they were written. And her responses! Well, you have the letters, so you know well how deeply she reciprocated the feelings expressed on the page. Then, at last, she inquired as to the source of your sadness. (I say "your" sadness for the letters were conceived and constructed with the purpose of making a romantic arrangement between the girl and yourself. I'd never been part of a matchmaking before, though my mother used to speak of such things, and I found that I very much enjoyed it.)

Before next contacting her, Victor instructed me to write to Margaret Saville in England, sister of Robert Walton, and request that she send me a copy of the journal R.W. wrote to her during his last sea voyage. Since, as I'm sure you know, that journal contains your story, I was most anxious to see it myself. Mrs. Saville was more than kind and sent a cleanly typeset copy of the journal.

I wept for you, my dear friend. None who reads your sad tale could hold you in contempt, even in light of your many violent actions.

After sending the journal to Italy, I prayed each night that the girl would be as moved by your story as I. And it would appear that, sometimes, God hears such prayers.

Soon the girl's response arrived, and her love

for you, her compassion and tenderness, were tenfold what they had been before.

Allow me to impart this one last fact concerning her: there is no living man on this Earth who could be her love. Only you, being already dead yet alive, can fill the void in her life.

And so I was compelled to act quickly.

I booked passage on the SS *Cotapaxi*. Your fever was in its final stages. I would not have sent you on your way so soon were it not for the fact that no other ship will sail again for Italy until early next year, and to deny you the promise of happiness for even one hour longer seemed to me a sin of unforgivable measure.

I know not what fate befell the soul of your creator, for his visits ceased after we received the girl's response to Walton's journal. I can only hope that he has found the forgiveness he sought. Too much misery has already resulted.

And so, my friend, here ends my tale. I shall miss you, and pray that jubilation awaits you on the Italian shore. I take leave of you with these words from Gibran: "Love gives not but itself and takes not from itself, love possesses not nor would it be possessed, for love is sufficient unto love."

Your Friend,
J. Merrick

The creature carefully folded the letter and put it with the others.

He turned back toward the sea and saw the ghost of errant light dancing across the waves, imagined the reflections in the ripples to be the figures of himself and his beloved engaged in a waltz.

CYRANO

The radiant sphere of the moon shone down upon him, and he gave himself all the way over into its light.

And there beheld promise.

And there beheld sublimity.

And there beheld forgiveness, bequeathing it as well and saying, for the first time, the name of his creator with no hatred in his heart.

He looked at the letters in his hand.

He wondered if she would be as delicate and lovely as her script (she was even more so), if she would smile at the sight of him (she did, and resplendently, opening her arms for his embrace), and if she would ever wish to dance with him (there was music in the square when he arrived at her gate, and they danced; oh, how they danced).

He raised his arms above his head, the moonlight passing between his fingers to create silver rays which shrugged away the shadows; the sea-spray bathed his face, becoming the scent of perfume as it beaded against his skin; and he recalled having heard a fairy story about a puppet who longed to become a real boy, who wished upon a star, and whose wish was granted.

Aided by moonlight, he gazed inward, quietly saying the name of his beloved over and over, as if it were a prayer—"My dearest Beatrice, daughter of Giacomo Rappaccini"—until he found a solitary pinpoint of shimmering icestar in the night sky.

And toward it he whispered, in a voice so delicate that crystal could not compare, "Let me come home from my ghost."

And so he did, to treasure her for the rest of their days.

I'VE GOT HUGH UNDER MY SKIN

by
Rex Miller

It was warm in the observation alcove above the OR, and Peter Collyer stood up to shed his coat, which he'd put on because of the unseasonably cool late summer weather. He stood, waiting, until the doctor finished his conversation with the two young men—students, in all probability—who would be observing the surgical procedure with him. The doctor shook hands and his gaze fell on Collyer.

"Hello." His voice was resonant, loud in the small enclosure, but pleasantly modulated.

"Hello," Collyer said, smiling, "I'm Pete Collyer. I spoke with you on the phone about an interview?"

"Yes. Of course. Good to see you." The doctor said it in a tone that obviously meant it wasn't particularly good to see him after all, but he was used to that. *Popular Culture Magazine* was a powerful publication, but the mag had a well-deserved rep for tough interviews, to say the least. "As I told you I won't be able to give you much time—" He was shaking his head, getting ready to leave.

"No problem, sir. Just a couple of minutes is all we'll need."

"Well . . . we'll see. I've got to go try to work some magic for this fellow." He tipped his silvery-haired head toward the OR, where a skin graft was about to take place. "Man's truck caught fire. Anhydrous ammonia." The surgeon made a face and winced. "Severe third degree burns over much of the upper body. He was lucky he got out alive, but—" he shook his head again, "he needs some serious magic. This is going to be a major graft procedure, but apart from that the man has lost nearly a third of his left arm and part of the shoulder, so the trauma is quite devastating. So . . . I'll speak with you briefly after the operation."

"I'm grateful, Dr. Styne. Thanks." They shook hands and Collyer was impressed by the strength of the man's grip. He took a seat behind the students and listened to their hushed conversation. Styne, at 42, had his own reputation, and it was well deserved. He was said to be one of the best graft men alive. The students carried on a sotto voce play by play, so to speak, of the procedure they were about to observe, as down below in the brilliantly lit OR a sexless, faceless phalanx of green-garbed people began to occupy the room.

It was the operating theater of a famous teaching hospital with ties to a prestigious, monied college. Styne was chief of the surgical department.

Peter Collyer had done his own homework, he knew that Styne and the crew below would have taken a superficial dermal layer, called a split-thickness, with a dermatone—a very sharp knife—from the donor site. Plasmic circulation was involved, and the wounds to be repaired would heal—in theory—by capillary in-growth initiated from the wound edge. But the degree of success involved in the graft "take" or revascularization depended on the recipient site. Barring such things as chronic infections or vascular insufficiencies, split-thickness grafts were highly effective methods of wound coverage and closure. And there was no one better at the procedure than Frank Styne, MD.

He listened to the hushed voices discuss the problem areas that would be addressed: exposed bone areas where the wound was devoid of periosteum, substantial cavities where other types of reconstruction would take place. Their comments about Dr. Styne were articulated in awed tones. More than once the word "genius" was used. Abused descriptive noun that it was, Collyer suspected that it was at least partially accurate when applied to the man they were watching.

Styne made an imposing figure as he strode into the operating theater, slender, tall—the tallest person in the room and made more so by his slimness and perfect bearing—gloved fingers in the "hands up" position.

The doctor began almost immediately to work on the anesthetized patient, and the reporter from *Popular Culture* listened to him describe the procedure into a microphone as he performed the operation.

"The transposed muscle can't always fulfill its locomotor function, you see, but the synergistic muscles ... vascular pedicle ... aggressive extirpation or debridement ... anastomosis ... perfusion through the derm-subdermal plexus ..." Collyer's love for words and command of the language allowed him to follow most of the shop talk. He doodled idly on his notepad, thinking about what he would say to Styne and how he would phrase his questions.

An hour and twenty minutes later, the operation over, he was downstairs in Styne's outer office, waiting. It didn't take long.

"Come in, please," the tall surgeon said cordially. "Only a couple of minutes—sorry."

"I understand. I won't take up much of your time." The reporter went into the doctor's inner office. Styne turned, his body language cold and impatient. Since he did not invite the man to have a seat, Collyer remained standing in front of the large, high-tech desk that Styne used for a work surface. "As I told you on the phone, *Popular Culture* is running a feature piece on you in the next issue. I assume you're familiar with the publication?"

"Mm." Styne nodded, his features an impassive mask.

"You need to know the general contents of the forthcoming piece so that you can tell your side," Collyer began, choosing his words as best he could, "because of the nature of the allegations made in the article." He kept his voice soft.

"What sort of allegations?"

"Regarding your identity. The story will state that investigators have discovered you are not Frank Styne, But Hubert von Frankenstein, a direct descendant of the doctor who created the Frankenstein monster."

"That's preposterous!" the surgeon laughed, but his face had suffused with color. "Where did they get such an absurd notion?"

"I'm afraid the investigation was rather complete, Dr. Styne. You were traced back to New Rochelle, where you used the name—" he glanced at his notes— "Franklin Steen, and they were able to trace your family's history back through your father, your grandfather, his father before him—all their aliases and histories—it's been a long and comprehensive investigation." The doctor's stare was menacing, but he said nothing. Collyer smelled chemicals and a faint tobacco smell. "Would you like to comment for the record?"

"Why would you wish to invade my *privacy*, young man? I've done nothing to deserve your magazine's scrutiny. Why would you wish to hurt me?"

"We don't want to hurt you, sir. But—we're a news-related publication. Something like this is big news. You're a public person, because of the—uh—celebrity that attaches to your name, and people are curious about the Frankenstein family. The fact that you're a physician—"

"—saving lives, making an important contribution—"

"Yes. Certainly—that, too. No one suggests otherwise. But don't your patients deserve to know your real identity?"

"You know that isn't possible, Mr. Collyer. Don't act naive. If people found out ... if they thought I was ..." he sat behind his desk. "Please. Don't do this to me."

"Do you deny that you're the great, great grandson of the man who created the Frankenstein monster? The *real* monster?"

"That book was a *joke*—don't you see? He was a *great man*—a true *visionary!* My God! They made his work into a—mockery! There was never a monster. He made phenomenal steps toward achievements that science never had the courage to even consider: the first experiments involving discorporate intelligence, recombinant DNA, revivification, a multitude of pioneer disciplines. He was a *brilliant* man." The reporter was furiously taking notes, and a tiny recorder was catching it all in his pocket. This was more than he'd hoped for.

"But he stole cadavers and—"

"Oh, my God, man, there was none of that. You're confusing fiction and reality. The Frankenstein name has been slurred by generations of scandalmongers who besmirched one of the great founding fathers of science for the sake of gossip. Stolen cadavers indeed—it was a different world back then—life was cheap. You didn't have to steal cadavers from the graveyard or the mortuary, they were in abundance—all that was fabricated."

"You're saying the story about the creation of the monster is utter fiction?"

"There was no monster. There was achievement.

Glorious achievement. The work that was done back then made my work in there today possible—do you want to ruin that? Do you want to make it impossible for me to save countless other lives? You have no idea of the breakthroughs my family made in so many areas—"

"No one wants to stop your work, Dr. Styne, but if all you say is true wouldn't you wish to clear your family's name?" Collyer had taken a seat in front of the desk. The office ceiling was divided into grids, four by eight foot rectangles of white sheetrock, with what appeared to be steel ribs. "Frank Styne" reached under his desk and triggered one of these and as the journalist sat down and asked his question the area in front of the desk was suddenly sealed off by four walls of solid steel that fell with a resounding crash onto the floor of the soundproof office.

"What the hell?" Collyer jumped up and began beating on the steel walls. "HELP! SOMEBODY HELP ME!" He didn't notice the opening in the steel wall that fit against the front of the desk. It was a dark hole, down low, and the exhaust pipe feeding from the doctor's desk opened into the aperture. There was no light in the steel box, but even if there had been some, the gas was invisible. It took about forty-five seconds before the toxic agent caused Peter Collyer to lapse into unconsciousness, and another three minutes or so to kill him.

Styne went out and made sure nobody was waiting in the outer office, returned, opened the enclosure, and began preparing the donor for the dermatone. He was going to have to move on again—but before he did there'd be time to take one more for the graft bank. There was always room for some more bones down in the scraps vault. By the time the story ran, Dr. Frank

Styne would be long gone. It was good of them to give him some warning.

Later, when he was leaving the building for the last time, a nurse asked him if Mr. Collyer from the magazine had found him all right.

"Yes, thanks. But he didn't stay long. I guess I must have done something that got under his skin."

BRIDE OF FRANKENSTEIN: A MODERN LOVE STORY

by
Richard T. Chizmar

CLASSIFIED MATERIAL
The following are excerpts from a journal found in the suspect's residence:

June 3
 The time has finally come and I can barely contain my excitement. After weeks of careful planning and preparation, I am almost ready to proceed. I brought in the final load of equipment and supplies from the university early this morning, and I found what I needed from the hospital clinic yesterday. Everyone at the hospital acted delighted to see me, of course, but I could tell they were uncomfortable with having to face me after all this time. They were stiff and serious, and so careful with their words; even the expressions on their faces were fragile masks. I know they were laughing behind those masks. They have always laughed at me. The final piece of equipment is due to arrive here at the house some time tomorrow after lunch. UPS has been very good to me. The basement looks wonderful and is well on its way to becoming fully operational. I must remember, though, to buy a couple of big fans

later this week; I'll have to scrub the floor some more, too, to keep the dust down. The air downstairs is much too musty to work in for long stretches of time, but that should clear up. The overhead lights I picked up were a good fit, but I'll need at least one more. It's all finally coming together.

June 6

If I am discovered, they will surely think I am mad. Of that, I am quite certain. But they do not share my vision, and they do not feel my pain. Of that, I am also certain. I do not concern myself with the danger of discovery; I plan to be painstakingly careful. Besides, there are so many other things that call for my attention. Strangely, I find myself wondering what my peers would think if they could take a peek into my secret world. I think of that arrogant bastard Fred Benson, his tiny rat face squinting in the bright basement light. Eyes flashing wide when he finally realizes exactly what it is he is seeing, grabbing his heart and swooning the way he does when he wishes to make one of his dramatic scenes. I especially like to envision what the ice princess Jennifer Taylor's reaction might be. I crack up just thinking about that! She would probably take one look and drop stone cold to the floor. What a sight that would be! But all of this is harmless curiosity. Of course, I do not care for their opinions. They never did understand. Sure, they acted compassionate for a time. Expressed what seemed like genuine sympathy. Told me to keep my chin up. But, then, when I didn't bounce back to their idea of a normal functioning human on their own damn timetable, they sent Charlie Cavanaugh—as if that moron knew anything at all about the pains of lost love—out to the house to give me the old "life goes on" speech. No, sir. They know nothing of my misery. Nothing of the darkness that has enveloped my heart.

The lab is complete now. Everything seems in fine order. Tomorrow is Saturday. I will make my move in the morning.

June 8

It was so easy! So damn easy! If a single sliver of doubt that my vision was true and honorable existed before yesterday's events, they are certainly gone now. This must be my destiny! I am so filled this beautiful spring morning with hope and wonder and the tingle of sweet, sweet memories, I feel I could burst! Yesterday was as mentally numbing and physically exhausting as any day I have ever known, but after just a few hours of sleep, I feel more than sufficiently rested. Indeed, I feel rejuvenated, enlightened. Body and spirit.

I found her only miles from here. A dear, sweet woman. A classic beauty with thick, flowing hair the color of sun-sprinkled wheat and the lean, tan body of an athlete. After I did what I had to do—the hardest part—I gently placed her in the back of the van and covered her with the flannel blanket Marilyn and I always used to spread for picnics. Drove carefully home and backed into the garage. Carried her in through the breezeway and down into the basement. Spent most of the night checking and rechecking the system, then hooking her up. Today will be a busy day.

June 9

Spent the past eighteen hours with her. I'm drained, but not at all discouraged. If I am to break new ground here, I must remain strong. Looking at her, I can't help but daydream about Marilyn—wonder what we would be doing if she hadn't left me ... what our lives would be like. I find myself thinking of one day in particular ... back when I was very young, the first semester of my final year of undergrad school, I think. We'd awakened that Saturday morning in each other's arms, eaten a light breakfast outside on the back porch. Spent the afternoon downtown, walking hand-in-hand, munching soft pretzels and snow cones, browsing in the book and record shops, playing video arcade games in one of the sidewalk mini-malls. Hours later, our legs begging for mercy, we'd stopped for dinner at one of our favorite Fells Point seafood restaurants and watched the boats cruise the harbor, their white and blue and red lights dancing a private show for us as we enjoyed our meals. We'd slowly walked the streets home, her head on my shoulder, and made wondrous love for over an hour before finally falling asleep. It had been a truly magical day, full of life's simpler pleasures. The kind of pleasures you had to be in love to understand and fully appreciate. The kind of pleasures Marilyn blessed me with each and every day for over 35 years ... and then took away so cruelly.

June 12

Something is wrong. It's not working. I checked and rechecked the entire system and cannot locate a problem anywhere. I wonder if, perhaps, I am the problem. I'm not thinking clearly enough, I know that much. My vision is blurry, and I keep hearing Marilyn's voice down there, but now I can't understand her sometimes. It's almost as if she's going farther away from me instead of coming closer. And I keep seeing things ... a wave of a finger, a blink of an eye, a twitch of a nose. But it's not possible ... not yet. I just need some rest tonight. That's all. I will keep at it in the morning!

There has been no mention of the missing woman on the television news. I've watched the Channel 11 spot every day, and taped the other two channels. Nothing.

There was an article in the *Sun,* but this is the city, so something like this merits a mere three paragraphs of mention on page 9. Off to bed now. But first I'll say a prayer that I dream of Marilyn and that I find the problem tomorrow.

June 19

I had no other choice ... I had to go out and find two more. It wasn't as easy as the first time, I had to drive out to the country this time, but I did it anyway. I made it back safely, and they are waiting for me in the basement. I should have known that Marilyn's sweet voice was telling the truth—that the first woman was not the one. I was not the problem; she was. She had been telling me that all week, but I wouldn't listen. Wouldn't listen to anything she was saying. Now I know better and have two specimens to choose from; I only pray that one of them will work out. I'm starting to feel the pressure now. Things are going to heat up in a hurry, I'm sure. Three incidents in just over two weeks will make this big news by the morning paper. I can't risk the chance of going out and finding another ... please let one of them be the one!

June 20

Success at last! The third woman is perfect! She's so much like Marilyn that it's almost spooky. And her voice is so strong and clear now; so chipper and cheerful, just like when she was here with me. Before I hooked her up today, she begged me to carry her upstairs and let her sit in her favorite old chair for a while. I obliged and promised her only fifteen minutes, but ended up rocking and humming to her for over thirty. She's safe and sound in the basement now. Finally, all the pieces are in place. Soon we will be together again!

June 21

Must keep it brief tonight. I haven't felt this drained since residency, when the thought of a good night's rest was a fool's dream. The procedure is progressing magnificently, if a lot slower than I expected. It seems the only matter I overlooked was the lack of an assistant, and the delays that could possibly arise because of that. Nonetheless, I am supremely confident, and will continue in the morning when my strength allows. Soon, my love.

June 23

My God, it's over! I've failed! They have come for me! The alarm is sounding upstairs, and I can hear the angry shouts of the men and the hungry cries of their dogs. They are pounding on the door and I fear they will break through at any moment! It rips my heart that I am so very close to eternal love but I will never feel her tender lips on mine ever agai—

* * *

Excerpted from the June 25 press statement issued to all media by the Baltimore City Police Department:

At approximately 9:25 a.m. on Monday, June 23, state and local authorities arrested Doctor Francis Einstein at his home in the 1400 block of Federal Hill, and charged him with numerous offenses, including trespassing, theft, and graverobbing.

Evidence seized at the scene indicates that Dr. Einstein, 35, is responsible for the three "body snatchings" that have taken place in city and county cemeteries over the past three weeks. In each incident, cemetery personnel reported that they were surprised by a white male and knocked unconscious with what was thought to be a rag soaked in ether. Each time, when the employee regained consciousness, the casket lay open and the body was missing.

Additional evidence found in the residence indicates that Dr. Einstein is also responsible for several robberies at the University of Maryland's School of Medicine, including the theft of a human brain from a Neurology research lab.

As you will all soon see (the residence is still an active crime scene and will not be released to the media until 9 a.m. tomorrow), the basement of Dr. Einstein's home has been constructed into a makeshift laboratory facility, with twin stainless steel operating tables, a functioning life-support system, and various other unidentified medical equipment. Dr. Einstein was found hiding in the basement and placed in custody, and all three bodies were discovered near by.

After extensive questioning, police psychiatrist Donald Gaines reports that Dr. Einstein's only official comment is: "I did it all for love. I did it for my Marilyn."

Gaines explains: "The woman he is referring to is Marilyn Caroline Einstein, his deceased mother. For reasons unknown, she took her own life six months ago (gunshot wound to the head), and according to his former partners at his medical practice, Einstein never recovered from his loss. He was still on emergency medical leave at the time of his arrest. Neighbors and friends report that Einstein was extremely close to his mother (his father died when he was seven years of age) and had never left the home he grew up in, even after he earned a national reputation as a surgeon.

"I'll try to have more details for you all on this later, but the initial story at least is that Dr. Einstein claims he saw a vision and heard a voice inside his head some time ago that told him he could bring Marilyn back if he found the right body and a functioning brain ...

that he could somehow reanimate her. Apparently, he believed the voice to be that of his mother because, he claims, it told him things no one else could know about himself. The voice also told him that she was as sad and as lonely as he was and that she was sorry she committed suicide and that she longed to return to life again. When Einstein's initial reaction was one of doubt, the voice became angry, told him that it was his destiny and that it was for this reason that his mother originally named him Francis. The voice told him that his given name was Doctor Francis Einstein ... then repeated over and over and over again that his common name was FrankEinstein ... FrankEinstein ... FrankEinstein.

"After a short time, Dr. Einstein became convinced that he was indeed the Frankenstein of myth and legend, and he set out to recapture his mother's love."

Dr. Einstein is currently under police guard at City Hospital's Psychiatric Department, where he is awaiting further testing.

* * *

Page one headline of June 26 evening edition of the *Baltimore Sun*:

FRANKENSTEIN LIVES!

SPECIAL EFFECTS
by
Terry Beatty and Wendi Lee

Daniel Cherkas couldn't believe he'd left the door to his studio unlocked. With all of the valuable items stored inside, he'd always kept the place locked up tighter than the lids on his cans of liquid latex. Maybe he'd just been too preoccupied with this current project to remember to lock up when he'd finished working late last night. At least he hoped that was the case. If the studio had been robbed or vandalized, he'd never recover from it. He could replace all of his equipment, could even recreate his sketches and sculptures, but the memorabilia would be impossible—hell, half of it wasn't even his, but borrowed from collectors. He said a little prayer as he flipped on the lights.

The gaunt yellow face of the Frankenstein monster glared down at him. He let out a deep breath. Thank God the framed and matted one-sheet was still here. He'd borrowed the extremely rare and incredibly valuable poster for the 1931 film from a friend—and it would have been the first thing taken if some collector-without-a-conscience were to break in here. Daniel promised himself he'd have an alarm system put in as soon as possible. He didn't ever want to have a scare like that again.

He had been working a little too hard lately. The public expected a lot from him these days, and he had no intention of letting them down. Movie fans, especially *monster* movie fans, knew the names and work of all the great makeup and special effects guys, from Jack Pierce to Rob Bottin. But Daniel Cherkas was the first one to become a household name, as famous a name in horror as Stephen King or Clive Barker. Sure, Lon Chaney, Sr. had been a superstar in his day, but he was an *actor* wearing his own makeup designs. Daniel was the first non-actor in his profession to become as famous as the creatures he helped create.

Daniel looked at the awards case that stood next to the framed poster. It was full of statuettes and plaques from all sorts of organizations, from fan groups and his peers, lauding him for his work on *Face of the Phantom*, *Quasimodo*, and *Blood of Nosferatu*. And the movies had been good, good enough to propel him to the top of his profession. But now he had to top himself. He had to recreate Frankenstein's monster. And he was stuck.

Everyone in the world knew what the monster looked like. It looked like Boris Karloff wearing Jack Pierce's classic square head, bolts-in-the-neck, trademark and copyright by Universal Pictures makeup design. Hell, even with other actors such as Bela Lugosi and Glenn Strange taking turns under that makeup, even playing it for laughs opposite Abbott and Costello, or using the monster to peddle soft drinks in TV commercials, the original had lost none of its power. Sure, there had been Frankensteins before and after Karloff—Thomas Edison had made a silent film of the story as early as 1910, with Charles Ogle playing a gangly fright-wigged monster, and Christopher Lee, his face pale and scar-covered, gave an energetic and frightening performance in 1957's *The Curse of Frankenstein*—but it was Karloff that stuck in everyone's mind. Daniel Cherkas was no exception.

He had surrounded himself with Frankenstein memorabilia in his studio. Movie posters, Halloween masks, toys and photos of every version of the creature ever produced shared space with the casting and molding materials that lent a decidedly pungent aroma to Daniel's studio. He had even borrowed, from the Ackerman collection, life masks of many of the actors who had played the role. He had wanted to avoid any similarity with any previous version of the character, using Mary Shelley's descriptions from the original novel as his basis. First, though, he had to exorcise those other versions from his own mind. But he couldn't do it. He kept coming back to Karloff, damn it.

He sat on a stool in front of his work table and stared at the rough Plastilina bust that he had started the night before. It was still in a very rough form, the green modeling material just slapped together as a foundation on which to build a face. He dug his thumbs into the bust, hollowing out eye sockets, and building up the brow and cheek bones. He spent only a few minutes pushing and pulling until a distinct face started to form. He sat back and studied it. It looked like Boris Karloff.

"Shit!" he hollered, pounding his fist into the bust, smashing its features into some grotesque parody of a Dick Tracy villain.

"Having a bad day?" The voice was deep and guttural. Daniel nearly fell off his stool, startled to hear someone else in the studio. He turned around and saw a huge misshapen man with long black stringy hair, yellow skin and pale watery eyes—an animated caricature of a corpse. His vision blurred and he fell unconscious to the floor.

"I'm sorry. I didn't mean to startle you." It was the same voice Daniel had heard before he fainted. He was coming to now, and was seated in the office chair that went with the desk at the back of his studio. The intruder was squatting in front of him.

"Didn't mean to—Jesus, man, you scared the hell out of me!" Daniel said, pushing against the arm rests of the chair in order to sit up straight.

"I read that you were planning to make a new film of Shelley's book. I wanted to speak to you," said the visitor. "It seems you're having a difficult time with your makeup design. I looked at your sketches. They all look like Karloff."

"Yeah. Yeah. Tell me about it. Listen, I ought to be pissed at you for breaking in here, but this makeup of yours is incredible. I've had other guys want to work with me, but nobody's been this good. I can't believe I'm saying this, but you're as good as I am."

"Mr. Cherkas," the visitor spoke, a wry smile on his black lips, "this isn't makeup. I *am* Victor Frankenstein's creation."

"Come on, quit yankin' my chain," Daniel said, almost laughing. "Is this latex or . . ." He touched his visitor's yellow face and felt the warmth of real skin. "Oh, God," he said, his eyes growing wide in realization. "You're not kidding, are you?"

"I'm afraid I've never had much occasion for humor, Mr. Cherkas. My life, in fact, has been singularly devoid of it. Despite the Hollywood portrayals, I assure you I've never chased Abbott and Costello around a haunted castle."

"But this just isn't possible. I mean, you're not real. You're a character in a book," Daniel said, trying to convince himself that this was some sort of latex fume-induced hallucination.

The creature stood and moved its twisted form over to the work table. It hoisted itself up and sat next to the punched-in bust.

SPECIAL EFFECTS

"Perhaps I should tell you the whole story—or more precisely, the rest of the story. You know of my beginnings, having read Mary Shelley's book. It's all true, of course, aside from an embellishment or two. Artistic license, I suppose, or perhaps the result of getting the story secondhand. It was the Englishman she calls Walton, whose letters frame the book, who told her the tale. I don't know if she ever believed it to be true, or simply considered it a tale worth retelling. It's the only one of her books that remains in print, you know.

"I would have liked to have met the young lady who told the tale so well," the creature said, "but by the time I was even aware of the book's existence, I had been away from Europe for many years. So many, in fact, that she would have been cold in her grave the first time I read my own story. Perhaps it's just as well. People tend to be frightened by my appearance. You certainly were.

"You know that I told Walton—though that was not the man's true name—that after causing the death of Victor Frankenstein, I intended to put an end to my own miserable life. That was my intention, and yet, when I had built my funeral pyre and lit it ablaze, I could not throw this misshapen body upon it. I, who had murdered man, woman and child—who had even destroyed my own creator—could not bring myself to end my own life. Frankenstein had instilled in me a life-force so strong that I could not destroy it, even with my own grotesque hands.

"And so I traveled across the sea in the belly of a ship, hiding, as I have done now for the better part of two centuries, in the dark, alone. I made my way to unsettled areas of this continent, living as a hermit in the forest. I lived in caves or deserted cabins. Yet as civilization encroached upon me, I was continually forced to desert the homes I had made.

"I did live for some time on a farm in the midwest. Like the old man Shelley called De Lacey, the farmer was blind. He took me in and I worked the land for him in exchange for my room. I had to stay hidden from his family, of course, but they rarely came to the farm. It was there that I discovered the Hollywood version of my life. There was a battered black and white portable television that his children had left behind. As you can imagine, it would be difficult for me to attend a screening at a movie theater—though I have done so a few times, bundled up in winter clothes to hide my ugliness—but I eventually saw all the versions of my story on the late night "Chiller Theater," complete with used car commercials and sad attempts at humor by a so-called 'horror host.' I'm afraid they had little to do with the truth, though dear old Boris did bring a certain dignity to the role.

"But my old blind friend, like all men, had a limited life span, and with his passing, I had to move on. And now I find myself with no place left to hide but the back alleys and the sewers of your cities."

"But why are you here?" Daniel interrupted.

The creature stood and shambled back to where Daniel sat. It leaned forward and looked Daniel straight in the eye. "You've promised to give your public a Frankenstein they've never seen before. I can help you do that. Study me. Sketch me. Take castings of my face and hands, deformed and horrible as they may be. Do what you must to show me as I truly am. And when you are done, I have but one request of you."

It was no surprise to the crowd in the Dorothy Chandler Pavilion when the award for best special effects makeup went to Daniel Cherkas. His work on *Frankenstein's Experiment* was the most amazing thing anyone had ever seen. It far surpassed his previous work,

SPECIAL EFFECTS

and had done something that had been considered impossible—given the public a new face for the Frankenstein monster. The only thing the crowd found at all odd was when Cherkas included among his thank yous, "Dr. Frankenstein's creation, without whom this would not have been possible."

But there was one member of the audience who didn't find it odd at all—a lanky man, dressed impeccably in tie and tails, his toupee so carefully crafted that it was impossible to spot, his contact lenses giving him eyes as blue as the sky. There was a smile on his chiseled and elegantly handsome face, and he applauded Cherkas wildly, not for the makeup job everyone had seen on the movie screen, but for the one no one but he would know about, the makeup job that allowed him to sit here and smile and applaud with face and hands made of foam latex and acrylic paint, with craftsmanship so fine and delicate that no one would ever suspect the truth. And if you looked at him closely, from just the right angle, you'd swear he looked a little like Boris Karloff.

A DEBT REPAID
by
Larry Segriff

It was cold in the hospital parkade where I waited, but I barely noticed. Outside, the snow continued to fall, large, white flakes drifting through the light of the street lamps and merging into a pure, inviting blanket on the ground.

It made me almost homesick to watch the falling flakes—that and a variety of other, less pleasant emotions—but I couldn't tear my eyes away. Not until I heard the sound of her heels clicking solidly against the cold, hard concrete.

It was time.

I was careful not to be seen. I was masked, as always, but still I did not want to leave any more information behind than I had to. Over the years, my excursions into cities like this one had been rare, but even so I had learned a certain respect for the authorities: both their technologies and the doggedness with which they wielded them. I recognized that doggedness all too well, and had resolved long ago to avoid it as much as possible.

I waited until her key was in the lock and then came over the wall where I'd clung for so many hours in the shadows. As always, I moved as silently as the snow upon the wind.

I came from behind her as she was opening the door. One gloved hand cut off her cries while the other tore away her coat and her starchy white uniform.

A DEBT REPAID

Her struggles were ineffective, and within moments I was pressing myself into her. She shuddered, as much from my coldness as from the act itself, I think, and redoubled her efforts to get away, but I held her easily.

It didn't take long. I couldn't allow it to. When I had finished, I transferred my grip to her neck and squeezed ever so lightly. I wanted her unconscious, not dead.

Then, laying her gently upon the front seat of her car and covering her up against the chill of the night, I fled once more into the welcoming darkness.

The low, brick building loomed up out of the night to greet me and I smiled. In those moments when I stopped to consider my actions, I sometimes felt I had chosen the man within as much for the aesthetics of this building as for the work he'd done over the years.

As usual, I examined the place carefully before entering, looking for any signs of trouble. There was only one car parked in the lot, one that I recognized as his, and no other tracks in the new-fallen snow. I took the small amount of time necessary to climb to the roof, but found no evidence that people had been up there.

He was inside, and he was alone. I smiled beneath the latex of my mask and went in to join him.

His back was to me as I came in. I could see he was working, but I also noticed his shoulders stiffen at my entrance. He knew I was there, but he wouldn't turn around until I forced him to.

I pulled off my mask and slipped it into one of the large outer pockets of my overcoat. My gloves went into the other one. He knew me; there was no need for a disguise here. Besides, I liked him to see my face. It kept him off guard, and made it harder for him to conceal his thoughts.

Silently, I walked around him and stood facing him. There was a gurney between us, his hands busy with the figure that lay on top of it. He kept his gaze down, pretending to concentrate so that he wouldn't have to look up.

I, too, lowered my eyes to regard the body before him.

It was a girl, maybe sixteen years old. Naked, she showed the early signs of his handiwork: a tracing of red lines on her torso, but he had not yet made any incisions.

"The ancient Aztecs used to draw lines like this," I said, lowering my hand to trace imaginary circles upon her chest. "The only difference was, the people they drew them on were still alive." My hand lingered upon her left breast.

I could feel his anger before he spoke. "My God, where's your respect? She's dead!"

At that I lifted my gaze and met his. I could see the horror that rose up within him, momentarily dimming his indignation. "She's dead," I agreed. "But you know she doesn't have to be."

He shuddered at that, his anger draining away, and his eyes fell from mine.

"I can't," he said after a moment, his voice very soft in the cold, cold room.

"You must. Otherwise . . ."

Suddenly he flung his marker at me with all his might. The distance between us was no more than two feet, and his attack caught me completely unprepared. Still, I plucked it from the air before it could strike me. He sobbed then, and turned away.

I smiled and finished the markings myself.

"You know this can't possibly work," he said after a time. "Different genetic material; different blood

A DEBT REPAID

types; you just can't make a person like you would a quilt."

I shrugged, glancing down at myself. Obviously, I knew no such thing. Still, I had no reason to argue with him. "Then you've nothing to fear, have you?" I said.

He had no answer to that. I let another minute pass before continuing, "Will this one contribute?"

At that he looked at me, and I was very nearly touched by the torment I saw on his face. Miserably, he nodded. "I intend to use her ovaries. She's the youngest one that's come in on my shift, intact."

I nodded and gently cupped her sex with my right hand. Hard to believe, after all this time, that I was holding a whole new race beneath my palm.

He grimaced and turned away.

"When?" I asked, my own voice barely above a whisper.

He didn't answer.

I sighed. Removing my hand, I reached out and turned his face to meet mine. "5250 Richmond Street," I said. "A wife named Gloria and a baby daughter, eight months old, named Jessica. If you'd prefer, I can take one of them—or both—back with me."

It was an empty threat. No human could survive in the frozen wastes where I lived, but he didn't know that.

Anguish twisted his face into a mask almost as horrific as mine. A single, harsh sob escaped his lips.

"When?" I repeated.

"Tomorrow," he said. "I'll be ready when my shift starts tomorrow."

I released him and he jerked away, but not before I saw the cold, silver tears upon his face.

I nodded and spun back toward the door. "Until then," I said and, slipping on my mask, disappeared into the falling snow.

* * *

An hour later, I was on the roof of an apartment building, watching the snow come down. It was one o'clock in the morning, and few cars moved on the street below. My mask was in my pocket, for in places like this I didn't fear being seen. The flakes that fell on my face took a very long time to melt.

Would he understand, I wondered? If I could lay out all my reasons before him, would he understand what I was doing? Would anyone? Would it matter to him if I pointed out that, for the first time, my children—if any were born—had a chance to live? Always before, when I came back to the cities, I knew that any child who looked like me would have been killed, quietly, at birth. Now, though, things were different. Now there was a chance.

I'd tried other ways. I had lived in any number of places, from the simple Inuit of the far north to the sophisticates in the world's largest cities. I'd tried masks and cosmetics. I'd even considered surgery, but there was too much about me that was simply unalterable. At times, I had asked for friendship; at others I had simply accepted their fear; but everywhere it had been the same thing: failure and rejection.

Now I was trying something new. The lowliest of beasts had their mates. The worm in the field, the snake, the skunk, all had others to join with. Even Man, that most hateful of creatures, had companions to comfort him. All but me.

But soon, now, that would change. One way or another.

Thinking such thoughts, I pulled on my mask and slipped over the side of the building, looking for a window I could force. The night was fleeing, and my mission was still unfulfilled.

* * *

A DEBT REPAID

5250 Richmond Street was a small, ranch-style house with a lot of trees surrounding it. The neighborhood was quiet, only one dog barking madly as it picked up my scent, and that was at least five houses away.

There was no snow tonight. The temperature had dropped to near zero, but I was not cold as I stood among the shadows and watched the darkened house.

He had left an hour ago, a little earlier than he usually did. Maybe he was stopping at the store for some donuts. Or maybe he was planning to betray me.

Over the years, I had come close to my goal many times, but always some last minute twist had foiled me. That was why I stayed, watching his house.

At the first sign that all was not right, I planned to go in there and kill his wife and child.

Half an hour after he left, the lights went out, one by one. Another half-hour had gone by, and nothing had moved. I was starting to think things were safe, that maybe things were going to finally work out, when the police car came rolling by.

It was moving slowly, shining its spotlight all along the houses. I cursed silently and slipped deeper into the shadows, watching and waiting.

The low brick building looked unchanged from the previous night. Again, there was but a single car in the parking lot, but the snow had all been plowed away. I could not tell by looking whether he was alone in there, or if he had a small army of policemen to help him in his cause.

I went in. I had no choice. If I left now, alone, I had lost anyway.

He was seated at a desk near the door, his head bowed over a newspaper. He did not look up at my entrance.

I pulled off my mask, slipped it into my pocket, and moved up beside him.

"Well?" I demanded.

He didn't look up. He didn't speak. He simply rose from his chair and walked back toward the operating room. I followed without a word, but my senses were stretched for any sign of betrayal.

She was on a table in the very center of the room. Naked, I could see that she was beautiful, perfectly formed in every way. Gently, oh so gently, I reached out and touched her face.

"You've done well," I said, "though you did it out of fear and not out of kindness, still you've done well. I shall not forget."

His only reply was to connect the instruments surrounding her. They were not the same ones used on me, all those years ago. These were new, but built on the same principles mentioned in the diary I'd found. I could only hope that the notes had been complete.

I was vaguely aware of his hand moving toward the switch that would decide it all, but I could not watch him. My gaze was focused solely on that cold and lovely face.

He muttered something, a curse, perhaps, or a prayer for failure, and then her eyelids fluttered. I saw the change take place, and an exultant cry ripped from my very soul.

One of the monitors beside her started to beep, and I heard him gasp. "My God!" he cried. "It worked!" Then he turned to regard her and he gasped again, this time in horror.

He staggered back from the table toward the door and much as I wanted to stay with her I knew I couldn't. She was a newborn babe; it would take time before she could even move, much less get herself into trouble. At the moment, he was the threat I was concerned with.

I followed him as he raced to his desk and collapsed into the chair. I was right behind him all the way. Mankind cannot abide my sort. That had been proved to me many times in my life, and while I did not think there was much he could do, I wanted to take no chances.

He surprised me. He made no effort to reach for a weapon or the telephone. Instead, he put his head on his arms and started to sob.

It took him the better part of five minutes to regain his composure. When at last he was able to raise his head, I tensed. This was the moment of his resolve. This was when he would make his move.

"Take her," he said.

"What?" Of all the things he could have done, that was the last I'd expected.

"Please," he said, his shoulders slumping, "just take her and leave."

There was something false about him, though, something that seemed insincere and made me suspicious. "You've cheated me, haven't you?" I said, my voice sounding harsh even to me.

"No," he said, but he would not meet my gaze. "I've done all that you demanded. I swear it."

I shook my head, my hands forming themselves into fists. "I do not trust you," I said. "I know your kind too well."

A single, wrenching sob escaped his lips, confirming my direst fears. I seized him, plucking him from the chair as though he were a child, and held him dangling before me.

"What have you done?" I demanded. "Will she die?" I thought of all the things he could have done to prevent her from living very long and slowly, almost involuntarily, I started to squeeze.

"No!" he cried. "I swear it! She's fine, all her organs intact, exactly as you requested."

"But?" There had to be more to it than that. My grip tightened even further.

A certain resolve seemed to come into him, then, a defiance, perhaps, or an acceptance. He placed his hands upon my wrists and lifted his gaze to mine. "You asked for a companion," he said. "Oh, you were eloquent, that night when you first arrived. You complained that, in all of nature, only you were alone, and, in threatening my family, you gave me reason to help you. I did. I have created a companion for you, a woman to be all things to you. All things but one."

His gaze, still locked with mine, hardened. "She will bear you no children. I performed a tubal ligation on her last night, when I installed her ovaries. She is quite healthy. Nothing will stop her from receiving your love. But she will bear you no children, now or ever."

Almost without thinking, I shifted my grip to his neck. His eyes widened, the awareness of his own mortality shining within their depths. I squeezed, once, not intending to kill, but in my anguish I may have squeezed too hard. It had happened before.

Laying his motionless form upon the floor, I quickly stripped off his clothes and took them in to my bride. Like me, she would be able to withstand the cold, but there was no reason for her to be uncomfortable.

She lay as I'd left her, her arms and legs twitching with the beginnings of voluntary movement. It would be some time yet before we could converse.

I dressed her, speaking all the while in as soft and comforting a voice as I could.

"You will be my wife," I said to her, wrapping her in a blanket and lifting her gently into my arms. I also picked up the instruments of life. If my seed did not take root, I would need them again.

A DEBT REPAID

He was still unmoving when I passed him on my way out. My anger had passed, but still I was glad I'd let his wife live when I'd finished with her. He had robbed me of my children. Perhaps she would give them back to me.

"Come," I whispered to my virgin bride. "It's time to go home."

Holding her tightly, I slipped out into the darkness, hoping the future would prove brighter than the past.

A LOAF OF BREAD, A JUG OF WINE

by
Brian Hodge

The only great figures among men are the poet, the priest and the soldier.
The man who sings, the man who sacrifices and the one who is sacrificed.
All the rest are good for the whip.

—Baudelaire

She thought of him as a secret friend, or in more fanciful moments when she dared risk the sin of impure thoughts, a secret admirer. Theirs was so far a relationship conducted via place, not proximity. Perhaps he had heard her voice, but Sister Giselle had never heard his, and likely he knew her face, while his was a mystery that she found easy to dream of in idle moments. Which was improper, of course, she was the bride of Christ, and there was room for no other.

Were it not for the stable, doubtless they would have had no relationship at all ... whoever he was.

She had been born to the farming life in a countryside still healing from the scars of the Great War, and as a girl she had known much toil. Now, given her youth and experience with beasts of burden and her farm-girl's strength, care of the horses fell to her. Certainly, Father Guillaume had more pressing obligations in the village and the surrounding countryside, and Sister Anna-Marie was getting too feeble.

A LOAF OF BREAD, A JUG OF WINE

Giselle did not mind. Horses belonged to God's flock, too, and the scents of hay and oats took her home again, if only in her imagination. She could talk to the four horses while currying them, while drawing them fresh water, while feeding them, talk to them as she might friends who stood patiently by and absorbed every word. They seemed wise and caring, with gentle souls beneath their muscular flanks, and placid brown eyes that seemed nothing if not protective.

Pity, then, that they could not speak in return.

Who has been caring for all of you before I can get to you? she would ask. *And is he as kind and gentle as I believe he must be? For you never raise a fuss.*

It began perhaps three weeks ago, Giselle leaving the cottage that served as their priory and realizing the horses were already well cared for and lacking for nothing. One day, and the next, then a third. Asking around did nothing to assuage her curiosity, and served only to whet it. Father Guillaume had been distractedly amused, had smiled and chuckled with vague superiority. "Perhaps the Lord has seen fit to send an angel."

She hadn't thought it nearly as funny as he had.

The next day, this unseen angel began to leave loads of fresh-cut firewood, as well. Giselle's first explanation was that it had been one of the villagers of Château-sur-Lac, slipping about to perform Christian duty in absolute anonymity. But then, how to account for the fact that *someone* had been spending nights in the stable? More than one morning she had found a nest of matted hay along the far, rough-hewn wall, and when she lay a hand upon it she fancied it to still be warm from his slumbers. From then on, each night she coaxed Sister Anna-Marie into preparing a plate heaped with whatever remained from the evening meal, and she would set it on a tack shelf in the stable, out of reach of equine muzzles. And mornings she would set out a small loaf of fresh baked bread, perhaps a wedge of cheese, and a small crockery jug filled with wine drawn from the casks in the cellar below their cottage.

Never did the food remain untouched, and never did she see who came to claim it.

How mysterious. And how thrilling.

"Could it be that your secret friend is a refugee, mmmm?" Anna-Marie smiled impishly at her suggestion, then went back to preparing another evening plate with stewed chicken and vegetables and grapes. She never had to be coaxed anymore; the old nun was likely enjoying this intrigue almost as much as Giselle. "Perhaps he fled one of the coasts."

Giselle hadn't thought of that, though it made sense. It was a time of war, but so far Château-sur-Lac had seen little of it. To them the war was planes, far overhead. More than two years ago, France had fallen and Hitler had danced his little jig of victory. Marshal Pétain had signed his armistice with Germany, and only France's north and west coasts had been occupied, the interior spared. Father Guillaume had been furious, had called the man a traitor to his people. Giselle had, at the time, only just taken her vows, and tried to deal with it more philosophically. Tried to look at it as she might, say, a drastic measure in medicine ... as with cutting off an infected limb to save the rest of the body.

As ones who followed a man who had died upon a cross for no fault of his own, surely they could live with sacrifice.

And so she fell to wondering: What sacrifices had been demanded of her mysterious ward, whom she had never even seen? Had he been forced to forfeit love and the creature comforts of home and hearth, to rely on the bounty of nature and the kindness of strangers for each meal? Had he been forced to trade the company of his fellow human beings for that of animals, or none at all?

Perhaps he had been a soldier, separated or deserted from his unit in the confusion of Dunkerque, with no choice but to now live and travel by stealth. Or maybe he had been an artist, living in some garret on the Left Bank of Paris until he gave it up for life in one of the more peaceful coastal cities—Cherbourg, or Brest— and since the coming of the Germans, had submerged his disillusion with humanity in the countryside.

Oh, she felt she knew him already, knew his story. She *had* to—she'd come up with so many, it had to be one among them.

And probably she would have been content to continue on his own terms, providing the meals until the inevitable day when he moved on and she found the food cold, untouched ... were it not for the gift.

On a chilled November morning in the third week since his arrival, an hour past dawn, Giselle wrapped her frayed cloak about her and left the cottage. Behind her, Sister Anna-Marie groaned of stiff knees and wrestled fresh logs onto glowing embers. The heavy door thudded shut and she was alone with the world. On the rear stoop sat bottles of milk and cream, left by one of the villagers. She glanced around, like a wary cat, then dipped her finger in the cream and quickly licked it clean.

Giselle scurried along the path back to the stable. In the distance, a late-rising rooster called. The morning stillness was a fresh and living thing, the air full of mist that clung to the skin and brought a shiver. As far as the eye could see, a pastoral tableau of rolling hills and flat fields, the distant lake that had given the village its name, and woodland that encroached upon it all with the patience of aeons. She would die here someday, Giselle knew, and be grateful for the life spent here.

The path curved back, halfway toward the church and the stone rectory that sat behind it. At one of Father Guillaume's windows she saw the yellowish gleam of an oil lamp.

In the stable, the horses stood placidly, each with a heavy blanket draped across its back as they breathed out soft moist clouds. She spoke to them, called them by name, then crossed over the earthen floor to the shelf for the empty plate.

Beside it, positioned with such care that it sat perfectly straight, was a doll. With winsome painted eyes, it gazed out somewhere just over her head. For a moment, Giselle dared not violate it, then reached to gather it in her arms. It looked and even smelled of age, with thin, limp clothes that nevertheless retained a certain grandeur of pre-revolutionary court gaity. Its head and limbs were porcelain, its complexion milk white but for a rosy blush upon each delicate cheek.

A gift? It must be. For her. For her.

"Are you still here?" she called out, and went running around the stalls for the far wall. As she passed, one of the horses whuffled noisily. "Have you stayed this time?"

The nest was empty. Just a shadowed bed of hay, and nothing else. And was he even now crouched outside, within some sylvan hideaway, spying for a glimpse of her when she emerged with the doll in her arms?

She fingered her rosary and prayed for a moment. This was coming perilously close to courtship. Worse, in some hidden cleft within, she wanted it to be so.

Giselle knelt beside the matted hay, lay a hand upon it, felt the fading, radiant warmth. *His,* and may God the Father, Christ the Son, and the Blessed Virgin forgive her, but she did long to feel it from the source itself. If only once, just once.

She counted, as she might measure a horse, handwidths down along the matted area where his back and shoulders would have lain, then the tapering length of his legs. She had thought it before, but it occurred to her once again:

He must be enormous.

When she left the stable, doll in hand, it was with the taste of delicious fear that she was about to surrender to forbidden curiosity.

Night, barely a moon, the entire countryside dipped in black that seemed to run and pool.

She had kept herself awake for an hour by pinching a spot on her thigh, and for another hour beyond that simply by lying in the darkness, contemplating her faltering courage, and wondering where it might lead if she *did* creep out the door and dare look her refugee in the face. Perhaps he had entertained similar thoughts, was right now lying out there with a deliciously miserable heart and hoping to hear the sound of her footfalls.

A few feet away, Sister Anna-Marie snorted in her sleep and stirred, then fell silent.

The back door might wake her—there was this to consider. And maybe tonight *would* be better spent sleeping, there was always tomorrow night....

Oh, *enough.* There would *always* be another tomorrow night. Of what good was trepidation? He was but a man, no doubt a shy one, certainly kind at heart. No harm would come from their speaking, and meeting one another face-to-face so that she could at least know what he looked like. The advantage was his, there.

Giselle eased from her bed, drew her cloak about her

and, creeping barefoot across the cold floor, carried her shoes to the back door. From a kitchen shelf she took a lamp and matches.

Out the door, quickly, quietly as she could shut it, and then she was hurrying along the path. The stable loomed ahead of her, a sagging black square punched in the night. At its door she stopped to light the lamp, then slipped inside.

A muted glow surrounded her and cast a tilting shadowplay on the walls, and she eased across the hard-packed earth. The deep bellows breath of sleeping horses was the only sound as she passed them in their stalls. To the far wall, then ...

She stopped.

He was there, lying on one side with his broad back to her, curled beneath a heavy horse blanket which rose and fell with his own steady breath. She could see little of him, the man himself, just a great head of shaggy black hair.

In a young life whose course had run slowly, so straight and free of genuine surprise, this was new: that the risk of change came down to a single moment. She had but to take the step into the next, or turn around and retreat and forever wonder.

Giselle cleared her throat, loudly: "Excuse me? Sir?" And louder still, "Sir? Are you awake?"

A sluggish flex of his shoulders, a stirring of his legs. The moment crawled by, a slow eternity, then whipped ahead in sudden flurry. She thought she saw his face, half turning back her way as he opened one sleepy eye—

And could she trust the lantern's glow, the peculiar shades of color that it sometimes cast? Was that grimacing cheek indeed a sallow yellow? She saw but a glimpse of it, and there was no time to decide. A groan of terrible anguish came scraping forth from the cavern of his chest as he threw the blanket about his own head and scuttled back against the stable wall. He drew his knees in toward his chest and, with head lowered beneath its makeshift veil, held himself together like some trembling fortress.

"Leave me," he said. "Leave me to my world, and go back to your own. If you wish to do me one last kindness ... then let that be it. Please."

Giselle took a step forward without even intending to. She was drawn to misery like moths to candles; it was more than her calling, it was the *reason* for her being. This man spoke in a voice so lashed with agonies, his words were almost secondary, and she could no more leave him than she could deny Christ.

"I mean you no harm," she said. "I've tried to show you nothing but goodwill. Surely you know that by now, don't you?"

"I know it, yes." His voice seemed near to breaking. "But this was when I was a stranger to you, who moved by night. There have been others, whose hearts have been kind enough ... until they see me for what I am ... and at once their hearts turn murderous."

"Then they've missed what's obvious to me. That your heart is far kinder than theirs." Giselle took another step closer, and another, and knelt just a metre away. "What could change them so?"

Beneath the blanket, he seemed to recoil. "My countenance ... it is more hideous than you could possibly imagine."

"I've seen and tended to faces afflicted by disease, and all the injuries that can happen on farms. I never once quit loving the person behind such a face. So I promise I'll not turn away from yours." When she got no reply, she tried another route. "I don't even know your name."

Again, a heavy stirring beneath the blanket. "I ... I

was never given one. So, in time, I gave one to myself, the only name that would suit me: Nomad."

Had he been so abandoned as a child, no one had even bothered to grant him the simple gift of a *name?* This was more than sorrowful, this was a moral crime. She told him her own, then: "Let me see you, Nomad. Please, let me see you."

He seemed to consider it awhile, like a king weighed down by ponderous burdens of the heart. Then the lowered head rose, the blanket with it. "Move back a few paces, then, if you really mean to see me for what I am."

And he stood.

It was one thing to contemplate his enormity of stature in impressions left in a bed of hay, quite another to behold it in person. He seemed to simply keep uncoiling from the stable floor, taller, and taller still. She'd always thought herself big-boned, born to robust farming stock ... yet there was someone who stood nearly three heads taller than she.

One brutish hand rose from within the blanket, to pull it slowly away, and for the first time she met his dull and watery eyes. Saw his yellowed skin, his blackened lips, the tangled cascade of coarse hair whose locks bunched about his shoulders like throttled snakes. His face was like none she had seen, ever, more total in its noble ruin than any ravaged by disease or wound. And her heart shattered for the sufferings others must have heaped upon him; for no matter how powerful his shoulders or broad his back, both most surely have broken under the strain.

Giselle groped inside for words, but there were none. We are all beautiful in the eyes of the Lord? How easy to say, with her own complexion like milk. The last thing Nomad needed was to hear sanctimonious platitudes ...

So, instead, she stepped forward to where he stood atremble, reached up, and touched his face. Which soon dampened with his tears.

"There are hours yet before dawn," she said. "Please share with me where you've come from."

In the hour past dawn, Nomad refused to leave the stable with her, and no amount of coaxing would draw him out to join her in a walk to the rectory. Father Guillaume should be told, but moreover should be introduced to this wandering soul. Such conversations the two of them might have, what endless lifetimes of humanity had Nomad witnessed, as an outsider. If anything, humanity could *learn* from him, and benefit. Let it begin with her, and with the Church. Let it begin here.

"But why?" he pleaded with her. "You have your hopes and your optimisms, but these are born of your naivete. You have seen so little of the world, you have no way of knowing how much it can hate. Of hope and optimism I have none ... because instead I have experience. I *know* the reception I'll meet with."

"For everything and everyone, a place," she told him. "This is what I believe and I believe because this is what I've seen. No one can be truly happy until they find that place. I *am,* because I *have.* I belong to God, and to the Church, and to Château-sur-Lac. And if I can help you find that place for your life ... then it will prove that mine has fulfilled some of its purpose as well. Don't you see?"

He said he did, and that he dared not turn his back on her before she had her chance to try.

Giselle ran from the stable with her cloak billowing behind her, into the fresh damp chill of morning. She raced along the path to the rectory, whose window was filled with the jaundiced glow of a lamp.

How unlikely she would be doing this if other circumstances had asserted themselves. That Nomad was nothing as she'd imagined was a blessed relief. His ugliness and profound misery were easy to contend with, compared to the handsome face and shy, seductive demeanor that might have been his. And had he possessed these, had he been that Parisian artist in self-imposed exile? Perhaps she would still be making this trip to the rectory, though to instead confess and mourn her broken vows.

She banged on the cottage door, and when it opened, Father Guillaume stood as she had never seen him. He had already donned his cassock, but had yet to shave, his thin-jowled face seemed to sag, his graying hair was still mussed from the pillow. And behind his round spectacles ...

"Have you been *weeping?*" she asked.

"Yes." He peered at her as if only now realizing who it was. "You're out of breath. You, too, have heard?"

Giselle frowned. "Heard what?"

Father Guillaume waved it aside briskly, almost gratefully, and wiped at his eyes. "You're out of breath. There must be a reason. Come in."

She crossed the threshold and they sat at the scarred old table where the Father took his meals when he preferred to dine alone, with his Bible or his meditations. A fresh log was beginning to blaze away in the fireplace, atop old embers.

"The man who's been passing his nights in our stable," she began, "the one who's done so much with the horses, and left so much firewood behind for his keep ... he's no longer a stranger. I've just now left a conversation with him that lasted for hours. Father, he's more deserving of our pity and our help than anyone I've ever met. *Ever.*"

Giselle recounted the long and sorrowful story, of

one man created by another, then rejected not only by his creator but the whole of humanity, as well. Condemned by fate to wander for nearly two centuries, as he neither aged nor died, as people and their reaction to him did not change, only the world around them. And she thought of Michelangelo's ceiling in the Sistine Chapel, of that immense paternal deity reaching out his muscular arm to touch the fingertip of Adam. What jealousy would Nomad feel were he to see that? And given paints and brushes, what would his own rendition look like: extended fingers become a clenched fist, with the back of the creator turned away in abhorrence?

When she finished, Father Guillaume slowly rose from the table, moved idly toward the fireplace where he warmed his hands and shook his downcast head.

"I've heard of . . . of . . . *it*. I can't bring myself to call it 'him.' And for years I thought the story itself was not much more than the product of a fevered mind." He moved across the room to a cabinet of plain oak, very old. Here Father Guillaume kept his meager wealth of books: his Bibles and history, and old volumes by Aquinas and Spinoza and others. His finger glided over spines and he removed one aged volume and returned with it to the table.

"It's a jumbled collection of letters and a journal and a recounting of much of that very story you just told, though in this case, from the mouth of Victor Frankenstein. This was written by an English sea captain named Walton who encountered both of them on the frozen north seas. I found it not long after the end of the Great War, at a bookshop in London. I thought at the time I might send it along to Rome, so that it might be condemned for its blasphemies, its heresies, but . . . but I never did. I never in my most fantastic dreams believed it to be true."

Father Guillaume lowered his head a moment, rubbing bunched fingers into his reddened eyes, then looked up. "You must drive it away, Sister. Tell it to leave."

Surely her ears deceived her. Even so, not her eyes. The Father's face was stern and unyielding. "Nomad is *not* an 'it,' Father, he's a man. Maybe his beginnings were different than yours and mine, but he doesn't feel any less. He doesn't need love and mercy any less. On the contrary, he needs them even more."

"*He,* then," said Guillaume, harshly, "*he* is an abomination in the eyes of God! *He* has no right to exist!"

"But he does. No matter how quick you are to turn away, he still will be there."

"This abomination you're so quick to defend ... it deliberately murdered a child in Switzerland. Maybe more than one."

"And here at home," she explained, "Gilles de Rais murdered many dozens of them. He went to his trial and execution repentant. Would you be the one to judge him beyond forgiveness?"

Father Guillaume simply glared, would not answer.

"I thought not," she said gently. "Then please ... why not extend the same mercies to Nomad? He's certainly had none of the advantages of an aristocrat who should have known better."

"But his birth was more atrocious than that of the most lowly peasant." Father Guillaume pushed away from the table with a groan of misery, and despite the disappointment, she felt mostly pity for him. What had he endured to leave his mind and heart so closed on some topics? "Very well—he's done no one any harm in the three weeks since he first came to hide here. I suppose it would be unchristian to drive him away. But Giselle ... please keep him out of my sight. And if he wishes to go, don't discourage it."

A LOAF OF BREAD, A JUG OF WINE

She winced. "You have no more charity for him than that?"

"On the contrary. I think it's far more than he's accustomed to."

Oh, but the Father's arguments were slippery ones. Certainly she had pushed her luck challenging his authority to the degree she had. At least there was something to build on, and perhaps over the next few days his heart would soften.

She readied to leave, then stopped at the door, remembering. "Father? Why were you weeping when I first knocked?"

He stood in the center of his cottage, looking lost within his cassock. He seemed to want anything but to answer. Finally, "Did you hear the motorcar just before dawn?"

Giselle shook her head. "Nomad and I, we were deep in our conversation."

"A cousin of Henri Sanson, driving in from Nantes to bring Henri the news. Henri came to me ... and I should think that most of Château-sur-Lac knows by now." The Father shook his head and sought his chair. "The Allies have invaded North Africa. Germany has decided to break the terms of the armistice ... and occupy all of France. The war? It's come home, Giselle."

Her knees weakened at the threshold, and she steadied a hand against the doorjamb. What a fragile cloak was security; it felt as if, for two and a half years, they of the interior had made their own separate peace, then lived much as before. Ripped away, now, and they had no promise of anything. Only this: Their lives as they knew them were all but over. And how would they be treated by those first troops of the occupation who came down into their shallow valley to claim it for their own?

At the moment, she felt suddenly as if she had more

empathy with Nomad's life than that brought by hours of conversation. She now understood how it must feel to await a life of indignity and loathing. This country knew already, even if it had come before her time: the German army made harsh masters.

"I'll toll the bell," she said. "We should all gather. We should pray."

"Yes," he murmured, and nodded. "Yes. We should." He drew a long breath that trembled with impotent rage. "What anyone prays for silently, in their own heart, is between them and God. But I will have *no one* in my church praying for a single German ... unless it's that he find his way to the border. Or an early grave."

She thought to argue—didn't Germans, too, have immortal souls?—but the urge passed after a moment. His rebuttal would be swift—the Germans had forfeited their souls the day they decided to invade Poland—and would leave no room for objections.

So, instead, she left, for the church, for the rope, for the clarion bell that would unite them all. If peace during war they no longer had, they at least had each other.

While Nomad, it occurred to her, had no one.

It came, soon enough: the war.

More planes overhead. On tranquil mornings and still evenings and moments during the day when cows fell silent and conversations ended, from the roads just beyond the valley came the sound of mechanized caravans. The low mingled rumble of engines and rolling tires and the crushing tank-treads of the Panzer divisions ... these would drift down the gentle slopes on crisp November air, like the first drafts of a wind that would soon turn bitter and furious. It was, Giselle thought—and Sister Anna-Marie agreed—almost

A LOAF OF BREAD, A JUG OF WINE

worse this way than if the Germans had arrived in the village immediately. They had no faces this way, no eyes to beseech in hopes of finding pity. They could only be imagined, and invariably imagination conjured ogres in uniform.

This climate of fear ... in it, did Nomad feel more at home?

Giselle had been forced to lie to him to spare his feelings, telling him that Father Guillaume soon would meet with him, but that he was ailing, and for now it took all his strength to give heart to his parishioners. Nomad did not question, and from her lips, at least, it was believed.

She tried to get him to move into the priory, where he could at least enjoy the warmth of a fire; they would fix up a corner for him, or perhaps a nook in the cellar. But no, he steadfastly refused, preferring to remain in the stable and the daily company of the horses who, he said, never judged or turned their eyes away or cried out at the sight of him. When parishioners came up the hill, from the sprinkling of cottages and farms below, to seek spiritual guidance from the Father or the sisters, he was careful to wear an empty grain sack, cut with eye holes, to protect them from a possible fright.

His was the life least changed by this shift in the tides of war, and Giselle tried to spare him an hour or two each day, simply to talk. He listened wonderfully, and spoke with a hesitant and self-conscious eloquence on more books than she could ever hope to read ... Milton and Plutarch, Dante and Dickens, Descartes and Steinbeck and Twain. Of countries he knew, but little of borders; he crossed at timber lines and often did not realize it until he overheard a new language spoken.

War? Nomad had lived through them before, and for him they were no different than peace. He was an aberration to invader and defender alike, and in that spirit, Giselle supposed, he lived under a constant declaration of war from all nations. Their talks opened more than her eyes, it felt as if they shed light into her soul as well. . . .

Until at last the occupation came to Château-sur-Lac.

It was preceded by the sounds of battle, the fabric of the day rent by machine gun fire and the crack of rifles, the dull thud of grenades and explosions greater still. Two columns of ominous black smoke rose in the distance. A partisan ambush, no doubt; prayers for its victory resounded through the village.

And went unheard.

The battered victors came over the hills and streamed into Château-sur-Lac, sons of the Hun from a generation before. Teutonic faces grimed with soot and sweat and blood; gray tunics and coal-scuttle helmets and high black boots; carbine rifles and Schmeisser machine pistols and potato masher grenades. And every man who had just lost a good friend to partisan fire had replaced him with a lethal anger burning in his eye. Peasant blood would run just as red.

Barely over twenty of them, all told, half a dozen surviving wounded, the rest able-bodied. Teenage boys fought alongside hard, seasoned veterans.

The villagers were rousted from their homes, forced to gather in the central village green—such as it was—before the tiny cafe and bakery. A battered but still operable motorcycle came roaring up the hill to the church. Out of the sidecar leapt a private who rounded up priest and nuns at rifle-point, and began to march them back down to join the rest while the cyclist buzzed a circuit around rectory and priory and barn to make sure they had missed no one.

The thought of Nomad, gargantuan child that he was

A LOAF OF BREAD, A JUG OF WINE

in some respects, back there alone, elicited surprisingly little worry in Giselle. In his vast span of days on this earth, he had learned nothing quite so well as how to hide.

Pity the rest of them had not learned so valuable a skill.

They were gathered within a perimeter of uniforms. Some in tears, others in sullen quietude, most of the older ones calm and resigned, as ones who were watching history repeat itself. Father Guillaume moved among them, as did Giselle and Anna-Marie, but how much comfort could cold hands provide under the watch of muzzles colder still?

The officer who came striding forth from a tight knot of his men silenced them with a pair of shots into the air from his Luger sidearm. His face was tightly seamed; prematurely graying blond hair strayed from beneath his helmet to cling wetly to his upper forehead. When he spoke, he had no need of an interpreter; his French was deliberate but no less understood.

"I am Untersturmführer Streckenbach," he called out, "and you will give me all the cooperation due the Third Reich. Who refuses, will be shot. In a few moments you will be questioned and asked to surrender whatever weapons you may have in your possession. Who refuses, will be shot. Your homes will then be searched. Who is found to be lying ... will be shot. Understood?"

Giselle stood with clasped hands and listened to the scarcely audible murmuring around her. How little malice the man actually spoke with. He might have been placing an order in the bakery.

"For tonight," Streckenbach went on, "your home will be ours. We have just suffered the loss of our radio at the hands of some unfortunate countrymen of yours. For their actions, I do not hold you responsible. For your own, you will bear every responsibility. Until a messenger can be dispatched to send back new orders and evacuation for our dead and our wounded, you will accord us your hospitality."

He suddenly craned his neck, scanning faces in the crowd. "Where is the priest . . . ah, there you are." Beside her, Giselle felt Father Guillaume go suddenly rigid. "I wish to see you in a few minutes." The lieutenant flicked one finger toward the door of the cafe, and in a moment a young private was at his shoulder to ensure he found the way.

Giselle met his eyes only once as he was led away from the crowd. The Father's eyes, resigned and bitter, retained something crushed as well. Something broken that could never be restored. Did they kill priests to demoralize an occupied village? She prayed not. There was no need. Château-sur-Lac was full of compliant people.

She continued to pray until her concentration was shattered, as two soldiers departed on motorcycle and in sidecar, down the road and away to the west, buzzing like a horsefly until they were gone, simply gone.

Servant of God or not, Father Guillaume looked for things to hate about this man. This Hun. Oh, there was plenty to find. He hated the small scar that curled out from the corner of the left eye, hated the cleft in his chin. He hated the straight posture and the blue of his eyes and the gray of his uniform and the sharp tangy sweat-smoke smell of him, and most of all he hated the very fact of this man's existence, and how they were now forced to breathe the same air in this rustic cafe. *I can never eat here again,* thought Guillaume. *I'll see him and smell him even then.*

"You despise me," said Streckenbach. "Your eyes make no secret of it, and I find it perfectly understandable. I don't ask your goodwill, only your cooperation. Wine?"

He poured from a bottle and savored the bouquet and nodded quietly as Guillaume told him no. He then gulped like a Philistine at a stream and Guillaume hated that, too.

"Occupying officers often seek out the mayors of the villages they enter," the lieutenant told him. "That may be of value, but I find greater worth in men of God. You priests are natural born mediators, sworn to keep the peace. You know the hearts of your flock better than anyone. Better than I can ever hope to."

Father Guillaume's stomach curdled. "I'll tell you nothing about a single one of them."

Streckenbach refilled, toasted him ironically with the glass and poured it down. "Nor do I ask that of you. As I say, you hear their confessions and know their hearts. You know who lives peacefully, and you know who's prone to ... impulsive behavior. What I require of you is to keep them pacified, any among them with, shall I say, *ideas*.

"Regardless of what you may think of me and the army I serve, I have no desire to leave dead villagers behind. Whether or not I *do*, is largely your responsibility. Understood?"

Guillaume shut his eyes and nodded slowly and agreed. How sad a day this was, and would that he had been born deaf so that he would not have to hear himself acquiescing like a toady.

"Dismissed," Streckenbach said, and of course that was but the most recent thing to hate.

As they were his people, and he their shepherd, he went from home to home to comfort whom he could. Some families had been forced out and into the cottages of neighbors, as their own homes were appropriated for makeshift barracks and, in one case, a ward for the wounded.

The pile of confiscated weapons grew, with hunting rifles and shotguns and pistols, even implements of daily life on the farm such as pitchforks and scythes. Their lives were no longer their own in Château-sur-Lac, and even God seemed very far away.

Late afternoon, Guillaume left the heart of the village and trudged back up the hill to his church and rectory. For a minute, at the very least, he stood over and contemplated ruts dug into the earth by a heedless motorcycle. He stamped them flat, smoothed them over until no trace of tire remained, then bypassed both home and church. Onward, to the cool dim recesses of the stable.

He found it inside, that hateful thing whose very existence mocked the divine creation beneath its feet. It stood in one of the stalls, stroking the sculpted neck of one of the horses and murmuring into its ear; beside it the beast looked like a Shetland pony to a normal man.

Such was his first sight of this abomination: the ghastly face, the gigantic stature, the clothing that looked crudely sewn together from existing garments to meet the task of covering its outsize frame. Guillaume saw, and could believe in devils.

"You came," it said, like a child who feared to trust its own delight.

Guillaume swallowed down his disgust and tried to offer a reassuring smile. "You doubted?"

Nomad patted the horse's mane, then hurried out of the stall with great jerking movements. Crossing the stable with the self-conscious embarrassment of one who lived in the humblest of abodes yet sought still to be a proper host. The sight was a travesty of everything human, and at last it bid him join itself, seated on bales of hay.

"Giselle?" it asked. "Is she . . . ?"

"Come to no harm."

And how could something so appalling as that face show such relief? It must have been a trick of light.

" . . . yet," Guillaume added, and yes, that face showed its true wretchedness at once. "With the Germans, who can tell what they will do? Who can wake up each morning with the assurance that there is no bullet or bayonet for them that day?"

Nomad plucked loose pieces of straw from the bale, let them fall to the floor. "Is there no love in them for anything good and kind and gentle?"

"None. They love only conquest."

Guillaume watched the thing go through the motions of thought and anguish. These seeds he was planting were falling on fertile soil, he could tell, needing only the proper watering to bear the terrible fruits for which he hoped.

He pressed on: "You have a great and tremendous rage within you, do you not?"

"I once did," said Nomad, in a voice of something lost. "I once, long ago, told my creator, 'If I cannot inspire love, I will cause fear.' And how I devoted myself to that heinous mission. But now I believe that even devils must tire of provoking suffering, when suffering faces are all they see. And I have even come to believe that those same devils must despair themselves as amateurs when compared to the likes of Mankind. You have, yourselves, taken over their task with so much more efficiency." Nomad lifted his gaze, then his arm, to the stable door and beyond. "How many wars have I seen? I no longer remember. So what fear can I cause that would not be welcomed over an invading army?"

"Ah," said Father Guillaume, and he must not be swayed by this creature's pretense to remorse, "but what of the fear you might bring to the invading army itself? Is it possible that your natural inclinations might then be put to a greater good?" He let that sink in, then clinched it: "If for no other's sake than that of Giselle."

The thing turned a wide, watery eye upon him. "How can you wear those robes and ask this of me?"

"I care more for the oppressed than the oppressor. It's no more complicated than that." He drew a breath and tried not to choke on the next words. "And if you do this for me, for Giselle, I will then offer you my hand, in friendship . . . and in love."

"Love," said Nomad, musing the sound and taste of the word, as if something foreign. "Then I ask one thing of you beforehand. Please, allow what I do to be a holy task. Bring me your sacraments."

Guillaume drew back, could not help himself. *"What?"*

"The bread, the wine. The blessing."

This thing was asking too much, and for what? He doubted very much that it even possessed a soul, and surely, in all its years, no priest would have offered it baptism. He would play no part in desecrating the Eucharist. Would not see his church reduced to giving legitimacy to monstrosities which by all that was right and holy should not exist at all. He would not, *would not*—

"As you wish," Guillaume heard himself say, and felt his feet take him to the door.

She came suddenly awake in the night, and moved only enough to reassure herself of the warm, familiar nest of her own bed. She blinked, then looked over at Sister Anna-Marie, whose slow and even breaths continued undisturbed.

A LOAF OF BREAD, A JUG OF WINE

Had she been dreaming? Something had pierced sleep.

There—*again,* and Giselle sat upright in her bed, as at once the world expanded beyond her to include the whole of her village.

From below, down the hill, came the crack of a rifle, lonely and desolate and full of terrible foreboding. A cry, then, of mortal anguish, and next a sudden rip of machine pistol fire. The after-ring of each sound hung in the silent crystalline perfection of the November night.

Giselle cast aside the quilts and bolted from her bed, then wrapped her cloak about her and didn't even bother with shoes. For a moment she paused near Anna-Marie's bed, in debate. The old nun slept deeply. Well, let her sleep on. Perhaps she was dreaming of fields in summer, and youth.

She ran into the night, the grass chilly and damp beneath her feet, and as the sounds, with increasing frequency, continued to roll up the hill, she pounded on the Father's door. There was but a moment's pause before he called calmly for her to enter. He sounded as if he had been awake all night.

Giselle shivered within her cloak, and found him sitting at his table. No lamp burned, but he had left the curtains at his dining window pushed aside. He was a black cassock and a pale face immobile in a silver-blue flood of moonlight.

"Sit," he said, with hand proferred toward a chair. "We'll wait."

"Do you not *hear?*" she cried. "They're killing the people—"

"No." Slowly, Father Guillaume shook his head. "They are defending themselves. And I dare hope they finally know the taste of defeat." He tilted his ear—such bliss!—as if the faraway crash of shattering wood were a faint strain of music. "After so many lifetimes of avoiding the eyes of men, how silent and stealthy must that creature be, when it wishes. And how powerful."

Giselle felt her knees go weak and she collapsed onto the chair he had offered.

"And what lengths it will go to for the sake of love."

"*You* set Nomad to this killing?" she cried. "How could you? *How could you?*"

"Because it is what Nomad does, Giselle. It is what Nomad is." She sought his eyes but they were beyond seeing; his round spectacles were flat replicas of the moon. "In my own heart God is first, and my flock second. On their behalf, He did not answer. So I turned to one that would. Though perhaps ... Nomad *was* the answer to prayer."

Bile rose in her throat and she forced it down. "How dare you presume such a thing."

Father Guillaume spread his hands. "Samson slew an army of Philistines with the jawbone of an ass. Did it just happen to be there? And God smiled. So before you judge ... *listen.*"

She had no more heart with which to argue—it hurt too much. Hers must be the same as the grieving hearts of mothers who see their sons grow out of playful innocence to be hanged as convicted murderers. All mourn for the dead, yes, but they mourn no less for the passing of what potential might have been fulfilled in the living.

And so she listened.

To the frantic cracks of rifles, the bursts of automatic fire. Here a scream, there the concussive blast of a grenade. And still the cries went on. The brittle sound of splintering, as she learned to distinguish wood from bone. Learned to distinguish cry of fear from cry of mortality, and the breaking point in a long suffering wail when the former became the latter.

And so she listened.

As the deliverance of Château-sur-Lac went on, and on, and on.

They did not leave the table until after moonlight waned to give way to dawn, and for two hours or more it had done so in silence. Dawn came with none of its usual innocence and hope, but instead a pall of guilt and apprehension, heavy as clouds.

"Get up, come along," Giselle told him. "At least see what you've done."

They left the rectory and trudged out upon the hill, far enough beyond the church so that it did not block their view of the village below. Beneath the lightening sky they gazed down upon an eerie tableau where nothing moved but a wafting haze of smoke, and in a place or two, the licking tongues of dying fires. Several bodies in gray uniforms lay strewn about, more than one broken into impossible angles. Another hung limp in a charred black hole blasted through the stone wall of a cottage. Yet another had been slammed halfway through a roof. One in the street appeared to have been driven entirely through with a shattered length of timber. And the rest? Giselle hoped not to have to see them, inside their charnel houses.

"Where is everyone else?" said Father Guillaume. "I dared thought by now they would be rejoicing."

"They're terrified even to look out their own windows. Would you be any different, if you didn't know?" Giselle looked at him without pity. "Be proud. He served you well."

She left him to dog her footsteps through the clinging mist, and returned to the rectory, the warmth of its fire that had fed well through the night. Giselle huddled at the table and wondered why she had not gone back to the priory instead, then realized she had more to say. She waited until Guillaume hunkered at the fire to add a fresh log.

"Tell me," she said. "How do you justify this before God? Aside from your feelings about the Germans—oh, I know *those*—but instead, Nomad? How do you justify condemning him to carry such added burdens to his soul?"

Father Guillaume straightened at the fireplace with a weary groan. "Nomad doesn't *have* a soul, Giselle."

"By what authority do you make that decision?" she cried.

"By the authority of the Church!" He returned to the table and sat heavily, angrily, in his chair.

"Then the Church is wrong!"

Guillaume pointed wildly in the direction of the village. "That creature was never conceived like a man. Even a horse, or an ox, or a dog comes into this world by natural birth, but we don't consider them to possess souls. How much lesser a being than them is Nomad, then? In Nomad I endangered nothing. *Because there is no soul within to endanger!*"

She drew into herself then, feet like ice, heart like broken fragments of stone. There would be no arguing with the Father, for there was nothing in his mind left open. And what *of* Nomad? She could not believe that he, too, lay below in a cottage, one more casualty of the night. Had he wreaked his havoc, then fled, unable to face her? He had to know she could forgive him anything.

Sadly, though, there were more immediate and pressing matters to be concerned with.

"What of the Germans' reinforcements?" she asked. "They *will* come, you know. Later today, tomorrow.

A LOAF OF BREAD, A JUG OF WINE

How do you propose to explain where the first have gone?"

"It's not our duty to explain anything a German decides to do," he said. "We take the bodies and we bury them, or hide them beneath haystacks, or haul them by ox-cart to the lake and weight them with stones and sink them to the bottom. We clean up their blood. And they remain the secret of this village. For as long as it takes. . . .

"They were here, and they left. That is all we know."

Giselle tried to keep from shivering. Dawn was cold, but this priest's heart was colder still. How gentle he had seemed, for years, while concealing the scheming heart of a murderer.

She was about to leave his table when she heard a scraping outside the door. Heavy feet upon flagstones, unsteady, and then the door swung open.

He filled the doorway, Nomad, then entered with the slow and painful gait of one who ignores wounds. She sought his eyes, and when their gazes met, the yellow smoldering fury in them seemed to soften, and she knew him capable of tears he would never allow. He had purpose, and now, at least, she was not it.

He strode past her, and after a brief pause to glance about the cottage, continued to the bookcase where Father Guillaume's dusty and cherished volumes sat like wise old friends. One arm swung up, to add something to their company.

"For the love of God!" Father Guillaume suddenly screamed. "You brought that here? *Here?*"

Giselle shut her eyes, quickly, grateful she could, so she did not have to see those of Lieutenant Streckenbach staring dimly from across the room. His mouth hung frozen half-open in perpetual surprise, and by now the skin of the head was waxy and pale.

"I thought you would be pleased," explained Nomad, in loss and sorrow and the pain of lifetimes of broken promises.

He shuffled a few more steps to sag to the floor, before the hearth, and when Giselle moved to help him he seemed to plead with his eyes, *No, I am beyond your help forever,* and she could only gaze upon him in tears. His rude clothing was splotched with blood, surely not all his own, but then, surely some of it had to be. How many wounds could such a formidable body withstand? How many bullets, how many blows, how many piercing slivers from the heart of a grenade?

From the floor, he looked over to Father Guillaume, who sat in his chair, shocked into silence by a revulsion beyond even his own comprehension. Had Judas looked this way, Giselle wondered, in realizing the enormity of his crime?

"I *have* a soul," said Nomad, in blood and quiet dignity, and she then wondered how long he had been outside to listen. "I do. I can feel it, and I know that is what it is, because nothing else could ache so deeply. Though I may not have been born with a soul, I know that I have built one of my own over time. With every year I live . . . with every deed, with every sorrow and indignity and wound I suffer, with every humiliation and hour of loneliness . . . I know I build that soul a little more. These things that tear human hearts to pieces? These are my bricks, and my mortar."

Father Guillaume managed to find his voice after all. "You take much for granted."

Nomad seemed almost to laugh. "And you do not?"

And thus Giselle wondered: did she, as well?

For a while Nomad turned his head to gaze into the fireplace, where the fresh log was beginning to blaze anew. "I planned once to kill myself. On the frozen north seas, I left my creator behind in the bed where he died, and I told the captain of that vessel that my only intention was to then build my own funeral pyre, and climb atop it, and let the winds take my ashes to the sea. What a fine dream that was...

"But as I made my way south again, another dream took hold, and on that day when snow and ice were behind me, and wood to burn before me, I knew I could not. Because of my incomplete soul."

He stood, a long and painful process, and left the comforts of the hearth.

"Every day I build that soul a little more. And whether it takes another year, or ten, or a thousand, only then will I consent to die. So that I can stand whole before whatever God there may be ... and demand of Him one thing: *'Why?'*"

Giselle bit her lip and drew blood. Better this pain than that of having nothing to say to him, no balm to soothe either an anguished brow or soul. With eyes shut, she felt his vast presence pass her side, then pause, as a huge, callused palm caressed her cheek with such tenderness it belied the fury of the night.

"I remember something from a poem," he said. "A poem about love, and simple pleasures. I remember but a few words ... 'a loaf of bread, a jug of wine, and thee.' I once dared hope that even these simple things would not be beyond me, if only for a day." He withdrew his hand and reserved his last baleful look for Father Guillaume. "Only poets tell no lies."

Giselle lowered her head to the tabletop as she listened to the thud of the door and the scrape of his unsteady feet across flagstones as he was lost to the mist, the smoke, and the everlasting dawn.

A spellbound wretch
In his futile gropings,

Brian Hodge

In order to flee a serpent-filled place,
Looking for light and a key;

One damned descending without lamp,
On the edge of an abyss whose stench
Betrays the wet depths
Of endless stairways with no rail ...
—Baudelaire

PISS EYES
by
Rick Hautala

Transcript of a conversation with Ajut, a member of the Inuit tribe. Part One:

I am an old man now, but when I was a child, I recall fondly how my mother would tell us children stories at bedtime. These stories were told to entertain us and, at times, to frighten us into good behavior; but no tale she ever told us scared me half as much as something that happened during my eleventh year. This tale was told to me by Ootek, my father's brother, and it was all the more frightening because he insisted that it was true.

Now, I never believed him, of course; not until a year later, when he took me out onto the ice and showed me the fire-blackened hull of the big wooden sailing ship from the south. Then, in my twelve-year-old wisdom, I allowed as how *some* of his tale might have an element of truth in it ... but not much.

I understand now that I no doubt didn't want to believe what I heard, but I will tell you the tale as it was told to me, more than sixty winters ago, and you can judge for yourself. In fact, we are within a two day journey of the old ship, so if you would like, I could take you there to see it.

I remember food was scarce that year, as it often is for the People. Kaila the Provider had not supplied our men with nearly enough seals and whales during the annual summer hunt. For long periods of time, the sky remained dark and cloudy even during the summer, when the sun never sets. When winter came, and snow filled the sky and covered the ground, and the wind howled like a woman in pain outside our igloos, we remained inside our igloos many days at a time. Only a fool would dare to go outside when Paija the Evil One was prowling about, looking for anyone foolish enough to brave the long winter darkness alone.

Ootek, my father's brother, lived alone. His wife, Howmik, had died the spring before when the ice upon which she was walking split open beneath her weight, and the *inua angkuni*, those great ghosts who live below the ice, caught her by the feet and dragged her under to dwell with them. No one can gaze long upon the faces of the *inua angkuni* and keep his thoughts straight afterward. Howmik was alone at the time, so no one saw any of this happen, but what happened proves that the *inua angkuni* are always looking for someone foolish enough to be out on the ice alone. Howmik's footprints were found on the edge of ice near the open water, and everyone in our village could read the story those tracks told.

Throughout that winter, Ootek kept very much to himself, rarely coming to visit even when we offered to share with him the meager supplies of our food. During the long, dark winter, he made a habit of going out for long walks in the night. Even when wind howled like Amow the wolf, and the snow drifted like thick smoke across the ice, he would go outside, telling no one where he was going or what his intentions were. My father suggested to my mother that Ootek's wife had returned to Ootek in the form of an *ino,* and that he was spending his time sporting with her in the frigid darkness. Of course, I believed him because I

PISS EYES

know many truths about the spirit world. Just because I am now a Christian, it does not mean that the spirits and demons of my people have all disappeared.

After supper one night, my sister and I had been put to bed, but I was unable to sleep. I remember that I felt a sharp tingling in the air, like on those days in the summer, when lines of fire reach down from the sky and touch the earth, and the booming sounds like that of shifting ice fill the air. There was a different smell in the igloo, too, like the stinging in the air after it rains. I grew fearful and was unable to sleep, but I dared not disturb my mother and father, who were talking in hushed tones near the whale oil fire on the other side of the igloo. My father was sharpening the point of his harpoon. As I lay there, huddled under my caribou blankets, my childish imagination carried me away. And then, beneath the howling of the wind, I began to hear something else—a low, distant moaning sound, coming from outside. Just then, our dogs began to bark loudly.

Of course, my first thought was that the *inua angkuni* were moving about, moving invisibly from igloo to igloo, looking in on everyone and trying to decide who—if anyone—they would take with them next. Naked and shivering, I huddled beneath my warm caribou blankets, knowing that if *inua angkuni* looked in on me and I saw them, I might never again be right in my mind.

Suddenly, a scream loud enough to be heard above the roaring wind and barking of the dogs filled the night. I sat up in bed and looked at my father, feeling only a small measure of relief when I saw that his eyes were wide with fear, too. I knew that he had heard the sound as well as I.

"Ootek," he said simply, staring at my mother.

I remember how his wide-open eyes glistened darkly

in the reflected light of our small fire. He laid his harpoon aside and made a move to put on his outside clothes, but my mother held him back by both arms and begged him not to go outside.

I remember the twisted torment I saw on my father's face as he considered what he should do. If, in fact, his brother was outside and in danger, he of course must try to help him; but if the *inua angkuni* were nearby, to go outside meant that he, too, risked death ... or worse.

After what seemed like a very long time, my father twisted out of my mother's grasp, pulled on his thick snow pants, coat, boots, and mittens, and went outside. The wind died down to a whisper, and the dogs stopped their barking the instant he went outside. After that, I could hear nothing else, not even the heavy tread of his boots in the snow. He was gone for what seemed like a very long time to me, and I began to cry softly to myself, thinking that maybe my father had joined his brother on the journey to the land of the dead. But some time later he returned. I will never forget the look I saw on his face when he told my mother what he had found.

"Yes, it was Ootek," he said, shifting his gaze away from my mother as though he were afraid to look her in the eyes. "He has seen Paija, the Evil One."

Well, my friend, it is time for our meal. I will tell you more of this after we have eaten.

Rev. Robert Crocker's journal entry, July 14, 1964:

I've been traveling with Ajut and his family for a little over three months, now, as they journey across the ice toward their summer hunting grounds. There is a stark beauty to the Arctic, but after days of unending daylight, when the nights are marked by nothing more

PISS EYES

than the sun's grazing swing close to the western horizon, a mind-numbing monotony begins to set in. Here in these vast, endless stretches of ice, it amazes me that Ajut and his hunters seem to know at all times exactly where they are and where they are going. They seem to have an uncanny, some might think almost supernatural ability to navigate by an internal compass; either that, or else they see a remarkable diversity in this landscape which, to my civilized eyes, seems to be nothing but vast stretches of wind-blown snow and ice, and then more snow and ice.

We travel much of the day, and in the evenings, after talking with Ajut and other members of his tribe, I am busy transcribing the stories he tells me. I am particularly interested in the one he began to relate to me earlier today. When I expressed some skepticism, he repeated his promise to take me out across the ice and show me the remains of the burned wooden ship. As if *that* would prove his tale. I don't see the connection, but he insists that the ship is no more than a two day trip from where we are now. He has promised in the morning, that is when the red ball of the sun rebounds off the flat, western horizon, we will go there, and I will see for myself the proof of his tale.

I wonder, though, if there really *is* a sailing ship nearby. What could it possibly be? Could there be a sailing ship, perhaps a whaler from more than a century ago that got ice bound? How could it have not been destroyed in all this time? Ajut is nearly seventy years old, and if, as he says, the ship was old back when he was twelve, it would have to be at least a century old. Why hasn't it been crushed or buried by the shifting ice, or destroyed long ago? It is a mystery to me, but much about these people, the land they live in, and their sense of the spiritual is mysterious. Perhaps

I'll know more when—and if—I get to see that ship the day after tomorrow.

Transcript of a conversation with Ajut. Part Two:

In fact, my father's brother, Ootek, had not seen Paija, the Evil One, but he had seen an *ino,* one of the "great ghosts," as our people call them. From that night on, his mind was never right. He didn't become *shaman,* as often happens when men of our tribe encounter one of the gods or spirits of the ice. Instead, he became only a little bit crazy, like a man of the People who has had too much to drink of the white man's alcohol.

Sometime shortly after that night, Ootek told me about what he had seen that night on the ice. His wanderings had taken him far and wide on his solitary journeys. A great distance to the north of our summer village, he had discovered the place where a ghost lived within the hull of the ship from the south that had been cast up onto the ice. Ootek told me he once caught a glimpse of the *ino* there, lurking in the darkness inside the ruined ship, but he was fearful for his life and left as fast as he could. But the *ino,* being a spirit, could travel much faster across the ice than he could, and when Ootek arrived back at his igloo, which was near to ours, the *ino* was there, waiting for him.

He told me the ghost stood at least eight feet tall, and had long, flowing black hair and wrinkled, gray skin. He described to me the *ino's* skin, which he said was shriveled and cracked like that of a corpse that had been buried for a long time in the ice. But the worst thing about him, he said, what had let him know that this was truly a demon were his eyes.

His *eyes!*

Huge and bulging, he said they were, and stained

PISS EYES

with a milky, yellow glaze. I joked with him, and said that his *ino's* eyes must have looked like the snow where one has relieved himself, but when I asked if his *ino's* name was "Piss Eyes," Ootek didn't laugh. He told me in a stern voice that I should show respect for the spirit world. He then told me he had screamed because he had seen the demon moving in silence among the igloos of our people, looking for his next victim to claim. In my mind ever since that day, though, I have always thought of Ootek's *ino* as Piss Eyes. He warned me that if I didn't show more respect to the *inua angkuni*, they would come to claim me during the long, cold winter night. Perhaps, he said, the *ino* was looking for me that night! For a long time I was fearful of that happening, but—well, as you can see, I have lived a long time, now, and I have never in my life encountered Piss Eyes.

My friend, if we are going to make the journey to the old ship, we will be gone for five or six days. Let us pack our provisions and begin now that we are well-rested.

Rev. Robert Crocker's journal entry, July 17, 1964:

After traveling across the ice for two days, I am absolutely exhausted; but before I rest, while Ajut builds a small, temporary igloo for the night, I must write down what we have found.

At least some element of Ajut's and Ootek's story is true. There *is*, in fact, an old sailing ship out here in the middle of nowhere on the ice. I am amazed that Ajut could find it so easily. It was as if he had followed a clearly marked path straight to it. The ship looks like at one time it had been a grand, three-masted sailing ship. It might possibly have been a whaling ship, but, as Ajut told me, it has been nearly destroyed by fire except for a large portion of the hull, which is heeled over onto the frozen ground. Drifting snow and ice have all but covered the blackened hull.

Amazed as I was to see something like this, where the flat, snow-covered ground stretches to the horizon in all directions, I asked Ajut how far we were away from open water. He told me that it is still more than a two day journey to the open sea, so I have no way of knowing how this ship got here. Perhaps we'll never know.

Exhausted as I was from our traveling, I set out to explore the derelict. Inside the fire-blackened hull, sheltered from the elements like the interior of a small cave, I found evidence that someone had indeed lived within this ruin some time in the past. After staring at the bright glare of sunlight on the snow for so long, it took a long time for my eyesight to adjust to the darkness; but as I wandered about inside the ship, I found to my horror what were obviously human remains scattered about. Many of the bones had been stripped clean of flesh and broken lengthwise, apparently to remove the marrow. It was obvious, even to me, that this was not done by any scavenger. My first impression, as horrifying as might be, was that the survivors of this shipwreck from some long ago, forgotten time had been trapped here and, in a vain attempt to survive, had resorted to eating human flesh.

The thought nauseates me even now as I write it.

I hurried out of the ship's hull, back into the white glare of the snow, but I have vowed, tomorrow, after I have rested, that I will go back into the ship and try to discover the identity of those poor souls who were reduced to such a horrifying end, and tonight I will say a prayer for them.

* * *

PISS EYES

Transcript of a conversation with Ajut. Part Three:

As I told you yesterday, I have never seen Piss Eyes myself, but beside Ootek, who died more than twenty winters ago, there are several members of my tribe and other tribes who have reported seeing him, at least at a distance. Of course, the People believe that there are many spirits who wander out here on the ice, especially during the long winter night. It is only a fool who would want to get close enough to identify any of them.

There is a man named Kakumee in our tribe. He died many winters ago, too, but he said that one time he had seen and actually spoken to Piss Eyes. I know this could not be true because if he had, in fact, seen and spoken to an *inua angkuni,* if he hadn't died right there on the spot, he would have never again been in his right mind. No one can speak to one of them and live. But Kakumee used to tell us how, many years ago, when he had been traveling across the ice to a fishing hole, he had seen the dark figure of a man off in the distance. Because the *inua angkuni* seldom appear in broad daylight, Kakumee had guessed that this must indeed be a man, although he said the being stood at least eight feet tall. The man or spirit saw him, and as he approached, Kakumee saw beneath the being's ice-fringed hood a face that was gray and wrinkled like that of a dead person. He also said that the spirit's eyes—because as soon as he was up close and got a good look at him, he saw that he was no human being or even a white man—were glazed a bright, milky yellow.

As yellow as the eyes of Piss Eyes!

By gestures, Kakumee said the creature made it clear to him that he was hungry and would allow Kakumee to live if he shared his meager food with him. When a spirit demands anything, it is wise to give it to him. Piss Eyes appeared to be very thankful for the food, but then, Kakumee said, again by way of gestures because the language the spirit spoke was like nothing Kakumee had ever heard before, the spirit made him understand that he would kill Kakumee if he didn't provide him with his sled and dogs.

Now, as you can no doubt guess, to be left out on the ice far from camp without any means of transportation is almost certain death, but Kakumee had no choice but to give Piss Eyes his sled and dogs. He almost died during the long trek back to the tribe, but he lived to tell his story many times around the lodge fire. Of course, maybe members of the tribe never believed him, and they thought that he had made up this story to hide the fact that he had lost an entire team and sled, nearly the entire measure of a man's wealth, out here on the ice.

Rev. Robert Crocker's journal entry, July 18, 1964:

As tired as I was, I slept poorly last night. The wind howled around our makeshift igloo, whistling with a shrill whine that rose and fell in plaintive, hollow notes. I couldn't help but think that it might be Ajut's *inua angkuni*. In the morning, after a breakfast of dried caribou meat and tea, I dressed warmly and went out to the ship's hull to begin exploring. After walking around the perimeter of the ship several times, making hurried sketches of the ruins from several angles, I took a small oil lamp, lit it, and entered the split side of the hull where the day before I had seen the human remains. This time, I was better prepared for what lay within, and although the thought of the horror that had occurred here some time in the past made my stomach

PISS EYES

turn again, I moved past the human bones and proceeded deeper into the hollow belly of the ship.

It seemed obvious to me that the sailors, whether they were whalers or explorers, had indeed tried to survive here for some time before succumbing to the hunger and cold. The obvious remains of cannibalism made it clear to me that, as each man died, the survivors partook of the dead man's flesh. Why they never tried to leave the wreck and travel south seemed obvious; they must have known that none of them would ever make it back to civilization. Why, then, I wondered, as I looked around the insides of the scorched ship, why would they prolong the inevitable by engaging in such an unholy act as cannibalism?

But I already knew the answer.

They, like all of God's creatures, had clung desperately to life, no matter how futile or foolish the attempt might seem. Perhaps, I speculated, the last survivor, crazed with loneliness and hunger, had tried to burn the ship to stay warm, or perhaps he had tried to burn it with himself inside. This seemed a likely scenario except for one significant fact: the broken bones inside the charred hull had shown absolutely no evidence of having been burned. It was obvious that whomever had eaten the human flesh and dug out the bone marrow had done so after the ship had burned.

No matter how long and hard I pondered this desperate situation, I knew that it was and would remain a mystery for all eternity. In the grand scheme of things, it was as if Ajut and I had never discovered this antique ship and never pondered the fate of the wretched individuals who lived and died here.

I made my way slowly through the interior of the ship toward the stern, guided by the flickering light of my oil lamp. I passed through a warren of wrecked rooms and storage areas where much of the wood making up inside the ship had been stripped, no doubt to be used as firewood by the survivors. Deep inside the bowels of the ship, I noticed some things on the floor that did, in fact, look like fire-blackened bones, but I didn't investigate them too closely.

I lost track of the time as I wandered through the wreck, trying to muster up some images, some indications of the fates of the men who had been here so many years ago, but finally I gave up, knowing that the secrets of what had happened here would remain locked in ice and time forever.

Suddenly, I heard Ajut calling my name from outside. After signaling that I had heard him, I started back toward the opening in the ship's side, moving carefully so I wouldn't fall over or bump into anything.

Perhaps it was the hand of God that directed me to place my hand on a particular cross beam, but whatever it was, I suddenly shouted aloud and jumped backward when something white suddenly fluttered in front of my face. The frantic motion as I fell backward almost extinguished my lamp, but after a few seconds, it burned brightly again. At first I though I had merely knocked off an accumulation of snow, but after a moment, once the initial rush of fright had subsided, I saw that I had knocked down a folded piece of paper that had obviously been stashed up on top of one of the cross beams.

Ajut called out my name again, sounding extremely concerned or excited. As I bent down to pick up the paper, I shouted to him, assuring him that I was unhurt. I took a moment to unfold the paper and noted that there was writing on both sides of it. The script was small and cramped together with no margins or paragraph breaks. It was written in French, but fortunately I had studied that language in college, and even at a cursory glance, I recognized several words and

PISS EYES

phrases. I was trembling with the excited speculation that this might be a page from a survivor's diary, or perhaps from the ship's log. Hopefully by reading this, I could glean some idea as to who these people had been and what had happened to them out here on the ice.

As I stepped out of the darkened ship into the open, a sudden blast of cold wind took my breath. My eyes instantly began to water from the stinging brightness of the snow that surrounded me. It took me a moment or two to notice Ajut, who was standing some distance from the ship and waving excitedly to me as he pointed with one hand toward the sun-hazed horizon. I tried to see what he was indicating, but my vision was still nothing more than a watery blur. He kept yelling excitedly as he pointed out across the rippling expanse of ice.

"There he is, see? Someone is out there on the ice, Father Robert," he called out as I slowly made my way over to him.

In all the time I had known Ajut, I had never seen him this agitated or excited. He was practically jumping up and down as he pointed toward the northern horizon.

"He is gone now, but he was there! Did you see him? I tell you, I saw him go by."

"Who?" I asked, still dazed by the sudden brightness and unable to think clearly. "What are you talking about?"

"I'm sure it was Piss Eyes," Ajut said, practically shouting. "I saw Piss Eyes pass by. He was driving a sled, being pulled by a team of dogs. Do you mean to tell me you didn't see him?"

"No," I replied, shaking my head as though dazed. "I didn't."

Of course, I immediately suspected that Ajut was

having a joke at my expense, but after tucking the folded paper into my parka pocket, we walked out in the direction he had indicated. More than a mile onto the ice, we saw the fresh, clear impression of dog tracks and the runners of a sled.

Ajut knelt down and inspected the tracks carefully. "That sled was carrying a great weight," he said. "And I could see, even at this distance, that the man in the sled was very tall." He stroked his chin thoughtfully. "If it was Piss Eyes ..." He lowered his voice as he stood up and, squinting, scanned the distant horizon. "If it truly was him, we would be wise to start back to rejoin the tribe as soon as possible."

We went back to our temporary shelter to settle down for the night, but before I went to sleep, I translated the page I had found.

Journal, date, 18—? ... Unknown.

I have been dwelling here in this realm of ice and snow now for I don't know how long—an eternity of misery and suffering. The nights are long and cold, and the days are no better. Measuring time by the sun makes no sense here. Long, eternal hours are spent in darkness, and when the sun rises, it weaves and bobs along the horizon like a blazing red disk that casts no warmth. Almost all of the time, my stomach, my entire being growls with hunger and suffering. Following the death of my creator, I wandered I know not how long across the ice, intent on killing myself out here in this vast desert of snow and ice. My wanderings eventually brought me to the northernmost point of the globe, and there I sought death, but no matter how loudly I cried to the heavens to let the spark of life inside me ex-

PISS EYES

pire, I ever clung to life, knowing that it must be the will of all living things to stay alive. At one point, I had been intent on building a funeral pyre and destroying myself, but this far north where trees do not grow, I could not find anything with which to do that. No wood, and no spark to kindle it. From time to time in my wanderings, I have seen pass by those native people who are suited to living here in the frozen North. On occasion, I have encountered one of them and eaten their food in order to sustain my miserable existence. At times, I have been forced to steal their dogs and sleds. In time, I came to think that I must stay alive, that it must be my creator's will that I could never allow death to release me from the agony and torment that I so richly deserve. I have no idea when it was that I found this abandoned sailing ship which I have been using as a home. These ruins had sustained the bare existence of these nameless men for some time, but they were all dead by the time I found them. After rummaging through their supplies, I found in the captain's quarters this single sheet of paper, a quill, and ink, which I thawed over the fire I made by using the iron and flint I also found in their supplies. After writing this short account of my miserable existence, I lit the ship on fire, intending to throw myself into the flames to destroy once and for all the abomination that I am, but as flames licked the dark, frozen sky like hungry tongues, I was again unable to destroy myself. I must live, I realized, even if it was to consign myself to this frozen wasteland for all eternity where I will dwell in the solitary agony of what I am. This is my punishment for having destroyed my creator.

Rick Hautala

* * *

Transcript of a conversation with Ajut. Part Four:

We were lucky to have seen what we have seen and still be alive to tell about it. Even now, as the wind howls around our shelter, I can feel the presence of unseen spirits, moving about on the ice. I know what we have seen must have been Piss Eyes because I remember what he looks like as clearly as if there was a picture inside my head from the way my father's brother described him to me.

Yes, we are very lucky to be alive and still in our right minds. Tomorrow morning, we will leave this place to rejoin the tribe. I have already shown you more than I promised. Once we are back with the tribe, I will tell you more stories.

Rev. Robert Crocker's journal entry, July 22, 1964:

I doubt that mere words will in any way convey the true depth of horror, of pure terror which Ajut and I experienced following our evening meal after I had explored the burned ship's hull and translated the paper which I found there. Totally exhausted, we settled down to sleep. The igloo was illuminated by the single, teardrop-shaped flame of a whale oil lamp. Sleep came fast, as it always does, to Ajut, who dropped into a heavy slumber almost the instant he lay his head down. I, on the other hand, lay there shivering as I listened to the steady hiss of wind and blowing snow outside. Usually, I find only stark beauty, not terror, in this desolate environment, but on this night I was unaccountably filled with agitation and nervous speculation.

Could that truly have been Piss Eyes that Ajut had seen out on the ice? I had seen nothing except the ev-

PISS EYES

idence of sled runner tracks in the snow, but I knew my companion well enough to know that he would not make light of the situation. True, at times he and other members of his tribe have shown a remarkable sense of humor, but Ajut's entire demeanor seemed not to be that of someone who was attempting to perpetrate a practical joke. He was obviously nervous and on his guard. Before settling down to sleep, he told me that we might have made a mistake, making our shelter so close to what had been—and obviously still was—the dwelling place of a spirit. Perhaps our presence will anger Piss Eyes. I showed Ajut the piece of paper I had found inside the ship, and I explained to him how it indicated that white men from the south, people like me, had been living here, but he would hear nothing of it. He insisted that we should leave this area immediately upon waking so as not to anger the spirits. I can tell by Ajut's reaction to all of this that my mission here to bring him and his people to Christianity will take a great deal of time, perhaps longer than my lifetime.

Sometime after I had drifted off into a thin and disturbed sleep, I awoke to hear our dogs barking wildly. The instant I opened my eyes, I saw that Ajut had his rifle in hand and was already up and crouching in front of the igloo opening, looking outside in an attempt to see what had disturbed the dogs. My first thought was that it might be a polar bear wandering nearby. When I asked Ajut what was the matter, he silenced me with a quick hand motion.

We sat for long minutes, waiting for the dogs to stop barking, but they were barking and leaping about, frantically pulling at their leashes as though they either wanted to attack whatever was in the vicinity . . . or else run away from it. Gripping his rifle tightly, Ajut was getting ready to go outside when the side of the igloo behind me exploded inward. After that, everything happened so fast, it is still nothing but a blur to me. Through the shower of ice and snow, I remember seeing a huge, dark figure lunge at me. In a shattering instant, I was startled by the sudden report of Ajut's rifle, sounding close to my ear. The sudden brightness inside the igloo stung my eyes, and I had no idea whether or not Ajut's bullet had hit its target. The whole world was spinning crazily around me. As I fell backward, I saw Ajut bolt his rifle to try to fire again, but no sound followed. I guessed that the chamber had jammed.

My mind went blank with panic.

One of the few clear thoughts I had was that it must be a polar bear, crazed with hunger, that had attacked us. I saw thick, long arms reaching out for me, but in a single, shattering instant, I realized that they were not paws, but large, human hands. A powerful grip took me by the shoulders, picked me up, and shook me roughly as a voice roared in my ears.

At the time, I thought Ajut was shouting to me, but then I realized that the sounds, unintelligible as they were, must be coming from the creature. Wide-eyed with terror, I looked up to see a terrifying countenance, glaring down at me. My first, fleeting impression was that it was the twisted, ugly face of a dead man. I was repulsed by the creature's hideous features, its flared nostrils, its snarling mouth; but what drew and held my attention was the creature's eyes. They stared at me with a violent gleam of bright, burning yellow.

I sensed more than saw Ajut as he charged toward the creature. Still clamped in the monster's violent embrace, I saw Ajut swing the butt of the rifle over his head, but as it came down in a whistling arc, the creature casually swept the blow aside. The impact sent Ajut staggering to one side where he hit his head hard against the side of the igloo and fell down.

"Ou est le papier?"

PISS EYES

The words exploded in my ears, and I thought for a dizzying instant again that it was Ajut who had spoken, but he was lying facedown on the hard-packed snow floor, and I could see a bright red splash of blood on the snow. I looked into the creature's face again and was nauseated by the sour, rotten stench of its breath. All strength drained from my body when I saw the snarling anger in the creature's yellow eyes.

"Ou est le papier?" the beast bellowed.

It took several moments for my terror-stricken mind to register that this ... this *creature* was actually speaking French. Stunned into silence, all I could do was nod my head to signal that I understood that he wanted to know where the paper was. I had absolutely no doubt what paper he meant, and I was simply hoping that he wouldn't kill me before I could give it to him. I couldn't recall the French words for, *It's in my pocket,* so I shouted in a hoarse voice, "Oui! Oui! Le papier!"

Grunting softly, the creature eased up its grip on me and lowered me to the ground. My first impulse was to go to Ajut and see if he was still alive, but the instant I started to turn away, the creature grabbed my shoulder and dug its fingertips painfully into my shoulder hard enough to make me cry out.

"Vite!" the creature roared. *"Le papier! Vitement!"*

Trembling with fear, I reached into my parka pocket and extracted the folded piece of paper. My legs almost gave out beneath me, and I almost lost consciousness as I handed the paper to the creature, who grunted as he snatched it out of my hand.

"Merci," the creature said; and then, without another word, it shouldered through the gaping hole it had made in the side of our igloo and disappeared.

I stood there for a moment, absolutely stunned. I watched numbly as the creature dashed out across the ice at a speed that was much greater than any normal human being could run. Within seconds, it seemed, it was nothing more than a black speck on a sun-glazed horizon. A low groan from Ajut drew my attention, and I turned to aid my fallen companion.

Rev. Robert Crocker's journal entry, July 26, 1964:

It's been four days since the monster attacked us. Fortunately, Ajut's injuries appeared to be minor, and he was able to navigate us back to the tribe. Aside from a sharp headache and a purple bruise the size of a baseball on his forehead, he seems fine. Last night, I went to him and asked if he would tell me more tales of his people and their beliefs, but he flatly refused. When I pressed him, he finally spoke to me in a low, even-toned voice. Not once did he take his gaze away from the small, flickering flame of the whale oil lamp.

Transcript of a conversation with Ajut, a member of the Inuit tribe. Final Entry.

You say, Father Robert, that you came here to teach us your religion, to bring us the truth of Christianity. During our time at the old sailing ship from the south, I have seen you embraced by an *inua angkuni*. You looked the spirit straight in the face—you spoke with it in a language I have never heard before, and you did not lose your mind when you looked into the spirit's yellow eyes. You not only lived through this experience, but as far as I can tell, you are still in your right mind. This makes me think one of two things: either your religion is very strong and it has protected you from the spirit, or else you never were in your right mind in the first place.

I have much to think about. The demon may not

have touched you, but he left some of his evil inside my head when he touched me. I can feel his evil spirit, shifting about inside this painful swelling on top of my head.

Please leave me for now. I have much to think about.

Rev. Robert's Crocker's journal entry, August 3, 1964:

Apparently Ajut's injuries were worst than they appeared, or maybe he was simply too old to survive them and it was simply his time to go. The Lord alone knows, and He moves in ways that we cannot always understand, but regardless, Ajut died shortly after I spoke with him. I can't help but feel responsible for the death of this man. I hadn't known him for very long, but in the short time we spent together, I recognized a strong and loyal friend, and I grieve his loss as does his entire tribe.

But many of the things he said to me have made me question exactly how strong I think my faith is . . . and it makes me wonder.

Ever since I began my conversations with Ajut, and after seeing what I have seen, the events that occurred out at the ruined sailing ship have become confused in my mind. They are making me begin to question the very foundations of my faith. In spite of the confusion that day, I think I know *exactly* what I saw; it was an extremely tall, ugly, gray-skinned man with yellow eyes who spoke and, apparently, wrote in flawless French.

But how can that possibly make sense?

How can anyone or, if he truly is not human, any*thing* exist out there, alone in this frozen, barren wasteland?

How in God's name does it survive? How does it stay warm? What does it eat?

Since the events of that day, especially following Ajut's death, I have begun to see that life up here in the north—even life in the spiritual world—is very different. My sleep has been plagued by terrifying dreams that awaken me several times during the night. I sit in the frozen darkness, sweating and panting heavily as a wrinkled and scarred face with glowing yellow eyes—*Piss Eyes!*—drifts in the darkness in front of my vision. Sometimes I watch as the features on this horribly ugly face gradually melt into the smiling face of my dead friend, Ajut.

After considering things for several days, I believe I finally know *exactly* what I saw out there on the ice. I did indeed see and was touched by an *inua angkuni*, one of the evil spirits the Eskimos believe inhabit this icy realm. And I have decided that, with or without the help of anyone from Ajut's tribe, I must go out onto the ice and search for this creature, whatever he may be, whether man or spirit or demon. I will search for it until I find it.

FALLEN ANGEL, MALIGNANT DEVIL
by
Billie Sue Mosiman

My Beloved Sister,

—I write to you of my misery at the news of your recent illness. I fear we both have reached beyond our prime years and are on the slow sad descent toward embrace with our creator. How many times this year alone has the archenemy pneumonia come to be your bedside companion? As for me, my cough has not abated nor, according to my good doctor, will it. It is the most bitter potion of later life to recognize the waning of the physical strength. The virility of my soul is as strong as ever (as is yours, I pray), but the body falters too long before the spirit. Did we ever once think, even a fleeting thought, that we would grow old as our loving parents who watched so meticulously our little childhood games?

But I have more to tell you than this common haggling we all have with the dimming of the light. It is most important to me that I share my lifelong obsession with someone at last, and there is no better candidate nor understanding friend than you, dear Margaret.

I ask you to remember twenty years past my ordeal on the ship carrying Dr. Frankenstein into the northern regions where he searched for the great monstrous being whom he had created. I sent you letters, hoping to divest my mind of worry and woe on that perilous journey. No one has been able to forget the tragedy of

Frankenstein's unfortunate passing, least of all me. That bone-cold fearful trip, the coming revolt of my crew, and then! Then the being himself appearing in the very room where his master had just momentarily given over his ghost to heaven's hands.

I cannot forget. I admit to dreams, incessant, unrelenting nightmares of that very day, and the look of him—the scent, the agony, the pitifulness of him that was made from death to live again.

I admit another failure of heart. Until the being appeared standing at the side of his dead master, I really did not believe my good friend could be telling the entire truth. How could anyone, nay even a genius so great as our Dr. Frankenstein, actually create from human limbs a new personage to walk the earth? Only God could breathe life into inanimate clay. Oh, yes, I know I am a modern man and even twenty years ago I knew the precepts of science, but even science has its limits and I have never forsaken our God, Margaret, I would dread eternal damnation were I to completely cast out my faith.

Yet there he stood, majestic in height and visage. I told you before how macabre was the meeting, how my heart trembled like a butterfly caught within my chest. Just one glance at his face told me this was an aberration of nature. Never could there have been born to woman a being with such beauty and yet such horror as loomed before me! The alabaster of his skin that appeared to shine with a tinge of yellow, like a slab of cold marble left to discolor in the hot sun. The pale glow of his eyes that reflected high intelligence, but not without a sheen of low cunning. The graceful movements of his long tapered fingers as they reached out without tremor, then drew back like darting sparrows from the silent mask of death that lay over his master's features.

FALLEN ANGEL, MALIGNANT DEVIL

I tell you, I have not been able to forget, cannot eradicate from my mind that strange and glorious encounter with what never should have walked the earth with mankind.

I know I have not written of poor Frankenstein and that last fateful voyage into what might have been my own graveyard of ice, but this does not mean I have not grieved my friend, or wandered late in the nights throughout my home, lost in reverie and wonder, cloaked in the remnant of old fear.

You see, dear Margaret, I did not know it all these years—I tried denying it to preserve my sanity!—but I am no less a man obsessed with that being who threatened to burn himself on a pyre in the far north regions, than his creator was when alive and under assault.

The thought that has sustained me, given me wild little hopes and incremental spasms of pure excitement, has been that the being I saw leap from the ship to the floating ice, that being who stalks my dreams and dogs my days—he might yet be alive! Do you think it possible, or have I completely lost my mind?

I can hear your answer now, whispering across the long miles. You necessarily will think me mad. The being promised before God he would do away with himself. Yes, I know this was told to me and when spoken, I believed it with all my heart. There stood before me a man-made man, an abomination, and knowing his full evil, he said good-bye to Frankenstein, good-bye to the world that would not have a part of him, and I knew he meant his threat to perform self destruction. Yet. Yet, Margaret, the one idea I cannot rid myself of is this: What if he weakened in his resolve?

Oh mad, mad, yes, you'll think age has caused a slippage of my mind, that time has brought me dementia as on a platter along with aches and muscle cramps and sleepless nights. But I am not truly mad no more than was Frankenstein. Like him, my view of what life is and what life can be has been broken and remolded to fit the true facts. I have looked upon the face of the profane, held conversation with a heartless murderer, and it did not drive me insane. Why think it could happen just from twenty years of wonder and rambling thought?

Since my health has improved somewhat and my fretful cough kept under control with mild poultice and sweet stinking syrup they sell at the local prescription palace, I feel strong enough to make one last venture into the question that has burned within me for these twenty long, mostly undistinguished years. Does he still live and breathe? Does that magnificent being lie scattered to the winds, a few bones scored with fire left behind, or did his pride eschew suicide at the last? And how will I know unless I pursue either his ashes or his footsteps across the frozen tundra?

There is small reason to dissuade me, Margaret. I don't wish to bring you more pain than you already suffer, but you must understand this thing I feel compelled to do. Will you forgive me if I take a ship and supply bearers for one last trek into the white wilderness of the north? Will you find it in your heart to accept that this is the only way I can live out what days I have left to me without becoming so disturbed I will have to be put away from society?

There are just the two of us left. I have lost all I loved since Frankenstein succumbed on my ship. There is no one to hold me here safe, crazed with unanswered question, but you, only you, my beloved. Would you regard me with less devotion if I made the one pilgrimage my soul most desires?

I will wait a fortnight for your reply and if you beg that I not search out the being for your sake, I will have to live on unfulfilled and wretched, stumbling

FALLEN ANGEL, MALIGNANT DEVIL

through the dark labyrinth that is my mind, my eyes seeking contact with heaven as the last reprieve. You know my hope has always been never to cause you alarm or a moment's sorrow, but if you could see a way to release me from guilt at my proposed voyage, if you feel strong enough to unfetter your brother from his familial attachment for this one last adventure, I will bless your name as a saint forever.

Your loving brother,
Walton

* * *

Walton accepted the glass of port offered to him by the Captain. "I trust this will settle my stomach. Nothing else has been capable of it." He drank a swallow, relishing the fine bodied taste upon his parched tongue.

"It surprises me the voyage has been so difficult for you. We all know what a fine vessel you sailed yourself, at the helm as her good captain, sir."

Walton sighed and lowered the glass from his lips. "I am afraid that was long ago. It has been many years since I've set foot aboard a ship."

"And longer yet since you've been this far north, I expect?"

"When I came back from these regions on my last trip where my crew considered mutiny and the ice mountained around the ship's decks like walls, I swore never to brave such utter misfortune again."

"Ah well, these waters are not as dangerous for our ships today as they were in your time." The Captain brought the decanter to the table where the overhead swinging lantern pierced the glass and threw prisms of colored light dancing onto the polished teak planks. "I heard stories of your last trip. Sailors I served with in my youth told us tales I scarcely believe."

Walton glanced up, then abruptly away. He tested

the port, willing his stomach to subside its rumbling. "Sailors favor tales that can be retold, tales never to be taken at face value, my friend."

"Yes, but the things I heard . . ."

"I dare say they weren't true."

The Captain eyed Walton skeptically. He was not a man to be put aside from curiosity. "The man? The great huge beauty who came to Dr. Frankenstein's cabin? He was a myth?"

Walton nodded. "A creature of fevered imagination. You must recall we were facing extinction. Had not the ice floes moved, we would have all died a cold death together."

The Captain drank his port in silence a while. The ship swayed gently through the swells, lulled by an open sea that had not seen a storm in three weeks.

"There were all those rumors of an 'experiment.' Dr. Frankenstein upon his death had a trail of gossip tagging at his coat. There were so many of his friends and loved ones who were so brutally dispatched. Strangled, weren't they?"

Walton knew he must escape this interrogation before too long. He distrusted the dark look in the other man's eyes. If anyone suspected Frankenstein's being actually existed, a new hue and cry would rise from the superstitious populace. Where the world might wish to kill the devil, Walton hoped to still all his questions about immortality, and the life waiting on the other side of death that only a man dead made to live again could answer.

"There are unfortunate circumstances in every man's life," he said finally in rebuttal. "My own second cousin was knifed in London while on holiday."

"So the stories are untrue. They are fabrications?"

"They have never been more than that."

"And you were in the cabin with Frankenstein's

FALLEN ANGEL, MALIGNANT DEVIL

body at the last and you did not see a tall elegant person who later leapt onto the ice to be carried away in the distance from your ship?"

"If I had, would I not admit it? My men saw all sorts of visions and suffered innumerable nightmares when for a time we thought we would perish en masse, surrounded by frozen silence, far from home. Even I thought once I saw a veritable flock of black birds rising from behind a cliff of an iceberg. Crows!" Walton rubbed his forehead as if to dispel a bad dream. He hoped his performance was believable. He'd not want rumor sailing back with this captain to alert curious explorers to follow him.

"Yes, well, I understand the strain you and your crew must have been under. I was in the Straits once myself on a long voyage when a typhoon overtook us. The mind plays wondrous games when under threat of annihilation. Some men claimed an angel with a wingspread a hundred meters wide swooped down from the top of a monstrous wave and lifted our ship from a deadly trough."

Walton finished his port and, satisfied his stomach had been revived to normalcy, begged the captain's pardon for his early departure for bed.

In his cabin, he took out the writing materials and sat at the small desk attached to the wall. He penned in his painstaking script:

Dearest Margaret,
The trip so far has been uneventful, though far from boring. Just tonight the captain of this ship thought to examine me about the rumors brought back to the mainland from my trip with Frankenstein. Here it is twenty years after the fact, and still those stories will not be put to rest. I admonished my crew to forget what they had glimpsed so briefly, to hold fast to their

tongues or evoke ridicule for a tale so unbelievable not one common man would take it as truth. Yet here we are, and the captains of ships sailing north to sea repeat gossip of an unlikely creature who visited my ship and then left it like a madman, flinging himself off to become flotsam upon a triangle of sheer ice.

I put the captain's curious nature to rest, I pray, but I know my entourage and many cartons of supplies indicate I am trekking into the wildest reaches of the north, and my lie about scientific measurement of the wind velocities across the steppes of the plains does not satisfy every inquisitive mind who knows of it.

Oh, if only I can be left alone!

Nevertheless, I must tell you that despite the lingering spells of coughing I withstand and the regular stomach upsets that I ply with port and strong mind control, I am so excited to be on my way at last to find either the monster or his bones, that I hardly sleep. Adrenalin races through my body and clouds my brain day and night.

I hope this finds you well from your bout of sickness, that you do not fail to pray for my soul, and that you know my love resides with you even as the waves press me onward to an uncertain future. This quest has such hold of me, but not even physical ailment, interrogation, or the fear of finding that which I seek can delay me in the least.

Your devoted brother,
Walton

* * *

Walton had hired bearers to carry his supplies north through a wasteland of snow and ice. Across great flat plains they trekked, spidery shapes struggling across open tundra, beset by winds so cold it froze the bits of hair the men had failed to shave from their cheeks and

FALLEN ANGEL, MALIGNANT DEVIL

chins. White blinding light swept down from across the far mountains so that tinted glasses and goggles covered everyone's eyes from the pain and possibility of an eyesight loss.

Where he was going, Walton did not know, save north. He consulted the compass every hour, making sure the troop of tired and bedraggled men not lose their way. At each towering snow bank, natural ice cave, or deep crevice they came to, he paused to search the white pristine realm for evidence of habitation.

His hired men were beginning to balk, to hang back and walk in sullen groups to speak among themselves in whispers. Walton felt their reluctance growing with each new day, and he despaired that he would find anything to prove to him Frankenstein's being was either dead or alive before his companions, like the crew of his last ship, threatened to abandon him to his intractable mission.

He would die alone. They must not leave him now!

It was twenty-two days into the trip and four of his men had turned back, slipping away in the night while he slept, when Walton chanced upon an artifact that made his heart leap with joy. Just at his feet as he trod relentlessly up a slippery hillside of ice, he spied something glinting in the torturous white sunlight. He bent to retrieve it, to peer at it closely. Finally he raised the tinted goggles and turned the item over in the palm of his gloved hand. It was a flint stone, shaped by human hands, chiseled by other rock, perhaps, but unnatural in shape. The being had done this! He was close by, surely. He had found flint, thus fire, had discovered a way to survive the cold and ice that would have claimed him if his suicide had not.

Walton smiled a little smile, his lips just curving slightly beneath the covering of wool over his mouth. He looked back over his shoulder at the men coming along behind him, and quickly shoved the stone into a pocket.

The thrill was such to spur him to ever greater expenditure of his energies, and that day he covered two more miles than on most days before. His bearers grumbled and called out pleas that he slow down, but nothing could hold back Walton's immense desire to find the dark treasure of the north.

It was near sundown, when the night came dropping over the plains like a black sheet, that Walton found the place he had dreamed might actually exist.

Around the bend of a mountain's foot, he happened upon a curved wall of ice, the south side of another ice cave carved into the mountain's belly as if someone had taken a giant scoop and hollowed out a cavity. He hurried forward, racing the dying sun to the lip of the wall. Grabbing hold of it with his left hand, he swung around to see the vast opening.

There!

In a great gaping hole with a roof overhead of shining ice reflecting the last shards of sunlight, was the evidence that Walton had always hoped would be found. It was all primitive, disorganized, but recognizably made by human hands for human comfort. There was a bed of limbs against a far wall, taken, Walton surmised, from some far region in the area where trees must grow. There was a cold dead heap of coals indicating fire for warmth and cooking. There was a cave man's ax, made of a length of timber and a sharpened stone attached to the head with sinew strips from an animal's hide. There was a pile of bones, tiny ones and larger, gnawed for nourishment and then discarded all in one place.

This is where the glorious being lived.

And he lived yet! The coals were not scattered, the

bed undisturbed and ready for a man to lie his head down for a sleep. He lived, he lived!

The first men to catch up with Walton wandered into the cave and began looking around with disbelief. Some shuddered. Some laughed and then abruptly lost the impetus to laughter. One, the leader of the hired men, a bear of a man with biceps as enormous as cannon balls, came to Walton and said, "What does this mean? Who or what lives here?"

"I don't know," Walton replied truthfully, "I hope it is the man I've come to find, but I don't really know."

"We were told you were a scientist."

"And that I am."

"Come to measure wind with strange instruments."

"I am afraid that was not quite the truth."

The leader glanced around before turning again to Walton. "You hunt a man who would live alone in this wilderness, someone who would live like an animal hibernating in a cave of ice? What manner of demon is this?"

Walton almost laughed in his man's face. Demon? *God* would more approximate the real character of Frankenstein's successful experimental being. He said, placing a calming hand on the other man's arm, "We'll have no talk about demons and such things. I have been searching for a friend of mine, someone who deserted civilization twenty years ago, someone I thought must by now be dead from exposure or starvation. That I've finally found his lair, and I admit it appears to be not unlike where a polar bear might take up residence, but now that I've found him, you cannot fully imagine my joy and thanksgiving. This man was once great. A learned man. He spoke fluently and visited all the great cities of the world. But something . . . tragic . . . caused him to turn his back on his fellow man, and I could not live with myself had I not made this ponderous trip to assure myself he still lived—or had finally found a restful peace in death. You do understand, don't you? You'll assure the others not to be afraid? We will return, all of us, just as soon as we can now. Our long journey is at an end."

The leader frowned trying to understand what was essentially an unreasonable and illogical story from the man who paid his salary, but after a moment, his breath pluming white and foggy from his lips, he nodded acquiescence the way a sheep will bow to the shepherd's song. "I'll tell the men," he said, and trundled away to the mouth of the cave where the rest of the party stood in wonder.

That night, with his lantern turned low to conserve oil, Walton could not stand the wait for the being's return to his home place. He took out the paper and began to write to Margaret.

Dearest Sister,
Through divine providence I have not been killed, beset by my churlish supply bearers, or dropped off an ice crevice into an endless cavern. The Good Lord has answered my prayers and taken me to the very place of my dreams. I am here in the cave where Frankenstein's monster has been living! If something happens to me so that I do not make it back to your loving arms, perhaps someone will bear this missal to your hands so that you will know I have not wasted my money and my last year of health. I did not waste those years thinking about this incredible being; my life was not a squandering of my precious time on the ridiculous notion that the monster still lived and walked on the same earth I did. I took a delusion—I know you thought me delusional!—and proved it to be reality.

He is here. Somewhere he is in this vicinity, roaming outside these icy walls, hunting for food or scouring

FALLEN ANGEL, MALIGNANT DEVIL

the snow for something to burn at his fires. There is evidence all over that he was here within the last forty-eight hours. The coals from his last fire lie just as he left them. His bed of dried limbs where he lays his head is a long dark rectangle behind me, and his ax made from materials at hand (wood and stone and what appears to be strips of rabbit skin) leans against the freezing wall.

I cannot tell you of my exuberance, how this makes me feel to be in the abode of the man I met that once and who ever after ruled my thoughts. It is like happening upon a casket of jewels when you are destitute. Or having been adrift at sea on a trembly raft for forty days and forty nights and finally making landfall upon a paradisal shore. I feel as grand and full of passion as I am sure Frankenstein felt when first his creature moved and drew the first breath of life.

My men are in a dreadful mood and though I've sought to reassure them I have found a lost friend, I can see them even now at the mouth of the cave, their backs to me, and by observation of their agitated movements know they are plotting to flee upon the slightest provocation. Margaret, dear, we may have progressed with our science and philosophical knowledge a long way from the days of idle witchcraft, spells, potions, and fear of the dark unknown, but these men are but a step from hysterical mutiny. I have seen it before when on my ship in the sea that brought me into the north, and it is an unmistakable aura, a miasma of anxiety and trepidation that first seeps and then overwhelms men when they face a rip in the veil of natural events.

My joy is tempered by my own fear of how the men will react upon encountering "my long lost friend." I expect a wailing and a cringing, for this being who has been in the studio of my mind for twenty years still causes me to shiver when memory takes me too close to the surface of his true person. You know I have been at a loss to describe him except to tell you there is an instinctive drawing back from him, though his beauty is astounding. He inspires that dread all men harbor of the grave, he rankles the perceptions of what a man should be, and it is his "new life" that Frankenstein gave to him that causes us lesser mortals to quake and to turn away to evade seeing what God, in His mercy, dared not create out of dead parts.

I grow sleepy, dear, or I would write more. The fire, after my long day in the fierce biting cold, causes my head to droop on my shoulders. I have eaten heartily of potatoes cooked to a mush and a chewy jerky of that fine venison I brought from the last outpost. I am too happy. I feel a consuming warmth invading my body from my toes to my graying hair; I am content as a man can be who once—no, many times!—thought he was mad to follow after a nightmare, just to wrestle it from the dungeon into the full luminous glare of corporeality.

I hope the being does not find me sleeping, but I must rest now, and write more later when I know, beyond any doubt, I have done this good and righteous thing by coming to claim Frankenstein's world-shaking creation.

Your most devoted brother,
Walton

* * *

The first he knew of the commotion, one man was dead.

Walton rose from the robes covering him near the fire and shrieked along with his men, the sounds issuing from his mouth without volition, so great was his terror.

FALLEN ANGEL, MALIGNANT DEVIL

Out of the blackness of the cave's opening stood the thing Walton most feared and yet adored. Two of the men rushed toward the imposing figure, but the being brandished a length of raw corded wood that struck them on the heads, knocking them back into the cave where they sprawled on their backs.

"Don't!" Walton called, anguished that it had come down to this, that his dream so easily slipped into fiendish nightmare. He didn't know if he called to his innocent men or to the monster, but neither of them listened.

A harsh ear-splitting bellow rent the air and another man was in the monster's big hands, held off his feet from the floor of the cave, struggling mightily to save his life. As Walton rushed forward, he could see the tendons bulging on the monster's great arms and the veins filling to bursting point from the hapless victim's throat.

"Let him go! Don't you recognize me? Don't you know me, Walton, your master's friend? I'm WALTON. Hear me or as God is my witness, I will shoot you down without hesitation." Walton held a pistol on the monster, but whether he could actually kill with it, he did not know.

The monster's face turned slowly toward his voice and as his full features were presented, Walton felt the gun wobble in his fist, felt his stomach turn over, and his mind fell back as if from a blow. What horrible malignant devil was this thing that held his gaze as though in a vise? The beauty was still there, hiding beneath insane eyes that knew no language or obeyed no laws. The skin was smooth over the wide cheeks. The lips, compressed in rage, were black as they had been when Walton first saw him, but an unearthly hardness made them look carved from heavy stone.

"Please," Walton said, his voice pleading softly. "Let him go."

The man dropped and his feet went out from under him. He hunched over his knees gasping in breath. Walton watched in suspense as the man came to his feet and ran for the outside, disappearing into the night. Suddenly it was clear Walton and the being were alone together. One man lay on the ice floor, but he was obviously never going to run or move again. His neck was broken, his head angled incorrectly, eyes staring. All the other men had fled in fear for their lives. A despair filled Walton when he realized they had taken with them most of the supplies.

"Now what shall we do?" Walton asked quietly, coming closer to the being and reaching out tentatively with his fingers to touch him. "Don't draw back, I won't hurt you. I never meant to cause harm. Do you remember me now? Do you recall that meeting in the ship's cabin where your master died?"

A cry of anguish and of buried rage arose from the being's chest as it staggered away from his touch into deeper shelter of the cave.

Walton, overcome with pity, approached him again. "Do you still miss him? Do you still live with regret that he died?"

It occurred to Walton the being probably had not spoken aloud for years, maybe he had never spoken again after leaving the ship. If that was true, he might have forgotten by now even how to speak, how to form the words he had once so exquisitely voiced.

It was amazing that he had even remembered Walton's face. The recognition in the being's eyes, just as he loosened hold of his victim's throat, had been unmistakable. There was a shadow of humanity that thrust forth and defeated the fury of the animal the be-

FALLEN ANGEL, MALIGNANT DEVIL

ing had become to survive in the north. He knew Walton. Oh, he knew him.

"I came to find you," Walton now said. He saw the monster lower himself before the fire and stretch out his marble white hands to the flames to warm them. "I knew in my soul that you had too much pride to destroy yourself on a pyre the way you said you would. You are a majestic creation, built from flesh and blood, given life again, and you couldn't end it, could you? I knew, someway, that you still lived. And now I've found you."

The first efforts at speech were like gears grinding and flooded streams gurgling over their banks. The monster made guttural sounds, shook his great shaggy head, threw out his arms in frustration, and tried again and again to overcome the limitations of his unused vocal cords.

Finally the words he tried to bring forth were just intelligible enough for Walton, leaning in close and paying strict attention, to decipher.

"You ... should ... shouldn't ... have ... come."

"Yes, I should have come. I had to come. Destiny meant it to be. I've spent my life obsessed with you and what you might be doing if you lived. I dream about you, I write about you. I could not die not knowing you better."

"I ... I ... am ... a dangerous ..."

"You do not have to be dangerous. I've thought about your former deeds of murder and evil and came to the conclusion that had I been outcast from man, unloved, hated, feared, reviled, I might have done the same as you. What man can be set apart from the world and still be compassionate to it? Yes, you killed Frankenstein's friends and the ones he most loved, and he never forgave you for it, he died cursing you, but haven't the years alone taught you anything? Have you not come to terms with our God and asked to be relieved of your murderous desires?"

A look of absolute scorn suffused the being's face. Walton drew back, uncontrollably shaking and afraid to stare into those yellowish eyes.

"I ask nothing.... of ... God! There is no ... God ... who would allow my creation in His universe."

Quietly, meekly, Walton said, "All things come from God, even you. And unto God you will return one day, as will we all."

The being reached out and with his bare hands thrust into the fire, scattered the burning coals all around the area between them. Walton jumped back so as not to catch fire to his clothes. He stood, looking down at the bowed head of the most incredible creature ever designed by the mind of man. *Those arms,* he thought, *come from another human. Those legs, that torso, the massive distinctive head upon the broad shoulders. They all belong to men long dead. I do not believe Frankenstein could have known what he was intent on creating.*

"You ... must ... go away." The being left the twinkling bits of coal and moved to where his bed waited. He lay upon his back, one graceful arm flung over his eyes to blot out the night.

Walton followed. He would never give this up. He knew now the same fire of ambition that drove Frankenstein. He must take this bounty, this remarkable genesis of a new man to show the world. The being had spent twenty years paying for his crimes. He was a different creation than he was when he jumped from the ship, devastated by his master's death. He was not as articulate, his hair was uncut and filthy, his clothes consisted of animal skins, his mind was desolate and empty, but he was a complete and total wonder, a demi-god.

FALLEN ANGEL, MALIGNANT DEVIL

Walton said it. "You will be a god before the people. If you return with me, they will hail you as they would a majesty, a king. I have money, plenty of money. I will fill a coffer for you, give you rooms, buy you a wardrobe. I will introduce you to the greatest men in the world and watch from the sidelines as they go down on their knees before you. There has never been another like you in the history of the world. Time has moved on and in this modern era you will receive the glory you never received before."

The arm lifted wearily from the being's face. He turned his head slowly, and for just a moment, Walton's heart stopped in his chest. The look he saw in those cold eyes congealed the blood in his veins, weakened his knees, and if he could have made a move to flee as had his men, he would have run out into the pitch black darkness begging for God to save his soul.

"You ... want me ... to be ... *your* god. That is what ... you ... want."

Walton felt his eyes filling with grateful tears that the truth, once and for all, had been brought into the open for him to hear and to welcome. What the being said answered all the questions Walton had asked himself over the years. It told him, finally, what his real motive was in the perilous undertaking to find the great being. "Yes," he whispered, falling down to his knees in worship. "Yes, you are my god, I want you to come with me and lead the way and teach me all you know."

The arm moved back over the stony terrible face. Walton stretched out before the dying embers of the scattered fire and gave in to sleep. He knew, felt it in his bones, in his molecules, that his wish would be granted.

* * *

Billie Sue Mosiman

Dear Margaret,

I send this letter with the wild hope you'll receive it before the news travels as far as your fair city. I have found Frankenstein's monster and he has agreed to accompany me back to civilization. He is a frightening person, a fallen angel, a malignant devil, all the names he called himself when in the cabin as his master lay dead, but he is also the most magnificent and awesome creature the world will ever know. Imagine if he is studied and scientists of today can make more like him! We will revive the dead and have them walk. We will restore life, overcoming the dark night that takes our souls, stealing them away into the universal silence.

What reaches will our imaginations take us next? What wonders will we perform, greater than our Jesus whose miracles we still venerate?

It has been many days since we left together from the being's hovel in the ice cave. My bearers all escaped, never to be seen since. I have no supplies, my kerosene is gone, my food, my medicines, but Frankenstein's monster is as brilliant as he is beautiful and he finds food for us to eat, and provides the fires to keep us through the long hours of night.

We should come into the first village along this bleak plain of constant winter tomorrow. I have advised my friend (Yes! He is the best friend I might have ever hoped to have.) to cover his face when we enter to hire passage across the cold seas home. I fear the reaction of man until I prepare them for what they will see upon looking into his face. He has changed and there is more death lingering about him than there was twenty years ago. I am growing used to him, in a small way, but still when he stares at me with those unwavering pale eyes or when he suddenly reaches to

FALLEN ANGEL, MALIGNANT DEVIL

touch my flesh, I can't help but automatically recoil as if he were a snake with fangs full of poison. If I can't help my own reactions, I know others would be compelled by revulsion to smash him to his death rather than deal with the unholy feelings he causes to stir in a man's heart.

I hope you will also prepare yourself for I expect meeting him will scare you into speechlessness. I rush to assure you he is not dangerous and means no harm unless you were to raise your hand to him, or displease him in some other manner, for he is more like God than we are, and we know we cannot trifle with God.

I must sound mad and sometimes feel that I have fallen over the precipice, truly, but I am filled with envy, loyalty, and yes, stupendous fear, of bringing back the one man who could change the entire world as we know it. I am not mad, dear Margaret. I am bringing home the Savior.

Your loving brother,
Walton

* * *

Walton walked alongside the tall powerfully-built monster as they entered the village of fishermen and small men of commerce. Even with his face covered with a length of wool wrapping, his eyes necessarily peeked from the hood, and something about the way he carried himself, how he moved like a strong dancer, how he tucked his hands into his coat—all these nuances combined to give off an air of dread and loathing that caused passersby to move aside, to turn and stare, to whisper behind their hands.

Walton most feared the trip home and how to get his prize there without mishap. If he could have put the being into an iron cage and transported him the way he would a vile man-eating cat from the dark continent, he would have done it. Of course, there was no man who could do such a thing to a god, not one who dared try it however much he thought it might be the best way.

"Are you thirsty? Shall we go into a pub for an ale before I buy our passages?"

Asked not to speak, the being nodded. He took a hand from his coat and held the wool over his face tightly together.

"I haven't had an ale for two months. I suppose it's been a lifetime for you." Walton chuckled a little, but the sadness of it caused him to break it off in mid-chuckle. To live without the comforts of man was high punishment and it had robbed this creature and caused him the most extreme loss and agony.

Once inside the pub, Walton took off his hat and threw back his heavy cape. He had eaten nothing but rabbit and wolf for weeks. His mouth watered for the bitter ale and the hot steaming stew full of thickly chopped vegetables. He ordered two plates and two ales from the slovenly woman who came to serve them. Then he looked around, feeling alive again instead of frozen and half starved for community. He knew he must look a sight, unwashed, bearded, his cheekbones prominent from the restricted diet. But the men in the pub were not looking at him, not one of them, uninterested in the aging man with the big appetite. They were deathly silent and stared, of course, at Walton's companion wrapped mummy-style in wool, hunkered over the odd little rough table, his head in his huge hands.

Walton cleared his throat. "Hello, gentlemen! We've come from across the tundra and it was a worrisome trip. We've been out on a hunt. It's wonderful to be back with all of you and to share a drink with everyone. Woman! Fill the glasses! I will pay the bill."

FALLEN ANGEL, MALIGNANT DEVIL

Still the men made no move to be at ease and none answered Walton's generosity. "Oh, my companion, here?" he asked, hoping to head off any sort of scene that would undermine his plans. "He's suffered from frostbite and I dare say he won't be uncovering himself for some time. It ... well, it affected the tip of his nose, you understand, and we're to see a doctor as soon as we have something in our stomachs."

As a body the men rose from their tables and stools. They came toward Walton, who felt increasingly nervous. He looked up into faces all around him that showed no smiles, not even a welcoming word. "What's wrong?" he asked. He felt, rather than saw, the being push back the chair slowly. He put out a hand to stay him, but it was shaken off.

"This is the monster," one of the men said in a grave tone. "We were warned he would be back. Your men told us of him. And here he is, we know that much. He is an abomination before heaven."

The being stood, surrounded by the men, and Walton tried to rise, but hands came down sharply on his shoulder blades and kept him fast to the chair. "You don't understand," he said. "This is ... Frankenstein created a ... you have to listen ..."

The being said, his voice so loud that it reached and resounded from the low rafters, "I told you, Walton. I told you it would end like this and you wouldn't believe me. You insisted on worshiping that which God finds loathsome."

The monster swung out to make way for the door, but he was overpowered, there were too many enemies to defeat, and as Walton watched in horror, the men rode the large creature to the floor, screaming at him, beating at him, stabbing at him. The room was a melee of violence and bloodlust, the scent of fear mingled with fury. The creature cried out, his cries drowned by the clamor of his attackers. Walton broke from his chair and joined in, tried vainly to pull off the frenzied crowd beating the life from their victim, and at last, knowing he was losing the one thing that had made his life worth living, he shouted his misery as his heart broke, shattering to splinters in his chest. He fell, was rolled aside, and lay there in tremendous psychic pain, panting, weeping, cursing in his mind the Supreme Creator for ever allowing him to meet and to know of Frankenstein's freakish, godlike mortal.

In a short while the violence abated, the roar of the men fell to reverent whispers, and Walton heard the last words uttered from the throat of the dying beast.

"This is what I hadn't the courage to do! I leave this world to enter into the darkness from whence I came . . ."

Walton turned onto his side, got to his knees, and crawled over to the broken body. Where Frankenstein had delicately stitched the limbs together there were now bloody rents, an arm was detached from shoulder, leg from groin, lifeblood pouring, soaking into the hovel's wooden floor.

"Don't go," Walton cried. "I came for you. I dreamed of you. I lived for you. Please don't leave."

There was one last flicker of life in the otherworldly, washed-out eyes. Walton saw in them a brief embittered despair and then a yielding to fate that carried whatever soul the monster had owned across the separation between life and death into the vast, unknowable, unreachable beyond.